# *The*

# PRETENDER'S

# LADY

*The*

# PRETENDER'S

# LADY

*A Novel*

**Alan Gold**

YUCCA

Yucca Publishing books may be purchased in bulk at special discounts for sales promotion, corporate gifts, fund-raising, or educational purposes. Special editions can also be created to specifications. For details, contact the Special Sales Department, Yucca Publishing, 307 West 36th Street, 11th Floor, New York, NY 10018 or yucca@skyhorsepublishing.com.

Yucca Publishing® is an imprint of Skyhorse Publishing, Inc.®, a Delaware corporation.

Visit our website at www.yuccapub.com.

10 9 8 7 6 5 4 3 2 1

Library of Congress Cataloging-in-Publication Data is available on file.

Cover design by Yucca Publishing

Print ISBN: 978-1-63158-048-2
Ebook ISBN: 978-1-63158-058-1

Printed in the United States of America

# The Skye Boat Song

Written by Sir Harold Boulton (1859–1935)

*Speed bonnie boat, like a bird on the wing,*
*Onward, the sailors cry*
*Carry the lad that's born to be king*
*Over the sea to Skye*

*Loud the winds howl, loud the waves roar,*
*Thunder clouds rend the air;*
*Baffled our foes stand on the shore*
*Follow they will not dare*

*Though the waves leap, soft shall ye sleep*
*Ocean's a royal bed*
*Rocked in the deep, Flora will keep*
*Watch by your weary head*

*Many's the lad fought on that day*
*Well the claymore could wield*
*When the night came, silently lay*
*Dead on Culloden's field*

*Burned are our homes, exile and death*
*Scatter the loyal men*
*Yet, e'er the sword cool in the sheath,*
*Charlie will come again.*

# Prologue

The Island of South Uist in the Outer Hebrides

November 1737

She stood tall on the rock, her strong legs wide apart to brace herself against the biting evening wind. Her hands were clenched in defiance on her hips, her tartan skirt whipped by the strengthening flurries, her Clan Macdonald scarf and beret proudly proclaimed her heritage.

She stood silently in contemplation, breathing deeply as she prepared to address the multitude. They had gathered before her, thousands upon thousands of her countrymen and women. Although she was only fifteen years of age, she knew that her voice mustn't fail her in the hour of her calling; she'd been rehearsing the words for days, and now was the moment when she would cause the people of Scotland to rise up against the German kings of England.

Despite the mounting howl of the wind presaging a winter storm, she knew that if her words were to inspire, she must be audible to the crowd. She must shout to be heard above the roaring sea and the pounding waves. Only by being heard, would her words wash over the throng, to elevate and embolden them by her passion.

She looked at the assembled faces, row upon row of proud Scotsmen and women: Macdonalds and McLeans, Stuarts and McMillans, McAdams and McGregors. Rugged men and beautiful women in their traditional clan tartans, a vast army with swords and shields ready to defend Scotland with their last drop of blood.

Tribal leaders who hadn't spoken to each other in generations had all gathered on a sandy beach on a remote island to hear the words that young Flora would use to rouse the entire Scottish nation and free them from the oppression of the evil king in London.

And so she began, loud and confident, proud and magnificent. "Hear me well, my countrymen and women. Listen to my voice, for I speak to you of great and important things. William Wallace, our leader, our national hero, won a great victory at the Battle of Stirling Bridge fought exactly four hundred and forty years ago. Vastly outnumbered, Wallace and Moray routed the English Army led by the monstrous Earl of Surrey. The blood of the English glistened on their swords and is still fresh despite all the centuries that have passed; centuries in which we Scots have been enslaved by the English."

She could see women beginning to weep, and men, strong and robust men, trying to mask their tears. But she had to continue.

"And just as our greatest hero led our nation to victory, so too will I, Flora Macdonald, lead our armies and undo the terrible damage being done to our proud Scots heritage by King George, who sits on his throne in London. Yes, I may be but fifteen years old, but only I, Flora Macdonald, can save you from the monstrous injustice and evil that these foreigners have brought to our sweet land . . ."

Suddenly, a voice from the bowels of hell drowned out her rallying cry. "Where in the name of sweet Jesus are ye, Flora Macdonald, you numpty scunner. Didn't I call ye not fifteen minutes ago to come back and prepare the hame for the daddy's supper?"

Her mother stood in the doorway of their nearby croft, screaming at her, loud and angry above the screech of the gulls. She realized that her daughter was again play-acting. "Dear God, what are you doing on that rock? Ye'll be the death of me. Come inside this instant or I'll tan your wee cunny, you pot-addled wastrel."

Her mother disappeared back into the house. Furious at being prevented from rallying the Scottish people to her cause, Flora jumped down from her platform, making nearby bemused gulls, razorbills, and gannets scatter and launch themselves into the wind and sea spray.

How dare Annie McDonald interrupt her! Didn't her mother know that today was one of the most auspicious of days for Scotland? She'd been practicing her William Wallace speech for a week now, and just as she was about to get to the highpoint, rousing the assembled millions to a fever of zeal, she had to retreat to prepare the house for her father's return from his work. But what good was food and drink when the Scottish people were trodden down by the heel of the English soldiers?

Followed by her audience of pliant dogs, Flora walked the short distance along the shoreline until she reached her home. She opened the door and was greeted by the smell of freshly baked griddlecakes and oatmeal. And because it was a Saturday, her stepfather had slaughtered a lamb, which meant that tonight's stew would contain a choice cut of meat. She smiled. Saturday's supper was the best of the week, and they'd have some more money when Hugh had sold the rest of the beast to the nearby townsfolk.

Flora stood at the door, and watched her mother, Annie, red-faced from the heat of the caldron, busying herself in preparation for the return home for the night of the rest of her family. Annie felt a sudden squall of cold November air enter the house and looked around to see her splendid daughter framed in the semi-darkness. She straightened her back and walked to the table with a plate of freshly baked bread.

"Lass," said her mother, as the Flora began to busy herself preparing the house for nighttime, "why do you do it?"

"What?" asked the young girl as she helped her mother set the table with spoons, bowls, and knives for her brothers, her parents, and herself.

"You know what! Why do you talk to yourself? You're always going off to the sea and standing on some rock and shouting at the waves like some moon-cranked loon. What do you say? Who do you think you're talking to?"

"Nobody."

"Then why, girl? As a bairn, you were always been so full of life and fun, but now you're breaking down the doors of womanhood, you don't play with your wee friends anymore. Time was, you'd run naked down to the sea with your lads and lassies at the drop of a hat and the lot of you behaved like draggie rooks. But now, there's nary a friend drops by and all ye do is play outside alone, pretending that you're queen this or princess that."

"It's what I like to do, mother," she said.

"But darlin', you're losing all your friends. They're off playing and you're all alone with your play-acting. I don't know what's to be done."

"I do have friends. Lots of friends. We sit and talk when we don't have chores. But . . ."

Before Flora could continue, the door to the croft suddenly opened, and her stepfather, Hugh, walked in. Normally a man who greeted the evening with hugs and kisses for his beloved family, on this evening, he was quiet and simply nodded to his wife and Flora.

"You're troubled, Hugh! What's happened?" asked Annie.

Hugh sat in his chair, the straw-filled cushions bursting and in urgent need of repair and refilling. Flora brought him his two drams of whisky and sat by his side to warm herself by the fire. Still not answering, Hugh reached over to the griddle hanging above the nook and took one of the twelve cakes warming there. He bit into it, washed it down with the whisky, and nodded to Flora, who immediately brought over the flask and poured him another two drams.

"For God's sake, husband, what's happened? You're frightening me."

"The Queen is dead. The terrible news came through by dispatch this afternoon," he told her.

Flora and her mother looked at each other. Both remained silent, trying to understand why such news would affect Hugh so badly.

"That's terrible," said Flora feebly. "But why is it terrible, father?"

"You know how dependent that fool down in London was on Caroline. She was the only good mind in the whole of the court. Without her, the king will be lost and prey to all the knaves and scoundrels who'll want to profit from his adversity."

Flora nodded. "That is indeed terrible. But why is it terrible for us?"

Hugh sighed. "Don't you see? King George hates and detests his son Frederick, who's next in line. Frederick is a useless scoundrel. He'll conspire, probably with Sir Robert Walpole to replace George and rule in his place. My betting is that the prime minister will convince the Parliament that George is incapable of ruling alone and will demand a Regency, which will effectively put Walpole in charge of the whole country as well as the throne. And that'll make the prime minister the most powerful man in the land. He's the most corrupt man in all of England and Scotland, and sure as chickens lay eggs, he'll come up here looking for new sources of wealth. Scotland will be raped afresh by Walpole and his minions, for if he takes control over the king and the government of England, it's us who'll suffer."

"But won't the Parliament stop him?" asked Flora.

Hugh smiled and stroked his stepdaughter's hair. "The king's a ninny and Walpole and his cronies have just been waiting for the Queen to die so that they can pillage Scotland anew. It was only Caroline whispering into the king's ear that stopped the nonsense going on. But with Caroline now gone, God only know what's going to happen."

"Then surely now is the time for us to fight against English rule, father," said Flora. "Like William Wallace four hundred and fifty years ago, we must rise up and march to do battle with the English. We must sharpen our swords and prepare . . ."

"Don't talk molly mush, girl," said Hugh. "We're not going to rise up, and we're not going to raise an army. And stop mentioning William Wallace, if you please. He caused the deaths of thousands of brave Scotsmen, and for his service to his country, he was hung, drawn, and quartered. I don't fancy that death for any of my friends. If we even raise our voices, the English will come marching up here with an army fifty thousand strong, with cannon and artillery, with horses and God only knows what else. We'll be slaughtered. No, our only hope is that George remains sane and doesn't turn into a lally brain."

Hurt by his rebuke and the repudiation of her hero, Flora stood, and walked in silence over to the kitchen area to carry the stew, oatmeal, and other food to the table. But one day, she vowed, she'd prove her father wrong. One day, he would apologize and admit that when Scotland was at its lowest ebb, when all was hopeless, it was Flora Macdonald who rose up and led her people into a sunny and free upland. One day.

# Part One

# Chapter One

July 1745 – Eight years later

It was all his. By birth. All of it. The Prince of Scotland braced his body against the ebb and flow of the waves as the small rowboat plied a path between the underwater banks of kelp and seaweed. He stared closely at the shoreline of the island, momentarily visible now that the early morning mists were rising to reveal silver-gray rocks, scrub grasses, and desolate hills. The morning winds were not yet sharp enough to sweep the mist with its heavy stench of salt and the reek of rotting sea grasses. He shivered in the chill of the morning air, then glanced into the water and shuddered again at the sight of a glistening field of kelp, a meadow of drowned corpses, dead fingers commanding the tide to wave him on, then back . . . forward then retreat . . .

As the land drew into sharper focus, huge white-gray boulders of granite formed an impenetrable barrier along the hilltops. Again, he shuddered. His father would have quipped that somebody had just walked upon his grave. The stench of seaborn rot, the drowned kelp, and thoughts of the peril he was in made the young man shudder once more, suddenly overwhelmed by feelings that had been growing in him throughout the journey from France—that his mission was doomed from the beginning, and a rational person would return to the sunny uplands of Umbria and Tuscany and the naked breasts of wholesome girls and the warmth of the Roman air. Here, in Scotland, that same deity who'd encouraged him in

2

his mission had changed his tune. Charlie was suddenly beleaguered by the feeling that the deity was telling him not to land.

Born in the frenetic mania of Rome and an intimate of the cities of Italy and France, any cosmopolitan man would have been disheartened by the look of desolation before him. This was no Tuscan countryside with its hillsides corrugated by precise rows of fertile vineyards, nor was it the sunny uplands of the Loire with its rich and fruitful soils and grandiose castles, its gentle valleys, and charming towns. This was a land devoid of people and animals, a rock abandoned by God and all his angels.

But the Prince of Scotland was no ordinary man, and despite the cold and the disconsolate nature before him, he forced his mood to change so that his companions would perceive nothing of his concerns. A leader's insecurity spread like a contagion and he knew he must avoid any semblance of doubt at all costs. As his boat drew closer and closer to the shore and his first footfall on his realm, he smiled and nodded to those who looked up at him.

The rowboat's keel ploughed the field of water grasses, and he listened to the voice of his new land. The only sound that could be heard was the screaming of gulls and the sea's gentle susurration as its foam grasped at the sand in defiance of the receding water. Pitching forward when the boat dug a furrow into the beach, the Prince of Scotland saved his dignity and himself by grasping onto the outstretched arms of his courtier, Achille della Valle. The prince crossed himself, bowed his head in hope of the Lord's blessing, and jumped into the water, walking the few steps up the beach to stand on a tussock of grassy land.

Charles Edward Louis John Casimir Sylvester Maria had been rudely dubbed Bonnie Prince Charlie when introduced to the Scottish guide who boarded his ship in France, the Doutelle, in order to guide it safely through the narrows and shallows of the Outer Hebrides Islands. Now he stood for the first time in his life on the land that he should, by rights, have inherited at birth. The fetid sea behind him, Charles breathed deeply of the warming air and smelt the freshness of the earth. From the stability of the land, even the spume of the waves and the smell of the salt air were now pleasing. He said another prayer to the Almighty who had allowed him to meet this day.

He stood silent, looking up at the hills that rose above the coastline, and heard his small party unloading the boat and carrying its contents up the shore.

"Gentlemen," he shouted above the shrieks of the seabirds, "there's much time for work, but little enough time to thank the Lord God for delivering safely a Stuart back to his rightful kingdom. Come and pray with me awhile and sing an orison to the Maker of all Things. Raise you voices, gentlemen, and join me in singing *Benedictus qui venit in nomine Domini* . . ."

The eleven men who had accompanied the prince fell to their knees, and the royal priest and chaplain began the chant.

Not two minutes into the song, the party was interrupted by a crude shout from the nearby hillcrest overlooking the beach. In surprise, they raised their bowed heads and saw a huge bearded middle-aged man of fierce mien, wearing the Macdonald tartan, standing with legs spread apart, hands on his hips, looking at them in bemusement.

"And what in the name of God in his heavens do ye think you're doing here on my land? Are ye smugglers? Shipwrecks? What? Speak before I come down there and separate every man jack of you from your manhood . . ."

In a pre-arranged subterfuge, Achille della Valle shouted back in broken English, "Sir, we are Irishmen accompanying our priest to bring enlightenment in the name of the Lord to your Island's people."

The Macdonald stood immobile looking down at them from his vantage point on the crest but began shaking his head in disbelief. Then he burst out laughing. "Away and boil your head, you mutton mouthed arse fiend. You're no more Irish than I'm a Chinaman. You'll be Charlie, the young chevalier, here from France. You're the boy who calls himself heir to our throne."

Prince Charles, stunned at the man's audacity, mortified that he'd been so easily discovered, got off his knees and stood tall and proud before the man. "And whom do I have the honor of addressing?" he shouted.

"Alexander Macdonald of Boisdale speaks with you. And where is your army? You were supposed to be bringing ten thousand Frenchies. When will they be landing? I see none of their ships?" The Macdonald took gigantic strides down the dune until he arrived at the beach and stood proud before the landed party.

Charles was about to address the Scotsman when he heard a murmur of discontent from his crew who raised themselves from the sand at the Macdonald's approach. "The army that the king of France promised me has, unfortunately, failed to be raised. There is no army following. The king is afraid of setting his troops upon the sea with the potential of storms and bad weather."

Again, the enormous Scotsman burst into laughter. "You're talking shite, boy! The French haven't sailed with you because they're terrified of the British Army. And you, my bonnie young Italian, would best serve yourself and us if you were to get back onto your tatty wee boat and return to your hame the way you came. Without an army, you'll never get the Scots lairds to agree to rise up against King George. Nobody's going to risk their bollocks for a naïve boy who arrives in a row boat with barely enough soldiers to scratch his arse."

"Sir," said Charles. "I am come home. I shall not be leaving."

The Scotsman looked at the prince, then at the group and sniffed contemptuously. For weeks, it had been rumoured that the invasion was coming. Now that it had arrived, it was even more farcical than any Scotsman would believe.

"No, laddie," he said, "This isn't your home. You were born in Rome, so put away these ideas of ruling Scotland and return to a sunny land where the ladies are welcoming and the wine flows freely. For years, you've been spreading the word about coming here to rule Scotland and England, but that's all it's ever been, boy; just pish from a soft cock and wind from a bellows. By heavens, but you're an arrogant fellow. You arrive and expect us to follow you when we've all heard of your reputation for drinking and womanizing. You're no king, Charlie, and we Scots need none of your sort on our land. Go home, boy, and play at being a prince."

The crew behind him began to rise angrily and Prince Charles heard the sound of swords being withdrawn from scabbards. "Master Macdonald," he said, knowing that he had much to accomplish in these next few words, "this is my home. It was stolen from my grandfather James II and from his son, my beloved father James III. I am here to reclaim this land in the name of the Stuarts in order to place my father as rightful heir onto the throne of both Scotland and of England. If you will join me in throwing off the yoke of oppression and ridding England and Scotland of these damnable Hanoverians who have usurped the throne and the royal succession ordained by God Himself, then we shall succeed faster. But if you refuse to join me then I shall still succeed, but the task will be harder, the journey to London longer, and you will lose out on the spoils of the victor."

The Scotsman looked at the young man long and hard, his face wearing an inscrutable mask, his thoughts indefinable behind his thick glistening beard. The wind suddenly arose and the Scotsman's kilt fluttered against his muscular legs. But it was the corners of his eyes that crinkled fractionally that told Charles that the Scotsman was more bluster than fearsome and his aggression had been nothing more than testing Charles' resolve. Suddenly the Macdonald's mouth beamed a welcoming smile.

"You've got balls, laddie. That I'll say for you. You've come here without the king of France's men yet you're still puffed up like a cock partridge; I have to own that it takes guts to land on these shores and think of raising an army. You may be a bully-rook, but you've a pretty turn of phrase, and I've no doubt but that you'll turn the heads of some lassies as you roam the Highlands. But it'll be a damnable hard job winning over the Lairds of Scotland with words alone. We've no great love for the fat sausage eaters down in London, and God only knows we want rid of them, but its guns and cannon and an army we need to fight them, not your playmates yonder," he said gesturing to the prince's crew.

"But these are strange times, and who knows, Charlie, maybe you can turn the lairds' heads as easily as you seduce the Italian lassies, so you may have a chance. But I'll not join you, Charlie, though no doubt there'll be some who'll happily seize the opportunity. And I'll not stop you getting to the mainland, though God knows if it becomes known that I've assisted you, Chubby George will come looking for my bollocks."

The prince knew that it was as much as he could expect, and in gratitude, he shook the Scotsman's hand. "Thank you, Alexander Macdonald. I'm sorry you won't be joining me, for I'd like to have one such as you by my side when I take to the field against King George. But knowing you won't oppose me is a benefit that I won't reject. Now, my Lord of the Islands, perhaps you could see me to a house where we can rest and eat and prepare for our journey further on to my realm."

Again, the Macdonald burst out laughing. "Your realm! Only by the good grace of the Almighty, all the lairds of Scotland, and your ability to defeat King George II, will this ever become your realm. You've an uphill struggle, laddie, and you're beef witted if you think you'll open up anybody's ears without ten thousand Frenchies behind you."

Then he pointed to the prince's Italian and French supporters who stood and listened in amazement at the way in which the ruffian spoke to their prince.

"And especially when half your crew are dressed like flax wenches going to a fling. Still, it's your problem, just as long as you don't make it mine."

He shrugged his shoulders, laughed, turned, and led the way up the beach to where the small island village was situated.

Mr. Casaubon's Coffee House
Edinburgh, Scotland

A Month after the Bonnie Prince's Landing, 1745

Despite the condensation that obscured much of her view through the small window panel, she knew him from the pamphlet she had picked up inside the apothecary's shop just the other day. The caricature on the pamphlet showed him as fat and pampered, with what appeared to be a ruddy face and wearing a wig askew as though he were a pisspot incapable of walking a straight line from drinking a glass too much of malmsey.

Yet from the words he'd written, she knew him to be the very cleverest of men, and although he dealt in moral philosophy, whatever that was, he would have a better understanding than anybody within her society of how she should greet the news. She had read and re-read the pamphlet he had written, and on the third or fourth time, she finally understood what point he was striving to make.

She had been directed by the apothecary to where he and his friends normally met in the mid-morning, but now that she stood outside the very windows of the very coffee caravan in which he sat drinking with his friends, her courage failed her. How could she just walk up to one of the most brilliant men in Scotland and simply introduce herself?

It was all so easy when she was a young girl, growing up on her island in the Hebrides, running around naked in the cool summer air with her friends, boys and girls, and feeling as if nothing in the world could stand in her way. In those days, she could go up to anybody, speak to anyone, dare to do whatever she wanted. Her mother Anne had said that she was a wild free spirit, and could never be tamed. But in her fifteenth year, she'd changed and become introvert, preferring to be alone with her dreams, isolated in her thoughts. And she seemed to be continually angry; angry with the way Scotland was controlled by the English, angry with the failure of the Scots to rise up and free themselves of the yolk of English suzerainty, and angry with the men and women of Scotland who just accepted their lot without rising up to fight for their rights.

In the years since, while she'd been in the employ of the wife of the laird of the Macdonalds as friend and companion, she'd grown and had come out of her shell, but still burning in her, now more like embers rather than flames, was her desire to see Scotland free. One day, she thought, one day . . .

Some of her mid-teenage shyness was still with her and she was diffident about approaching such elevated gentlemen. She knew that ladies in polite society, especially ladies in England, were very reticent and their manners were precise and they showed themselves as coy. Yet she was not just Scottish, but from the Islands, and women from the Western lands were known to be forward and to speak their minds with an honesty that was generally not present in the high society of Edinburgh and Glasgow and the other towns and cities of Scotland. For Edinburgh was a University town, and contained some very clever people.

Although a Gaelic speaker, she was well educated and spoke passable English and French and Latin and could easily read the newspapers and journals, and she sang beautifully and played the harp and the spinet. But she was bedevilled because of her station in life. She was little more than a companion to Lady Margaret Macdonald, wife of Sir Alexander Macdonald who was one of the most important men of her clan, though in her dreams, she saw herself as both a lady in society and a woman who discoursed on weighty matters with men.

Yet without more of an education, how could she approach a man of his brilliance and ask him the question that was on the lips of all Scotsmen from the Highlands, and to which she could not find an answer within herself? But now that she was here, soon having to return to Skye, this was her only opportunity to hear the opinion of a truly clever man, so approach him she must. She knew in her heart that she couldn't return to the Islands without an answer, though as matters stood today, she didn't know whether to side with Sir Alexander, who was against the Young Prince Charles Edward, or to support Lady Margaret, who was a Jacobite and favoured the replacement of the Hanover interlopers in London with the Catholic Stuarts.

She saw through the misty window that he was seated with two other gentlemen, all drinking coffee; on tiny plates beside the cups were little cakes that the gentlemen picked up and relished with each mouthful of the coffee. They were in earnest discussion, embroiled in some matter of impregnable discourse. Her heart thumping, she pushed open the door and heard the bell tinkle. Some looked around at the newcomer but not the three men seated at the far side of the room, for they were too engrossed in their discussion to concern themselves with who came into and who left the establishment.

As she entered the coffee shop, she was immediately affected by the warmth and the smells of the food and drink, but repelled by the stench of the tobacco smoke rising from all the pipes, as though they were peat fires in the gloaming. Beneath the roof of the shop hung a low cloud of brown-gray pipe smoke. Trying not to cough, she stood close to the door and then sauntered along the walls so that she could glimpse his face. It was a kindly face, and the ruddiness that she'd perceived from the caricature was in reality a redness of the cheeks and the forehead, brought about by a good life and lots of laughter. She breathed a sigh of relief, for his eyes twinkled like those of Caleb Macdonald when he told a story late at night around a fire, and Caleb had a good temper and was kindly and open. Maybe Mr. Hume would be just as kindly, just as open, and accepting, despite having the narrow set eyes and the large nose of a footpad. Yet still she held back, waiting for a breach in the men's conversation that would provide an entry point for her.

At last, they seemed to take a break from their debate, and Flora Macdonald walked as boldly as her legs, though not her heart, allowed and stood before the table, looking each man in the eye. Each glanced up at her and smiled, seemingly bemused by her sudden appearance. Women were a rare sight in a coffee house, especially one so young, comely, and rudely dressed.

"Good day, Gentlemen. My name is Flora Macdonald. I am from the Outer Hebrides Island of South Uist. I have come to seek out Mr. David Hume. Might I know which one of you gentlemen is Mr. Hume?"

The men remained silent until one spoke and asked politely, "Tell me, Mistress Macdonald, does this Mr. Hume owe you money or any other debt or a service that has been promised but not delivered?"

She caught the twinkle in his eye, and shook her head. "Mr. Hume is unknown to me as I to him. He owes me nothing, but if he'll speak with me, then it is me who will owe him a debt of gratitude."

One of the men stood, and pulled a chair from another table, offering it to her. She sat.

"Mistress Macdonald, I am Mr. David Hume," he told her. "I have the honor to present myself to you."

He held out his hand, and she shook it. Hume noticed that she had a slender, delicate, and warm hand. For an instant, he'd imagined that the hand from a Hebrides woman would be as crude and rough as the skin of a goat, but hers was like a silk glove. And she was a handsome lass, buxom with a fresh and lovely skin, beautiful glistening black hair, and a sunny smile.

"These other gentlemen are my good friends and confreres, some members of their School of Common Sense, a school where I am not a pupil. May I introduce Mr. Adam Smith and Mr. Thomas Reid."

She knew their names vaguely. When she'd lived in Edinburgh, she had read of their names in newspaper articles, but she knew nothing about them other than they were at the University and were acquiring a reputation throughout England and France. She turned her attention to Mr. Hume, but before she could ask her question, he asked her, "Might I persuade you to take a cup of coffee with us. It's really very good."

She smiled and nodded. Hume turned and indicated to a servant, who immediately brought a cup of the steaming black liquid. Flora sipped it and grimaced at its bitterness. "Dear God in heaven, is this what you spend your days drinking? I wonder at all the fuss. If I'd wanted to drink tanning acid, I could have stayed at home!"

The three men laughed, and Mr. Smith said hurriedly, "It's an acquired taste, Miss Macdonald, but once it's acquired, it's very hard to reject."

She sipped it again under the amused scrutiny of the three men, and found that the second taste was marginally less bitter than the first, and she could indeed begin to perceive a flavour that was unnoticeable in her first sip. But regardless, she could never see coffee becoming as popular as ale or whiskey.

"Now, ma'am, perhaps you could tell us why you've sought out our illustrious companion, Mr. Hume," asked Mr. Reid.

She breathed deeply, as though about to breast a mountain, and said, "The other day, I read a pamphlet containing your thoughts, and I would favour your advice concerning the landing of Prince Charles Edward Stuart. You've written on the causation of one event happening after another. In your pamphlet, you said that when an event follows after another, most people think that there is a connection between the two events and that the first event makes the second event follow on from the first. But you dispute that. You say that even though we perceive one event following the other, we don't perceive any necessary connection between the two and that we can only trust the knowledge that we acquire from our perceptions."

The three philosophers looked at her in amazement. She continued undaunted, "Yet surely the event of Prince Charles landing will cause the English to attack Scotland, or so my stepfather Hugh believes. Will it, or won't it? I mean, the very fact that he's here will lead to England sending their troops up into the Highlands and there'll be a slaughter, won't there? Yet in your writings, as far as I understand them, you say that because one event follows another, it doesn't mean that they're connected."

Hume smiled and nodded. "You've read *A Treatise on Human Nature?*"

Flora shook her head. "No, I've read the pamphlet that tells something about it."

"I'm afraid, Mistress Macdonald, that matters such as the future of events are a great deal more complicated than that. Causation and consequence determine a particular event that follows upon another. If you stand and scream out that I'm a thief and that I've just stolen your purse, we can be well assured that as a consequence of the event of your shouting, a guard from the Castle will enter these premises and arrest me. If I light a taper and put it to my pipe, we can confidently expect, as a result, that the tobacco will burn. But these are matters that are ascertainable from evidence that comes from our experience. What you're asking is whether or not a particular event will lead *ipso facto* to another event, and when we're dealing with the nature of human decision, experience cannot be relied upon.

"The landing of young Charles may or may not lead to the English sending up their troopers, although as your father suggests, it's highly likely. If they do, the Scotsmen in the Highlands will undoubtedly rise up and there'll be a terrible battle. This, though, has little to do with my treatise. If you want an answer to what will happen now that the Young Pretender has landed, I'm sorely afraid that you'll have to have coffee with King George, rather than a dullard like myself."

She burst out laughing. Her laugh amused the three men. It was a tinkling laugh and had once been compared to the water of a stream tripping over the stones of a brae. "Dullard? It's told that you're the cleverest man in Scotland."

"Were I that clever, I shouldn't have been passed over for a professorship in Moral Philosophy at our very own University," he said.

"You were passed over, Hume, because you wouldn't recant your treatise and everybody thought that you were an atheist," said Adam Smith.

Hume turned to Smith and then back to Flora. "My young friend, Mr. Smith, is profoundly influenced by his studies at Oxford University and its God fearing Professors. He has lost his keen eye for what is happening in his native country of Scotland," he said. "We are governed not by man's or God's law, but by the dictates and whims of the clergy. I have always feared living in a theocracy. Had I been alive at the time, I would have cheered loudest and longest when old King Henry told the pope to go hang himself. Regrettably, hatred for the papacy has given birth to fanatical men such as Mr. Luther and Mr. Calvin and Mr. Knox. Now, it appears, our protesting Presbyters have turned into incarnations of popes, and we Scots are, in all but name, governed by the Church. Soon we will be suffering under the bony outstretched hands of a Scottish Savonarola."

Flora had no idea what he was talking about and sipped her coffee again. She was beginning to warm to its bitterness. "So you and your friends are unable to tell me what will happen now that the Stuart has landed."

Thomas Reid shrugged his shoulders and said, "Not with any certainty, I'm afraid, ma'am. But the likelihood is that many will die as a result of his impetuousness."

"Then what shall I do?" she asked. "Do I support my master, Sir Alexander, who believes that the Stuart should return to France and not provoke the English, or do I support my mistress Margaret and stand for the Jacobite cause?"

The three men looked at each other until Adam Smith said softly, "I'm afraid we're only philosophers, Mistress Macdonald. Our thoughts are those that originate from a rational mind. A mind, ma'am, that is the very opposite of that of a king or of a prince."

## THE PALACE OF ST. JAMES, LONDON

His Royal Highness, King George II sat in increasing impatience in the Audience Hall of St. James's Palace, and listened to the stultifying tones of Henry Pelham patronizing him as though he was a mere princeling instead of a monarch who had been ruling England for eighteen years. If Queen Caroline were still alive, she would no doubt already have sensed her husband's imminent explosion and would have moved to sit by his side and stroke his arm to quell his rising temper. Calming him down was the only way to prevent a Hanoverian outburst that would cause the recall of Parliament and further fulminations by the damnable anti-Royalists in their libellous pamphlets adding to the litter in London's filthy streets.

So the king was forced to listen to his prime minister droning on about this issue and that matter. George never truly understood why, as the king, he should be bothered with issues that were, by rights, the responsibility of the prime minister. Try as he might, he couldn't prevent his mind wandering to matters outside of the palace. No matter how important Pelham considered the issues brought to the royal attention, the dreadful little prime minister didn't have the voice or manner to make his audiences sufficiently interesting to stop the king's thoughts from wandering. He began thinking about the new uniforms he'd ordered for his detachment of guards; then he thought of battle plans and ways of manoeuvre in a war field; from there, he thought of the hunt he would enjoy in Richmond Park this coming Saturday. He sighed involuntarily and deeply regretted the onerous duties of a king, when all his friends always seemed to be having so much fun and left the running of their estates to competent managers. All his friends seemed to do was accept the money their tenants paid and live in the precincts of the court enjoying his royal patronage. Yet as king, he was forced to pay attention whenever Pelham felt he needed to bring a matter to the royal attention.

Since the death of Caroline eight years earlier, life within the court had become utterly boring. He missed her keen sense of humor, her brilliance, her ability to judge issues that he found difficult to understand, and her ability to advise him on the proper course of action. Since her death, he had sought consolation outside, rather than inside the court. And it wasn't just with his mistresses, for no woman could satisfy him in the bedchamber like his wife Caroline had been able. And she, a lusty woman, had enjoyed his performances just as much. So his dalliances with his many lady friends were little more than a relief, and although he enjoyed their company, none had the wit or judgment that he had always come to enjoy from his long-dead queen.

Still, he mused, not all of the pleasures of life had departed with her death. Just the other day, the king had indulged in a new sport, and he was eager to return to it. It was all so exciting. A goose was hung upside down by its legs from the branch of a tall tree, its neck and head covered in grease and oils, and despite its squawking and twisting, a horseman had to ride at high speed toward it, grasp it by the neck as he passed, and attempt to pull off its head. It was far more difficult than the king thought, and on the few occasions that he had managed to clasp the bird while riding at speed, his hands had slipped off the goose's neck six times before he finally gave up. The more the animal shrieked, the funnier the game became.

He and ten other lords and ladies of the court had spent a merry afternoon until Lady Albemarle had finally managed to dig her fingers into the pathetic animal's neck and tug off its head. The game had the unusual distinction of providing both entertainment and a good feast. After that, he'd watched some bear baiting by a pack of wild dogs in the pit in Windsor Park before returning to the draughty corridors of St. James's Palace.

And now, instead of being outside of these monstrous walls riding in the park or visiting one of his lady friends, the king was forced to sit on his throne and listen to a man who really should have been a fishmonger importuning customers in the streets, or a cobbler, or a clerk in a counting house, drone on about this and that. Yes, of course, they were important issues, but when Walpole or the Earl of Wilmington addressed him, they knew how to make their topics interesting. But Pelham . . . he was so boring that sometimes the king found himself asleep during the audience and having to be woken by one of the court.

Where, George wondered, were the real men of England? Why did he have to be served by men such as Pelham, mere functionaries who carried as much grace as a village bailiff or a costermonger in a small shop in Pimlico? Where was Walpole, dead these past few months? Where was Carteret? Where were the great and decisive men of Hanover who understood the need to keep France in a state of neutrality? Only his damnable British counsellors, and the British people it seemed, failed to understand why he had committed money and troops for the safety of distant Hanover against the damnable French.

Something that Pelham said attracted his attention and his mind was forced back onto the here and now of this interminable audience. "It appears, Majesty, that this young man landed on a remote island on the westernmost shores of the Hebrides. Our spies in Paris tell us that he sailed with two ships, the Elisabeth and the Doutelle. The first ship carried his munitions and a treasury that had been supplied to him by the king of France, but this ship was set upon by the dogs of the British Navy, the *HMS Lion*, a 54-gun two-master man o'war, which did so much damage that the Elisabeth was permanently crippled and forced to return to France. Any rational and normal invader would, having lost so much, return to the land from whence they came and regroup, but not this headstrong boy. Instead, he refused to make passage back to the bosom of the king of France and the bosoms of his many mistresses, and so the second ship carried the Young Pretender onward to the islands until the boy landed in a rowing boat with a handful of courtiers and a priest."

"And his army?" asked King George.

"No army, Your Majesty," said the prime minister still reading from the notes his secretary had given him for the audience and refusing to look up into the king's eyes. "It appears that the king of France, though promising the Young Pretender an army, decided at the last minute that the sea between our nations was too rough for his troops to set sail, and so he ordered them to return to their barracks. Undaunted, the boy continued to sail, obviously intent upon attacking our realm with his few . . . his very few."

The king, and the court following, burst into laughter. "He marches upon us with a rowing boat full of courtiers. Is he mad?"

"It appears, Majesty, that he is intent upon raising an army from amongst the lords of Scotland. However, he has already alienated many of these gallants because he refuses to heed proper advice. He still insists upon beginning every conversation with whomever he meets by repeating the motto of the House of Stuart, *a Deo rex, a rege lex,* which means . . ."

"I am not an uneducated man, Mr. Pelham," the king hissed. "I speak passable Latin. It means 'the king comes from God, the law comes from the king.'"

The lords and ladies of the court looked at the king in anticipation of the sudden eruption of a quarrel between him and his prime minister. They knew in how much contempt the king held Pelham and were hoping for his exasperation to turn into an explosion. But Pelham continued to refuse to look at the king and maintained his indifference to their ranks by reading from his notes. George's body seemed to slump further into his throne at the calculated insult.

"When the young man was ashore, my spies tell me that he demanded fealty from those around him, but he was rejected. He claimed at every vantage point that his family were the rightful monarchs and stewards of the realm . . ."

"So the Stuart wants to be a steward, eh Mr. Pelham. Eh!" said the king and burst out laughing. The court joined in, the ladies in their crinolines banging their closed fans against their hands in approbation, the gentlemen in their fine silks raising their hands and shouting out "*hurrah!*"

When the noise of the court had quietened, Pelham looked up at the king, then back at his notes and continued with his audience. "Indeed, Your Majesty. The boy has now traveled inland and has gained a foothold in the Highlands. My spies in Scotland tell me that he has sent letters of demand and requirement to all the clan leaders telling them of his arrival and stipulating their fealty to his cause. However, your government doubts that the Scottish lords will rally around him. The Presbyterian church is strong in the south of the Scottish lands and is an important buffer for us in England against the more brutish of the clans."

In surprise, the king exclaimed, "The Church? What has the Church of Scotland to do with the landing of this young man? Good God, Mr. Pelham this isn't going to turn into another religious engagement between Protestants and Catholics, is it? Surely the Catholics of England have accepted the results that were obtained after the Battle of the Boyne? The Irish have accepted the result, and the Catholics of Scotland aren't so firm in their beliefs that they'll oust the Presbyters and all the councils that run the affairs of that nation, are they?"

For one of the few times during the incessant audience, Pelham looked up from his papers and addressed the king directly. "Majesty, there may or may not be a strong Catholic following among the lords of Scotland. But the land is more tribal a clan than religious and holy. The tribes prefer to dance to the tune of Scottish pipers rather than bow to the dictates of Mr. Knox and his disciples; yet for all that, the Presbyters are held in high regard. However, and this is my reason for concern at the landing of this youth, I am informed that Catholicism still runs strong in the hearts of many in Scotland, and it is always possible that they see the divine right of kings having been broken by the accession of King William from Orange and his wife Mary. As Your Majesty might know, Mary may have been the daughter of England's Catholic James II, but she professed the Protestant faith. According to my agents in Scotland, there is an undertow in the currency of affairs that says that they'd rather have a Stuart on the throne of England and Scotland than a Hanoverian."

The king of England raised his voice to argue, but Pelham talked over him. The court was stunned by the man's arrogance, and even more surprised that the monarch allowed it to happen.

"However," Pelham continued, "the wishes of the Scottish lords are difficult to ascertain. The Young Pretender to your throne might not on his own be able to convince them to join him in an adventure against your rule; but as you know, there is nothing that the kings of France and

Spain would like to see more than the triple tiara of the pope placed high above the Crown of Britain. This boy has landed in order to replace Your Majesty with the Crown of the Stuarts, just as his father, the Old Pretender did in his attempt to replace your father with himself nearly forty years ago. We understand that Prince Charles has landed intent on placing his father on your throne as James III of England and VIII of Scotland. And there's no doubting that it's in his young head to crown himself Charles III. Whatever fealty he has toward his father is surely tempered by the simple fact that he will soon be the heir to the throne if he defeats Your Majesty's armies, should the circumstances arise. I have no doubt that this is the reason he has embarked upon this perilous mission."

"Be it reason or treason, Prince Charles must be stopped," demanded the king. Lady Winchelsea, one of the ladies of the bedchamber, thought that the rhyme was another of the king's quips, and burst out laughing, but stopped immediately when she realized that she was the only one.

Pelham nodded. "Your government will listen carefully to your thoughts in this matter as we always do, Majesty, and then we will act in the best interests of Britain. There are a number of alternatives. Either we could allow his folly to play itself out and for him to be rejected by the lords of Scotland, returning defeated and humiliated to France and Italy; or we could send a small expeditionary force to greet him, arrest, and imprison him, and embarrass the king of France at the same time. The choice, Majesty, is yours."

King George II looked around and saw that the entire court was staring at him, waiting for him to make a decision. He glanced to his left to consult his wife Caroline, but when he saw her empty throne, he was overwhelmed by dejection. If only she hadn't died.

AUGUST 1745

If courage defined the difference between bold action and craven acquiescence, then surely her audacious stance would bring results. Despite her stepfather's disapproval and her mother's consternation, and even

disregarding her own concerns about being so closely and publicly identified by such a course of action, Flora knew in her heart that this was the
moment for which she'd been born.

A dispatch rider had given news to Hugh that the Prince of Scotland
had written letters to the leaders of the clans, but their response had
been tardy—no, not tardy, utterly and totally and callously and indiffer-
ently silent. The young prince had been completely ignored by the clans
and was waiting every day for some sign that his life's mission wasn't to
be dashed on the rocks of the Scottish shore before he'd had a chance
to reach the pinnacle of the Highlands. But Flora knew the clans well
enough and understood that they'd be reluctant to embark on a war with
England without the support of the French or Irish. Hugh had told her
in no uncertain terms that landing without King Louis' army spelled certain defeat for Prince Charles' plans to regain the throne for the Stuarts.
But Flora wouldn't allow that to happen. Not while there was a morsel
of Highland air in her lungs. She'd told her employer the news, and now
was her moment.

"So," said Lady Margaret Macdonald to her young companion, "what
is this magnificent conspiracy you're involving me in? And why must I
say nothing to Sir Alexander?"

"Ma'am, as you know, the lairds won't rise up unless they're pushed.
Their lordships are reticent because the prince hasn't brought with him
any artillery or men. Yet we Scots have more than enough to drive the
English back off our land."

Lady Margaret looked at Flora in suspicion. "Go on."

"Well," said Flora, "what if the women of Scotland were to rise up?
What if they were to force their menfolk into supporting the prince?"

Margaret laughed. "And how precisely do you think that we women
could do that?"

Flora grinned. "The wives would threaten to withhold their womanly
favours from their menfolk until the men agreed to go to war behind the
prince."

This was too much for Lady Margaret, who burst out laughing. "Like
Lysistrata in ancient Greece? But Flora dear, Lysistrata arranged for the

women of Greece to withhold their lovemaking in order for their men to stay at home and stop fighting, not for them to go to war."

"I don't know who this lady is, but if it worked in ancient Greece, there's no reason it couldn't work in modern Scotland."

"*Lysistrata* is a play, darling. She isn't real. And there's no way in the wide world that a Scotsman would allow his wife to refuse him her duty on condition he'd go to war."

Downhearted, Flora nodded and continued with her tapestry.

"However," said Lady Margaret. "Like you, I believe that Charles' arrival spells a moment of destiny for the Scottish people. I believe fervently that we must be the masters of our own destiny in our own land. And I do agree with you, as well you know, that the Jacobite cause is worth fighting for if we're to remove the English yoke from our necks. So while I don't think I'll advise the other wives of clan leaders to do as you've suggested, I will write to them, and point out the importance of the prince's rallying cry and why they should encourage their husbands to comply with his wishes. But withdraw their sexual favours? I think not. Scotswomen are known to be lusty, and I can assure you that my request would fall on deaf ears."

She burst out laughing again and asked Flora to fetch her a fresh duck's quill, several nibs, two pots of ink, and a quire of paper.

# Chapter Two

It was already after noon, and his confidence was fading rapidly. Another few hours and the sun would drop behind Loch Shiel and then the chances of anybody coming before the middle of the following morning, if at all, were remote. Since he'd landed by rowboat at noontime on Loch nan Uamh and had been met by the laird of Morar, who stood at the head of 150 of his clansmen and made the prince's honor guard, he'd marched up the Glen expecting to see crowds of Highlanders cheering on his venture. But the entire glen beside the River Finnan had been empty of almost anybody other than the occasional crofter and his family.

The prince had spent some time with one of the families, but the laird advised him to walk onward to Glenfinnan in case any Highlander had accepted his invitation and was coming to meet with him. This he did, but the man who walked besides the banks of the river between the grand hills that formed the valley, was a very different man to the expectant youth who'd landed at the mainland lochside not four hours earlier full of hope and excitement for the future.

It was nearly a month since he'd first made landfall on the Island of Eriskay in the Hebrides, and Prince Charles Stuart had suffered rejection by almost everybody he'd approached. He had left France expecting his arrival to be welcomed, but from Island to Island, and now on the mainland, every lord and chieftain he'd met had told him to return home, assuring him that they wouldn't join him in his venture, especially as he'd come without a French army and with no money to purchase loyalty.

In desperation, the prince had sent letters and messengers to all of the lairds and clan leaders of the Highlands, informing them of his presence and asking them to meet with him at Glenfinnan. But he'd been here four hours, and not one man had arrived. The laughter and expectation amongst his small party who had traveled with him slowly diminished as the time wore on and now was completely muted. They sat there, looking at the ground or each other, not daring to look Charles in the eyes. Soon, their confidence in the venture would evaporate completely with the warmth of the day, and then there would only be the silence of defeat in the air. He was lost without having fired a single shot.

Now that they were at the meeting point, there was nothing to do other than sit down and rest. The Macdonald escort quickly made themselves at home around their campfires drinking whiskey and ale, commenting softly so that he couldn't hear what they were saying; but he knew right well what their conversation was all about.

By the time the late of the afternoon had arrived, Prince Charles was prepared to admit that the Highlands would never rise to his call to arms. Without a French or a Scots army, there would be no fight, no conquest, and no throne. He sighed deeply, wondering what to tell his father, and what to tell the French king. To return in ignominy was more than he could bear. As soon as he was able, he'd escape to Italy and bury his head in the bosom of a young woman.

The prince, resplendent in his black silk shirt and black trousers, wearing a Stuart tartan scarf that had been woven for him especially for this day by a Scotsman in Rome, drank a dram of whiskey to fortify his courage in what he knew he now had to announce to his friends, the laird and the escort. But as he recharged his glass from the flagon, he noticed a movement high up on the hill overlooking the Loch. Thinking it must be a stag or a bird in flight, he drank another glass, but then looked up and saw that it was a man who had climbed and was now standing motionless on top of the ridge. It was a Scotsman wearing a particular tartan, but too distant for the prince to make out to which clan he belonged.

In interest, the prince stood and looked up at the lone man. It caused others to stop their quiet conversations, and to follow the prince's eyes. Others stood, and joined the prince, looking upwards.

If he'd come at the prince's behest, then he would be first of what might be many. He wore the MacLeod tartan except for the beret that was MacCrimmon. He stood on the hilltop looking down into the valley, not moving a muscle. Then he reached around his back and pulled forward bagpipes, took a deep breath and blew air into the skin. For long moments, all that could be heard was the moaning of the pipes as they filled with air. Then the piper lifted the tube to his mouth, pushed on the skin with his arm, and started playing. It was too distant for his face to be seen so the prince didn't know whether he meant good or ill by his tune. But when Charles looked about him he saw some of the few men of his honor guard smiling and nodding, and he knew that the lone piper was an omen of good things to come. One of the party of Macdonalds stood and walked over to him, whispering, "He's a MacCrimmon, the pipers to the MacLeods of Skye. This is a great honor, sir. When he's finished his tune, you must go forward and hail him thanks."

"But what does it mean?" asked the prince.

The Macdonald smiled. "It means, Charlie, that the MacLeods are coming."

The piper stood on the hilltop for several minutes until he'd finished playing "The Gathering of the Clans." His music had filled the vale with the voice of the pipes and the hope that the piper brought with him. As the last notes faded from the hills and drifted over the smooth inlet of the sea, the prince walked forward, and shouted, "I thank and commend you, Piper, for the honor you have bestowed on me. Come join me, sir, and I'll drink to your health."

The piper stood there for several moments; then he tucked his pipes away over his shoulder, and slowly descended the hill. But he was not alone. For after him they came in their twos and threes, climbing over the crest of the hill and descending toward the gathering on the shores of the inlet; then they came in their dozens; and as the afternoon progressed into dusk, they came over the hills in their hundreds.

Then came the Clan Cameron, and by the count of them there were at least eight hundred fighting men, with the Laird Lochiel at their head, marching proud and defiant. His men advanced down the side of the loch in two columns of three men deep, and beside them in chains, marched English prisoners who had been recently taken in a small battle at one of the many Forts the English had built to constrain the Highlands.

The sight of them filled his heart with such a joy as he'd not previously experienced. His father had failed to land on Scotland's shores when he and France had tried to take back the Scottish throne for the Stuart. But the son was now standing on the hallowed ground that God Almighty had ordained that he and his father rule and as the men gathered around him, looking at him as though he was some exotic beast from a distant jungle, he knew in his heart that his moment had come at last.

He could barely breathe as he stood and watched the Highlanders continue to come over the hills in their brilliantly colored tartans, their swords and daggers gleaming in the last of the afternoon sunshine. He felt that the very God Himself was telling him that this time the shame of the Stuarts would be avenged, the Hanoverians would be sent packing home to Germany, and Scotland and England would again be his family's realm. The long exile would soon be over. He and his father could return to their Island and all would be back to the way it should always have been.

The Laird Lochiel marched to where Prince Charles was standing and bowed his head. It was a curt nod, in no way subservient but a sign to all the men gathered that Charles was recognized as the rightful Regent of Scotland, here on behalf of his father the rightful Stuart king, and that the battle with the Hanoverians was about to commence.

"I come with my men to fight by your side, Your Highness. There are hundreds and hundreds more on their way. But midday tomorrow, there will be thousands of Highlanders gathered to march on the English encampments and claim Scotland for ourselves and the Stuarts."

His men shouted in approval, and Charles Stuart walked forward and grasped him by the hand. Then he hugged him and said, "I am resolved to raise the Standard of my family on this Glenfinnan spot and declare war against the Elector of Hanover and all of his adherents. We men of Scotland will rid our island of these usurpers and once more, the blood of the Plantagenets, the Tudors, and the House of Stuart, as determined by God Almighty Himself, will course through England and Scotland like a cleansing river and put an end once and for all time to foreign interference in the ruling of our great nations. Today, gentlemen, we meet in peace in the majestic hills of Scotland, but tomorrow we will march in fury and war toward the enemy, and he shall know of our zeal and righteousness. This I swear in the name of the House of Stuart, your rightful kings."

A huge roar erupted from the assembly, and one of the prince's party unfurled a silk blue, white, and red flag that he thrust into the ground, eliciting another roar of approval.

As the men of the Cameron were cheering, the prince looked up at the darkening sky and saw torches breasting the hilltops. There was sufficient light still to determine from their colors that these were the Macdonald of Keppoch, and he estimated that there were at least three hundred of them. Behind them came the Macleod, then some of the MacDougalls, and finally, despite the dark, came some MacEwans and then some MacGregors and then men of the Wallace clan.

What had in the early afternoon been a cold, solitary and silent glen had suddenly turned into a meeting of the clans, with fires up and down the hillsides, thousands of men shouting and laughing, and pipes competing with each other for dominance of their voice.

The young prince stood for long moments looking at the gathering and wondering how his father might have felt, had he been fortunate enough to have landed in Scotland all those years ago. His heart was nearly bursting with pride as he re-entered his tent and sat down to drink a glass of wine with the Laird Lochiel.

The two men, different in age by thirty years, looked at each other in satisfaction. "Why did you come," asked the young prince. "I landed on these isles and was rebuffed by almost everybody I spoke with. I was forced to write letters asking you to meet me here. I fully expected you to reject me, as did everybody else. Yet you and the other lairds have suddenly presented me with an army and the likelihood of a resounding success. But why? Why did you suddenly change your minds?"

The Laird Lochiel sipped the Madeira and smiled. It was such a simple question and such a simple answer. "The fact is, son, that you shamed us all. You arrived to claim your heritage and we all treated you as though you were carrying the pox. Your letters made us realize how far we've fallen under the rule of the damned Germans in London. And truth to tell, our wives and loved ones told us that we were unmanly to allow you to stand alone and face the English; that you were fighting for your crown, and it was our duty to fight beside you.

"Look, lad, we have no love for the Union with England. It was imposed upon us by Queen Anne because she died without an heir and she just wanted to ensure that the damned Hanoverians ruled the land so that a Protestant arse would warm both the thrones of Scotland and England. And for years we've lived under the rule of fat George and his father before him. They speak neither English nor Gaelic, but a German language that is like listening to two dogs barking at each other.

"So when you landed and wrote your letters, you made us feel guilty that we had been sitting idly in these Highlands all these years suffering the heavy foot of those in London. And when your letters roused our wives and they started digging us in the ribs to join you, well . . .

"Laddie, you made us realize that we should be ruled by one of our own and that the kings of Scotland go back beyond the time of Robert the Bruce. And because our wives, all of our wives, seem to have come out in your support, well, that's something that we Scotsmen can't ignore. You have much to prove to us, laddie, but you're a Stuart, one of us, and for that alone, we owe you our allegiance and our swords."

Charles nodded and sipped his wine. "I shall not let you down," he said softly. "Nor shall I let down your remarkable wives."

The Laird Lochiel smiled and said, "The time for words is now. The time for deeds is tomorrow. Then will we know whether or not you're fit to be king."

The prince slept well that night, and as dawn broke on the following morning, he made a special point of visiting the fires of every clan and paying his respects to every laird and leader. During the day, he and the men he now considered his generals discussed the tactics for taking on the English. The questions were apparent to everybody, but the answers were speculative. Should the English be drawn to the Scots Army or should the Scotsmen march to where the English were encamped? Should the forts be attacked first to rob the English of the ability to stab the advancing Scots Army in the back? How should the army be fed? Was it right to steal the food and animals from the fields of honest Scotsmen and women, or should it be first paid for, and if so, how without the French treasury to support their venture?

But the most pressing question was one concerning weaponry. The English had munitions, cannon, horses, and cavalry and highly trained artillery. The Scotsmen had little more than dirks, broadswords, mismatched guns, Lochaber axes, pitchforks, and a particularly nasty double-edged dagger that the Highlanders concealed in their socks called a mattucashlass.

"This has been our problem all along," said the Donald of Lochiel, the Laird of the Camerons. "We have men of courage who are used to fighting in the hills and valleys, but we're not a regular army, and taking to the field against the mouth of a battery of cannon is likely to lead to a slaughter of our good men. If only the French had sent over artillery, we could have met them on equal footing."

"Then we'll have to use subterfuge," said the prince. "We'll have to draw them to us and ensnare them in a trap. There are enough valleys in the Highlands for an army of thousands to fall prey to a hundred Scotsmen high on a hillside raining gunshot down on them. How valuable will their artillery and cannon be to them if they can't raise them higher than the height of their shoulders?"

The others around the council table nodded. They all knew it had to be done, but the question was whether the English Army would simply fall into a trap and allow themselves to be led to the slaughter. And knowing the English, the likelihood was that their tactics would be to draw out the Scotsmen from the Highlands and slaughter them on their terrain. It wasn't a happy prospect.

ARMADALE

ON THE ISLAND OF SKYE IN THE OUTER HEBRIDES

SEPTEMBER 10, 1745

Her stepfather looked at her in increasing anger, and her mother feared that Flora would go too far and provoke him to such anger that he'd hit her. If that happened, and knowing the girl's temper, she would hit him back, which would likely cause him to do something that they would both regret. She'd not seen her daughter or her husband this angry at each other since Flora was a young girl who'd run away to the mainland for some fun and laughter, despite the prohibition of her father; and when he'd dragged her back kicking and screeching like a barn owl by the scruff of her neck from a boat about to leave the Island's dockside, she'd sworn oaths at him, which would have terrified even the Lord God Himself.

Annie Macdonald's only option was to intervene, although she loathed doing so, knowing the pride that grew in both of their strong heads. And knowing husband and daughter as well as she did, the likelihood was that they'd turn their anger against her, a prospect she didn't relish. But she had to do something to take the sting out of the air.

"Now listen to me, husband Macdonald. And you too, daughter. I'll have none of your shouting in my house. Whether you're for or against the coming war, you'll maintain a civil tongue in your muttonheads, or you'll find that you're walking around with my boot in your backsides, and neither of you will relish that prospect, I'll be bound. So lower your voices and mind your tempers. Is that understood?"

They looked at her in astonishment, but she drove the point home. "Hugh?"

He nodded. She turned to Flora, who nodded reluctantly.

Hugh continued to look at his wife, then at his stepdaughter, and knew the perils open to him unless he calmed down. Only rarely did Annie lose her temper, and when she did, he knew that he was in rare trouble. But he had to make the situation patently clear to both of them in case they still nurtured hopes that they could turn his head and make him run with the rest of the hounds of the Islands. Deliberately lower-ing his voice, he almost growled, "Let it be understood by both of you that by reason of my position as Commander of the Royal Militia of the Western Islands, it is my sworn duty to prevent the young prince from advancing through our land. I have to prevent his success. If my actions insult your sensibilities or your emotions, then I'm sorry, but it's something you'll have to accept. It's the price I'm willing to pay for our security. A security, I might add, young lady, which you have severely compromised by encouraging Lady Margaret to write all those damnable letters to the clan leaders. That was an enormous folly, girl, and I just pray that we don't live to rue your actions."

"It was the right thing to do. It's roused all Scotland and it'll be the death of England. And yes, you may have your duty, father, but in your heart, you're a Jacobite and you know it. How can you command your troops to kill your very own fellow Scotsmen, brothers you'd follow if you had a choice?"

Hugh Macdonald breathed deeply in a brave attempt to retain con-trol of his anger. He remained seated at the table and ate some more of the breakfast oatmeal. He was about to answer, but instead took another long draught of his ale. There was so much to do this day, now that the Stuart was marching on Edinburgh, and the last thing he had time for was an internal disputation with his willful stepdaughter.

"Flora, darling, let me try to explain something to you so that you can understand it from my position. All the men of the other Macdonald clans have rallied around the young man. He's marching with a couple of thousand Highlanders. He's full of bull and bluster, and nothing spurs a man on to exaggerated heights like being at the head of an army prepar-ing for battle. He's rallied our brethren and men from the other clans and they can smell the sweet perfume of victory."

"So shouldn't you be joining them instead of supporting that fat German bastard in London who . . ."

"Listen to me, Flora, for the sake of sanity. All the Prince of the Stuarts has done is raise an army. He has yet to raise an arm. Don't you understand, girl, that King George won't allow an assault against him in Scotland or England or anywhere else. He'll move heaven and earth before he allows a Stuart to take what the Hanoverians own. If George allows the Stuart to take Scotland, it'll give too much encouragement to the Tories and the Jacobite sympathizers in England who hate the Germans and who only need the barest of excuses to rise up against them. They hated his father, the first King George, and they hate this one even more. He's fat like you say and indolent and stupid and since his wife died, all brains seem to have left the palace. But like any king, he'll fight tooth and claw to retain what he's got.

"If he allows any Stuart success on English territory, then the movement against him and his clan will grow stronger and stronger until he'll have to go scuttling back to Hanover. His father might have loved Hanover and taken his mistresses there for fun, but this George is more settled in England, and he'll want to stay. Which means that he'll throw everything he owns against the attacks of Prince Charlie, and Charlie simply doesn't have the men or the guns or the armaments or the treasury to meet such a challenge. The young man may win a skirmish or two, but he'll lose the war, as sure I'm sitting here right now, and when he does, there'll be hell to pay for any who supported him. You women don't understand war, nor appreciate the deaths that will result. But let me promise you that if this young chevalier has his way and is all puff and glory, then there'll be thousands of widows and fatherless children in the Highlands come next Christmas."

"But . . ."

"Does your muddle-brain not understand what that will mean, love? Can't you see the dangers of me taking side with Prince Charlie? As sure as the mist will rise above the sea in the morning, if I take the field beside the Stuart, I'll eventually be on the losing side, and our lives will be over. Fat George in London is just looking for a reason to march into Scotland and put an end to the truculence up here against his reign. But while so ever I'm commander of his militia in Skye, and we remain loyal to England, we have a chance of being left alone if disaster befalls the mainland and the isles."

He returned to eating his breakfast oatmeal but knew that both his wife and daughter were looking at him. Wondering.

Flora, too, didn't want any further argument, but since her return from Edinburgh and especially as a result of her long discussions with Mr. Hume and Mr. Smith, she had decided that her politics must enable her to be a covert supporter of the Jacobite cause and just pray that young Charles Stuart was successful. But with her stepfather's attitude, Bonnie Prince Charlie's success could mean disaster for her family. It was a murderous dilemma.

"Father, whilst you feel you must do your duty, surely in your heart you want an end to the oppression of Scotland? Don't you want to breathe free Highland air and not have English lords and generals tell you what you may and may not do?"

Before he could answer, she continued, "Whilst ever there's a chance that Prince Charlie could succeed, surely we Scots must support the rightful claimant to our throne. Can't you see that?"

Hugh Macdonald looked at his intelligent and handsome stepdaughter. All those years ago, when he'd abducted her mother as a young widow-woman, Flora had come to him as a young stripling, and it had been the delight of his life to watch her every moment as she grew into one of the most respected and talked-about young women of the Isle. She was attractive, assertive, feisty, and forward. She breathed the air of resolution and carried a demeanor of audacity, whether she was in conversation with her equals or her betters. Hugh prayed that when she wed, if she ever wed, it would be to a man who was strong and determined in order to temper her brazenness, for if she married a chicken-hearted caitiff, she'd become a shrew before the cock had stopped crowing, and people avoided shrews like the plague.

Ever since he'd carried her mother off kicking and screaming, punching his chest and swearing Hugh's eternal damnation for all eternity, these past twenty years had grown into a time of quiet and unending love between them. And every day of his life with his wee girl, Hugh had looked on in amazement as Flora had grown from a stripling full of wild excitement into an educated, comely black-haired black-eyed beauty, pursued by all the young bucks and giving herself occasionally and then only to the bravest and most gallant.

Of course he knew that she was right; Hugh's heart and soul lay in the success of the Stuarts and ridding the Scottish hills and vales of the heavy boot of the English, but the impetuous boy had come to Scotland without an army, without money, and with only the slimmest of chances of winning against one of the mightiest armies in the world. No matter what the romance of joining his fellow Scots in the adventure, Hugh more than any others had to use reason in place of the patriotic fervor that was rampaging through the clans like some disease.

"It's a pity that you stayed in Edinburgh those few days after Sir Alexander returned to the Isle, Flora, for the people that you met have turned your head and filled it full of dreams," he told her softly. "Those in the University or in the great Castle can sit on their silken trews and take sides and no harm will come to them; they can plant their chairs on the edge of the battle field and cheer on whom they want, and only shed a tear if the result goes against them. They'll write their sonnets and poems and rue their misfortune.

"But it's a very different matter for those of us in the middle of the battle, for it's our guts that will be skewered, our limbs torn off, and our lives destroyed. And when our blood is seeping into the ground and the birds are plucking out our sightless eyes, your perfumed university friends can go back to their fine houses and their salons, and they can drink their coffees and say 'tut tut what an awful thing to have happened.' But remember lass that it's women like your mother who'll have to drag home the corpses of the men they love out of the stinking mud of the battlefield and bury them or try to find their bodies in unmarked graves. No, Flora darling, romance soon evaporates when there's a bullet flying toward your head or a cannon ball ripping out your innards. And it's for that reason and that reason alone, that I am staying as I am and not transferring my allegiances to the side of the Stuarts. When this boy's rash adventure is over, I want my family intact and living, not dead and glorious."

"But what life is worth living if we have to live in disgrace?" Flora asked quietly.

"There's no disgrace in living, lass. If the boy wins, we'll continue to prosper on Skye. If he loses, the same will happen. We Hebrideans have lived on these rocks, man, and boy, for more generations than there are blades of grass. We owe nothing to anybody and that's the way it'll stay, regardless of whether a Stuart or a Hanoverian rules in England. But while so ever I'm master of this household, I'll continue to do what's right for my family, and if that means commanding the royal militia in these Isles and fighting the insurgency, then so be it."

"And if it means that our branch of the Macdonalds will be hated and our name will be spat whenever it's mentioned?"

Hugh shrugged and returned to his oatmeal. There was much he had to organize and he had no more time for such discussions.

Flora looked imploringly at her mother. She knew that her sympathies lay with Prince Charles, yet she had been surprisingly quiet during the conversation, unlike the time she'd shouted for joy on Flora's return from Edinburgh when her daughter had given her all the latest news and gossip concerning Charles' landing and the gatherings of the clan at Glenfinnan. It was all the talk of Edinburgh that thousands of Highlanders had rallied to his flag and were slowly gaining supplies from crofters, and they were arming themselves with guns by attacking the English forts; now they were marching toward Prestonpans near Edinburgh.

The early victories of the Stuarts had seemed all but too easy, and while she was still in Edinburgh, Flora had queried those who knew of such things. She'd asked why it was that the English troopers were in such short supply in the Highlands, and why there were so few Scotsmen loyal to England to hold back the Stuart march. She was told that many Scotsmen had been co-opted into the English Army as the Black Watch when they were told by their commanders that they would only fight in their own country. But in a duplicitous fashion typical of the English, the Scottish regiment had been withdrawn down to England two years previously, where they were needed to fight a threatened French invasion that never materialized. The clever people of Edinburgh were now taking wagers on how quickly the Black Watch would be sent back up north to defend their own territory against the invasion of the Stuarts.

All of this information was like manna from heaven for her mother. She relished every word Flora told her and not just about Prince Charles and his adventures but also of the food she'd eaten, the cafes she'd entered, the houses into which she'd been invited, the parties at which she'd been a guest, and especially the new fashion of dances from London and Paris that Flora had been taught.

For Flora and her mother, Edinburgh was the very epicenter of the universe. The young woman had brought back bolts of the latest and most fashionable cloth to make dresses, and she'd also returned with newspapers and pamphlets, some in Gaelic and some in English, which she and her mother would consume for weeks on end to find out what was happening in the rest of the world.

But when all the gossip had finished being discussed and she was satisfied as to the details of Edinburgh society, Annie Macdonald asked her daughter to repeat the information she most wanted to hear, the latest news of the advance of Prince Charles.

Yet now, just when Flora most needed her mother to argue by her side and stand firm against Stepfather Hugh, she was almost silent. Normally a woman of powerful emotions who expressed her feelings vehemently, Annie Macdonald was obviously torn between two of the four people she loved most in the world and unwilling to fall to one side against the other. She felt like Flora in regard to the need for Scotland to be ruled by a Stuart, well, anybody but the fat Germans from Hanover, but she knew in her heart that it was a doomed enterprise, and so her rationality demanded that she sit on her husband's side of the table. Yet to do so would be to alienate her daughter, so Annie decided that silence was the most prudent adventure.

Not that the argument was clear-cut for Flora. Listening to her stepfather defending his decision to fight on behalf of the Hanoverians, she had suddenly become very angry at his rationalizations and it had sealed her determination as a supporter of the prince. When she'd returned home from Edinburgh, she too had been torn between emotion and rationality, but now her path was set. She was not normally antagonistic toward Hugh Macdonald, but in this case, she truly believed that it was one thing to remain neutral, but another thing entirely for her family to be a traveling companion of the Hanoverians. For then they would be hated by their friends, and that was something she could not countenance.

PRESTONPANS, SOUTHEAST OF EDINBURGH

SEPTEMBER 21, 1745

It was late at night, well past the hour when he normally retired, but nothing he could do would induce sleep. He'd tossed and turned and stared at the ceiling of his tent, but his mind would not settle. The young woman from Edinburgh who'd tried to bring him comfort had cheered him, but when his needs had been satisfied and she was sound asleep snoring gently, he found that the lass in his bunk was more irritation than consolation.

The question that plagued his mind, as it addled the minds of his generals, was whether or not his carefully constructed plan would work. Since the English commander, General Sir John Cope, had landed at Dunbar a few days earlier, it had become obvious that Prestonpan would be where his battle was to be fought. Charles' scouts told him that they were opposed by only two thousand, five hundred soldiers, most of them shabby and marching in ill-formed routine. It was a ragbag collection of men, barely an army at all. Yet they had amongst their rabble some well-armed foot soldiers and a battery of fierce looking dragoons. But the real threat came from the six 1½-pounder galloper guns along with six small mortars that could do horrible damage against an army of sword-waving foot soldiers charging across a field.

Prince Charles and his three thousand men had come to within sight of General Cope's army the previous afternoon. The Scot's Quartermaster and Adjutant-General, John William O'Sullivan made the unilateral decision to send a small contingent of the Camerons into a nearby

Churchyard on the northern corner of Prestonpan in order to scout out what the English were doing. It was folly, and the men were immediately fired upon by the 1½-pounder cannon.

Furious, Prince Charles and his advisor, Lord George Murray ordered the troops' immediate withdrawal until the morning when Charles, looking at the lay of the land, decided that the attack must come from the west. It was a potentially murderous and well-chosen battlefield, which gave very great advantage to the English. They had two high stone walls on the right of where they were encamped, a bog on their left and the sea behind them. And as if these obstacles weren't enough, there was some sort of a moat in front that would slow down and delay any headlong attack and cause terrible injuries to the prince's men. But the English had drawn the battle lines, and only a fight to the end could now ensue.

He had been in a state of inertia and depression, ruminating on the casualties and losses his men would suffer until Lord George Murray entered his tent and nodded. Prince Charles wondered why Murray had a grin all over his face. He told the prince that a certain Mr. Robert Anderson from the village of Prestonpans had approached him and told him that he had known the area since his childhood and that there was a secret path through the bog, which would take the prince's men behind the English where they could attack in surprise and without the artillery guns being used against them.

The decision was to set off before dawn, at four in the morning, and by sunrise, they would be behind the English. The Scots had no advantage of cannon or other artillery, and so this subterfuge would enable Charles to let loose the fury of Scotland at the Englishmen's backs. There would be no time for the English to turn around their artillery, and even if they did, they would be firing their heavy guns into the English as well as the Scots.

It was a good plan, reliant only on whether the information from Mr. Anderson was correct and whether an entire army could march in the pitch black of night through a bog in total silence so as not to alert the enemy and then be ready at first light to blast them to kingdom come.

Which was why the Prince of the Stuarts couldn't sleep.

THE PALACE OF ST. JAMES, LONDON

OCTOBER 1, 1745

It was a mood that pervaded the entire palace, one that nobody could breach. Even the estranged and hated heir to the throne, Frederick, Prince of Wales, had said that he was willing to try to speak with his father for the first time in months, despite the fact that he relished the misery that his father King George was currently suffering.

Courtiers tried to distract him with suggestions that they go hunting together or that they play cards; his mistresses had whispered suggestive and immoral proposals into his ear, but they were received unheard, as his mood was so deep, his depression so great, that nobody was able to alleviate his suffering.

Every time a member of the prime minister's council made a suggestion, it was met by a shrug of the king's shoulder, and the hapless man was dismissed with a curt warning to wait until the return of the Duke of Cumberland. Every time food was served, the king sampled morsels and wondered aloud what his son, the Duke of Cumberland, was eating at that moment.

During periods of quiet in the audience chamber, when the only hint of a sound was the noise of whispers behind fans, the king would suddenly shout out "You are all fools and knaves and the only real man in my kingdom is my beloved son the Duke of Cumberland, and while he is on the continent fighting the French you're all here trying to gain greater advantage from me."

Shocked, the court would stare at the monarch, who would then slump back into his throne and retreat into his enveloping silence, mumbling occasionally to himself.

It had been two days since a messenger had brought the news to the prime minister. Pelham immediately sought an audience with King George and informed him that the army of General Sir John Cope had been soundly defeated on a battlefield outside the Scottish city of Edinburgh by the army of the Pretender to the throne of Scotland and England. The king looked as though he was suffering an apoplectic shock as Pelham informed him that the Scots army had come up in the middle of the night behind Cope's emplacement and as the sun rose, had opened fire with their few guns, but that the vast majority of death and destruction had been occasioned by the use of the Scot's claymores, vicious double sided broadswords that hacked and slashed through the ranks of the English soldiery. In utter fear and terror, the English soldiers had run away, leaving only a handful of officers and their men to fend off the Scottish attack. It had been a rout, and General Cope had escaped and was now hiding his head in shame and disgrace. The Scots, Pelham told the king, were now in charge of Edinburgh and were heading south to cross the border intent upon rousing the treasonous English Jacobites to their cause and marching on London with the intent of laying claim to the throne.

Pelham had experienced only a few monarchs in his time of service and didn't know what to expect when such bad news was brought. Fat old Queen Anne would have flown into a blue funk and have been comforted by Marlborough. The first king George wouldn't have understood because he only spoke German and French, but his advisors would probably have advised him to abandon England and return to the home of his heart in Hanover. So Pelham had no idea how the second George would react. But no matter what anticipation he might have conjectured, he would never for a moment have imagined that the king would mumble some inaudible words and then retreat into a catatonic state as though he was looking into the very jaws of hell itself. It was even more of a mystery, for this very king himself had led the English Army on the continent and been seen to be a man of valor and action. Yet now he looked like a man who had seen a ghost, and no matter what the prime minister said or did, George wouldn't or couldn't speak; and so in the end, Pelham had to rise without leave and retreat back to his offices to discuss with his Cabinet and his advisors the growing menace posed by the unexpected forward thrust of the Jacobite.

Everything changed in an instant when the Duke of Cumberland, the second son of George and the late Queen Caroline, burst through the doors of the audience chamber of St. James's Palace in the Mall, and marched without leave or announcement to the plinth upon which the monarch's throne was placed.

"Majesty," he shouted theatrically as he drew near to his father, "I am returned from Flanders to save England from the Scottish barbarians and quash the Pretender's ambitions for your throne.

As though the king was suddenly awakened from a deep slumber, he opened his eyes, looked up, and saw his favorite son William Augustus walking rapidly toward him.

"A miracle," the king whispered. "England is saved. My military genius son has returned."

The king stood, an amazing sight to the assembled court, and opened his arms as the duke paced toward him. "Everybody, sing Hosanna and shout hurrah in reverence at the arrival of the saviour of England."

Bowing before he embraced his father, the twenty-four-year-old Duke of Cumberland, still sweating from his frantic rush by horse from Dover on the English coast, quaffed a cup of wine and said, "Has the Pretender advanced over the border? What's happened to the coward General Cope? Has he shot himself yet? If not, give me a pistol, and I'll do it. Have the damned Jacobite Catholics in England roused them-selves? What's the state of preparedness in the northern cities? Has the Pretender joined up yet with any French troops? What's the role of Louis and the damnable Frenchies in all of this? What are our generals doing to marshal their forces? Where are they deployed? Eh?"

The questions erupted one after the other, but nobody held the answers. All the king continued to say was "England is saved. My son, my real son, has returned."

Less than an hour later, Prime Minister Pelham, having been informed of the Duke of Cumberland's arrival in London, rushed to St. James's to greet the commander in chief of the English army. For the first time in weeks, he was utterly delighted with some good news. Now that the young man had returned, the morale of England would rise, and some backbone would return to the British army.

"Your Royal Highness," said Pelham, shaking the young man's hand. "I'm truly pleased to see you. We're sorely in need of your military skills. Have you had a chance to decide on how the war against the invaders will proceed?"

"I've ordered the Black Watch to return from the South Coast to meet me in the Midlands so that we can assemble other forces and march north against Prince Charles. I'll not let him march too far south or it'll be a devil of a job to drive him back over the border with Scotland to where he had the audacity to land."

Shocked, Pelham said, "But the Black Watch is needed to protect our south against the prospect of an assault by the French. After all, it's the French who have been encouraging this Jacobite uprising. You must realize, sir, that their intention is for our armies to be divided and so distracted that the king of France can prepare for an invasion of our land."

"It's a risk I have to take, Mr. Pelham," said the duke. "The Black Watch is a powerful group of fighting men and will put the fear of the Protestant Almighty into hearts of the Popish Scotsmen assembled against us. And it'll send their damnable English Catholic supporters into a blue funk to return to their houses and hide under their beds. If the French do attack us in the South, we shall have to marshal our forces to deal with it in another way. I can't have my best troops sitting and looking southwards over the sea when we're under assault by waves of Scots from the north. It's one of the risks of war, Mr. Pelham."

The prime minister nodded, hoping that the risk wouldn't end in disaster. It would be hard enough quelling the growing sentiment for a rebellion against the Hanoverians in England and fighting the advancing Scots; but if England was attacked in the south by the French, then heaven help the hindmost.

LONDON, A STREET JUST OFF PALL MALL

OCTOBER 5, 1745

It began as a tune hummed by the occasional hawker as he strode from door to door carrying a huge wicker basket of his knives or kitchen linen or lettuce and cabbage on his back. It was soon picked up and sung by barrow boys as they pushed their carts laden with vegetables or meat or fish in the early morning along the rutted tracks and between the horse-and cattle-dung, which was ever-present on central London streets.

Soon governesses and maids who worked for the families of wealth and means in fashionable villages like Chelsea and the Borough of Kensington along the banks of the Thames were teaching both the tune and the words to the children in their charge.

The way in which it began to spread through all levels of English society gave the playwright, lawyer, and wit, Mr. Henry Fielding, an idea for a journal that would rouse the patriotic spirit of the nation, damn the Catholic Jacobites, and at the same time show just how serious was the threat from Prince Charles Stuart. It also encouraged him to begin sketches for a bawdy book that he might name after the central character, Tom Jones.

But Jones' amorous adventures were secondary in his mind to the morale of London, which was suffering at the advance of the Young Pretender's army of wild mountain Scotsmen. So frightened were Englishmen about marauding frenzied men in kilts wielding hideous swords and pikestaffs, that Fielding was determined to do something about it, while also restoring his faded reputation as a writer. A month after hearing his costermonger, Bert, mangling the words and singing a bastardized version of something that should have been in every Englishman's heart, Fielding published the full text in the first edition of his new pamphlet, *The True Patriot*. Everybody who could read purchased the magazine, in which he had reprinted the words to "Rule Britannia" so that every true Englishman and woman would know what they were singing.

And he was gratified to hear the barely literate Bert shouting "Rule Britannia," "Britannia rules the waves," "Britons never never never shall be slaves" to every customer and passer-by. And as Britons joined in, and the voice of the English rose loud above the melee of the streets, the Scottish army, about to be joined in battle by the Duke of Cumberland, suddenly didn't seem quite as fierce.

# Chapter Three

Flora Macdonald could barely contain the excitement that threatened to overwhelm her. She felt blessed every time she received some news of the adventure and wore both a huge grin and a new skirt of calico, which had most recently entered Edinburgh from the city of Calicut in India. She'd made it to celebrate the prince's victory just outside of Scotland's capital and was skipping through her morning chores before going to be boon companion to Lady Margaret Macdonald. The previous evening, when she returned to her home in the late of the evening, far from being tired, her mind raced with the prospects of Charlie's victories, and she couldn't wait until she was with the Lady Margaret today to see if there was any later news.

Being a good and dutiful daughter, she knew she couldn't gloat in front of Hugh Macdonald, for he had grave responsibilities, and now that the prince was already over the border of England and was marching past Carlisle and Manchester and would soon be in London, Hugh's problems were vastly exacerbated. He had gambled on the failure of the Scottish uprising against the hated Hanoverians, and he had lost. Thrilled as Flora was with the success of her prince, she was also nursing concerns that when King George and his detestable brood packed their bags and fled back to Hanover, the fury of the empowered Scots might be turned against those in the Highlands who had rejected Prince Charles and his father as their new monarchs.

The Macphersons, the Camerons, the Stewarts of Appin, and the Robertsons had all come out strongly in support of Bonnie Prince Charlie. But the Macdonalds of both Sleat and Clanranald and the Macleods of Dunvegan had pitched their flags against him, and there was growing anger and bubbling hatred between the clans.

So late that night, when she arrived home in the darkness and cold of the November day, she knew to expect a reception that was vastly different from the mood she felt in her heart. Every day recently, she'd returned home to find her mother Annie quietly preparing the stew and her stepfather brooding in the chair by the fire, smoking his pipe and complaining about the stupidity and incompetence of the English. And she wasn't disappointed this night, even though she had received information that was bursting out of her breast.

As she opened the door to the house, she was met by both the aroma of cooking and the growing gloom that was now part of her household since the prince's success in the battle just outside Edinburgh eight weeks before.

Hugh Macdonald looked up and acknowledged his daughter as she entered the house. She smiled at him, walked over to the fireplace, and kissed her mother's cheek, glowing from the heat beneath the caldron in which the stew was bubbling. Beside the huge pot was a smaller one in which oatmeal was gently warming.

Flora bent over and kissed her stepfather. "Have you heard any recent news?" she asked, knowing that he wouldn't have heard of the latest success of the Jacobites. She asked out of respect for the man she so loved.

Hugh shrugged. "You'd have a better chance of finding out what's happening than I would, for riders go to Sir Alexander before me," he said softly. "Have you heard anything today?"

Flora told her parents, "We did have a rider from Fort William who conversed with Sir Alexander. I don't know much of what was said, but he did tell Lady Margaret, and she told me a little. It appears that as of yesterday, or maybe the day before, the Highlanders were approaching Manchester and there was little to stop them marching on London."

Her father looked at her in amazement. "But they were only just now at Carlisle, just over the English border. The siege . . ."

She smiled and said, "The siege is ended, father. The Aldermen and Council of Carlisle surrendered after only a few days. The prince is in control of the Castle and now his men are well south of the city. He's left a small contingent there to ensure the city stays loyal to him, but now there's nothing to stop him on the road between us and London. He's going to win, father. We're going to be free."

"You're wrong, child," said Hugh. "He may have won Prestonpans and Edinburgh and a few other poorly defended cities, but going to London is folly. I've heard that there were furious rows when his council told him as much when they'd just taken Edinburgh. They begged him not to go further. They said that he should remain and consolidate his victories and begin the defense of Scotland against the certainty of English retaliation. But he was so arrogant and certain that God was on his right-hand side that he ignored their advice and he's marching into the jaws of hell itself, and taking good Scotsmen with him."

Flora began to interrupt, but Hugh continued, "The prime minister's brother, the Duke of Newcastle, is in command of five thousand troops recently returned from Flanders. And King George's son, the Duke of Cumberland controls that many and more who are even now marching north to meet the prince on the field of battle. Rumour has it that Prince Charles only commands six thousand men, and his commanders, especially General Lord George Murray, have begged him not to be so foolhardy as to try to take London. But he won't listen even to a man of Murray's skill, and onward he marches. His supply lines are stretched to breaking point, and there are no crofters in England who'll supply him with victuals. He'll have to battle for every mouthful of food and dram of whiskey. It's madness."

But from the timbre of his voice, Flora knew that even though the information her father had was probably correct, his analysis didn't take into account the certainty that the Catholics of England and Wales and probably Ireland would rise up in a biblical multitude and that thousands and tens of thousands of English Jacobites, who hated the Protestant king, would march to join him. Even if they had pitchforks and pitted themselves against English cavalry and artillery, the huge numbers of Jacobites who were oppressed by the Hanoverians would bring certain victory.

"But what if he is victorious, father? What will happen to you? To us? How badly will it go for the Macdonalds when a Stuart's arse sits on the throne in London knowing that we opposed him?"

Hugh didn't answer, but reached into the inglenook of the fire and knocked the tobacco from his pipe. He filled it slowly from his jar and lit it from a taper, looking at his anxious daughter and wife all the time. "One thing I promise to you both. Nothing will happen to this family while ever I'm the head of the household. I might have planted an English flag in my garden, but your sentiments are well known. If I have to spend some time in a Glasgow prison for making an error of judgment, then so be it. But the Macdonalds will rally around you and you will want for nothing."

It was the first time that Hugh had ever mentioned the prospect of prison. Would that it were the case, Flora wouldn't have been so concerned for the fate of her family. But she knew just as well as her mother that Hugh, and probably they, would be viewed as a family of traitors, and traitors were hanged if they were lucky. If they weren't so lucky, they'd also be drawn and quartered. Just like William Wallace. And it wasn't a prospect she looked forward to.

THE GEORGE INN, IRON GATE, DERBY

DECEMBER 4, 1745

He'd entered the town in the hope of finding those loyal to him. Yet the streets were empty, as though citizens were hiding from an invader rather than a liberator. It had been as Lord George Murray had predicted, yet he'd steadfastly refused to believe what was fast becoming obvious.

Nobody, it seemed, had rallied to the call of his campaign. His flag had failed to inspire the Catholic residents of England. Nor had the French or the Welsh come to support him with men, arms, or money.

Devastated, humiliated, he rode his horse along Iron Bridge Road until he reached the George Inn where he dismounted and entered, followed by his generals, clan leaders, and advisors.

The innkeeper looked at the sudden arrivals in concern. He'd known that they were heading toward Derby but hoped that they'd continue on to Nottingham, a larger and more important city. But for some reason, they were here, and he was concerned that they might use arms against him. But nothing could have been further from the truth.

"Landlord, my name is Prince Charles Edward Stuart. My colleagues and I require a private room, food, and drink so that we can discuss certain matters. Might we impose upon your hospitality?"

Before the innkeeper could answer, the prince took out his purse and tossed two gold Louis onto the table, more than enough to pay for all the food and drink that the party could possibly consume. The landlord welcomed the prince and showed him upstairs to a large room that the town council occasionally used for its deliberations.

Lord George Murray was about to follow the prince up the stairs and begin the planning of the next section of the campaign, when he felt his arm being held by his aide-de-camp, the Chevalier Johnstone. The chevalier nodded and indicated for his general to remain downstairs for a moment.

When they were in private, the chevalier whispered in his ear, "General, you must make the prince see reason. To go on without support from the English Jacobites would be madness. It'll result in our slaughter."

Lord Murray nodded. "I know, laddie, but he's a headstrong young whelp and he stopped listening to my counsel long ago. If he trusted me, he wouldn't have replaced me as commander in chief after we reached Carlisle."

"Because you tried to tell him the truth about the stupidity of marching further into England? But he reinstated you, sir. Surely you still have some influence."

The general smiled. "He reinstated me only because the Highland lads wouldn't serve under a nincompoop like the Duke of Perth. Even Bonnie Charlie realized that if an army has no confidence in its leader, it won't fight."

"But if we continue on to London . . ."

The young man's words were drowned out by the prince yelling from the upper floor of the Inn. "Lord George Murray, we're waiting on you."

The war council was about to begin. When he entered the room, he saw that the ten most senior men of the Jacobite army had been gathered, as well as the prince's political advisors. The mood was somber. Everybody had come to England expecting the Jacobite Catholics to rise up and greet the liberating army with plaudits and flowers and for the menfolk to down their tools, pick up weapons, and march shoulder-to-shoulder with their army. People had spoken of one hundred thousand, even two hundred thousand Englishmen, both Protestant and Catholic, rising up against the hated Hanoverians.

Yet wherever they rode, the streets and laneways had been empty, and only curious children had come out to see what was happening; and most of these had been dragged back kicking and screeching into their homes.

A few hundred Manchester men had accreted to the prince's army while he marched south, but nothing like the thousands and tens of thousands who hid behind their window curtains as he rode past. All had assumed that the English disdain, bordering on contempt for the Hanoverians, would cause them to welcome a Stuart return; but it seemed as though the people of England were biding their time, waiting to see which army would be victorious, before they came out in their multitudes and supported the victor.

As they had passed through Bolton, then Manchester, then along the old Roman road to Derby, the elation of the troops and the confidence of the commanders had ebbed like a tide. They had been given a welcome in Manchester, but it was half-hearted, and more out of fear than admiration. It was as though the guardian angel who had overseen their Scottish triumphs had suddenly withdrawn himself and disappeared when they crossed the English border.

"Well, gentlemen," said the prince, trying to sound a great deal more confident and authoritative than he currently felt, "I've called this council together because of the growing opposition amongst some of you to my decision to continue marching toward London. This place," said the prince looking around the upper room of the Inn, "is not particularly conducive to important discussions, and soon we shall move down the road to Exeter House, which is being prepared for our stay tonight and which is more appropriate for our deliberations and the making of battle plans. But before we move on, let us refresh ourselves with English food, wine, and ale in this Inn and speak of the immediate needs of the army. So, gentlemen, your advice please. Let's hear from the naysayers so that we can eliminate their thoughts and opinions and then go down to Exeter House to discuss our divine project. I beg you to remember that while we might be suffering temporary adversity, our triumphs have been ordained by God Almighty himself, and it is my intention to fulfil *his* command, which is to restore my father and my family to the throne of England."

He looked around, and as he had predicted, while his Scottish generals were downcast, his Irish political advisors were smiling fit to burst.

"Why begin with those who oppose you, Majesty. Better to let me begin," said Athol O'Malley, one of the Irishmen who was supporting his cause, "by congratulating you on your brilliant strategy so far. Who would have believed that an army of loyalists could have succeeded in coming within a hundred and twenty miles of London with such speed and economy? Nary a man-jack lost, nor more than a couple of bullets spent, and already we've got the English in such a flapdoodle that they're hiding in their rooftops and under their beds. Since our brilliant victory at Carlisle, we Catholics . . . we loyal Jacobites . . . have encountered almost no resistance, and we've taken Penrith, Kendal, Lancaster, Preston, and Manchester. Majesty, it's the greatest act of military genius since the Roman Emperor, Julius Caesar himself, landed in England and quelled the rebellious Druids."

His sycophancy had been predictable, and none of the military men raised a voice in argument.

"I thank you, Athol, but I'd also like to hear your opinion of what should happen to the campaign now," he said to the Irishman.

"Now? What does *now* mean, your Majesty? Is there a difference between yesterday, now and tomorrow? We're marching ahead of six thousand of the toughest and most skilled men against an opposition that dares not show its face. We've won breathtaking victories against the English usurpers in Prestonpans, in Carlisle and elsewhere along the way. What is to stop us from reaching the outskirts of London within two weeks and putting the boot up Georgie's arse? Where's his mighty army? Still bogged down in Flanders or dealing with the issue of the succession in Austria? I tell you, Majesty, that there is no English army that dares oppose us. The Black Watch is watching for the French and if the English had withdrawn troops from Europe why haven't they stopped our assault on London? The fact of the matter is, Majesty, that King George is more concerned about what's happening in Hanover than he is in safeguarding his English throne . . ."

Lord George Murray banged his fist on the table, shocking all around. "The fact of the matter is that you're a fool and a knave and downright dangerous, and you should be locked up in the stocks and have house-wives throw rotten cabbages at your rotten head," he shouted at the Irishman.

Shocked by the outburst, Athol O'Malley stopped talking, and the prince looked up in surprise that his normally polite and gentle-manly commander in chief had made such a crude and uncharacteristic statement.

In silence, knowing that everybody was looking at him, Lord George Murray said, "The man's a fool, Prince Charles. Old King Henry VIII paid his jester Will Somers two shillings a month to give him such advice and make him laugh. This arse-licking dog-hearted codpiece of a ne'er-do-well is not clever enough to be a jester, but he's a damned sight more dangerous to you than a regiment of crack English artillery. He'll spin words around your head until you're blinded by flattery, and if you're of a mind, you'll believe him. Then we'll all be killed and the whole of England will wonder at your stupidity."

The prince stood from his chair intent on scalding the general, but Lord Murray continued, "I don't care whether you like what I'm going to say or not. If you don't, I'll happily resign your commission and return as a volunteer to the ranks. But before I go, you'll listen to what I have to say and then we'll take a vote as your council, so that everybody here will be absolutely clear as to what I believe.

"It was folly to cross the border with England. You should have stopped in Scotland, defended Edinburgh, and drawn a line so that the Stuarts would be kings of the North. We could have spent the next five years ensuring the support of Ireland and Wales, and maybe even France, which would have given muscle to a proper Jacobite uprising. Then, ahead of an army of twenty thousand or more, you could have attacked England and thrown the Hanoverian off the throne. But no, Charles, you're an impetuous youth, and against my advice, you've marched south expecting the Catholics to rise up and join you. Well they haven't! And there's no sign that they will, nor that Wales or France will come to your rescue. The French have sent a token handful of men and supplies, but not enough to engage in real warfare.

"We've thundered south like wild-eyed stampeding cattle with barely a thought to arms or supplies or what the English Army will mount against us, and now we're in the midlands of England with a force of men a third the enemy's size, hundreds of miles from safety, with three-pounder cannon that wouldn't even put a dent in a crofter's hut, no rifles, and our only arms are muskets with no ammunition.

"General Wade is marching down the Pennines with six thousand men to try to cut off our march forward. The Duke of Cumberland is fast bringing up the advance with five thousand soldiers should we try to group on the Welsh border, and there are at least six thousand men marching up from the South Coast, and God only knows what other troops and militia are being raised against us. And this arse-licking catchpenny toad of an Irish ninny," he said, pointing an accusing finger at Athol O'Malley, "this shite-stirring fistle of a mankie drool, is pressing us onwards to London. What? Does he think that London is quaking in fear at our advance? They must be sitting in their coffee houses, rejoicing on our imminent destruction, laughing at our naivety for thinking that we could have caused England's Catholics to rise up and fight for us. I tell you, Charles, that if we don't turn around immediately and head back to Scotland, there'll be six thousand Scottish widows cursing the name Stuart from here unto eternity."

The Lord Murray breathed deeply and sat down on a chair. He had said his piece. He had planted his flag firmly in the soil. If the meeting went against him, he would be destroyed as a military commander. But in all good conscience, it was a risk he had to take. For the sake of Scottish men and women everywhere.

## THE PALACE OF ST. JAMES, LONDON

### DECEMBER 4, 1745

Prime Minister Henry Pelham set out early with his brother, the Duke of Newcastle, on a long walk from Whitehall to St. James's Palace, taking in a large swathe of central London in order to find out how the hearts of Englishmen and women were beating.

The two men could have taken a carriage, but Pelham insisted that they walk so that they could more accurately enter the crowds in the streets and enable them to gauge the mood of their fellow Londoners. They walked into a couple of coffee houses on their way and found the mood in both to be unusually somber. Normally beehives of gossip, noisy establishments full of laughter and banter, today everybody was talking about the coming invasion and the slaughter that would undoubtedly take place when the wild Scottish men with their claymores and daggers entered the city and raped and pillaged as they'd done up and down the length and breadth of England. As they left the first coffee house, the duke had commented to his brother on the quiet of the establishment. "It's more like a damnable Quaker's Meeting House than a coffee shop."

In case it was an aberration and to gain further information, Pelham had insisted that they visit a coffee house on Tyburn Road. But this shop too was patronized by people who also spoke in subdued tones and speculated on whether or not they could sleep safely in their beds that or any other night. Even though they had only visited two establishments, from these and the tenor of people in the streets, it was obvious that the stampede of the marauding Highland cattle had caused London to panic. People were speaking openly and in confident tones about the thousands of English women and girls dragged out of their homes and raped by a dozen or more Scotsmen, who then rejoiced in inflicting the most horrendous death by skewering them with pikes and swords. And all this while their menfolk in chains were forced to watch the degradation of their womenfolk before themselves being butchered. Prime Minister Pelham knew from first-hand reports that it was all nonsense, of course. It was even said that the prince insisted on paying for food and lodging as he progressed south. But that didn't stop the rumors.

The two men continued to walk past Tyburn Gallows where five cut-purses were swinging in the wind and then south down Park Lane, into St. James's Park and then on to the palace where courtiers opened the doors to admit them. The king's equerry nodded for the two men to enter, which surprised Pelham.

"Aren't you going to announce us, General von Hinton?" asked Pelham.

"For what purpose?" asked the Equerry, his heavy German accent more pronounced than the prime minister remembered hearing it in recent months. "There's almost nobody in the Audience Hall; they've all scurried away like frightened mice to their country estates. There's only the king and a few others, and they're so busy packing up and deciding with what to flee that they won't even hear me if I announce you. Just go in, Mr. Prime Minister, and announce yourself."

"Extraordinary," said the Duke of Newcastle and opened the door for his prime ministerial brother.

When they entered the Audience Hall, normally hissing with the sound of courtiers whispering behind their hands or their fans, there was only the sound of their footsteps echoing against the walls. It wasn't until they were halfway along the room that the king looked up from his writing desk and noticed them. They were shocked by his appearance.

Normally resplendent in a different military uniform every week, bejewelled and bemedalled, today the king was dressed in little more than his trews and nightshirt and was devoid of his wig, even though it was already the middle of the morning. His hair was ruffled, and most surprisingly of all, his face was completely un-made-up. He looked more like an elderly barrow boy than a king of England.

"Ah, Prime Minister. I can't decide which of my English crowns to take with me. And shall I take the Sceptre with the Dove or the Sceptre with the Cross. Or both? What do you think? And the rest of the royal jewels. What's your opinion?"

"My opinion, Majesty?"

"Yes, Mr. Pelham, what should I take?"

"But where are you going, sir?"

The king looked at Pelham as though he were deranged.

"To Hanover."

"But . . ."

"London is besieged, and the monarchy must continue. I shall be in Hanover until these barbarians are defeated."

"You're leaving?" said the Duke of Newcastle, barely able to speak the words.

"Of course. Now, gentlemen, your opinion. What jewels should I take with me to protect it from the Scotsmen?"

"None," said Pelham. "You mustn't go. This is madness. Majesty, what you are about to do is an act of rashness and great folly. To think of leaving London now would be an evil mistake. Sir, a king should lead his people in time of woe. To even contemplate leaving the capital at a moment such as this sends a signal to your people that all is lost. People will think that you're a coward, despite the great courage Your Majesty showed not two years ago when you led your armies against the French at the Battle of Dettingen. Yet now you seek to leave your people and travel back to Germany. How could Your Majesty think of such a thing? All London is frightened of the advancing Scots, and so this is no time for the king to leave his nation. Unless, Majesty, you truly believe that Hanover is where your heart lies and the seat on which the royal buttocks should reside. If that is the case, Sire, please inform me, and I'll travel to the north of London and welcome Prince Charles Edward Stuart who will prepare the throne for his father who will, by your abdication, become king of England."

The Duke of Newcastle was stunned at the impertinence of his brother, whom he'd always considered more of a shopkeeper than a prime minister. He looked at him with new respect. But the king felt no such respect!

"Kindly remember, Mr. Pelham, to whom you're speaking."

"I remember only too well, sir, that I am addressing the king of England, the inheritor of a throne on which sat the greatest of all monarchs our world has ever known, true leaders of their people whose Houses bore such great names as Plantagenet and Tudor. Men and women such as Henry II, Henry VIII, and Queen Elizabeth, who, I might remind you, stood alone and in peril against Spain and defeated the armada. There was a true monarch. Indeed, all three and many more were the stoutest hearts of this country, monarchs who would never have contemplated sailing away when their nation needed them."

"But unlike them, Mr. Prime Minister, I am not just the king of England, but I'm also the Duke Brunswick-Lünenburg of Hanover and the Arch-treasurer and Prince-Elector of the Holy Roman Empire! My lands and titles are far greater than just being the king of England. Is it wrong for a monarch to be kept safe from harm when he is heir to such august offices? Am I to put myself in the front line of every battle? If I'm killed, who then will rule in my place? I have a duty to my people."

"Your Majesty put himself in the front line against the French at Dettingen," said Newcastle.

"And standing beside me were the Hanoverian army and the Austrians. Safety in numbers, my Grace of Newcastle. But who can countenance standing against pillaging wild men in skirts who rape and plunder. Madmen who carry terrible weapons that can tear a man in two and rip out his innards. What kind of a weapon from hell is that, Mr. Pelham? This isn't an army come to take London; this is a force of wild beasts. An army is composed of gentlemen and other ranks who are trained to fight gentlemen like gentlemen; they march in precise formations and fire their weapons only when ordered. But what army can fight against these . . . these . . . wild brutes from the north who have red beards and red eyes and arms and legs covered in thick untamed hair like those of a Bavarian mountain bear. The stories coming to me concerning these men and what they do to prisoners are terrifying . . . when I fought the French, I knew what I was fighting, and what would happen to me. The worst would be a bullet through my heart or a mortal wound in a saber fight. But these men from Scotland. They're not men, Mr. Pelham. They're animals. Who can tame them? Eh? Answer me that, Prime Minister."

"Your brave son, the Duke of Cumberland, sir. And other generals who are currently racing the length and breadth of England to do battle. My own beloved brother, the Duke of Newcastle who stands by my side and who will leave this very afternoon to lead his army. These are the men, sir, who will defeat our enemy.

"And as to these reports of murder and rape and pillage, they are untrue. False. Hateful lies to slander the Young Pretender. He may be our enemy, Majesty, but he is a gentleman. Stories of rape and pillage are coffee house gossip and tittle-tattle. And yes, they may be hirsute and wear kilts, but these are Highlanders. They live a crude life in crofts and huts. But not all Scotland is like that. There is great intellect in Scotland, and the officers who lead these men would, I'm sure, be gentlemen of courage and wisdom. Men who probably live and thrive in the cities of Scotland, such as Edinburgh, which are replete with cultured gentle men and women.

"This Scottish army under the Pretender has fought a few engagements in Scotland and on the border of England, and they've not only fought well, but fairly."

"Fairly," shouted the king. "Fairly? How can you say that when in the battle outside of Edinburgh, they crept up like cowards and dogs in the middle of the night, and shot our Englishmen in the back? What's fair about that, Mr. Pelham?"

"It was a tactic that I'm sure the English generals would have employed, had they known to. Sir, there has been no question that the Scotsmen have behaved like barbarians. Yes, they are right at this moment in the town of Derby, but they will soon be met, maybe around Leicestershire, by General Wade or your son, the duke himself. We have vastly superior numbers, superior artillery, cavalry, rifles, and equipment. Our men are fresh, whereas the Pretender's troops have marched themselves into exhaustion. They're ill-equip, and almost nobody in England has risen to join them. They came here anticipating a mass uprising of Catholics, and your loyal subjects have rejected Prince Charles Edward Stuart and all of his vaunted ambitions to put his father on the throne.

"Yet Your Majesty is filling up your royal ship in the Thames with the treasury and heritage of England in order to desert his country, just when you should be standing firm and showing the people your bravery."

"My treasury, Mr. Pelham! I am England and England belongs to me. I am taking the crown and the jewels with me for safekeeping. The very last thing I want is for the damned Pretender to capture the crown and place it on his unworthy head," King George said, his voice raised almost to a shouting pitch.

And Pelham shouted back, "His head will be worthy of your crown, sir, if the throne is empty and he occupies it by right of conquest. Then the crown truly will be his, for he will have fought and won and deserve to be crowned king of England.

"It beggars my understanding and defies my belief in the divine right of kings and our heritage in the ancient monarchy of England that Your Majesty could even contemplate leaving your people at such a time, just when the battle is about to commence? Especially when in all likelihood Prince Charles will be soundly thrashed by the sturdy oaks who are your loyal subjects and who will lay down their lives for you!

"But what will your subjects say when they discover that you have scurried off to Hanover to protect yourself? You'll be a laughingstock. When you return in disgrace, you'll be mocked and hated in the inns and coffee shops and salons in London and the provinces. It won't do, sir. It truly won't."

The king stood from his chair and came to the edge of the plinth, his face puce with anger, his body shaking in rage. The only time he'd ever been spoken in this manner had been by his detested and long-dead father. "They hate me now, Mr. Pelham, just like they hated my father, and they hate my son. So what's the difference? They hate anybody who wasn't born in England. I can't help the fact that I was born in Hanover. Is that a reason to scorn me and my family? It seems that the only friends I have in this damnable country are my courtiers, and they've all deserted me at the first sign of trouble. All England lets me know how much they hate me. I'm mocked in the newspapers and on the stage and in the streets. So why should I stay and defend these people who are my subjects?"

"Not true, sir," said Pelham. "The English people might not have taken to you, or your heir, but your second son, the Duke of Cumberland, is loved and admired. He's a brave and respected commander of our finest men."

"My younger son is a wonderful man. Would that my oldest son and heir were such as he! But what I say to you is true. I'm not the idiot you make me out to be, Mr. Pelham. I know that I'm hated for sending English troops to help decide the Austrian succession. I know they detest me for sending three hundred thousand pounds to Princess Maria Theresa to help her fight against the French. But the English forget that I'm also the Elector of Hanover and that my father was invited to take the throne of England. Invited, Mr. Pelham. But it would have been better if we'd stayed where we were, instead of enjoying the ridicule and contempt of all England."

The prime minister sighed. "Whatever disdain the people had for you, sir, will be as nothing if they learn that you've deserted them in their hour of need. But you can turn that disdain around if the Britons see you as their leader in their time of crisis. I tell you, sir, that the Pretender Stuart won't advance much further south toward London before he's stopped by the duke, your son. And then the tables will be turned so quickly that all England will cheer for the family from Hanover who saved them from the Stuart family from Scotland. You'd be amazed how patriotism can make the people rally around a king. Please, Majesty, trust your prime minister in this matter. I have your interests at heart. Do not desert England. Do not vacate your throne."

ARMADALE

ON THE ISLAND OF SKYE IN THE OUTER HEBRIDES

DECEMBER 20, 1745

She sat on the rocks watching the fishing boats bobbing up and down in the sultry water. The heavy gray sky, a weak sun only a suggestion beyond the drab clouds, and the bleak menace of the thick and sluggish sea made her feel as though this was the very end of days. The morning was morose and the dark clouds, pregnant with rain, hung over the island like a fist of doom. Wrapped in two woollen shawls and a long thick skirt, still the icy chill managed to reach into her clothes and make her skin shiver.

Twice her mother had called from their house along the shoreline; twice she'd ignored her plea to come back to the house and eat her breakfast. Exhausted from barely having slept that night, confused and angry with life itself, Flora sighed deeply, picked up a stone lying at her feet, and tossed it into the lethargic water. It sank to the bottom without making more than the smallest splash.

A crunching sound of gravel and stones told her that somebody was approaching from behind her. She turned, looked up, and saw Hugh standing above her. But she looked back to sea and buried her head in her hands. The very last thing she needed was his gloating.

"Lass, come up and eat your breakfast. Your mother's worried about you. I'm worried about you. Come back and join us, darling."

"I'm not hungry, father," she said, her voice barely audible above the morning wind that was beginning to blow stronger as the day began to grow older.

He looked at his stepdaughter and sniffed the air. He didn't like the portent of violence that he could smell presaging a coming storm. For Hugh, who had lived beside the sea all of his life, the smell of a storm was as distinct as the smell of salt in the sea. He could almost taste the anger of the Almighty.

"Lass, it's already a freezing cold morning, and there's worse to come. I sense a blizzard brewing over the mountains. You'll need food inside you to ward off the chill. Come on, Flora love. Don't be silly now. There's nothing you can do, and no harm will come to our family. Indeed, if there's any good for Scotland out of the whole sorry mess that your Charlie has created, then it's you and your mother who'll enjoy the benefits."

He sat beside her and put his arm around her.

There was no anger in her voice, only resentment. "Benefits? So we'll benefit while Bonnie Prince Charlie and his army flee back to Scotland to be rounded up like Highland cattle and humiliated by the king's son."

"And what's wrong with us benefiting? I said right from the beginning that the prince's mission was foolhardy and that he was bound to come to grief. He did well to get as far as a hundred miles shy of London, I'll say that much for him. He got much further than I expected. But even his own council of war saw sense when they assessed the situation, and forced him to turn around and retreat . . ."

"They're a motley crew of artless beef-witted clack-dishes," she said vehemently. "Cowards, the lot of them, who should hang their heads in shame at the disgrace they've brought to the prince and to all of Scotland."

"No! They're experienced military men who know when to fight and when to save the lives of those in their charge. They saw it was madness for him to continue traveling south and headlong into London like some crazed cow in heat, knowing that for certain he'd be destroyed and take thousands of Scottish lives with him. Barely a single Catholic Englishman rallied to the prince's support. The Frenchies have stayed away like the double-dealing bum-baileys we know them to be, and the Welsh and Irish are too frightened to leave their own lands for fear of George's retribution. So what chance did the lad have to reach London and live, let alone take the fight to them and put their armies to flight?"

"But William Wallace nearly succeeded . . . he took the fight to the English; he crossed the border and rode down into their lands and they were forced to beg him for peace," she said.

"Stories, lass, and nothing more than legend. Mere tales told by ignorant folk about a Scots hero, which our people tell to give us pride in ourselves. That's because we've been a vassal state of the English since the time of King Edward Longshanks. And don't forget that Wallace was hung, drawn, and quartered and led his men into disaster; it took Scotland hundreds of years to recover from his madness. I pray to God that Scotland doesn't suffer again for the madness of a pretender king."

"But that's not the case with Charlie. Oh father, he was so near. I could almost taste the sweetness of his victory. I was so certain that he could have scared off fat George and the rest of those mollyrooks down in London. It would have taken just one battle for him to win, and then we'd have a rightful Stuart on the throne," she said, her voice close to tears. "But instead of that, he turned tail because of the cowards who marched behind him, and he retreated in shame without having fought one single army on English soil to claim his family heritage. I'm so ashamed of being a Scots woman."

"Never say that," Hugh scolded her. "Never be shamed by what your leaders do in your name. And don't confuse a tactical withdrawal for good military reasons, with a cowardly escape. The Bonnie prince didn't escape, because he'd fought no army in England. He just made a smart move to fight the English on his own terms."

"But if he'd fought them, he could have won," Flora said, but the certainty in her voice was no longer there.

"And he still could, lass," said Hugh.

She turned around and looked at him, trying to ascertain his meaning.

He continued, "His supporters are right here, in Scotland. This is where he must stake his claim and be crowned king. He has the right to demand the return of Jacob's Pillow, the Stone of Scone. It's one thing for the Plantagenet kings to have stolen it and the Tudors to have kept it, but it's of no value to these arse-fiend kings from Germany. These Hanoverians don't understand the value of the Stone of Scone to us Scots, and I'm sure that in the pursuit of peace, they'll be willing to give it back as a token. And once the Stone is back on Scottish soil, your Charlie can be crowned rightful king and successor of Robert the Bruce. All he has to do is bring his army home, rouse loyal Scotsmen and women to the cause, and send the Duke of Cumberland and all the other generals packing. And then . . ."

He remained silent, but the look of eagerness on her face, which had been missing since she'd heard the news of his retreat, encouraged him to give her hope in the future.

"And then, given enough time and support, and assuming that he isn't reckless and stupid, and further assuming that King George and his successor are as unpopular tomorrow as they are today, there's no reason why King Charles Stuart couldn't raise a loyal army of Scotsmen and march south to be joined by tens of thousands of Englishmen who detest the Hanoverians, and claim the throne of both nations."

Flora looked at him in astonishment. "Do you really think he could? Right now, all that Scotland knows is that he's a failure. They see him flying to England like a bird and fleeing home like a rabbit."

Her father smiled. "Oh, the fine gentlemen and ladies in Edinburgh will no doubt laugh in their glasses of wine and their cups of coffee at his exploits, but the men and women of the Highlands will see things differently. In Edinburgh, they'll see a young, foolhardy, and impetuous man, but in the Highlands, we'll see a brave and resilient king. As the days pass, we won't remember his turnaround in Derby, but his successes in Prestonpans and the border skirmishes that he won so brilliantly.

"When Charlie returns over the border, it's likely all Scotland will rise up in his support. Then, when the Duke of Cumberland comes to fight him, he'll find a forest of prickly Scottish thistles arrayed against him, thorns stabbing him where it hurts most. I think it's likely that thanks to your Charlie, Scotland will finally separate from England and that the Stuarts will again be the kings of this realm. There's little enough support for our union with England anyway."

"But if he succeeds, you'll be branded a traitor," she said, her words little more than a whisper, barely audible above the growing voice of the wind.

"That's something with which I'll have to deal when the time comes. Now, lass, come away and eat your breakfast before there's not enough of you left to celebrate Charlie's coming victories."

# Chapter Four

April 2, 1746

It was an exhausted sun in a limpid sky that greeted her early morning walk down to the sea. Everything else—the new green grass, the leaves emerging on the sturdy branches of the trees, the smiles of the clan folk as they walked along pathways no longer snowbound and rock hard—was fresh and invigorating. But the sun was weak and languorous as though its efforts to shine and spread its light and warmth through the dead of winter had drained it of energy so that it neither shone bright, nor did it warm the newly bared skin of the inhabitants of the Island.

She sat on the rocks watching the fishing boats bobbing up and down in the sparkling water, but there was nothing bright in her life. Unlike the other folk of the clan who welcomed the end of the winter and the coming of the warmth of spring, Flora dreaded each day for the news it would bring. While their lives were dominated by repairs to their farms or homes and by the prospect of the coming dances and fairs in spring and summer, her life was dominated by the invasion of a young man from Italy.

Prince Charles had won some significant battles and his enforced retreat had been orderly. But now she'd learned that the Duke of Cumberland had come by ship near to Inverness on the far side of the country. And with him came thousands and thousands of troopers and cannon and artillery. Fresh troopers, well rested and fiercely armed.

But the prince and his Highlanders were exhausted after fighting other English generals at Falkirk; yes, the Highlanders had won the battle, but at the cost of most of their ammunition and any remaining strength, they had after tramping hundreds and hundreds of miles through the worst days of a terrible winter. And from what she'd been told by a traveling knife sharpener who'd visited Skye from the mainland, many of the Highlanders had deserted the prince after Falkirk and returned to their homes. They assumed that the battle for the prince had either been won and he would be crowned king of Scotland, or lost and he would be destroyed by Generals Wade or Ligonier or Cumberland or one of the other fat gentlemen soldiers from South of the border.

And Flora had just learned that the prince was due to leave Glasgow at any day now, where he had been resting and regrouping, and would travel to Inverness in order to meet with the duke and fight him. All of Scotland anticipated the coming battle. Many were convinced that after his run of victories the prince would easily win on firm Scottish ground. Others, such as her father Hugh, understood the exhaustion and depletion of the prince's army and were skeptical of his ability to win a major battle. When he and his friends met, they would say quietly and in confidence to each other, as though they didn't want the deity to hear, that the prince hadn't been properly tested by a real army and when he was, he would be annihilated.

Flora had argued vehemently, telling Hugh that the prince's brilliant victory at the Battle of Prestonpans would be sung by balladeers for all time; Hugh had smiled and said that if the Englishman General Cope hadn't been such a bootless clapper-claw, he'd have won the battle easily.

And now Flora had to tell her family the decision she'd come to. It wouldn't be easy. She had traveled on her own before, but not this far, and not on such a mission. Yet she had to do it. She had to be there if only to see him, if only to be one of the Scots who would cheer him on. It was her duty.

She stood from the beach and began to walk toward her family's croft. She practiced the words she would need to use in order gain their consent. And if their consent wasn't forthcoming, she would go anyway, though the arguments would be furious and bitter.

But the question that she knew Hugh would ask was one that she herself couldn't answer, for she simply didn't know why she was so drawn to a man she'd never seen, never spoken with, and about whom she knew practically nothing. Some stories put about concerning him were that he was excessively tall and muscular and brave and steadfast and a superb horseman and swordsman and shot, with a barrel chest and sturdy and shapely legs. He was said to be handsome and gallant and with gentle continental manners, yet with a subtle and witty mind.

Other stories told of him being little more than a dwarf, two heads shorter than a grown woman, that he spoke with a terrible lisp, and that he stank of French wines and was continually drunk; and worst of all was that he demanded pleasure from every woman who crossed his path, whether they were a ten-year-old scullery girl or a grand-matron in shawls sitting at a window and barely able to move. It was said, but she'd shuddered in disgust when told, that if a mother and daughter were introduced to him, he'd insist on having his way with both of them and at the same time.

So did she want to see him and wish him well because of a need within her to determine who was the real Bonnie Prince Charlie, or was there a deeper reason that she couldn't even admit to herself? Why go across the country just to gain a glimpse of him, when portraits of the young man would soon enough appear in some rich person's home when she accompanied her friend, Lady Margaret Macdonald. These would give her a good indication of which story concerning his looks she should believe. So that wasn't the reason; and anyway, she'd never met the king of England, but she knew that she'd hate him on sight because he was fat and stupid and he detested the Scots. So it wasn't because of curiosity concerning his looks that drove her need to see him, although the idea of seeing him in the flesh sent a *frisson* of excitement through her body.

In her own mind, in her nighttime dreams, she saw Prince Charlie as a tall and magnificent young man riding confidently on a blindingly white Highlands stag, holding tight to the huge beast's horns, charging up the steep hills of a distant glen, dashing and handsome and courteous, doffing his cap to her as he thundered by to the accompaniment of pipes and drums.

In her fancy, Flora would be standing on the top of a hillside as he galloped toward her; and as he drew closer, she imagined him holding out his arm as the beast raced by, hoisting her up onto the back of his stag to carry her from the hill where she'd been looking out to the far sea, and galloping toward distant and mysterious lands. And she'd ride behind him on the back of the stag, clasping him around his waist, feeling his taut muscular stomach as he rode the beast, her hands inside his leather jerkin, her thighs joining with his legs in an intimate embrace as he breasted the hill and took her home to deposit her with Hugh and her mother Annie. And for the hour-long journey that she straddled the beast's back behind her prince, while she held him tightly with her arms feeling different parts of his lithe and handsome body, they shouted to each other over the howling wind and talked about every subject conceivable. She advised him about his ambitions and what his first acts should be as king of Scotland, and he listened to her in respect and admiration. But even though these night dreams helped her to get to sleep, the reality was that in the morning, her bonnie prince was still struggling to get the Scottish people to accept him and most were more content to sit and wait and see what would happen.

So what was it that compelled her to want to go and see him, even if it was from afar? Was it because he could become her king? If so, why travel across the nation in a time of war, when all she had to do was to wait for his coronation and then she would see him soon enough when he went on a royal procession to Edinburgh or Glasgow and the whole family would travel there just to stand in the crowds and wave and cheer him on.

Perhaps it was her devotion to him as a loyal subject; yet how could she be loyal to a man they called the Pretender who hadn't yet earned the right to sit on a throne by defeating his enemies into submission? Not only was the English enemy all over Scotland, but at least half of Scotland viewed him as an interloper and wanted nothing to do with him.

So why was she even contemplating undertaking so perilous a journey when knowledge of the outcome of the future engagement would be known by the people of Skye within days of the final sword being sheathed?

And that was what she didn't know, and couldn't answer when Hugh would undoubtedly ask her the questions that had been running untrammeled through her mind. Why was she soon to pack her traveling belongings for a journey to Inverness in order just to stand and stare at a man she'd never met? A man she wanted to call king?

In her heart, the name William Wallace kept recurring. William Wallace, hero of Scotland, true man of the people, and one of the greatest lords of war that her nation had ever produced. Even after his capture by the English, when he was about to face death for treason, Flora had memorized his immortal words, "I could not be a traitor to King Edward, for I was never his subject."

How grand and glorious, she thought. And now her prince, her Charles, had come to Scotland and like William had fought and won, invaded England, and retreated to the safety of Scotland where he would become king and all would be well. And yes, she would travel across Scotland, just to see him.

A cormorant wheeled in the sky high above her head. She looked at it and envied its freedom. All it had to do was to head east, and it would be over Inverness in a day and would look down on the looming battle. Yet she had to brave an English army on the move, as well as Scotsmen and women who were suspicious of strangers in a time when marauders were on the prowl.

And again, the questions invaded her mind. Why was it imperative that she risk her life just to glimpse at the man who would be king? Was it because she detested being ruled by the English and wanted a Scottish king to rule over the land she loved so dearly? If that was the case, then why Bonnie Prince Charlie or his father the Old Pretender who hadn't even bothered to land in England the last time he invaded the country? How could men such as these be of the bloodline of Robert the Bruce or Alexander or William?

Charlie was more Italian than Scottish, more French than English and more Angle than Celt. Yet her mysterious and breathless passion for him to be her king was what drove her to the heights of joy at his successes and the depths of despair when she was told of the frustrations and difficulties he was experiencing. So maybe the reason she felt such affinity was because of the fact that a young man had come to reclaim that which had been taken from him. Here he was, the son of a man who by all rights should have been king of England and Scotland as well as Wales and Ireland, fighting not just for treasure and possession and land and religion, but for justice.

Yes! That was why she and so many Scotsmen and women had rallied to his cause when they heard that he'd landed all those many months back. Not because of his looks or the awe of his majesty, but because he was seeking justice for himself, his father, and his family. And that was why she would travel from Skye and across the mainland, north to Inverness, where she would stand on a hilltop and look down on Bonnie Prince Charlie and wave to him as he strode manfully forward into his battle for justice. And maybe, if she were truly lucky, he'd have time and the presence of mind to turn around before he encountered the English and look up to the hill upon that Flora would stand, and see this Scottish lass in the distance, dressed in Macdonald tartan, her hair and dress gently wafted by the April breeze; and maybe he'd have the presence of mind to smile in gratitude and thanks that she'd come all the way just to wish him God speed.

CULLODEN MOOR

SOUTHEAST OF INVERNESS ON THE EAST COAST OF SCOTLAND

APRIL 16, 1746

His Royal Highness, William Augustus, Duke of Cumberland, British hero of the battles against the French, third son by birth, yet most beloved of the children of George II and Caroline of Ansbach, was ready. As were his men. Hardened in battle, rested, fit, keen, and with new techniques he'd taught them in their use of the bayonet, volley firing, and cannon assault, all was in readiness for a great victory. He sniffed the mid-morning air and looked over the flat and desolate field upon which the battle would shortly take place and felt a peace and confidence that had been absent from his spirit since the moment he'd heard of the landing of this young upstart Pretender who dared to call himself Prince Regent. The Duke of Cumberland held him in utter contempt, knowing him to be a fop and a dandy and a man who preened himself in the courts of Paris and Rome, telling everybody who'd listen that his *effete* father and he were the rightful heirs to the English throne and that God was on his side. Well, the duke thought, soon the world would see whether God would arm the silly young prince with cannon and shot or whether he'd side with Hanover and blow the Pretender to pieces?

The duke had issued an edict that forbade any officer or soldier to refer to Charles Edward Stuart as either "The Prince" or "The Prince Regent," for that inferred that he had some valid claim to the throne of his father, and such a claim was and always would be bogus. The edict stated that Charles Edward Stuart was to be known now and for all times either as "The Pretender" or as "The Usurper." The duke had even instructed his chronicler to draw up a paper that was to be circulated to all Officers in his army showing the legitimacy of King George's hold on the throne and the illegitimacy of the claim made by the Stuarts.

But these were minor distractions compared to the coming battle. After days of practicing, waiting, marching, drilling, and more practicing, the duke knew for certain that he and his army were ready. And not only were the English soldiers primed to engage with the Highlanders, but many of the duke's soldiers in the front lines were Lowland Scots, here to join and fight with their English brethren in the defeat of a usurper who was attempting to divide Scotland from England. How would this bonnie young man feel when he took the field and found that he and his Highlanders and their French and Irish cousins weren't only fighting the English, but their own countrymen as well? William Augustus smiled at the thought of Charles' face when he saw not just English uniforms on the other side of the battleground, but Scottish tartans as well. He wondered how many of the wild Highlanders would turn and run when they realized that the fearsome Lowlanders, their eyes ablaze with hatred, were also against them.

Since the Duke of Cumberland had arrived at Edinburgh at the end of January to take command of the Royal Army from the incompetent General Hawley following his disaster at Falkirk, the duke had worked hard to ensure that no more disgrace fell upon the name of England. Prestonpans was unforgivable, but in fairness to General Cope, the Highlanders had crept like cowardly rats around the flanks and rear of the army in the middle of the night and at first light had shot Cope's men in their backs. Some judiciously placed sentries should have been positioned to warn of such an eventuality, but the damage was done, Cope had been court-martialed for cowardice and fleeing the field of battle, and justice had been served.

The loss of Falkirk to the Pretender, however, was a military disgrace and needed to be redeemed for the sake of English pride. In the three months since he'd taken personal command of the royal troops, the Duke of Cumberland had used those military skills he'd honed in fighting the French to ensure that nothing that the damned Highlanders could use against him would either surprise or throw his men into turmoil.

His army had marched north from Edinburgh to Aberdeen, supplied by ships of the Royal Navy. They had spent weeks in military exercises and training. In the meantime, the Pretender had been unable to take Stirling Castle from General Blakeney, and the duke was informed that the Highlanders had managed to capture two forts and were harassing English troops. Minor victories, he'd sneered over dinner with his commanders. Wait for the real battle, he'd assured them. And now the time had come.

When the duke had taken personal charge of the English military, it seemed as though a new spirit had infused the entire army, from his general staff all the way down to the lowliest of foot soldiers. He knew many of them by sight and had stood tall and proud with them when they'd fought together not three years past at the Battle of Dettingen. They'd called him Tommy Lobster in those days, and the affectionate name had stuck. He never knew why he should have earned that sobriquet, other than the fact that he'd been wounded in the leg and the bottom half of his body had been covered in red blood.

So here, on this desolate stretch of moorland, was where the duke was soon to meet the impertinent fellow who laid claim to the throne of the Hanoverians. Just because he was the grandson of James II, this young Pretender believed that he could take by conquest that which the English people had so sensibly removed as a right from his family.

It was already late in the morning when the Duke of Cumberland, seated high in the saddle on his favorite white charger, Mars, arrived at the head of his many regiments to inspect the field on which the battle would shortly take place. And what he saw shocked him. It was an open moorland, enclosed on two sides; one wall was to the north and on the south side was the wall enclosing Culloden Park.

Now why had the silly Pretender chosen such an unlikely ground on which to fight? It put the Scottish Highlander troops in terrible danger, because the field of battle was completely open to the Englishmen's artillery, and he knew from his scouts and spies that the Scot's army had almost no artillery. He shook his head as he rode Mars around the southern side of the battlefield, muttering to himself, *The Scots will be slaughtered.*

Yet here the Pretender had set down his army, and so here the duke would fight, taking every advantage of his enemy's stupidity! The duke shifted uncomfortably on his horse. He was still merry from the effects of the celebration of his birthday the previous night, and although it was getting to be late in the morning, he could still feel the wine dulling his mind. Too much alcohol and he'd eaten far too much pheasant and deer to feel comfortable. He felt a heaviness in his chest and had been unable to relieve himself before dressing for the engagement. But he knew from many previous battles that he'd feel better the moment the first volley was fired and the first sword was unsheathed.

Suddenly a messenger approached him, riding quickly from the left flank of the duke's command line. The man galloped swiftly up the hill to where the duke, now joined by his general staff officers sat mounted on their horses, watching the preparations. The regiments were forming in columns on the battlefield below. The duke noticed that Cobham and Kingston's Dragoons were well to the right flank, as agreed, but that for some reason Barrel's, Campbell's and Munro's Regiments had exchanged positions. Quite why, he had no idea.

Distracted, he noticed that the messenger had spoken to General Daubney, who was now approaching the duke.

"Sire, intelligence has been received that during last night, while we were celebrating Your Royal Highness' birthday, the Pretender's Highland Army tried to approach our camp and attack us. However, their maneuver was a disaster as the men became separated in the dark of the night and were bogged down in the mud. That was why our sentries reported nothing, because they didn't even come close to our lines. Having failed so miserably, they returned to their lines only very early this morning, and according to my spies, it appears that those many who attempted to attack us are now exhausted, filthy, and most have deserted in search of food and sleep, even before a single shot has been fired."

The duke shook his head in disgust. "So, Gentlemen," he said in a voice sufficiently loud for his commanders to hear, "they attempt the same trick as they used on General Cope at Prestonpans. I wonder when these dogs will have the courage to fight an honest engagement, like gentlemen."

As the English formed up into regimental attack columns, the duke and his commanders noticed movement on the opposite side of the field. Taking out his spy glasses, he focused on the last minute preparations the Scotsmen were making. After some moments of scrutiny of the enemy, he turned and looked at his officers.

"Is this a joke?" he asked.

They looked back at him and shrugged.

Again, he studied the Scottish lines and searched in vain for what little artillery he knew they had. He looked for the cavalry, the cannon, and other weaponry. There were a few cannon scattered amongst the Highland regiments, but a body of artillery that could mount a devastating assault on the English cavalry or infantry seemed to be absent.

He wondered whether it could have been hidden behind bushes or secreted somehow in another way as a surprise, but looking around the entire area with his spy glass, he saw that there was nowhere within cannon shot to hide an artillery regiment. It appeared that the Scottish enemy had failed to bring all but a few of the cannon they possessed to the battle.

And what was even more surprising was that despite the Scots having been there all morning, there seemed to be some dispute about who should be stationed on the left and right flanks. Whole regiments of men were still being moved hither and thither at the whim of their commanders while the English were setting up permanent positions for an engagement following a carefully planned strategy. What on earth was this pretender prince doing, the duke wondered.

Colonel Maxwell rode up and said to the duke, "Sir, if I might be so bold as to explain the deployment of the enemy."

The duke gave his permission for the colonel to speak.

"From the color of their tartans, it's simple to see who has joined the Pretender. In the front line, Your Highness will note that the Atholl regiments are placed next to the Camerons, then the Stewarts of Appin, then the Frasers, the Mackintoshes, the Macleans, the Maclachlans, the Farquharharsons, the Stuarts and then the Macdonalds.

"In the second line, Sire, the prince has placed his mounted regiments as well as a handful of regular Irish and French foot soldiers who have come over to join him. The rest are a motley crew of clans and mercenaries and freebooters."

"This is very good, Colonel. Please make a note of it, so that I can visit some of these clans when I've put an end to the Pretender's ambitions, and make known England's displeasure at their treason. But I don't understand Charles' tactics. Where is his cannon, Colonel? Where has he put his artillery?" asked the duke.

"It would appear, Sire, that what you can see is all the cannon that the Pretender has at his disposal. It's a sorry day for the Scots when they can't even fire cannon at us."

"Nonetheless, Colonel, we are both experienced enough in military matters to know that anything can go wrong on a field of battle. I want you to ride down and tell the commanders of each of the regiments that the Duke of Cumberland said that if there is any man who does not wish to fight the Highlanders, I beg him in God's name to go. I would rather fight with one thousand resolute men than ten thousand half-hearted. Kindly go now, Colonel, and pass on my words to my men."

Maxwell saluted and rode off. As he did so, the heavy April sky suddenly opened with a peal of thunder, a flash of lightening, and a soaking downpour began. Without being ordered to, the English dragoons and infantry hid their muskets and rifles inside their coats in order to keep their powder and firelocks dry. But the downpour was so heavy that the English commanders lost sight of the Scottish army on the other side of the Culloden field.

At midday, the duke ordered his commanders to ride down onto the sodden field of battle and prepare to engage the enemy. As though the arrival of the Duke of Cumberland was a signal for something monumental to happen, there was a terrifying roar. It sounded as though the very gates of hell had opened up, and the screams of a thousand men shattered the peace of the field as they rent the air. But even these were drowned out by a series of deafening booms heralding the Scottish artillery's cannon fire from its position. The balls screamed through the air. The target was the duke himself as well as the members of the general command. The shots, however, landed uselessly at least fifty yards short of their target and made a squelching noise as they sank into the boggy land.

"Load cannon with grapeshot and ball," shouted the duke.

When the gunners raised their flags of readiness, the duke shouted out "Fire!" and within moments, a cacophony of thunder exploded into the air and the entire battery of English guns was loosed upon the Scottish lines, fire spitting out of the gun barrels as grapeshot and balls flew into the Scottish lines. They, too, aimed for the commanders, but unlike the *effete* Scots gunners, these men were led and instructed by General Belford, England's finest cannon marksman who had trained his artillery regiment to be both deadly fast and lethally accurate, and dozens of Scottish Highlanders were instantly killed and wounded in the first three volleys that finished before the Scots had a chance to complete the reloading of their cannon from the first assault.

For half an hour, the cannon barrage continued. Only occasionally did the Scottish cannon fire back, and when they did the balls rarely hit their target. The English onslaught, however, was murderous, and Prince Charles looked on as his casualties mounted, men screamed in agony, and to his left and right, he could see Highlanders deserting the slaughter on the battlefield, wandering away in their twos and threes back to their homes and farms and highlands.

Now that the rainstorm had eased somewhat and the field became more visible through the cannon smoke, the prince waited for Cumberland to make the first move, so that he could study the technique of his approach, and judge his own tactics accordingly. But there was no attack, no move forward. Only the terrifying flames from the mouths of the cannon, followed moments later by the deafening sound of balls and grapeshot screaming through the air and finding their targets in the arms and legs and chests of the brave lads who had rallied around his flag.

Suddenly, Lord George Murray rode up, his face gray with anxiety and frustration. "Sir, we must attack. We're being slaughtered. The men are beginning to leave in droves. For our morale and to save what's left of us, for God's sake, we must move forward."

The prince nodded, raised his sword, and gave the order for the infantry and cavalry to advance. At the same moment, he sent his Aides de Camp to the other commanders up and down the line that they were to move forward at once.

When the Duke of Perth ordered the leader of the Macdonald's contingent to move forward at the charge, the Macdonald Laird flatly refused, telling Perth that he wasn't going to subject his clansmen to certain death in the face of the English cannon. Other parts of the battlefield, however, followed the orders of the prince immediately because it was judged to be more dangerous to stay where they were and be helpless victims of cannon fire, than to charge forward and come to grip with the enemy.

The Highlanders charge, accompanied by fearsome screams and clan war cries, put the fear of God into the English. First away was the

Mackintosh, led by Colonel McGillivray of Dunmaglass. He and his clan were followed by others who drew out their claymores and broadswords, target shields and dirks, and yelled evil and vicious oaths at the tops of their voices at they ran headlong into a battery of musket and rifle fire and grapeshot from hastily repositioned cannon.

But as though the power and superiority of the English forces wasn't enough, the ground was a bog from the rain, and in order to maintain the momentum of their charge, the leading Highlanders were forced to turn to their right and follow the road that passed tangentially across the moor. But this forced them into a wedge and obstructed other clans running behind so that soon the advance stalled into a crowded melee in which clansman pushed clansman into Culloden Park's wall, arguing furiously with each other as to who should proceed first.

Some clans did manage to get through and attacked the regiment of the King's Own, commanded by General Barrel. However, noticing the confusion and crowding in the flank, the artillery was trained on those who had managed to break through, and they were cut to pieces by canisters of ball and grapeshot.

Soon soldiers of both sides were engaged in hand to hand fighting, and the troops of the royal regiments used the new techniques of right-hand thrust and parry with their bayonets that had been taught to them by the duke. The Scotsmen resorted to their traditional method of swordsmanship but found that as they raised their arms to bring their swords crashing down on the enemy, their undefended bodies were pierced by the murderous points of bayonets and they dropped down dead without striking a single blow. This newly developed and shattering use of the bayonet was just as devastating to the Scotsmen's assault as had been the accuracy of the cannon.

Vicious and continuous attacks by the artillery and troopers under the command of Barrel, Munro, Wolfe, Bligh, and Sempill finished any hope that the Highlanders might have had of victory. In a matter of an hour, the hopes and aspirations of the Prince Pretender, Charles Edward Stuart, were shot to pieces and left in the mud and gore of Culloden Moor, along with many hundreds of the men who had rallied to him.

The prince, transfixed by the enormity of his loss and incapable of moving from his place, was virtually manhandled off the field to safety by his commanders when the result of the battle became obvious to everybody. It was urgent that he be moved far away, for the duke's revenge on any Scottish commander would be swift and terrible.

Looking around him at the death and destruction, the Duke of Cumberland took out a rag and wiped the blood and gore off his sword before sheathing it. He was experienced enough to know even before casualty reports that his victory had been overwhelming and that unless the Highlanders were foolhardy enough to raise another army, it was the end of the Pretender's dream.

And it had been as crushing a victory as he'd predicted. Few men on the English side had been killed, although Munro's regiment had sustained the heaviest losses of all the English regiments; yet from the numbers who had attacked, and now were straggling back, it would appear that at least a thousand Highlanders had met their maker by courtesy of the Duke of Cumberland.

He spurred his horse forward to examine the battlefield and was joined by Lieutenant James Wolfe, a pleasant and affable and very capable young man. As they rode together in silence, with the smoke of cannon and gunshot still heavy in the rain-sodden air, the duke noticed that a Highland man lying on the ground was struggling to stand up. His leg had been blown off, and he was whimpering, but his musket was close at hand and so he still posed a threat. The duke turned to Wolfe and said, "Lieutenant, would you kindly shoot that enemy soldier."

The young officer looked at his commander in horror. He swallowed before speaking but then said softly and deliberately, "Sire, my commission is at your disposal, but not my honor. I shall not kill a wounded man."

In fury, the duke was about to reprimand him, when a soldier some distance away noticed the movement and without thinking put a musket ball into the Scotsman's chest.

"A common soldier, Mr. Wolfe, has done what you failed to do, despite a direct order from your commanding officer. I think you might have damaged your career by your damned impertinence. I suggest that you retire to your quarters, sir, and do not join us in celebration of today's victory."

The duke spurred his horse onward and up the hill.

On a further distant hill to the right of the battlefield, a young woman dressed in the Macdonald tartan tried to peer through the fog of smoke and mist to see what was happening. She had been on the high side of the approach to Culloden Moor since early morning, eager to be a spectator at the prince's victory. But since the battle began, and especially with the pouring rain, she'd sat blinded under her oilcloth, and the scene before her had been clouded in mystery.

But now, by its silence and the cries of the poor wounded Englishmen, Flora Macdonald assumed that the battle was well and truly over. She had waved to the prince when he had ridden around inspecting his troops before the arrival of the English army, and she could have sworn, although she wasn't certain, that he'd smiled and doffed his cap.

So now she would trudge the long miles back to Inverness, go back to her room at the Inn, and see whether some kind soul would invite her to a party in celebration of the enormity of Scotland's success.

## THE PALACE OF ST. JAMES, LONDON

### APRIL 24, 1746

The journey from the northern approaches to the City of London had taken him much longer than he anticipated. When last he rode out of London ahead of a column of soldiers in order to deal with the rebellion engendered by the Young Pretender, the streets had been almost empty, as though every citizen was cowering under his bed. Only the occasional gallant had come out onto the street and shouted a patriotic wish of God's speed and good luck.

Today, on his return as hero of Culloden and the man hailed as the redeemer of England, the crowds were five and ten deep in places, cheering and shouting and throwing garlands of leaves in imitation of a triumph in the time of Julius Caesar. But he knew the difference. In ancient times, the Roman Senate had decreed that to counter-balance the hubris a military champion might feel, a slave should stand behind him in the chariot and while the crowd of Romans was adoring him, whisper into the hero's ear, "Remember, you are only a man."

The Duke of Cumberland, third son of the king of England, needed no such reminding. He had defeated the damned Highlanders and quelled the Pretender who was now scurrying like a dog with mange through the thistles and thickets and bracken of Scotland, hiding while the duke's army sought to bring him to trial in London and then execution on a public gallows. Soon the duke would return to Scotland and teach the rest of the rebels and clan leaders a lesson that they would remember for the rest of eternity. But his return to London, greeted with such relief and joy by the populace, would be a cause for fury and despair by his brother Frederick, the Heir Assumptive and with many in Parliament who would happily have seen an end to the rule of the Germans and their replacement with the French-backed Stuarts.

Parliamentarians, men of low birth and no breeding were not of concern to him. They were worth two pence each and could be bought and sold according to whim. But the Royal Heir Assumptive, Frederick, hated and detested both him and his father and had set up a rival monarchy in Leicester House where politicians and literary types were visiting him and his awful wife Augusta of Saxe-Gotha and plotting and planning against the rightful king. And it wasn't as though the hatred was just on one side, for the duke himself, as well as the king and his late wife Caroline, detested the lazy, malicious, heir. In private, the duke knew that the king had consulted with lawyers and his ministers about the rights of the first born to inherit the throne but had been told in no uncertain terms that primogeniture was absolute and invariable, no matter how awful the succeeding monarch was. They had pointed out the case of the succession of Edward II, an *effete* lover of men and the first monarch to be removed from the throne. Despite his wicked ways, and against his father's wishes, Edward had succeeded his father Edward

Longshanks, one of history's bravest men and known throughout history as *Scottorum malleus,* the Hammer of the Scots.

So even the most unworthy of successors like his brother Frederick couldn't be removed from his position as heir, despite his open rebellion against his father, the king. And that meant that despite the Duke of Cumberland having laid his life on the line for the sake of England and returning as a national hero, history would soon forget The Battle of Culloden Moor and the name of the Duke of Cumberland and instead would revere forever the name of King Frederick of England.

His friend, the Duke of Rutland, rode up to him as he led his detachment into White Hall on route to St. James's Palace.

"How is Your Highness? A great day for England."

"I'm in need of distraction, Rutland."

"Distraction? Surely not. This is great day for you and a great day for England. Look at the crowds. They're beaming with love and gratitude for your great victory."

"Crowds of common folk don't interest me. They move with the wind. No, what concerns me is Frederick. I'm vexed in my mind because of my despicable brother."

"Frederick? The man's a numbskull and a coward. He couldn't have contemplated doing what you did to the Scots, my lord."

"Yes, yes, I know, but my father can't have much longer on this earth, and then Frederick becomes king, and as younger brother, I'll exchange my dukedom for a title of prince of somewhere or other, but then what? Do you think he'll allow me to remain in control of the army? What? So I can raise an insurrection and remove him from the throne. No, he'll have plans for me, like the governorship of some remote part of our empire. Or he'll send me to Scotland to sit in Edinburgh Castle in daily fear of assassination."

Rutland shook his head. "But you're the hero of England. The people will never allow it."

Cumberland laughed. "The people? They'll have forgotten the danger by the time they're sitting in their inns tonight and drunk on ale and brandy. No, Rutland, I'll be finished when my brother ascends the throne. You see if I'm not."

But then he perked up and said, "Perhaps the best idea would be for me to allow my fat and incompetent brother Frederick to rule and ruin England and to force his return to our ancestral home of Hanover in the hope that he could make his name and reputation there. Or perhaps when the House of Commons had enough of Frederick's bungling, they'll remove him as they removed Charles Stuart and beg me, the Hero of Culloden, to return and save England from itself."

Rutland began to interrupt, but the Duke of Cumberland was in no mood to listen. He continued, "But these are matters to consider when my beloved father has died and George II is no more. In the meantime, we have the gratitude of all England to receive."

The duke arrived at the steps of the palace. The crowds were confined to the street and the courtyard was full of functionaries, guards, and courtiers who had come to greet the returning savior of England. He dismounted, shook numerous hands, said for the umpteenth time to anybody who asked that while it was a great victory and England was again secure, he had much work to do to ensure that the Scots never rose again, and forced his way through the adoring throng to the inner sanctum of his father's power, the audience chamber.

Like the courtyard and the corridors of the palace, this was full of courtiers and functionaries. Relieved that the war was over, they had returned in their droves, laughing at the fears of others, assuring everybody that they weren't for one moment frightened but had been forced by circumstance to leave London and attend to domestic duties in their country estates.

All bowed low as William Augustus, Duke of Cumberland, walked the long audience chamber toward the throne of his father, King George II. An aisle parted and George stood to receive his magnificent son. The king began to applaud, and immediately the entire audience chamber resounded to the thunder of acclamation. "Hurrahs" and "huzzahs" were shouted in his honor. Somebody yelled out "three cheers for the Duke of Cumberland," and voices were raised in respect for his achievements. When the noise lessened, somebody began to sing a new anthem that had been hastily penned in George's honor, "God

Save the King." Few knew the words, but those who did, sang loud and clearly.

Eventually, the duke reached the king's podium and walked up the few steps where he bowed and kissed the king's outstretched hand. He stood and embraced his father on both cheeks. Turning and being theatrical, he shouted out, "Majesty, I bring good news of the destruction of the Pretender's claim to your throne. His army of Scottish traitors and miscreants, of Irish and French mercenaries, has been destroyed. After such a victory, no man in Scotland will ever dare raise his fist to an Englishman again. Shame upon all of Scotland who supported the impertinent Charles Edward Stuart and his ambitions. He acquitted himself poorly on the field of battle and now he is in hiding, and my officers and men are hunting him down throughout the Highlands and Lowlands until he is caught, when he will be brought to London for trial and execution for crimes of High Treason. God Bless Your Majesty George II and all of England. God preserve the king and save His Majesty from all of his enemies."

A thousand miles north, having just returned to her home of Skye and before she entered her father and mother's house, Flora Macdonald breathed deeply. She would have to tell them of the disaster, as the news would not yet have reached the Isles. And when she did, she had no idea what would be the reception. She sighed. She'd done her crying; now she must get on with her life. She breathed deeply before whispering to herself, God preserve and save Scotland from its enemy, England.

# Chapter Five

His legs were aching fiercely; his arms and shoulders felt that they were carrying an iron cannon, and his mouth was as dry as the bones of a skeleton. The horses they'd stolen thirty miles north of Culloden Moor made them all too visible, and so now, and for the past week or more, they traveled on foot. Slow, painful, and exhausting but safer.

Trudging over Scotland without horses meant they had to carry everything on their persons. And worse, they couldn't use roads or tracks that would have made them visible for miles around, so instead, the party had to scale heights through the untamed heather and traipse across bogs and trudge through uncharted wilderness. Where cattle, rabbit, foxes, and deer went, so went they.

And it seemed as though the land would never end. Every time they climbed from the embrace of a valley up its steep hills to breast its precipitous heights, they'd stand on the loftiest point gasping for breath and look all around them for sight of the Englishmen. But at the same time, Charles was looking onward, ever onward, as one valley folded into another, one hill revealed the peaks of more and even more hills and mountains in the distant and as far as his eyes could tell, there was nothing ahead but what they had traversed behind. A never-ending vista of more and more hills and higher and higher mountains that they had to climb to avoid being arrested by the Englishmen who pursued the prince and his companions with a vengeance and sense of purpose as though they were demons from the jaws of hell itself. Their refusal to quit the chase told him in uncompromising terms what would be his fate were he to be caught.

It was the eleventh day and night since the disaster and he and his party were too exhausted and starving to continue another footfall. Yet his guide, who hailed from this area, insisted that he must scale at least the next two peaks before they had put sufficient distance between themselves and the English; then, and only then could they take a rest late in the evening, well after dark, in one of the valleys beyond. Somewhere ahead, his companion guide assured him, was where there should be at least a few Catholic houses whose owners might allow the party to rest in one of their barns . . . even in the house itself if they didn't recognize the prince.

As his aching legs and thumping heart somehow carried him higher, he used the method he'd created for himself to lessen the physical pain. He distracted himself by thinking of alternative strategies he could and should have used in the battle against the English on Culloden Moor. Placing the Macdonalds on the right instead of the left as they'd insisted; choosing a different location to the moor, one that offered better protection for his troops instead of the vast and open area that led to the slaughter of a thousand of his gallants; waiting until the French supplied him with artillery instead of thinking that he could repeat his success at Prestonpans. All so obvious now, but in the noise and fog of a battle, when so many voices were competing for his approval, it was so easy even for the best of commanders to make an error of judgment. And all that was needed was a single mistake and a man like the Duke of Cumberland would spot the weakness and exploit it with disastrous consequences.

Had it really been just eleven days since the catastrophe of the battle close to Inverness? Eleven long days of misery and grief, of confusion and panic, and still he was running like a terrified dog. Still the duke's men chased him over mountain and through valley. Every time he stopped running, confident that the English were no longer in pursuit, their telltale red coats, and tall white hats were spotted far into the distance, always heading toward him. As he and his men rushed to a new place over the difficult terrain, they'd arrive to find that a large party of English soldiers was already in the vicinity, having traveled openly and easily by horse on the major roads that were barred to the prince and his supporters for fear of them being exposed by traitors and turncoats eager to profit from the vast reward offered for the prince's capture.

Every time he rested overnight in a cave or a hut or under canvas in a field, he'd awake from the nightmares of his dreams and as he stretched and rubbed the morning dew off his face, he'd see the thin column of smoke on a distant hilltop telling him that the regiment was still chasing after him and that he'd have to leave immediately to prevent being caught.

Early in their escape, on the first day after his defeat at Culloden Moor, the prince and his followers, ten worthies who still supported his failed mission, stole horses from a laird's stables and rode *pêle-mêle* across land for mile after mile, northwest, always northwest; yet a day or two later, after they'd rested and thought themselves free, one of the party would shout in despondence that he had spotted the dread uniform of a scouting party from one of the Duke of Cumberland's regiments, and again the chase would be on. It was then that they decided to free the horses and travel less conspicuously by foot. Less conspicuous perhaps but a thousand times more arduous and exhausting.

He had spent his entire life, all twenty-six years of it, being told that he was an *émigré* from his rightful throne of England and Scotland; but now, for the first time, he wasn't just an exile and a refugee from his birthright, but a fugitive from his enemy. For the first time in his life, he was a hunted, rather than a haunted man. And he hated the experience.

They hadn't eaten since mid-morning the previous day and it was already approaching twilight. They were cold and starving and feeling the effects of weakness. Their packs, full of guns and ammunition rather than food, weighed them down, and so despondent were they that two of the party had already suggested that they attempt to negotiate a surrender rather than continue with the deprivation they were suffering. The idea was quickly squashed, not by the prince, but by Alistair Macdonald who had fought beside him on the battlefield. He'd reminded his companions that the only surrender the Duke of Cumberland would allow was the surrender of each man's arms, arms followed by legs, followed by his guts, and then followed by his head.

But more than the rest, Prince Charles Edward Stuart was aware that the price of £30,000 on his head for his capture, dead or alive, was a fortune that no crofter could resist, and so every man they met and who smiled was a potential assassin and confederate of Hanover.

They came to the ridge of a hill, sweating, filthy, and in utter exhaustion. On the top of the hill, the group threw down their packs and fell in heaps of tartan and sweat, panting like dogs in heat, clawing the air for relief. Although they were starving, their flasks were always full of good clean Scottish mountain water that flowed generously down the braes and into the numerous rivers and streams that lined the land. For a time, the water they guzzled filled their bellies, though soon they knew it would only sharpen their hunger.

Resting on his elbow, the prince noticed one of the strongest lads in the group, Strachan Macleod, standing and looking through his spy glass at the distant hills both from where they'd come, and where they were going. The young man looked down at the prince and said, "No sign of the bastards, Your Highness. I think this time we might very well have outrun them."

Alistair Macdonald, lying on his back to control the fierce aches in his legs, laughed and said, "No chance, man. Just because you can't see them, it doesn't mean they're not there. They'll always be there until we get the Bonnie Prince out of Scotland and back to France where he'll be safe and then the damned duke will return to London and turn his back on us and remember that his real enemies are the French and the Spaniards."

"Maybe so," said Strachan, turning a half circle and looking ahead to where they were going, "but there's a group of crofter's huts in the valley below. And there's light in their windows and smoke rising from their chimneys."

"And with a king's ransom on the prince's head, we can't afford to risk alerting anybody to his presence," said the Macdonald.

"Then I shall stay here, and you men go and beg for food and shelter. It's wrong that you are all suffering because of me," said the prince, his voice harsh in the early evening air from the exhaustion of the day.

"Go boil your head, Charlie," said the Macdonald. Good-natured impertinence had become a way of salvation in the hardships they were all suffering. "If a group of men wearing different tartans descend on an isolated farm, do you not think the owners might suspect that we're escapees from Culloden Moor? Of course, the news might not have reached these parts yet, so they could just take us for thieves and robbers and cutthroats, which would be less profitable than the ransom, but far more terrifying. No, lads, we cannot go down into the valley and beg."

"Then we're doomed to starve," said another.

"Not if one of us goes and spies out the feelings of the farmer. He surely couldn't be frightened of just one man, could he?" asked the prince.

"In these parts, Highness, one man traveling alone isn't a curiosity; it's a threat. No, I say that two men go down and talk to the farmer. Two is the right number because it means companionship. Then if the farmer is hostile, we'll know to stay away."

Whether or not it was a good plan, everybody was too exhausted to argue, and so Alistair Macdonald roused himself and took another man and disappeared down into the valley, singing a traditional Scottish Highlands song at the top of their voices as they went in order to warn the farmer long in advance of their arrival and to show him and his family that they weren't creeping up on him with ill-intent in the middle of the night.

The prince and his men lay low in the heather and watched anxiously from the top of the hill as their two companions ran and walked down to where the farmer's buildings were situated. There were five buildings altogether, spread out over the valley floor. They were beside a stream at the western most end of a long, narrow, and beautiful loch into which the stream flowed. The buildings were made of wood, although the farmer's house was larger than usual and made of stone; its thatched roof had recently been repaired. Cattle grazed the hillside and a dozen or so deer were penned up in an enclosure.

And the prince waited and waited as the light waned and his hopes fell. They'd been inside the house for the better part of half an hour and there was no sign that any movement was taking place. The prince and his men waited in silence, their breath baited in anticipation of a warm bed and maybe some food.

And then the door of the house was flung open, and Alistair Macdonald strode out as though he was the owner himself. He stood there enveloped in the light, scratching his belly, and laughed. The tall Highlander cupped his hands to his mouth and shouted into the hills, "Come down lads. We're among loyal friends here. There's food and drink and a fire to sleep beside. Come down immediately."

An hour later, the prince and his companions were crowded into the home of the farmer and owner of the valley and hills in Altnaharra in the northernmost reaches of Scotland. Much further north and they'd come to the end of the country with only the Orkney Islands to stop them from falling over the edge of the world. The home belonged to David Mackay, a spare and tall man in his mid-forties with an honest and windblown face, who had farmed the land like his father and grandfather before him, all of his life. A Catholic, a Jacobite, and a man who detested being ruled from London, he welcomed the prince with respect and sympathy for his losses.

Ingrid Mackay, red-faced from the unexpected heat in the room and the sudden additional cooking, and pregnant with their seventh child, served the ravenous men griddle and oatmeal cakes along with recently brewed ale and thick slices from a haunch of venison that had been curing in the smoke house for the past three weeks. Still hungry, they ate some salmon that David had caught the previous day and that he had intended to smoke as a celebration for the birth of his next child. But there would be plenty more fish in the river.

After an hour of ribaldry, laughter, and relief, when the food and ale and wine had been drunk and for the first time in well over a week the prince and his party felt both comfortable and relaxed, David Mackay asked simply, "How long do you think the ravages will continue, sir?"

The prince took the pipe out of his mouth and looked at the innocent Scotsman. "Ravages?"

"The duke's ravages."

The prince shook his head. His team of supporters, clustered around the fire on chairs and on the floor, looked at the farmer.

"Since your loss on the battlefield south of Inverness, the duke's army has been marauding through all of Scotland. Stories are being told of massacres of innocents. People say that the English soldiers are killing anybody they see on the roads. Men, women, and children. They're dragging people out of their beds, out of their houses and killing them if they suspect they've been supporting your campaign. Have you not heard?"

The prince felt his body slacken in shock. He looked around and saw the mask of horror on his companion's faces. He shook his head again.

"They say tell that hundreds and hundreds of Scotsmen have been murdered in revenge for your assault on London. It's said that the rivers and lochs of Scotland are running red with the blood of its people. And you've heard nothing of this?"

Softly, the prince said, "We've been on the road. We've been escaping the . . ." But he couldn't finish his words. Instead, he looked again at his companions who were equally speechless, and muttered, "Dear God Almighty, what have I done?"

THE PALACE OF ST. JAMES, LONDON

APRIL 27, 1746

"Everyone?"

"Everyone!"

"Even those who were loyal to your majesty?"

"Of course not, Mr. Pelham. Only those Highlanders who dared to raise their hands against my royal person. Only them, and also those in the Lowlands who are sympathetic to their cause. They rose against me, Mr. Pelham. They must suffer the consequences."

"But Majesty, these are tens of thousands of Scotsmen. Your subjects. A whole nation. Surely you don't intend . . ."

"Did not the Israelites destroy the Philistines?"

"The Philistine army perhaps, sir, but not the Philistine women and children. When the Romans conquered ancient Israel, they killed those who fought against them, but the rest of the population wasn't killed. Their lives were spared."

"Perhaps," said the king, "but the Romans expelled all of the population and left the ancient land barren and denuded of people. And that's what I intend to do to Scotland. Those who fought in the Pretender's army, who dared to raise a hand against me, their wives, and their children will be banished. Remember, Mr. Pelham, that the children of Israel were taken as slaves and spread throughout the entire Roman world. We won't kill women and children, sir, just enslave them."

Pelham stared at the king open-mouthed. "I . . . but . . ."

The king smiled. "My court composer, Herr Handel, is already working hard on an anthem to celebrate my victory. He's calling it 'See the Conquering Hero Come,' and he's basing it on some theme or other of the Bible. So you see, Mr. Pelham, that I'm not unfamiliar with the currents of history. Our defeat of the Scots will resound forever as our greatest glory."

"Glory, Sire, should be celebrated both in victory on the field of battle and in the magnanimity with which the defeated are used."

King George II shrugged, already bored with his prime minister's ministrations. "I'm using these traitors very well, letting the women and children be saved and deported. Let them be sent to America, or moved from the Highlands of Scotland to the coast where they can pick up crabs and fish. But those men who are not executed as traitors will vacate their farms and the lords will be stripped of their titles and the clans will be disbanded and that will be an end of it. Scotland will never raise its hand against me and England again."

"But sir, following such a great and glorious victory, this surely isn't the time for vengeance; now, when your Scottish subjects are at their lowest ebb, is the time to show nobility of spirit, to demonstrate to the world the greatness of a greater Britain . . ." said the prime minister, but he was silenced by the Duke of Cumberland who sprang up from his chair behind his father.

The young man walked toward the front of the plinth. Since his return, he had become emboldened, and he spoke his mind much more freely on matters of governance and politics.

"Magnanimity? Nobility of spirit? Come now, Mr. Pelham, what magnanimity or nobility would the Pretender have shown to my father or my family? What high-mindedness would this upstart Italian have exhibited to the citizens of London? There would have been a slaughter and butchery on an unprecedented scale. The streets of London would have run red with Protestant blood. Which is why we must now be firm and show our resolve and prove to the Scottish and Irish and Welsh people the folly of raising an army against England. The ringleaders will be put on trial. My men are at this moment scouring the landscape and arresting the clan leaders and traitors who supported the Pretender; they are being rounded up and caged and will be brought to trial for English justices to have their way with them. And I shall take great delight when they are executed, all of them."

"Trials, yes, Gentlemen," said Pelham, "but slaughter of innocents . . . I beg you. These aren't biblical times, Your Majesties. Women and children?"

"You weren't there, Mr. Pelham. You didn't see the men I faced on Culloden Moor. They were wild and fearless and had the look of madman in their eyes. These were less men than animals. And even though they have been beaten, they are not yet bowed. So for our victory to be complete, Mr. Pelham, the Scottish Highlanders and their leaders must be broken. Their spirit must be destroyed. Their ability to govern themselves must be nullified forever. The rule of the Scottish lairds will be replaced henceforth and for all times by the rule of His Majesty King George and all his successors."

The prime minister was about to say something, but remained silent as the Duke of Cumberland continued, "And you, Mr. Pelham, will introduce forthwith into the Parliament a Disarming Act that will forbid the carrying and concealment of all arms and armaments. The broadsword and claymore will become illegal weapons. Further, the wearing of the

Highland kilt, tartan, and plaid must henceforth be prohibited except if worn by a regiment in the service of the English Crown. I would further advise you, sir, that you should introduce an additional parliamentary act that will force all Scotsmen and women to take an oath of loyalty to His Majesty King George and to imprison those who refuse, to suppress Scotsmen meeting and gathering in numbers greater than five, and that any mention of the name Stuart shall be considered an act of treason against the Crown. As of this moment, the Celtic way of life is lost and gone forever. From now on, there is no more Scotland, only England."

Furious at the impertinence of the young man's interference in the governance of realm, Pelham hissed, "And is there any other measure Your Highness would wish me to impose? Sow the Scottish soil with salt, perhaps? Erect a hundred foot high impenetrable barrier on top of Hadrian's wall between England and Scotland?"

King George answered softly, "My son is currently the hero of England, Mr. Pelham. He is cheered wherever he goes. You, on the other hand, are seen to have been *effete*, indifferent, and powerless in the face of the enemy. The people have no love for you, yet they have both love and respect for my son, the Duke of Cumberland. After all, it was he who saved us from the Pretender, not Parliament and certainly not you. He asks for little, other than the security of my people to sleep soundly in their beds, safe in the knowledge that no more harm will come to them from the Scots. What he asks is little enough. Do it, Mr. Pelham, or you might have to consider your own future very carefully."

Some of the ladies in the court tapped their fans on their hands in support of the king's stand against the prime minister. But it evoked a surprising and brutal response from the king.

"Who in this room dares to comment upon my conversation with my prime minister," he shouted. The court abruptly became silent, ladies and gentlemen looking in shock as the king rose from his throne. Everybody dropped to their knees and bowed or curtsied in obeisance as the king stood before them.

"Which one of you dares applaud when I remind the prime minister of his duty to the people? Nobody in my court will comment ever again on matters political. You, all of you . . ." he said, pointing to the entire room, "were the first to scurry like sheep at the first sign of danger from the Pretender. Where were you when he was only a week's journey from here? Eh? Where were you? You'd all run like frightened dogs cowering in your country homes, leaving me and my son the duke, to fight the enemy alone. I, your king, was left alone in this court to plan the strategy that would save this realm. Alone, my good lords and ladies. Not a one of you stood beside me.

"And now you come back here when I and my son have faced down the Pretender's army single handed, risking our own lives and those of our commanders and brave men who fought beside us, and you walk around the court as though nothing had happened.

"Well let me tell you fine ladies and gentlemen of my court, that your king will not forget your cowardice. We will not forget this empty audience hall at the moment of our greatest peril, when I was all alone to determine the course of the coming battle. I will never forget the sight of my empty audience chamber when I and my son stood alone here to face the barbarians from Scotland.

"So there will be no more applause or comments from any of you. Is that understood? You can all return to your homes and mansions as far as I'm concerned, and I'll surround myself with honest and noble men and women who don't desert their king at the first sign of trouble."

He sat down, his face flushed. Two of the ladies in the middle of the audience chamber fainted into the arms of their husbands. But the majority stared hard at the floor, too ashamed even to look each other in the eyes.


ARMADALE

ON THE ISLAND OF SKYE IN THE OUTER HEBRIDES

MAY 5, 1746

It was while she was stirring the caldron and adding oats and extra water to thin out the stew that the idea became a reality. As she stirred, her mind thought and thought but couldn't come up with an adequate image. It was then she determined that she had to see in order to understand.

She had always had a vivid imagination. When she was a slip of a girl, the local school teachers would call her "the dreamer" and "the far-away child" as she'd always be staring into space or out of the window instead of practicing letters and numbers on her slate; when she went to school in Edinburgh to finish off her education, she was regularly reprimanded for wasting her parent's money because even though her results and marks were generally very good, she often didn't finish an assignment or hand in her homework and was always accused of being in another world, far away.

And just as on so many previous occasions, it was while she was doing some boring and monotonous task that she was struck with a stunningly simple and marvelous idea, which had to be undertaken straight away. She couldn't wait until her mother and father came in from the fields before she told them. Even though she couldn't see the image clearly, it was beginning to coalesce as an idea in her mind. She nearly burst in excitement, waiting for her parents to return. But when she told them, their reaction was not what she'd expected.

"You will not go. I forbid it. There are ten thousand English troops scaling every hill and valley killing every Scotsman and woman they find. If you think for one moment I'll allow a daughter of mine to go to the mainland, you're insane," Hugh said to her.

"I shall be going, father, and there's nothing you can do about it. I have determined that if I leave now, I can be in the lands of the Mackenzie or the MacDonells of Glengarry within the week," she said to him.

Her mother Anne said, "Your father is right, darling. This is an act of madness. You know what the Duke of Cumberland is doing. They're calling him the Butcher. He's slaughtering everybody. Thanks to the wisdom and foresight of your father, we on Skye won't be affected, but God only help those poor souls on the mainland. If you leave here, your life will be in mortal peril. And if you go to the prince, you'll be viewed as one of his supporters and that's an end of it. You'll be lost to us forever. No, Flora. You will not go. You'll stay here and be safe."

Flora stood from her chair and walked over to the chimneybreast, trying to retain her composure. How was it that she could see so clearly and yet her parents were so blind?

"But don't you see that the prince needs support now more than ever. If I went over there, it'd give him courage. I could guide him, cook for him, ease his pain. Father, mother, you must understand that he's our rightful king. He can reverse this misfortune and rise again. Once the Scots see what the damnable English are doing, they'll rise up in fury and . . ."

Hugh lost his temper completely and banged his fist on the table. "Rise up? What are you talking about, girl? Have you any conception of what's happening on the mainland? There's a slaughter taking place. Murder on a scale not seen in over four hundred years, not since the time of Longshanks after the disaster caused by your beloved William Wallace. Cumberland's soldiers are butchering our Scottish men, women, and children. Lairds are being dragged off their land; crofts are being burned; people are being rounded up like cattle and forced off their property. And all because of the pretensions of a lad who'd never set foot in Scotland for a single day of his life and who suddenly appears to claim a heritage taken from his grandfather dozens of years before. Away with you, girl, and dream another dream. You'll not go to the mainland. You'll remain here. If you try to sneak away, I'll follow you and drag you back by your hair."

She stared at Hugh in a rare fury. "You speak to me as though you were my father. Yet it was you who dragged my own mother by her hair when she'd been a widow for barely two years and carried her away and forced her to marry you. How dare you tell me that you'll drag me any-where, Hugh Macdonald?"

Anne Macdonald gasped at her daughter's impertinence. "Flora, apologize to your stepfather immediately. He's as much father to you as your own father who you barely knew. When your poor father died, you were only two years old. How dare you speak to Hugh in that manner?"

Knowing she'd gone too far and looking at the hurt in Hugh's eyes, Flora nodded and said softly, "It was wrong of me to say that, father. I said it in haste and I apologize. You are my father in all but flesh. And I do love you fiercely for the way you've brought me up and treated me as your own. But you forget that I'm a grown woman and not a child who you can command anymore."

"You're a grown woman to the rest of the world, but to me you are and will always be my child, Flora, as much as you were the child of Anne's first husband David. I love you now as I loved you when you first came to me as a bairn. Which is why I'm ordering you to put these ideas of going to the mainland and trying to assist Charlie out of your mind. He's brought enough destruction to Scotland. God forbid he brings destruction to my family."

The family descended into silence. Both Hugh and Anne knew that nothing could shift an idea once it was in Flora's mind. Hugh now considered telling the ferryman to forbid Flora from boarding his vessel; Anne was considering ways to keep her daughter's mind occupied so that thoughts of joining Prince Charles evaporated like a pond in summer. And Flora, for her part, wondered at the damage she would do to her parent's love of her when they came into her room and found that she'd disappeared in the middle of the night leaving only a note asking for forgiveness and understanding.


THE WESTERN HIGHLANDS

MAY 12, 1746

Even at a distance, Prince Charles Edward Stuart looked haggard and drawn when Lord George Murray first rode over the hill and saw him and his party in the valley floor. As he drew nearer, it was apparent that these men were suffering the effects of sleeping in the roughness of the landscape. The prince's once regal coat was filthy, his hair was long and devoid of the shine of pomade, and he had the look and feel of a poor crofter whose life is spent grubbing in the dirt for roots and vegetables.

Shocked beyond belief, Lord Murray fought to repress his distress at the change which had come over the young chevalier. Instead, he rode his horse toward the fire, dismounted, and greeted the prince with a kiss on both cheeks. The delight on the prince's face at seeing his former commander in chief was palpable.

Lord Murray greeted all of the prince's retinue with a handshake and said to him, "By God, sir, but it was no easy task finding you. No wonder you've managed to evade the English all these weeks. It was only by having men who held implicit trust in my good intentions that I was able to predict where you'd be."

"And how close are the English? We're so hidden here from information that I could be standing on the Moon for all that I know of what's happening in the rest of Scotland," he asked.

"The English are no more than forty miles to the southeast. They're following the Road to the Isles. We're well north and traveling in the opposite direction. However, sir, there's no telling when the Butcher will send a detachment up this way when he finds you're not where he thinks you are."

"Come, George, sit and take refreshment, as best as we can offer. Unfortunately the servants are not working tonight, so there's only a five-course banquet of fish and pheasant and a good beef stew and three kinds of puddings to ease our bellies and slake our thirst," said the prince.

Murray smiled, and a place was made for him to sit down before the fire. Special precautions had been taken to build a brush fence on all sides so that the light from the fire was hidden to a distant observer. Alistair Macdonald gave Murray a crude wooden bowl and motioned for him to take part of one of the three rabbits that they'd caught and roasted for their supper. There was nothing to eat it with, as the barley bread and oatmeal cakes that a crofter had given them a week earlier had long since been used up.

Lord Murray tore off a hind limb of the rabbit and ate it greedily. "It grieves me that Your Highness is reduced to such penury. Even a humble farmer can expect more out of life than what you and your party are enjoying."

"I shall soon shake off the hunting dogs that the Duke of Cumberland has sent after me, and then I'll somehow return to France and Italy," he said.

Lord Murray looked at the prince in amazement. "Return? France? But I don't understand, sir. I bring you news that ten thousand Scotsmen are ready and willing to stand by your side and rejoin you in the fight for your kingdom."

The prince looked at him in equal and utter amazement. "Ten thousand? Ten thousand you say. What in God's name are you talking about George? Are there still men willing to stand by me? What? Even after the disaster that was Culloden Moor?"

"Especially after the disaster. But more than that, Charles, they talk of your other successes, those battles you enjoyed at Prestonpans and Carlisle and Falkirk, and they talk of the way you came so close to taking London from the fat bastard George. Yes, Culloden was a disaster and some in Scotland think you're the Devil incarnate for what's happened to us since, but many believe that you're the rightful heir and hate and detest George and his evil spawn the Duke of Cumberland for what they're doing to us right now. And being Scotsmen, they're not willing to be slaughtered, but are determined to take to the field and fight."

His words disappeared into the early evening air. It was a warm night after a sunny day, but instead of their skin being berated by the icy cold of a Scottish winter or soaked by the sparkling rains of spring, they were now being eaten alive by Mayflies and midges and other flying insects that made their lives utterly miserable. The party of men thought deeply about the news that Lord George Murray had brought them.

"Ten thousand, do you say?" asked Alistair Macdonald.

Lord George Murray nodded.

"By God, Charlie, we could teach that bastard Cumberland a lesson or two. We could cut his balls off with ten thousand Scottish Highlanders."

"And Lowlanders," said Murray. "Those who don't oppose you seem willing to stand up in your defense and come to your aid. There's much ill feeling about what the duke is doing in the Highlands, slaughtering so many souls. There's a growing hatred toward him and the king in London now that more and more people are learning about these massacres."

"What do you say, Charlie? Do you want another go at the bastard? I'll be with you and ten thousand others," Alistair Macdonald said enthusiastically.

Softly, the prince said, "And how many more will die this time without artillery and ammunition? How many will be slaughtered by the duke's guns? No, lads, what we need is more than powerful intentions. We need reinforcements and equipment, none of which will come from Scotland. We need well-trained fighting men to pit us against the training that the duke has given his army, for without them, what chance will we have? And we need cavalry and artillery, which can only be supplied to us from France. That is what makes an army to counter the bastard Duke of Cumberland. Scotsmen are the bravest on earth, and they'll charge fearlessly into a cannon's mouth like none other, but they're not a modern army and today the bravest force of Scotsmen will easily be defeated by an army of British cowards hiding behind a wall of cannon. I shall go to France and raise a trained and professional army, and I will return to teach the Duke of Cumberland the lesson he deserves when I'm riding proud and confident at its head. So be assured, gentlemen, that until I have twenty thousand men behind me with those arms and munitions, then I won't make the same mistake and take to the field again.

"I regret, George, that we must tell our gallant ten thousand to return to their homes and wait awhile for my return. There'll come a time, soon I hope, when I shall take to the field against the false king of England and his bastard brood, but only when I have the backing of a full French army, some gallant Irishmen, and the Welsh to join with my beloved Scotsmen. Then, and only then will I show German George just which one of us has the right to be called king and to rule the people of Great Britain."

# Chapter Six

It had all happened so suddenly, her head was still spinning from the way in which her world had suddenly changed. One moment she'd been a free spirit, like a puff of sea mist, able to go and do what she wanted, planning to go to the mainland and somehow assist Prince Charlie in his goal; next she was an engaged woman with the responsibilities of building a marriage home, of having a family with children, and becoming the owner of an altogether more prestigious social position.

Oh, she'd known Alan Macdonald much of her life, and particularly well since she'd returned from school in Edinburgh as a young girl of thirteen. The two of them became great friends when she settled back on the Isle, going for long walks together on Skye's fractured shores and discussing the most pressing issues of life; they'd swum naked in the cobalt lochs and they'd fondled and kissed and she'd allowed him to touch her in certain private places which brought her joy; and for his part, Alan had taught Flora how and where to touch him to give him the greatest pleasure; and they'd shared their secrets with nobody.

Not that it was such a secret on the Island, for it was quite normal for intimate friendships to occur among Scottish children, even in their early teens, just so long as two issues were clearly understood and agreed to by the boys and the girls. The first was that if a pregnancy resulted, both parents would take responsibility for the bairn that would live with the girl's family until a marriage had taken place; and the second was that a Macdonald from the south of the Island of Skye would never lay with, or even touch, a MacLeod from the north of the Island.

Every child in his or her earliest years at school on the Island was taught of the massacre of the Macdonalds by the MacLeods on the Waternish Peninsular in 1578, and every Macdonald knew that the hated MacLeods could not be trusted. True that on this terrible day, the Macdonalds had earlier locked a worshipping party of the MacLeods into the Trumpan Church and set fire to the building killing everybody inside, but in the history of the Clan Macdonald, it was accepted that this act was well deserved and it was only the hated MacLeods who didn't realize it.

Though not an unconstrained child, Flora had kissed and fondled many a Macdonald lad and gone swimming naked with them while they were young, and it was viewed as charming and innocent. Maturity and her growth into a handsome young woman had brought with it longer and more settled relationships with some of the Island lads when she'd returned from the mainland.

And the Lord knew how fiercely fond she was of young Alan Macdonald, and had been sweet on him since she could remember. So when her parents had announced a week earlier that they were betrothing her in marriage to Alan, she'd viewed the arrangement as sensible, exciting, and correct.

At the age of twenty-four, she was ready to wed and begin a family. She was already many years older than the majority of other girls on the Island when they wed, and she was gaining the reputation for being too fussy in her choice of a husband.

Now that she was engaged, of course, her Jacobite plans were put on hold, and she'd spent the previous month concentrating on the nuptials and the visit she and her new husband would pay to Edinburgh. The more she thought about her parent's warnings and the worse the stories about what the Butcher of Cumberland was doing to the mainland

Highlanders, the more she realized that they were right, and going over the sea from Skye would quite possibly result in her death.

And one of her most important duties, a tradition of the Islands and one that she truly looked forward to, was for her and Alan to visit her brother Angus and other family members, to introduce her fiancé to them and gain their support. Angus had remained on the family property when his mother had remarried two decades earlier. Flora and Angus saw each other twice a year, and on each occasion she relished her re-acquaintance with her brother, his wife Elizabeth and their four wee bairns. And now Flora would be bringing home her own man, her husband to be, Alan; she would be an engaged woman, and as such, she would gain newfound respect in the small but close-knit Catholic community of Milton and all of South Uist.

When she stepped off the boat with Alan behind her carrying her satchel containing a change of clothes and some food for the long journey, she looked around her at the island she had once called her home. She knew the island and its people well, even though most of her life was lived in Skye. But this time, she immediately sensed that things were different. South Uist was a poor place, its inhabitants earning their money from making tweed cloth as well as gaining an income from farming the vast beds of seaweed that they gathered to make soap for the people of England. Normally there would be five, maybe ten islanders on the dockside to greet the boat as it came in from Skye. Today, however, there were no Islanders, but fifteen or more English troopers, all of whom looked at Flora and Alan with immense suspicion.

"Dear God in his heaven, what's happening," she whispered, and held her fiancé's hand tightly.

Alan was taller than Flora by a head. He enjoyed red hair and pale skin that had caused him to be mocked when he was a boy but was now attractive to young women especially on the mainland. Known for his fearlessness in hunting and sports, he looked at the soldiers with the same concerns felt by Flora and held his fiancée close to him as they stepped off the boat. "Whatever happens, stay close to me, darling, for these troopers look in no mood for frivolity. They're hunting for the Stuart."

"I know who they're hunting, fiancé, but why are they on South Uist? They surely don't think that he'd come to so remote a place as this, do they?"

Alan whispered as they walked along the jetty, "It's told that the prince landed here last year when he began his great adventure."

"On Uist? Dear God, the prince was treading on the land where I was born."

Alan looked at her strangely. Unlike her parents, who were by now well used to the romance attached to Flora's Jacobite sympathies, it was a closely guarded secret on Skye bearing in mind Hugh's responsibilities as commander of the local Militia charged with preventing the Jacobite uprising. Neither she nor Alan had had the time in their brief engagement to discuss the prince or their loyalty one to the other. Alan had joined the Skye Militia and had practiced marching up and down with a gun so he was probably not a Jacobite supporter. But as a Macdonald, he was no lover of King George in London, either. She would have to tell him sooner rather than later that her sympathies lay with the other camp. How that would affect him, she honestly didn't know.

They walked further up the jetty, and under the suspicious glances of the troopers, Alan whispered to her, "Flora darling, cling to my arm and stare into my eyes, as though you were devoted to me. Make them think that we're just a young couple in love."

She smiled and whispered back, "Darling, you're now my fiancé, which means that as far as anybody is concerned, we are just a young couple in love."

At the end of the jetty was a horse and trap with the driver ready to transport any who needed to reach a particular part of the Island. He recognized Flora, though he didn't know Alan.

"It's Mistress Macdonald, daughter of old Annie Macdonald, isn't it?" he shouted to her.

"It is indeed, David, and it's good to see you," she said. "And enough of the 'old Annie.' My mother is ten years younger than you, and I wouldn't call you old."

He burst out laughing and got down from his trap in order to help them in while the troopers listened keenly.

"And who's the bonnie lad with you? Is he your lover?" asked David.

"Lover and soon to be husband."

Because he was dressed like an Islander in a Macdonald tartan, and because it was obvious that he was not a bewigged and powdered Italian Prince, the troopers paid them no further attention, and Alan and Flora walked across the road and climbed up into the trap to be driven from the southeastern harbor of the island to her family home in the baile of Milton.

As the engaged couple stepped off the trap and paid David for his trouble, her brother Angus came out of the croft and looked at Flora as though she had just descended from heaven. She knew that her visit was both unannounced and unexpected, but from the look on his face, it seemed as though he'd been struck in the private parts by a club.

"But how in God's name did you get here so quickly? The boat only left for Skye this morning. How did you know?"

"Know?" she asked.

"To come here?"

She looked at him as though he was crazy. "What are you talking about Angus?"

"You're here because I sent for Hugh to come urgently."

"You sent for father?"

Angus nodded.

"In God's name, why?"

But before he answered, Angus looked at Alan Macdonald and his brow creased. "Who is this gentleman?"

Flora introduced her fiancé, and the two men shook hands. Angus hugged and kissed his sister, and invited the two into his small but comfortable home. Elizabeth had already come to the doorway when she heard the sound of voices, and she hugged her sister-in-law, curtsied when introduced to Alan, and invited them inside for ale and griddlecakes.

The conversation was kept deliberately light, ranging from wedding plans to the prospect of the traditional tour of the mainland they would take after the wedding, to where and when the young couple had first met, but both Flora and Angus were keen to expand on the earlier part of their exchange. The unspoken glances that ranged between brother and sister told Angus not to discuss that which was most pressing on his mind, but after they'd eaten and drunk, he suggested that Flora accompany him outside to meet the children on their return from the local schoolhouse.

When they were finally alone and barely out of the croft's pathway, Flora said urgently, "Now what on earth were you talking about when we first arrived? You've sent for father? Why?"

Angus said softly, "I thought you'd come because you'd received the message I sent for Hugh to come here over the sea from Skye?"

"What message?" she asked. "What's so urgent?"

"The island is full of English troopers . . ."

"I know. All Scotland's full of the damnable English. When we landed, we saw a party of them. What's afoot?"

Although they were completely alone and out of anybody's earshot, he still whispered, "The prince is here."

Flora looked at Angus in shock. "Here? On Uist?"

Her brother nodded. She felt her face flush with excitement and her heartbeat as though she was a young, lovesick girl. Her reaction embarrassed her.

"If he's caught," said Angus, "it'll be a disaster. The English are murdering Scotsmen on the mainland, and now General Campbell has come over to search the Island for him. If they find him here, they'll believe that we're party to harboring him, which will give them an excuse to murder every man, woman and child on Uist. It'll be a slaughter just as it is in the Highlands yonder."

"But why have you sent for father? You must know that he's in charge of the Skye Militia. He's sworn an oath to find and capture the prince. Other than you, I'm the only one in the family who believes in the Jacobite cause."

Angus shook his head. "Hugh puts the lives of Scotsmen above his duty to London. I've asked him to come here so that he can help me get the prince off Uist before the English find him."

"I must meet him," Flora insisted.

Angus laughed. "He's in hiding on the western coast. Word has it that he arrived three evenings ago in the belief that the English wouldn't look for him on Uist. But I think he's been betrayed by someone on the mainland, because early yesterday morning, a regiment of English troopers arrived, and now they're scouring the Island."

"Where is he?" she asked.

"I don't know. I've been told that if I want to get word to him, I'm to go to a cliff-top and light a damp fire. The smoke will indicate that those loyal to him want to meet him. Then he'll find us. That's all I know, and all I can tell you."

They walked on in silence until Angus, somewhat diffidently, asked, "What will your fiancé's reaction be if he learns the news? I couldn't mention it inside the house until I was sure."

She smiled. "He's not a Jacobite, but Alan is a loyal Scotsman and hates the Butcher Duke for what he's doing on the mainland. He'll never countenance such a thing happening on Skye or Uist. He'll raise a sword in defiance of the English when he understands what it is that you've just told me. I know him well enough to be certain of that."

The Headquarters of the Duke of Cumberland
Fort William, Scotland

June 15, 1746

It had stood for more than half a century, withstanding the wild Highlands weather, the hatred by the indigenous Scots who surrounded it, and most lately an assault by the Pretender who had failed to breach its thick stone walls. Now it was at the epicenter of the battle to destroy the last vestiges of Scottish manhood. It had become the headquarters of the hunt for the man who would be king of England and Scotland and who, if reports were to be believed, was hiding like a terrified and beaten cur in the thistles and thickets of Scotland. In a land with so many caves and rocky inlets, of lochs and hideaways, of thick forests and Catholic bolt-holes, it was no wonder that the scoundrel had so far managed to evade capture, always a step ahead of the duke's troopers.

But for the first time in three months, it was likely that General Campbell had him well and truly cornered. He'd made the fatal mistake of leaving the mainland for one of the islands, and that meant it was a simple task of building a cordon around the coast of naval vessels to interdict every ship and boat that sailed to and from the place, land a battalion of troops on the island, and march north to south until the rat had been driven from his nest. Then he'd be tethered, hauled in irons to London, given a fair trial for the treasonous cur he was, and hanged, drawn and quartered.

The Duke of Cumberland couldn't restrain a grin when he thought of the suitability of the penalty he had in mind for the traitor. Hanging, drawing and quartering had been introduced by Edward Longshanks in 1283 in punishment for the rebellion of the Welsh and two decades later he'd order the punishment used against the traitorous Scotsman William Wallace, another who had pretensions above his station; now King Edward's successor, albeit separated by nearly five centuries, was about to use it against another traitor to England.

An irritating high-pitched voice, like an annoying fly, drew the Duke of Cumberland back to the present. He was sitting in the cramped offices of the commander of the Fort, a certain Major Edward Dalziel, an affable if rather stupid and sycophantic young man, unsuited to any position of military command, yet who was here in control of the fort because his father had purchased the commission for a very high price and was probably telling his London friends about his son's sparkling career in the defense of England.

"Mr. Dalziel," said the duke, "kindly tell me why you think that the prince is no longer in Scotland, but is in France."

"Well, sir, Your Royal Highness, I mean, really, he is a prince after all, and a prince can hardly be expected to live like a vagabond and a footpad and a highwayman for all these months. He has some pride, after all, doesn't he, Your Highness. What say! Where are his servants, his retinue, his privy, and those facilities which all Princes require? No, sir, I don't think that any Prince could remain in such inhospitable circumstances for so long. Which is why I think that many months ago, in the dead of night, the king of France sent a ship which picked him up and now he's in Paris, licking his wounds from the thrashing you gave him at Culloden Moor. That's what I think, sir."

"And your evidence?"

The young man hesitated, smelling a trap. "Well, I mean, he is a prince after all, ain't he."

The Duke of Cumberland remained silent, wondering how long he should continue to be polite to such an idiot when he should be in the field leading his men from the front.

"Major, I too am a Prince. My father is a king. And if I'd lost a battle and was being chased by an enemy, I'd be jolly certain that I'd avoid capture, even if it meant sleeping on the bare earth with brambles for my pillow. You see, Major, the French king could not have sent a ship to spirit the Pretender away, because my navy has had these waters under scrutiny for a year now, ever since we had word of the prince's intentions, and there have been no sightings of any French, or Spanish ship sent to transport him to safety. And I might remind you that the prince has been sighted many times in the past few weeks, most recently on the roads approaching the Islands of the Outer Hebrides, which is where General Campbell is currently lifting every rock and searching every cranny for him. So thank you for your unsolicited advice, but I suggest that you return to your duties, and let me attend to mine," said the duke.

Unaware that he'd been reprimanded, the young major saluted, and before he left, said, "It was a pleasure to have tried to assist Your Highness. I shall write and tell my father of the conversation. He'll be most impressed that I've been discussing such important matters with one of your standing."

As the young man closed the door and left the duke alone, Cumberland determined that as the commander in chief of England's fighting forces and as the son of the king, he must do something more to improve the lack of professionalism of the army. He'd done much training of those men under his command, but other commanders simply thrust rifles and muskets into enlisted men's hands and told them to go forth into battle. No! Something must be done to raise the standard of the fighting man if England was to gain preeminence in Europe.

The navy was different, for there were some very able and experienced officers commanding England's fleet and because ships were at sea for so long, with barely anything for the men to do other than repair equipment and swab decks, training on board was ongoing. But the army was the home and plaything of far too many men like the idiotic Major who were the second or third sons of the aristocracy of England and whose purchased commissions equipped them neither to command nor to fight. Men like the major were hampering England's ability both to defend itself, and to field a proper fighting force in France or wherever they were needed.

Before Culloden, he had taken personal command of the artillery and dragoons, and had trained and drilled them to a peak of performance, working out new and efficient methods of using bayonets and of rapid rifle fire and much more. A few years ago, a Royal Military Academy had been established at the Royal Artillery Depot in Woolwich in London with the intention of training good Officers of Artillery and Perfect Engineers, but nobody had yet emerged from the Academy capable of going into the field. And until such time as they were available to him, the duke would have to put up with rich, feckless, and useless nincompoops like the major.

He was disturbed by a knock on the door.

"Enter," he commanded.

A dispatch rider opened the door diffidently, saluted, and gave the duke a vellum pouch sealed with the wax stamp of General Campbell. He waited for the man to leave before he opened it and withdrew its contents. He read the dispatch from General Campbell quickly, noting that it had been written earlier that morning. When he'd finished, he swore an oath. So the prince was still at large, despite the northwestern fringes of the Island of Uist having been searched thoroughly. The general pointed out, and begged the duke to understand, that the Island's coast was a mass of caves and inlets and the sea's waves made it utterly impossible for his soldiers to search every possible hiding place of the Pretender, especially if he were in the hands of friendly locals who knew the ins and outs of the Island.

However, General Campbell assured the duke that he was continuing the search and would not desist until the traitor was captured and presented to him for arraignment. In the meantime, the general wrote, he hoped that the duke was pleased with the fact that he'd given stark warning to the citizenry of the island of the dangers of hiding the fugitive by parading two men from one of the northern villages before all of the inhabitants, and hanging them in the Common, just to make an example of them.

The duke smiled and nodded, especially when the general wrote and told him that the effect was immediate and salutary, and he believed that a few more hangings might just turn the balance of the population's favor against the prince.

THE TOWN (BAILE) OF MILTON
THE ISLAND OF SOUTH UIST IN THE OUTER HEBRIDES

JUNE 20, 1746

Hugh Macdonald, his stepson Angus, Alan Macdonald, and three other men from different villages in South Uist, along with Flora Macdonald who had insisted she would not be left behind, waited and waited in the high moorland, a grassy duneland that was dominated by the shadow of the mighty Beinn Mhor, whose peak was hidden in the cloud of a coming rainstorm. They had been waiting since an hour after sunrise and would wait, carefully concealed from English and treasonous Scottish eyes, until nightfall. There was nervousness among the party, for news had been given to them the previous day of the hanging of two innocent men in a northern village. It was a warning, which they had taken to heart.

The previous day, white smoke from a fire lit on a western sea-wall cliff face had alerted the prince and his party to the need for a meeting. A certain Alistair Macdonald had emerged from the woods late in the morning to where the fire had been lit, and after determining the honesty of those who sought the meeting, agreed to bring the prince to a high plateau on the eastern foothills of mighty Beinn Mhor the following day.

Waiting for the prince's party, the six men had hidden themselves in the duneland to keep from the prying eyes of both General Campbell's ever-present troopers and of islanders who wanted the prince gone so they could return to the safety of their previous existence. For her part, Flora could barely restrain herself. Hugh had at first refused to take her with, telling her that it was no place for a woman. Alan Macdonald, skeptical at first of helping the Jacobite, but then convinced by Hugh that the prince had to be returned to France to prevent any further bloodshed like the execution of the two islanders, agreed that Flora must stay at home and endanger neither herself nor the party.

It was only Angus who argued on her part, saying that she was the only loyal supporter of the Jacobite cause, and as such she was more entitled to be there than any of them. And so the others had agreed to her accompanying them, provided she remain in the background and didn't make her opinions known. Furious at the overbearing treatment she was delivered, Flora nonetheless bit her tongue and agreed to their terms just in order to accompany them.

Hidden in the tall bracken, and cut off from the sight of the road by stands of trees, the party spied every approach to where they were lying in anticipation of the prince's arrival. It was the middle of the day before Angus whispered, "There's movement out of the northwest. Coming across the field. I can't see for certain, but whoever it is doesn't wear trooper's uniforms."

Everybody remained lying in the heather and bracken until Angus confirmed that it was a party of five men. "It could be the prince," he said. "They're not standing, but crouching over the moorland and being very cautious in the way they're walking here."

It took a further half an hour for the two parties to finally come together. When they did, they viewed each other from a distance with caution, standing apart and simply staring. Neither wanted to admit their identity for fear of treachery until Flora Macdonald, hidden from view, pushed past her fiancé and walked boldly forward to the front line. She stood, legs firmly apart, facing the newcomers and said simply, "My name is Flora Macdonald. Which one of you worthies is the Prince of the Stuarts?"

Beaming a smile, the Pretender also stepped forward, knowing that no traitors would bring a woman to a betrayal. He held out his hand and said gently, "My dear Miss Macdonald, I have the honor of introducing myself to you. I am the man you seek. My name is Charles Edward Louis John Casimir Sylvester Maria, Prince of the Stuarts. I say this to prove I'm not an imposter, for no actor could possibly remember such a name."

Flora burst out laughing, a signal for the two groups to come forward and embrace. But Flora continued to hold the prince's hand for a moment or two more than necessary. She liked its touch, hard from his rough living yet sufficiently tender and gentle to show that he had no need to prove himself a man. And the prince looked deeply into Flora's eyes and saw a girl masquerading as a woman, her eyes delighted at just looking at him, her manner coy and retaining a reserve which was right and proper. It was he who removed his hand from hers.

An hour later, the food was served, the light of its fire and the rising smoke hidden by a brushwood fence and a high canopy of bracken and ferns that caused it to be dispersed by the crown of branches high in the trees. The parties continued to exchange information, knowing that the chances of their being spotted were very slim. For the better part of the hour, the prince and his attendants, especially Alistair Macdonald, told how they had evaded the English troopers since Culloden Moor. As Alistair embellished, so the prince denied any bravery on their part, and instead paid tribute to the bravery and loyalty of the Highlanders who had given them food and occasional shelter, knowing the risks they faced from the Butcher duke's barbarians.

When they'd eaten and drunk and rested sufficiently, Hugh Macdonald said, "And what are your plans for quitting this Island, Your Highness?"

The prince took a final drink from a flask of ale and wiped his mouth. "I am assured by loyal messengers who have managed to reach me that the French have a ship which will be waiting for me when I reach the Island of Skye. I have to get there soon, for then I will return to Paris where I will demand of King Louis that he provide me with the arms and treasury he once promised to support my claim to the throne. Be assured, my friends, that had the king of France been true to his word, I would have beaten the English and would at this moment be sitting on the throne in St. James's Palace."

The party from Uist looked at each other in surprise, but Hugh indicated that he didn't want any debate on any future military mission. Instead, he said, "Prince Charles, have you any idea as to how you're going to evade the Duke of Cumberland's troopers and sail to Skye without being seen? General Campbell's men are everywhere on Uist and it won't be long before they're swarming all over Skye. The man's closing in on you fast. God knows that Uist isn't the largest island in the world and there are only so many places where you can hide. But with so many caves and in such rugged terrain, it's unlikely that he'll find you until you execute your move. Forgive the example, but you can't see a rabbit or a hare until it bolts from its burrow, and that's when I'm afraid you and your followers will be caught. When you make the dash for your boat and put to sea, then you'll have nowhere to hide and your life will be imperiled."

The prince nodded and said, "I was hoping that you gentlemen . . ." he smiled and acknowledged Flora sitting at the edge of the circle, "and lady, could advise me as to the best way to evade capture when I'm on the coast of the Island."

Alan Macdonald said, somewhat too abruptly, "You managed to find your way here. You shouldn't have too much of a difficulty finding your way from the coast."

Reacting to the tone, Alistair Macdonald asked, "I've been wondering this past hour why it is that two supporters of the English are here helping the prince. You, Hugh Macdonald, lead the Militia on Skye, don't you. And you, Alan Macdonald, are a member of that Militia. For what reason are you here in support of our cause?"

Without hesitation, Hugh answered, "The lives of innocents have been wasted every hour of every day since your defeat at Culloden Moor. Scottish blood is staining the heather. The only time we'll be safe is when the prince leaves the islands and the Highlands and returns to France and Italy. Forgive my bluntness, sir, but your pretensions have brought Scotland naught but misery."

"And His Highness' victories brought the Scottish people naught but pride, Hugh Macdonald," said Alistair angrily. "It was because the king of France and the Welsh and the Irish and even the Scottish themselves stabbed us in the back with the dirk of treason that we lost at Culloden. But don't forget our victories at Prestonpans and . . ."

"I forget none of your victories, Alistair Macdonald. But I deal in the present while you relive the past. And in my present, innocent Scots men, women and children are being slaughtered. And the only way to put a stop to the pain is for us to help the prince leave this country as quickly as possible."

Alistair sat up in sudden anger. "Are you mad, Hugh Macdonald? Are you insane? The prince and his father are the rightful kings of this country and of England. Every loyal Scot should sing their praises. If we'd been properly supported . . ."

"Alistair," said the prince softly, "I beg you to keep your temper. Hugh Macdonald speaks his mind, and for that, he must be respected. I assume that Hugh speaks also for the rest of you?"

Alan Macdonald and most of the party nodded in agreement with Hugh, except Angus and one of the other villagers. It was as the prince had feared. The Highland loyalty he'd enjoyed on the mainland hadn't been reflected since he'd arrived on the Western Isles. But suddenly Flora spoke up.

"Your Highness, I don't agree with my father or my fiancé or the others here. I believe that you are the true and rightful heir to the throne of Scotland and that as loyal Scotsmen and women, we should support your claim and rid England and Scotland of the Hanoverians and their breed. What more proof do you want of the wrong-headedness of the Germans being in charge, father, than what's happening in the Highlands right now. Innocents are being murdered by the butcher Cumberland. Surely that fact alone must give you cause to change your loyalties and support the prince and his father."

Prince Charles looked at Flora in admiration. She was both beautiful and passionate, and Alan Macdonald was either a lucky or a very unlucky man.

"You're mistaken, daughter," said Hugh. "I have no loyalty for the English. I'm a loyal Scotsman. But a Scotsman who predicted what would happen when the prince landed not fifty miles from here a full year ago. And I'm a loyal Scotsman who is now particularly keen to prevent the same massacres which are killing Highlanders, from happening to my people in the Isles. And the only way to do that is to assist His Highness in quitting Uist and Skye and sailing back to France where he becomes somebody else's problem. Forgive my plain speaking, Prince, but that's all you'll get from me."

Prince Charles could feel the anger rising from his party of supporters, but knew he had to force them to keep their tempers hidden. One enemy on the Island was sufficient cause for concern, but to have both the English and the inhabitants of Uist against him would mean his certain capture and death. And to make matters even worse, he'd been informed the previous day by a villager who'd come to the abandoned croft where they were staying to give them supplies, that several bounty hunters had arrived on the island intent on earning the £30,000 ransom on his head.

"I admire your honesty and candor, Hugh Macdonald. And you, Miss Flora Macdonald, have been equally brave and forthright in face of opposition from your father and fiancé, which shows me your true spirit and determination. But I am still left with the vexed question of how I shall remove myself and my party from the island of Uist and repair to Skye. Might I purchase a small sailing boat, and set off in the dead of night?"

Angus Macdonald laughed. "Do that and we'll be scraping your bodies off the rocks come morning. The tides here are treacherous and at nighttime, you'll mistake an inlet for the channel to the open sea and come to grief. No, sir, you'll have to sail by day and be guided by somebody born on Uist who knows its ways."

"And you can't take your party of ten men with you, sir," said Hugh. "Such a large gathering would be bound to cause a stir which would quickly come to the attention of the English. No, sir, you'll go to Skye with a guide and nothing more. You'll farewell your party here, and we'll ensure that over the next few weeks, we ferry them safely back to the mainland where they can find their own ways back to their homes."

His party was about to object, but when they saw the prince nodding in agreement, they remained silent. Alistair Macdonald softly grumbled to make known his feelings about abandoning the prince at the most dangerous time of his escape.

"And when shall I leave," he asked.

"When I can find a guide willing to risk his own, and his family's life to save you," replied Hugh simply. After a moment, he added, "And most probably the lives of his village."

"But father," said Flora, "the prince must be in disguise. He can't be allowed to appear as he is, even in those filthy clothes, for he'll quickly be recognized by the troopers. If he's not disguised, how will he get past the guards who are stationed at all the jetties all around the island?"

Hugh looked at his daughter and asked, "What disguise are you talking about, lass?"

She smiled. "The troopers are looking for a prince. Not a princess. Why not use some of my clothes and disguise him as a woman. He could be an Irish seamstress. We'll call him Betty Burke. We could say that Betty is the seamstress to the daughter of the captain of the Loyal English Militia on Skye, Hugh Macdonald. That'll make it even more unlikely that he'll be stopped and searched by the troopers.

"And I'm certain that once His Highness has washed and shaved, he could easily pass for a woman; he has fair skin and with the right clothes he could make a very handsome lass. That'll fool the English guards for certain."

Everybody, especially her father and fiancé, looked at her in amazement, and for a moment, Flora was mortified that she'd said entirely the wrong thing and had offended some arcane royal protocol of which she was unaware. But then the prince beamed and smiled and nodded and said, "You're a very smart and perceptive young woman, Mistress Macdonald. That's an excellent idea, and one in which I'll heartily participate. And will you be joining me on the voyage to Skye as my employer?" he asked.

She looked at him in shock. "Me? Under no circumstances. I'm here with my fiancé, Mr. Alan Macdonald, to visit my birthplace as is the tradition of my people, and we've hardly left the baile of Milton since we arrived. No, sir, but as an engaged woman, soon to be married, all thoughts of adventure must be put out of my mind. I have certain important responsibilities now to my husband to be."

He nodded and said softly, "A pity, but I quite understand."

# Part Two

# Chapter Seven

Flora Macdonald looked from one to the other, trying to appreciate what they were saying to her. She understood the words well enough, but how her father and her fiancé could even countenance such a proposition was beyond her ability to understand.

They were in the front parlor of the small croft. Elizabeth, Angus's wife, and their children were in the recently added extension to the house created by Angus for the additional space needed since the birth of their last bairn. He'd built it during the previous year and was now thanking the Lord because his house contained sufficient room for his stepfather Hugh, Flora's fiancé Alan, and of course Flora herself who was given pride of place on the floor next to the fireplace in the front room. His new addition was in the back of his existing house and joined to it by a narrow corridor. But when he sensed the tenor of the conversation his stepfather was embarking upon, he had quietly absented himself from the front of the house, leaving Flora alone with just her husband to be and her father. She didn't even notice his absence when she looked around the room, shaking her head, trying to clear away any misunderstandings.

"But why?"

"Because," said Hugh, "a maid doesn't travel without her mistress."

"So call the maid the mistress. Don't say that she's an Irish seamstress but that she's a lady returning to Skye. Or if you must, say she's my maid visiting Uist from the mainland and now that her visit is finished, she's returning to her husband and family."

"No," Alan interrupted, "don't you understand, darling. We could call her the Queen of Egypt for all it matters, because in whatever guise the prince takes, he'll arouse suspicion. A woman doesn't travel alone in such dangerous times. You're known on this Island as well as on Skye, and it won't seem out of the ordinary if you travel accompanied by your maid. To do anything else will arouse too much suspicion. It'll all be for naught unless Betty Burke travels back to Skye with you, her mistress."

"But why can't you say that my maid is returning to my home in order to be with me. But why do I have to go?"

"They know you're here," Hugh insisted. "They know you're on Uist. If Betty Burke travels without you, they'll want to know why, and the moment they begin to ask questions, the prince's identity will be discovered. He can hide in caves, but he can't hide his manhood."

"But father, they'll know I traveled here with my fiancé Alan, and not with my seamstress Betty Burke. I can't travel back with the prince, father. Surely you can understand that."

"We'll say she traveled back from Ireland where she was visiting her family and came to Uist in order to meet you and your fiancé here. We'll say that Alan is remaining on Uist but that you have to return to Skye to be with your mother," said Hugh.

Suddenly annoyed at all the contrivance thought out without consulting her, she snapped, "I'm an engaged woman, father. It's unseemly."

"These are difficult times, Flora darling," said Alan. "If the prince remains here and is caught, the entire population of Uist, including your brother and his family, may be slaughtered by the bastard English. Your father and I have talked this through at great length, but we can't see an alternative."

"And what of the danger . . ."

The two men remained silent. After a moment, she continued, "the seas and the tides. By rowboat. I'm not a sailor."

"Ach, girl, you're more sailor than some Admiral of the Fleet. Since before you could walk, you've been rowing and sailing around Skye," Hugh said.

"Aye, around Skye which has calm waters but not around Uist. This is an altogether different sea, father. You know the currents and the winds around here. They're a dozen times worse than they are on Skye. And you surely know the monstrous tides and waves. Skye's arse is protected from the Atlantic storms by North and South Uist and the outer Western Islands, as though God had placed a blanket around it, but there's no such protection for Uist. It suffers the full force of the winds and storms of the Atlantic. You know how many Uist fishermen have been lost to the terror of the sea. What's to protect a small rowboat putting out from these waters? There's nothing between Uist and the Americas but a thousand miles of fiercest ocean and the wildest weather in all of Christendom."

"Darling, do you think I'd risk the life of my most precious Flora unless it was safe. Firstly, Neil MacEachan has agreed to row you and the prince. He's strong as an ox and has done the journey a hundred times. He'll be another one of your so-called servants, though you must treat him kindly when you're alone, as he's taking a great risk. Treat him as a servant when you're passing an English trooper of course, but remember that you're only acting. Neil deserves the respect and regard of every Scotsman.

"Secondly, you'll set out in the early morning before the winds freshen, and by the time the winds strike up in the early afternoon, they'll blow you safely into the harbor at Skye. And thirdly, it's summer. It's June for God's sake. How often have you seen murderous winter's weather in June? It's stormier on a duck pond in the middle of a village than it is going out in the warm waters of summer."

Flora remained silent as she pondered her father's face. She turned to her fiancé. "And you, husband to be. Are you happy for your future wife to risk her life and liberty in such an adventure? Is this the sort of man I'm marrying? One who disregards his wife's safety?"

"Flora!" shouted her father. "What a terrible thing to say to Alan . . ."

"No, Hugh," Alan responded quickly. "She has a right to ask and a right to be told. At first, I was vehemently against the idea of your traveling with the prince, for all the reasons you've espoused. I said you and the prince should return to Skye on the larger boat as paying passengers. But as your father said, the English are now searching every boat that leaves the Island and he's sure to be found.

"Then late last night, your father explained to me precisely what he's just told you and asked for my endorsement of your participation. Darling girl, there's far less danger to you in accompanying the prince than there is danger to you in staying here while the duke's men are rampaging all over the Island, sticking their bayonets into anything that resembles a body. And your going with the prince gives him a much better chance of escaping, and that means that the lives of hundreds, maybe thousands of Scotsmen and women will be saved. Would I risk your life for no good reason? Of course not. But on balance, it's right for you to go."

She sighed. "Where is the prince now?" she asked.

"He's in a disused barn half a mile from here. He's well hidden," said her father.

"Take me to him," she demanded.

"No, the risk is too great. The English troopers are everywhere, and the local people can't be trusted, especially after the hangings up north. The fewer people who visit him, the greater the protection . . ."

"I said take me to him. I want to know whether or not he agrees with your decisions. I shall not go until I've spoken, alone, to Bonnie Prince Charlie."

Although it was a sunny day outside, there was a deep gloom inside the dismal barn. She'd insisted on entering alone once her father had spoken the password to let the prince know that his visitors weren't the hated Englishmen.

Tentatively feeling her way into the shelter through the dank light that fell in blinding beams through the holes in the roof, she cautiously inched forward, whispering "hello" to alert him to her presence. Prince Charles Edward smiled when he saw that instead of one of the Highlanders or Islanders entering his hiding place, it was the pretty young woman from Skye, Flora Macdonald. She was the girl engaged to Alan Macdonald, a handsome if somewhat forward girl who spoke her mind in a forthright way.

He was delighted that she'd come to visit him. Flora was so unlike the ladies of the French and Italian courts with whom he spent much of his life; ladies who devoted entire mornings and afternoons trying on new dresses and jewellery and wigs just so they could preen and parade coquettishly in the night time courtly festivities. No such coquetry with Mistress Macdonald, however, for on his one and only meeting with the young woman, she'd proven herself to be bold and seductively outspoken. It had taken him aback somewhat, but during the meeting on the moors, his eyes had always seemed to turn toward her when he should have been listening to her father and her brother. And in her innocence, she hadn't for one moment noticed that he had been looking admiringly at her. Innocence and forthrightness all in the one young woman! It wasn't something he was used to in the courts of Europe, but it was disarmingly attractive.

He smiled as she felt her way into the gloom of the barn and thought again about the ladies of the European courts. What would they make of her? No doubt, Mistress Flora Macdonald would be an object of both curiosity and ridicule. Yet for all the airs and pretensions and graces of the fine French and Italian ladies he knew so well, he found Flora to be . . . he searched for the correct word . . . refreshing.

The prince remained in hiding until she was well into the barn, and it was obvious that she wasn't being followed. She continued to look around tentatively, calling his name in a whisper.

"Good morning to you, Mistress Macdonald. How very pleasant it is to see you. I'd expected your father or your brother, but a visit from you is a joy to my heart."

He threw off the covering of straw, stood, and brushed his jacket and trousers as best he could, and jumped down from the loft. Flora smiled when she saw him and walked over, not to shake his hand but to pull the vegetation from his hair.

"Dear God, Your Highness, but you're a mess. Is this how you appear in the royal balls and parties I've read so much about?"

He laughed. "Indeed it's not, ma'am, for at those occasions, I'm bewigged and bejewelled, primped and powdered, gloved and glorious, and I look as immaculate as one of the Borgia popes. It's a shame you haven't seen me when I'm in my finery, Mistress Macdonald, for I'm the most beautiful of men. I smell of the perfumes of Araby and my trousers and coats are as colorful as the fan of a peacock. I'm a thing of wonder to behold, lean and beautiful, and all the ladies swoon as I walk past them."

She looked at him in surprise, and when she saw the edges of his mouth crinkling with suppressed laughter, she slapped him on the shoulders and said, "Och, away with you, you lying spleeny earth-vexing malt worm. You've such a way with words, I sometimes don't know whether you're talking from your arse or breakfast time. You make everything right side up sound upside down."

"When I'm in the company of sensible Highland women such as you, I'm always right side up, I promise you. Now, Mistress Macdonald, won't you join me in a seat?" he asked, pointing her to the loft where he'd been lying. "I fear there's too much danger if we're down here on the ground talking. I'd like to offer you some refreshments, but all I can serve you is straw from a field of oats, and that's a poor substitute for the ale and griddlecakes your brother was kind enough to bring to me this morning."

She climbed the rickety ladder first, and as she waited for the prince to ascend, she was shocked by the sudden realization that she was in the presence of a man who just a month earlier had been to her a distant and mystical event. Not a man or a prince, but an occurrence, a movement to free her and all Scotland from the clutches of the English. She viewed him not as a person, but as a personage so removed from her that even speaking his name was a kind of reverence to an otherworldly being. A month ago, had she met him in Edinburgh or in the streets of a village in Skye, she'd have fainted at being in the presence of one so great and mighty. And now she was swearing at him, hitting him on his shoulder, and preparing to lie alone on straw in a barn, something she'd only ever done with boys with whom she was romantic. It was ridiculous and extraordinary. But extraordinary times led to incongruous measures.

He sat beside her. Even in the dimness of the light of the barn, she studied his face and his body as he settled himself back onto the straw. He was handsome in a boyish way, pretty in a feminine manner, though she found the gentleness of his face quite appealing. So many of the young men of Skye and the mainland looked like young versions of their fathers, and she had grown up surrounded by boys whose faces turned into craggy, bearded, and wild Highlanders when they became men. The prince was certainly different, for he didn't have the rough stony looks she was used to. Yet for all his gentleness and femininity, there was a strength and intelligence in his face, as though ideas and books and conversation were more important to him than all the masculine things that mattered so much to the young men she knew.

Yet for all that, the poor laddie looked to be out of place in an island barn on the westernmost part of Scotland. Perhaps if she were to attend one of the Court events in Paris or Rome, she'd see him in his normal surroundings and would appreciate his beauty. All her life, she'd grown up surrounded by unpretentious men, devoid of powder and wigs and fineries. Only in Edinburgh, the epicenter of sophistication, did she ever see men and women dressed in finery, though a provincial, and not a courtly finery. Not even Lady Macdonald, for whom she acted as a companion, dressed finely when she was in Skye, but would don a ragged tartan skirt and warm woollen overgarments when she was in the yard chasing away the chickens and gathering the eggs for morning breakfast.

They made themselves comfortable and it afforded Flora the opportunity to have a second glance at Prince Charlie; it was then she decided that he was a lovely looking man. He had a high forehead and thick brown hair and a strong nose and pleasing happy eyes. If ever she gained an invitation to one of his parties and found herself alone with him . . . but she immediately put the thought out of her mind when he turned to her and said, "So why have you come here, Flora Macdonald? Delighted as I am to see you, there has to be a reason for your visit."

She hesitated telling him. Now her arguments seemed to be so selfish. Here she was, sitting next to a young man who'd risked his all to regain the crown stolen from him and his family by the English Parliament, and she was too mean-spirited and unworthy to offer him the little service he required.

"Is there a reason you're not talking to me, Miss Macdonald? Surely one who was so garrulous barely two days ago can't have lost her power of speech in so short a space of time?"

"No, sir, I haven't lost my speech. It's just that I came here to say something, and now I think I've changed my mind."

He nodded. "And what was it you came to say? And then tell me what it was that changed your mind. The reason I ask is that if my presence has so powerful an effect on a clever young woman, imagine how potent I could be in changing the mind of King George, were he to grant me an audience in St. James's Palace. Why, using the same powers, he might take one look at me and pack his bags and return to Hanover with his dastardly brood."

Flora laughed. "I came here to tell you that I didn't want to accompany you on your journey to Skye."

"But you've already told me that, ma'am. Two days ago, in the foothills of the mountain you call Beinn Mhor. You made it quite clear that as a woman soon to be wed, you . . ."

"No, that's not it. My father and my fiancé determined that the safest thing for you would be for me to travel by rowboat to Skye as your mistress."

The prince laughed. "I have many mistresses, Flora Macdonald, all of whom are in Paris or Rome. Adding you to their number would be a delight, but I fear your Mr. Alan Macdonald might object."

She looked at him and burst out laughing. Again, in a reaction which would later embarrass her, she hit him on the shoulder and told him "You gorbellied lewdster. You know what kind of mistress I'm referring to. But truth to tell, I refused because I felt the danger was too great for me. If you're caught, then it's the gallows for anybody found with you, and I'm not even wed."

"And you've now suddenly changed your mind? I think that your initial reaction was the correct one. This will be a very dangerous crossing, and I'd hate to put you in the line of danger. You're far too young and pretty to risk your life and liberty for one such as me," he said. "You'll soon wed Mr. Macdonald and have many beautiful children and a wonderful life in the Islands. No, ma'am, you shouldn't accompany me."

"But I've changed my mind, Your Highness. I've decided to go with you. Yes, it's dangerous, but it'll be far more dangerous for you if I'm not there as your mist . . . your employer. These troopers are suspicious of everybody, and a maid traveling alone will undoubtedly arouse their suspicions. If they see you, they'll undoubtedly search you, and how long will it be before they realize you're a man? But if I'm there, I can brazen it out and order you to the back of the boat while I deal with the troopers. So I've decided that I must put my fears aside and assist my Prince in his adventure."

Charles smiled and gently kissed her on her hand. "You are a fine and brave young woman, Flora. If the world was full of Floras and Hughs and Alans, instead of German Georges and Fredericks and Augustuses, the world would be a much finer and more fitting place. A place for heroes. I thank you, Mistress Macdonald. I'm proud that you'll be traveling with me. It makes my heart swell with gratitude and lights a beacon in this otherwise dark and troubled world."

It was many moments before she realized that he was still holding his hand. Even when she returned to her home to tell her family that she would, indeed, accompany the prince to Skye, she protected the hand from the touch of others. And lying on the straw mattress later that night before the glowing embers of the fire needed to warm the cool nights of summer, she looked at the hand, and in her mind's eye, she imagined the prince bowing to kiss it once more. She barely slept, her heart was beating so fast.

The following morning, as Angus was preparing to take a tray of food, concealed in a cart in case he was stopped by the troopers, Flora ran to the door and said, "Brother, I'll take that to His Highness."

"Don't worry, darling, it's no bother."

"You don't understand, Angus. If I'm to help Prince Charlie pretend to be both a woman and a seamstress, then I need to spend time with him explaining to him the many complexities of his role."

Angus looked at her strangely. "I think I'd better inform Hugh and Alan of this conversation. You know how particular Hugh is about these matters."

Flora shrugged and said, "It's of no importance to me. But it's important to the prince."

She waited while Angus disappeared inside the house. When he emerged a few minutes later, she fought to restrain her smile when he told her that both Hugh and Alan thought it an excellent idea that Flora should be the tutor to His Royal Highness.

She immediately rushed into the house and took with her a couple of bonnets, a cloak, and hood, a pair of her boots, stockings, stays, petticoats and a ribbon she often used to tie up her hair. She laid them carefully in the cart and covered them with straw. She pushed, hauled, and trundled with the beast of a thing over the rutted pathway which led toward the sea and in the direction of the barn, fully knowing the dangers if she was stopped by troopers. But she breathed a sigh of relief when the wheels cleared the final rut in the road and she was able to push the cart toward the old barn.

What a place for a royal head to rest, she thought, looking at the barn's shape, all bent and torn, it's roof shingles slipped and broken. It lay like the skeleton of a dead cow in the middle of the field.

Having seen her coming from his hiding hole beneath the rafters and ensuring that she wasn't being followed, the prince had jumped down and was at the door to greet her.

"My dear Flora. Again, it's both a surprise and a pleasure to greet you. Why is Angus not with you?"

"Because Your highness, I'm here in order to teach you the skills of being a woman. You might dress the part, but if you walk and swagger and posture like a man, you'll be exposed in no time, and then we'll all swing on the gallows."

He opened the door and enabled her to push the cart into the barn.

"You're right. I hadn't thought of that. I must learn quickly what mannerisms a woman exhibits which are different from a man's. How clever of you to have thought of that, Mistress Macdonald."

"Clever maybe, but practical, certainly. I've brought clothes which I want you to put on so that I can show you how to look like my maidservant."

Together, they threw the straw off the cart and exposed both the clothes and the food. Greedily he eyed the flask containing ale and the covered bowl with its oatmeal porridge, still hot from Elizabeth's stove.

"Dear God, but I'm ravenous. You just don't realize how easy it is to live and eat in a palace, where all you have to do is to look at a servant and they'll produce sweetmeats or a glass of wine or even a ten-course banquet. But living the life of a soldier is to understand the true privations which ordinary people suffer."

She laughed. "And how would you know of the privations of people in these parts? If it's been a bad summer and a cruel winter, grown men and women die of swollen bellies and starvation; mothers have no milk in their teats to feed their bairns; cattle starve for want of oat-cakes or grass in the fields, and a dead cow can mean the death of an entire family. You have no conception of what it means to go hungry Your Highness."

Chastened, he nodded and said softly, "You're right again, as usual. I'm thinking like a member of a royal house and not like one of his subjects. But in fairness to myself, Flora, I wasn't like the other generals

I fought against who were on the English side. Men like the Duke of Cumberland feast themselves into a stupor off the battlefield while their men eat stale tack and oats. I always ate with my commanders and insisted that my commanders shared exactly the same meals as were eaten by my men. You have to believe me."

She smiled and nodded. "I believe you. Now eat up your porridge or you'll be too thin to get into the bodice and petticoats I've brought along."

They hid the cart beneath bales of oat straw, which Flora told the prince was known in Scotland as groats, and carried the clothes, the food, and the drink up to the loft. She lay the clothes aside to be tried on after the meal, and she sat and watched the prince eating hungrily. As he did so, Flora poured him some ale and tore off a wedge of freshly baked oatmeal bread. Although she'd eaten not half an hour before, she couldn't resist a taste of the moist and deliciously aromatic food.

Unable to restrain herself, she asked the question that had been pressing on her mind ever since she'd met him in the moorland a few days ago. She'd asked the same question of her father, but he'd failed to give her an adequate answer, telling her that such questions needn't concern one such as her.

"How bad was it? Up there in the Highlands? After the battle at Culloden when the Duke of Cumberland was killing my countrymen? How bad was it truly," she asked.

The prince didn't answer for some time, and Flora thought that she might have offended him by asking such a question. But she knew that she was ignorant of these matters, and if she was to risk her life by exposing herself to the clutches of these English men, then at least she had to know of what they were capable.

He put his wooden spoon down on the straw and turned to her. "The duke was in London reporting back his triumph to his father when it began, although I must assume that he'd given orders for the massacres to happen. He was resolved to inflict terrible chastisement upon us, both with fire and sword, to ensure that Scotsmen and women understood the true nature of English rule and the folly of rising up against London.

"When he returned to Scotland a month after the battle, after he had enjoyed his many triumphant marches and banquets in London, he stationed himself in Fort William and Fort Augustus. From there, Flora, he dispatched detachments of his troops to devastate whatever they found. They destroyed the seats of the lords of Lochiel, Kinlochmoidart, the Macphersons of Cluny, Glengyle, Glengarry, and many others . . . just burnt them to the ground and plundered the houses and killed the crofters and tenant farmers and the lairds' families. And I'm also sorry to have to inform you that a certain Major Lockhart, an evil and cruel man, marched a detachment of men into the country of your kinsmen, the Macdonalds of Barisdale, and destroyed everything in sight. It was described to me as being a devastation worse than a biblical plague.

"Some of the men were killed outright, some were dragged off and hanged in public, some were loaded into galley ships and transported to the Americas; some women and children were forced to watch as their menfolk were killed or beheaded and they themselves were then beaten with the butts of muskets and were stripped naked and forced out into the frigid cold night so that they would freeze or starve to death."

Flora clutched her mouth and whispered, "Dear God. I wasn't told."

The prince nodded. "Either Hugh Macdonald wanted to spare you the grief or he doesn't know himself. And as if this devastation wasn't evil enough, it certainly wasn't an act of mercy to have left so many innocent Scotsmen and women alive. The reason the duke didn't kill everybody in the Highlands was because he felt that there was no point expending bullets or the time and energy of his swordsmen in killing everybody, for he ordered that all the cattle to be taken from the Highlands and driven south, where they've been purchased for ridiculously small amounts of money by Englishmen."

"But without cattle . . ." she said.

"Without cattle, there'll be mass starvation in the Highlands. Whole families, entire villages, will die long and painful deaths."

Flora wanted to say something, but she wasn't capable of speech. The prince continued, "And it's said that the denuded land will be filled with Englishman and sheep, that the English will be offered cheap farmland

and will build their farms on land where once Highlanders lived for a hundred generations. It's a tragedy that needs to be stopped. I started it, and it's my duty to put a stop to it," he said. She barely heard his last remark, which was said almost as a whisper.

Flora, too, remained silent as she tried desperately to absorb the extent of the English Duke of Cumberland's brutality. But try as she might, the images wouldn't come into her mind. As Prince Charles talked more to her of the death and destruction that the duke was meting out to the Highlanders, Flora closed her eyes and tried to envisage a land on fire, a land devoid of the horned long-haired cattle, a land where the mountains were forever silent, a land where the white bodies of men and women, naked and shriveled, lay dead in valleys beside streams that were crimson and black with their fluids. But she couldn't. All she could see when she closed her eyes was the white and purple of the heather, the regal crown of the thistle, and a distant piper wearing a clan tartan standing on a rocky ledge above a sparkling loch, piping a lament. She could imagine Scotland no other way.

She tried her best not to laugh, for she knew that if she ridiculed him, he might object to wearing the clothes she'd brought. Then her own life would be in as much peril as would be his. Instead, she turned away from him and bent down in order to pretend to find some article of undergarments so that she could stifle her laughter.

She turned back, but when she saw that the prince was grinning all over his face, it caused her to explode and guffaw. He was wearing nothing but his pantaloons and a large petticoat and looked more like a plucked and dressed chicken than a prince in a royal household.

"You look wonderful, Your Highness," she said, still in hysterics. "Were I a man, I would . . ." But she stopped short of telling him what she'd do and glanced down at the ground in embarrassment.

"If you were a man, ma'am, I wouldn't be dressed like this, for the danger of your misinterpreting my intentions would be too great. There are enough gentlemen in the courts of Paris and Rome, not to mention in the Vatican, who have attempted liaisons with me, for me to be exceedingly wary about being in a state of undress in the presence of another gentleman."

She stopped laughing, and carried a bodice over to where he was standing. "So am I to gather that Your Highness in no way inclined toward a liking for gentlemen," she said, knowing the statement to be impertinent. But the situation was so extraordinary that she didn't mind saying it.

"That is precisely what you might gather. I enjoy the company of men in gaming and sports and martial pursuits, and there's nobody better to be drunk with or to beat at cards than a gentleman of similar persuasion; but in my bed chamber, I am definitely inclined toward the shape and aroma of a lady and disinclined to know the crude and muscular form of a man."

She helped him put his arms through the holes in a bodice, and when she'd tightened the strings of the stays at the back, she saw that the front would immediately be perceived by an observer as being far too flat for a middle-aged lady.

"I'm afraid that we're going to have to fill your . . ." Somehow she couldn't bring herself to say the word.

"Bosoms?" said the prince.

Flora smiled and nodded.

"Some straw, perhaps?" he suggested.

She bent down and picked up two handfuls of straw. Then she pushed it down the front of the bodice to fill the area where a woman's breasts would normally fill out the garment. As she touched the soft skin on his chest, she fancied she could feel his heartbeat, until she flushed with the realization that it was hers.

The prince saw that she had suddenly blushed crimson red and said gently, "Tell me, ma'am, when will you and Mr. Macdonald be wed? I would very much like to send you a wedding gift."

She stepped back and said, "It's our intention to marry within the next two or three years. I know in France and Italy and the hot countries, weddings follow shortly after engagements, but in Scotland, it's long been the custom for young couples to enjoy much longer engagements.

Then we know for certain that the man we're supposed to be marrying is the right one. At any time during the engagement period, either party can withdraw without penalty. But neither party can have knowledge of the other, for fear of a baby born out of wedlock. The Kirk of Scotland is very strict on this matter."

Now he tried on the dress. It was one of her more drab dresses, a dress that she wore to go into town and to the shop when she needed supplies. It was brown and heavy and worn with a cloak, ideal for the cold winter winds that blew over Skye. In the height of summer, it was warm to wear, but it was the least impressive dress that she'd brought with her and a dress suitable for a lady's maid.

The prince struggled into the garment, and Flora helped him smooth it over the petticoats. She put the cloak over it and raised the hood to cover his entire head so that only his face was able to be seen. Flora pulled the hood even more forward so that only the most keen observer could perceive the eyes and nose and mouth of a Prince.

She fussed and adjusted the dress to fit the prince's body, pulled here and pushed there, until she was satisfied. But no matter how much he hid his face, his growth of beard was apparent. Flora said, "You'll need to attend to your ablutions before you step out. One look at a woman's face with those whiskers and the next step will be up to the hangman's noose," she told him.

"Yes, but aside from my face, how do I look? Will I pass muster in this outfit?"

She walked back over the loft until she was far enough away to see him from the perspective of distance. She smiled and nodded. "You'll do, Betty Burke. You'll do fine. Tell me, would you like to shave now, for my brother Angus sent over a razor and a bowl and some soap."

The prince told her that it would be good to wash. Flora climbed down from the loft and retrieved the razor, sharpening strop and a bowl, which she filled with rainwater from the barrel outside.

When she climbed back, she handed the implements to the prince, who looked at her strangely. "Forgive me, ma'am, but do you expect me to shave myself?"

Flora smiled and said, "of course."

"But I've never shaved myself. I've always had servants to do it."

She looked at him in surprise. "But you've been a fugitive for the past many months. How have you shaved?"

He grinned, somewhat sheepishly, and said, "One of the party always did it for me. Sometimes, I would implore the wife or daughter of a crofter, who would take pity on me. I know that men here shave themselves, but I have no idea how."

Amazed, she said, "Dear God, man, you just soap up your face and run the razor over it."

But he looked so downcast, like a scalded puppy, that she sighed and said, "Take off your hood and your dress, and I'll do it for you."

He sat on the floor of the loft, and Flora lathered up the brush and the soap and applied it generously to his face. Carefully she shaved off the growth from his cheeks, then underneath his chin, and finally beneath his nose. She toweled him clean and dry and examined her handiwork, running her hand over his face to ensure its smoothness. As she did so, he looked up at her, and she looked down at him. Again, she flushed but was annoyed with herself for being silly. She was a Scottish country girl; he was a Prince of the House of Stuart. She was the daughter of a crofter; he was the son of a king in waiting. He was a nobleman with a bevy of aristocratic mistresses; she was engaged to be married to a good and decent farmer who was of her clan. To even contemplate a liaison was too silly. Yet her heart was beating so fast that she was breathless. It was just too silly, and she determined to control her girlish emotions.

She stood back and said to him, "Now you look particularly handsome, Your Highness."

"You're very good to me, Flora Macdonald. I know I must seem utterly useless to one such as you, a woman who is so self-reliant, but as a Prince of the House of Stuart, I have servants to do everything for me, and except for my military training, I could no more look after myself than swim from one end of the ocean to the other. That's the cost and benefit of being a Prince, I'm afraid."

She replaced his bodice and dress, and then finally put the bonnet and hood over his head. And then she smiled and whispered something conspiratorial. Something that would infuriate her father and brother and fiancé, but would ensure her own peace of mind. She needed to see whether her family could be fooled by the subterfuge, for if they accepted the prince as a woman, then there was hope.

Sometime later, Hugh saw two women walking along the road, chatting and nodding to each other. Even from a distance, one of the women could easily be seen as Flora, but Hugh wondered who was the woman she was walking home with. He watched them as they came to the croft and then turned and walked into the pathway.

When she saw her father, she smiled and said, "Father, how nice to see you. I met Mistress Macduff, all the way from Fife, here to visit her daughter-in-law's family. I've invited her for tea. I hope you don't mind."

Hugh smiled and said, "Of course not. How do you do, ma'am. I welcome you to this house."

Mistress Macduff nodded and said a quiet thank you. Then she repaired to the front of the room and sat in a seat. "It's such a hot day, I hope you'll forgive me for sitting in your presence," she said.

"Of course, ma'am. May I fetch you a drink of water. Or ale? Or whiskey to ease the burden of the day?"

"Sir, ale would be grand," she told him. "My, but you've a lovely daughter. She saw me in the road and took pity on me. And she a Macdonald. I find it very gratifying, sir," the old lady said.

"Yes," said Hugh, "she's a lovely young woman and will soon be married to one of her clan. She's as good a daughter as you'd wish."

But Flora couldn't any longer hold in her laughter and burst into hysterics, to the amazement of Hugh. "Father, bow down in the presence of His Royal Highness, Betty Burke."

Prince Charles Edward threw off his hood, removed his bonnet, and smiled broadly. Hugh gasped.

"Do you think the disguise will work, father?" asked Flora.

But all Hugh could do was to nod in agreement. And even before the prince could say anything, Hugh gasped, "It's a wonder to behold, daughter. Now for God's sake, get His Highness back into hiding before we all become victims of the English Butcher."

# Chapter Eight

June 27, 1746

Neil MacEachan was a gruff man. Tall and muscular, he towered over both the prince and Flora. Yet for all his Highlander diffidence and restraint in the company of strangers, it was apparent from his manner that the red-haired Celt was fully in command of the situation, and regardless of the rank and privilege of the two passengers he was rowing over to Skye, both of them knew instinctively that on the sea, he was captain and they would listen to his advice.

After having been formally introduced in the house near to the coast where they had journeyed the previous night, Neil told them, "They say that there are English boats patrolling these waters. We'll wait for both the right tide and for a clear passage before launching the boat and pushing off from the shore. Last thing we want is for the fly grub English to spot us before we're in deep waters."

He remained in the house and waited and watched patiently as Flora again dressed the Prince of the Stuarts in a woman's dress in preparation for their journey down to the shore and then in the rowboat to take them to Skye. Once more, she shaved him to ensure that there was no growth of hair to be seen should a trooper remove his bonnet. Adjusting the ties and bows of the dress, she smoothed it over the broad petticoats, and stepped back and admired her handiwork. Unlike on the previous occasion in the barn, this time there was no frivolity, for his disguise was a matter of life and death for them all.

But she was interested in Neil's opinion of her handiwork, because if the dour and skeptical Scotsman could be fooled, then so could an English trooper. "So, Neil MacEachan, what do you think of Mistress Betty Burke, my seamstress and maid? Do you think she'll do?"

Neil shrugged laconically. "She'll do for you all right; mistress, but she'll nary do anything for me. I get no stirring in the groin looking at her. She looks worse than a knotty-pated skainsmate, but then I'm not going to wed or bed her, and so long as she passes scrutiny by the Englishmen, who wouldn't know a Highland cow from the nether side of a barn, why does it matter what I think?"

It was exactly what Flora wanted to hear. Neil would have told her soon enough if the disguise wasn't working. When Neil was ensured that the path to the coast was clear, the three walked cautiously down to the water's edge beyond the rocky foreshore and the line of vegetation. The site for departure had been chosen because of the proximity of large rocks and trees close to the stony beach, behind which the trio could hide in the event of an English patrol. For his part, Neil barely spoke a word on the short journey, but the prince noticed that the man's eyes were everywhere, seeking out the shapes of shadows and rocks in case they hid an enemy.

They arrived at the shore of the sea. It was a sparkling and clear day with a zephyr breeze and a hint of the perfume of heather in the air. The prince couldn't help but smile at the feeling of freedom, having spent the past many months hiding in filthy fields and dismal barns with companions who had drifted away, leaving him with just a small core of loyalists. Now, to see the clean and gloriously beautiful sea, to feel the wind of freedom on his face, and to hear nothing but the distant screams of gulls, was overpowering his emotions.

But caution was the watchword as Neil painstakingly trod a path to the beach through the rocks, ensuring few if any footsteps were left behind. After nearly fifteen minutes of complete silence, Neil turned back to them and whispered, "I'm told that General Campbell and his men are in the area. They must have got news that you were close by. They'll do everything in their power to prevent you leaving the Island."

Flora looked at him in shock. "But we were told that Campbell was on the other side of the Island and to the North. How in the name of all the saints could he have known to have come to such a remote place as this?"

Neil shrugged. Such matters didn't concern him. Only the reality of the moment.

"Mistress Macdonald," said the prince, "I think if that's the case, then it would be safer for you to leave now and return to your Hugh and Alan. I could not countenance any danger imposing itself on your person."

"I wouldn't hear of such a thing, Highness. I've come this far, and I'm not turning back now," she insisted.

She was about to say more, when suddenly Neil turned back to the sea. He listened for a long moment and then faced the prince and Flora, looking sternly at them. They knew to desist immediately from any more conversation. The prince looked at the Islander and wondered what he could see or hear. He looked over the sea and neither saw nor heard anything.

Suddenly, Neil turned to them and hissed, "Away and hide behind the rocks at the top of the beach. Boats."

The prince and Flora Macdonald immediately ran back up the beach and hid behind a huge boulder. Her heart was thumping and she was terrified. The game was over. Now her life hung by a thread.

Panting in fear and terror, Flora risked sneaking a glance around the rock behind which they all hid and saw nothing but the open sea, the waves, and the seagulls. She continued to scan the horizon, then she stole a glance at Neil who still seemed to be concerned, and then she looked back out to sea in case her eyes had deceived her. But no matter how long she waited and looked, she could see nothing but an unchanging skyline and the waves gently washing the shore.

And then in the distance, soft at first but growing steadily louder, the harmony of the sea's voice was disturbed by the sound of oars straining against the current. And then, around the headland, the prow of a boat slowly came into view. As the troopers rowed, more and more of the long boat became visible. It was a coastal ferrying boat, used by the Islanders when the sea was too rough for large sail to safely put into the harbor. It was containing fifteen soldiers, all heaving on oars. And it was followed in short succession by another, and then another, and finally a fourth boat. In each, there were fifteen troopers, all heaving on oars; and in the prow of each, clinging to the forward flagpole, was an officer with a spyglass, peering at the land for any sight of the prince and his party.

"How in God's name did you hear them so far away?" Flora whispered.

Neil shrugged.

"Thank God he did," whispered the prince, "for had he not, we'd have been spending the night in a dungeon."

The three watched the troopers in the rowboats go past, but even though they slowly rowed and disappeared beyond the headland on the opposite side of bay, the three remained hidden, just in case there were more boats, or the four that had just passed by turned around and returned in their patrol.

They remained in hiding for a further half an hour, watching the sea with intensity until Neil MacEachan said, "I think that it would be folly to put to sea during the daylight hours. I suggest that we wait until evening, say about ten o'clock when it's sufficiently dark in these parts, and then we'll be able to slip past them unnoticed."

Flora and the prince agreed with his suggestion. But what they didn't realize, and what he didn't tell them, was his concern over the sky. Flora might have recognized the signs, being born and bred in the islands of the Outer Hebrides, but the prince certainly wouldn't have known that the high and hazy wisps of clouds in the sky presaged the coming of bad weather within the next day or so. The sun was shining, the sea was relatively calm, and the man born in Italy, claiming kingship in Scotland believed that the sea would continue to be as smooth as a millpond well into the future. But Neil knew that they were in for a rough crossing, and had it not been for the urgency of getting the prince off the Island, he'd have urged them to delay for a couple of days.

They returned to the house, this time with a much greater sense of caution knowing that the English troopers were so close. As they entered the empty dwelling, a sense of deflation overcame the prince and Flora. They had anticipated rowing to freedom by now and putting land and the prospect of being caught well behind them. What they didn't want was the reality of being cooped up together in a house for the entire day, with nothing to do but contemplate the danger of their situation.

For the rest of that day, they sat quietly and ate and drank of the supplies they'd brought with them for the boat journey. Careful not to take too much of the food in case they were longer on the sea than they anticipated, they ate mainly berries and summer fruits that Flora enjoyed for their sweetness and also the sense of wellbeing they gave her.

Neil, for his part, told them that he would secrete himself behind the large rock, and try to understand how crowded The Little Minch, the stretch of water that separated the Outer Isles from Skye, was with the boats of the English troopers.

When he'd left, Flora and Bonnie Prince Charlie, as she now regularly called him, settled down to wait out the day. They talked, as though they were old friends about the differences in their lives; but although Prince Charles was heir to a throne, he assured her that he was far more fascinated in the life she led than she would be interested in the world of the European courts with their intrigues, their politics, and the perpetual nuisance of hangers-on and those trying to gain influence by attaching themselves to his coat tails.

Flora couldn't see how the life of a farming family in the Hebrides could possibly be as fascinating as that, but he told her, "I have no real idea of how my future people live, nor what they do. That's why it's of importance to me that you teach me the daily activities of my kingdom. And in terms of my own life, you must understand the constraints that courtly life brings with it. You imagine that because people like me are rich and powerful that we're free to do and be what we want. But you couldn't be more wrong, Flora my dear. I'm a victim of my history. My father made a few unsuccessful attempts to reclaim his rightful crown so that the monarchy could continue, as it should have been, as was ordained by God *Himself* when *He* instituted the divine right of king-ship. My father's failure placed an intolerable burden on my shoulders to right this wrong. Not only does my father and my family expect it of me, but the whole of Europe, especially France and Italy, eagerly awaits my success. Failure is unthinkable. Failure will destroy not just my family, but the hopes and dreams of the many supporters and followers of the rightful heir to the English and Scottish thrones."

"Forgive me, Charlie, but you've already failed. Culloden was a fail-ure, and the past few months of escaping the Duke of Cumberland weren't the hallmarks of a victor. I don't mean to be cruel, but what else can you tell your father and your supporters when you return to France?"

He nodded. Then he smiled. "You know, Flora, there should be peo-ple like you in the royal courts. People who see clearly and speak the truth without thought to consequences. Instead, we leaders are surrounded by sycophants and flatterers who seek only their own aggrandizement. What you say is patently the truth. But I can't be as honest and straightforward as you. It's called diplomacy, and truth and diplomacy lie at opposite ends of the bed. I will tell all of Europe that the reason for my failure was the lack of support I received from the king of France. Without any French army, I still managed to win many great battles, and I came within a stone's throw of taking London. I shall tell them to imagine what a great victory I could have enjoyed, had I been supported by French troops. But you and I will know the truth."

"Yes, and a thousand Scottish widows and orphans."

"You cut me to the quick."

"Perhaps, Charlie, but no Scot would accept your coming here as a victory for my people. And if you do manage to convince your royal friends of how close you were to getting back the crown, and if the king of France sent his army, how would you have got them to leave England? Do you think they'd have let you sit on the throne without your paying the price for their work? My father always said to be careful about lying with dogs, because you'll wake up with fleas. Once the French troops are on our soil, why should they leave?"

He looked at her in bemusement, but then looked toward the floor of the house and for some time remained strangely silent. Embarrassed that she might have offended him by telling him a truth that he refused to countenance, she said, "Sir, I hope I haven't said something which I shouldn't have said. I'm only a simple woman, not used to the ways of courts and politics. If I have, then I apologize."

He smiled at her, stood, and came over to sit beside her on the chaise longue. He reached over and held her hand. "Dear Flora. You tell me both what I already know and what I refuse to see. Sometimes, one is so driven by the overwhelming desire to achieve a goal that one closes one's eyes to other eventualities. I realized that the king of France was looking for a reason to control the Crown of England but my prayer was that he would do so through my proxy; his reason was only to return the nation to Catholicism, and I honestly believe that he would have been content to have a pact of amity between our nations.

"But how else could I have won back the throne for my father? Look what I came so close to managing on my own, without the king of France's help. Imagine what could have been done with twenty thousand well-fed, well-armed, and well-trained soldiers? But would I or my father have been masters in our own domain? That's something which until now I've determined to confront when my family was again sitting on its rightful throne in London."

Once again, Flora was shocked by the circumstance in which she found herself. A Prince was sitting on her chair and holding her hand. A Prince! And she nothing but a Highland girl who lived on a farm. Yet for a reason she simply couldn't come to terms with, she felt comfortable, alone in a strange house, both dressed like women and holding hands. For even though he'd finished talking with her, he continued to hold her hand. It was a warm and gentle moment. Not a passionate moment, but a time of sharing.

And she recognized something in him that she had not seen previously. She saw now that he was a man. Ordinary, confused, worried, and in desperate need of the love and comfort that a wife could provide. He wasn't even looking at her as he held her hand, but instead was sitting beside her as she reclined on the chaise longue, staring at the floor, lost in the conflicting images that were swirling around in his mind.

Softly, as though not wanting to awaken a sleeping baby, she gently pulled him toward her, reaching up with her other arm as his body reclined upon hers. She held him in her arms. His head was on her breast. She stroked his face. He allowed her to envelope him in her embrace. He didn't question or refuse but submitted to her arms and allowed her to protect him against the enormity of the events that threatened him every moment of his waking and sleeping life.

She sang a lullaby to him, something that she'd been taught by her mother Anne when she was a child, and which, now that she was engaged to Alan, she eagerly waited to sing to her own bairns.

Sitting in the depths of the boat, he was already seasick as it breasted the waves and plunged into the troughs, but he was determined to pull his weight. The Scotsman, though, wouldn't have it.

"No, sir, you will not row," said Neil MacEachan, feeling freer to speak at his normal tone of voice now that they were a league or more away from the land. "Unless you're an experienced rower, you'll only confuse my rhythm and increase the work I have to do."

"But Mr. MacEachan, surely four hands are better than two."

"Not when the hands haven't held an oar before. Half of the work of rowing is in the strength of your arms, but the other half is in the technique of how you dip an oar into the waves and maintain a constant pressure, letting the weight and momentum of the boat and the flow of the water do some of the work. You have not learned the technique, and all you'll do is cause me to row round in circles. No, young man, you sit in the stern and relax and by mid-day tomorrow, I'm hoping that the tide and the currents will have helped me row to within sight of Healaval Mhor on Skye."

Flora heard the interchange, but because it was so dark, she could barely make out the two men who were talking. When they'd left the Island an hour earlier, pushing the boat out into the waves and scrambling aboard in constant fear of gun fire from the shoreline, they'd lain in the bowels while Neil had pulled and heaved against the battering of the waves. But as they'd left, the sky was still gleaming with the light of the stars and the crescent moon even trailed its tendrils in the water. And as they rowed further and further from the land, the nighttime fires lit by the troopers on the cliff tops diminished until they became no more than pinpricks of light to the north and south of the point from which they'd departed. But soon the Isle was out of sight, buried five leagues into the horizon.

Neil looked up and was concerned about the disappearance of the stars behind the blackening of the sky. Huge thunderclouds were starting to roll in toward Scotland from the Western Atlantic Sea. Hard though they were to see against the already dark sky, natives of the Islands recognized the intensity of a coming storm from the smell of the air and the shape and dimension of the clouds. And these clouds worried Neil as he rowed toward Skye.

Facing him and looking forward to the horizon out of which Skye would eventually loom, the prince had his back to the Island of South Uist and the ocean from where the rapidly forming storm was approaching and didn't understand why Neil and Flora had fallen silent. When he offered to help row the boat and when his offer had been refused, he felt it was Scottish Highland self-reliance or churlishness and sat back to enjoy the journey as much as he could. Unlike on the land where the Duke of Cumberland's army could suddenly be everywhere, on the high seas, his small rowboat could detect the sail of a ship many miles away and could take evasive action to be enfolded in the arms of the waves and hidden from his enemy.

Settling into the dimensions of his Betty Burke dress, cloak and bonnet, the prince was lulled into a light doze by the swell as the rowboat rode gently up and down the peaks and troughs. But he was rudely awakened when the troughs suddenly became much deeper, and he was thrown around inside the boat.

"What's . . ."

"There's a storm coming," said Neil, having to speak louder over the increased noise of the wind.

"But Hugh assured us that in summer . . ."

Neil laughed. "Hugh can say what he likes, but the Almighty decides what weather we'll have. And right now, He's determined that we're in a wee open boat on the high seas with not an inch of canvas to protect us from a downpour. You offered to row the boat, Charlie. Now you can do something far more important and that's bail out the water which'll collect when the rain starts to sheet down. Can you do that?"

"Of course," said the prince.

"So shall I," said Flora and began to fuss around in the bottom of the boat, amidst all the ropes and anchors, to find two buckets that she and the prince could use.

Neil nodded and continued to pull on the oars, more strenuously now that the seas were so much greater than when they'd set out. The wind was rising in tempo and beginning to scream past the distant island as though a thousand ghosts were moaning and flying into the air toward them.

"We're going to be blown off course by the wind and the waves," Neil shouted. "I can determine roughly where we are if I can get a glimpse of the moon and the stars. But we need a break in the clouds. Even so, with no compass to guide us, we'll be miles out when we make landfall on Skye. I hope you haven't got somebody waiting for you at a particular point, Charlie, because we could be fifty miles to the north or the south by the time we reach land. Or we could be pushed so badly off course we'll miss Skye altogether. Then . . ."

He let the words hang in the wind. And then it began to rain. They were already wet from the splashing of the oars and the waves, but now solid sheets of rain began to fall from the lowering black clouds scudding across the sullen sky. Peals of thunder and vast explosions of lightning turned the black night into brilliant day for just an instant.

The first sudden colossal flash of light shocked Flora who screamed and buried her face in her hands. It was so vast, so overwhelming, and the surprise was so great, that for an instance, she reverted to the terrified child who would hide under her blanket in a thunderstorm. On land, she could protect herself from the violence of a storm by hiding in buildings. On the sea, she was in the midst of nature at its most violent.

Prince Charles immediately moved over to where she was sitting and threw both his arms and the seamstress's cloak he had been wearing around her, holding her into him as she had done earlier in the day.

"I'm all right. Truly, Charlie. I'm all right. I wasn't expecting it and it was so close and so sudden. I was shocked by the brilliance," she shouted. "It felt as though I was inside it."

He maneuvered his cloak over her head, but she said, "We haven't got time to try to stay dry. We have to start bailing before the boat fills with water and becomes too heavy for Neil to row."

They looked at Neil, and although it was pitch black except for the illumination from the lightning, they knew that he'd be straining with all his might against the mounting seas.

The rain and the ferocity of the wind increased with every minute. From a journey that started off as a simple row between islands over an undulating sea, only hours later they were in the middle of a terrible Atlantic storm with stinging rain hurtling down and filling the boat, boding their death by drowning at any moment. The prince couldn't believe his bad fortune.

The mountainous distance between the peaks and troughs of the waves threatened to overturn the rowboat with every pull of the oars. It was pitching and tossing like a leaf in a windstorm and in danger of breaking in two, its spine creaking as the waves reached enormous heights, three or four times that of a man. Flora whimpered in terror but forced herself to remain silent and not to display her fear in case it spread to the other two, for then they would truly be lost. Instead, to prevent herself from vomiting in the swells and to stop herself from crying out aloud, she concentrated her mind on bailing out the rapidly filling water. Neil was intent on trying to ride the waves so that the craft didn't suddenly find itself at the top of a peak, for he knew all too well that in these seas, a plunge down into a trough could break a boat into a dozen fragments. The lightning told him all too menacingly that it was a good twenty or thirty-foot drop from top to bottom, and no rowboat could survive that kind of a fall. He braced his feet to ensure that he wasn't tossed hither and thither.

Only Prince Charlie tried to keep up the spirits of the other two by singing a French song, followed by one in Italian. It was fortunate that neither Flora nor Neil spoke Italian, for the words were superbly vulgar. He only rarely got to perform it, for normally he was restrained by the etiquette of the courts, and could only sing these songs in a drinking party of his male friends. When he came to the part about the size of a man's member and the look on a lady's face as he exposed himself to her, he sang the words with much greater gusto as though daring the Almighty to take offense, come down to earth in person, and do something about it.

Time meant nothing to them as the storm maintained its intensity and the seas grew ever more ferocious. They were starting to suffer exhaustion, but rest was a luxury they couldn't afford, for any let-up from bailing or rowing would lead to their certain death. They were in the epicenter of nature at her most violent and unforgiving. The music of the moment was a cacophony of vast thunderclaps that shook the very sea itself, blinding lightening that illuminated their terror, and the rolling and pitching of their boat that threatened to toss them into the deadly waves as though they were mere puppets.

The continuous thunder and lightning lit the surrounding seas and the light showed the fear in all of their faces. They knew in their hearts that they were going to die at any minute, and for an instant, Flora welcomed death in place of the fear she was feeling. Her arms were like lead, her clothes were soaked and heavy, and her face stung from the constant spitting of the waves. The water's spume against her skin was like somebody throwing sand at her.

The violent sea, whipped up into a frenzy by the wind, was topped with white foam and spume, flecks of which were swept up into the air and carried in the wind like snowflakes. All three of them were completely covered in white as though they were exposed in a winter's blizzard. The near and distant ocean was a vision of hell itself. Wildness was everywhere, as was its sister, tumult. The thunderclaps rent the air as though a giant was beating on a huge drum, followed by growls from the belly of the most hideous monster in the depths of the ocean.

Not one single portion of the sea or sky was calm. When lightning enabled them to see beyond the confines of their boat, they felt they were in the clutches of a demented ogre; everywhere they looked, the waves towered above them and threatened to engulf their flimsy craft; the sea was a witches' caldron, and the very sky itself galloped as pendulous clouds raced across the firmament. They were in the midst of a nightmare, yet the awful ache caused by the bailing of the water just to keep afloat and alive, and the stinging pains in their arms and legs and bodies told them that they were very wide awake.

The tiny rowing boat was tossed from the crest of one wave to the crest of another as the huge tide swelled with the winds and seemed to make the very water expand and explode. When they were high on the crests threatened with cascading into a deep mid-ocean trough, they surged down the back of the wave into the depths to find a monstrous body of water towering over the boat and threatening to engulf them in its fury. It was only by the extraordinary oarsman skill of Neil that he managed to maneuver the craft out of a hundred potentially disastrous precipices into safer places, that they remained alive.

Occasionally they would see a large sea bird, an albatross, or a sea eagle desperately beating its wings in an attempt to reach land. And that was good for Neil, for it meant that, although they were prey to the tides and were tossed like flailed grain by a demented thresher, just by following the direction in which the birds were frantically flying to reach cover, he knew that eventually, God willing, he would hit landfall.

The storm seemed to go on forever, and in their exhaustion, they didn't know how they would carry on. To stop rowing or bailing was death. But there was neither life nor power in their arms or legs, and exhaustion had overtaken them. Their work was failing, and soon, very soon, they would face mortal danger as the boat filled with water became unmanageable, and soon they would sink.

But somehow, they continued. They drew on unknown sources of power and energy and managed to row and bail, row and bail, even when their minds were numbed into thoughtlessness. After the third and then the fourth hour, Flora and the prince found that their bailing of the water from the bottom of the boat had become so routine that they barely realized what they were doing. They were all freezing cold, their clothes stiff and heavy as medieval armor instead of the soft wool and linen from which they were made.

The work and the foul weather brought the three of them close to fainting from fatigue. Flora was biting back tears from the exertion of bucketing water from the bottom of the boat and tossing it over the side. Though used to hard work, she could no longer feel her arms in their leaden state. Her shoulders ached continuously, interspersed with stabbing pains as the rowboat pitched, and she was tossed roughly against the sides or thrown back into the bottom of the boat. Yet she knew that her pains would have been infinitely worse had Neil not been plying the careful passage that he was, riding the waves as best he could under the most appalling circumstances.

With all their exertions, the one thing they knew was forbidden to them was rest, for Neil still had to negotiate every mountainous wave every moment to prevent floundering, and the prince and Flora had to keep the boat as light and as free of flooding rain and seawater as possible.

Rowing, bailing, praying . . . rowing, bailing, praying. Praying to a deity who laughed at their plight with his thunderous voice and lit their terror so that he could see his playthings and their frantic attempts to survive.

Rowing, bailing, praying for what seemed like eternity. Not a letup, not a moment to rest. Their breath was heavy and labored, their bodies soaked by both sweat and the torrents of rain that continued to pour down, and their minds were continuously numbed by the gargantuan flashes of lightning and explosions of thunder.

And then, in a moment, something occurred that changed their circumstance. It was noticed first by Flora, and without any words, she seemed to communicate her sudden appreciation to the prince who also looked up and took notice of the change. They turned to Neil, whose face appeared to carry less anxiety, less strain. They even noticed him nodding in encouragement. It was as though a calming hand had suddenly been brought down from the heavens themselves. It was difficult to appreciate, because the change at first was very slight, but soon the time between lightning strikes became noticeably longer, and the violence of the thunderclaps, the noise, and the vibrations shaking their bodies, were less insistent; it somehow didn't sound as terrifying, nor did it rattle their bones or their hearts to the very core of dread.

They were working less hard and the rain seemed to be less solid. There were even moments when they were able to look up at each other and grimace, to stop doing what they had been frantically doing and take a moment's rest.

It wasn't sudden, and it took another half an hour of hard work, but by the time they had been on the ocean for six or seven hours, the wind had dropped, the rain lessened, the seas were much calmer and smoother. The storm had passed eastwards and was now flying beyond Skye and toward the mainland.

Neil pulled in the oars, slid down toward the waterlogged bottom of the vessel, and said "Dear God in heaven, but I have no arms left. I have the strength of a bairn and I can't row another yard."

The prince and Flora put down their buckets, and they too collapsed into the bottom of the boat, letting the craft follow the currents as it wished. They lay there, soaked, exhausted, bereft, and completely numb as the vessel drifted with the waves and the currents. The once black and menacing sky began to clear, and occasionally breaks in the dark clouds revealed a starry firmament. The crescent moon was gone, for it was only an hour or two to daybreak, but as time passed, more and more stars could be seen, and the torrential downpour had given way to a blessed and gentle shower.

Flora was the first to say something. "We've done it. Dear Lord, for a time there, I thought we'd all drown. I've never worked so hard nor been so terrified in all my life."

The prince raised his head, which was resting on a drowned anchor rope, but was too tired to speak. Neil was snoring, having fallen fast asleep from the exhaustion. And so, as the rain stopped, the boat meandered gently onward, as though it had been abandoned by its crew, or had come adrift from its moorings and was floating listlessly upon an empty sea.

When the sun appeared, they roused themselves. It came up over the Island of Skye, which was still nowhere to be seen, and within a quarter of an hour of its first rays, the entire ocean was clearly visible. It was calm and peaceful now compared to the way it had been in the middle of the night. There was still a considerable swell, but now the waves were gentle and there was only the occasional white cap to be seen in the distance. Gulls were wheeling around, and a blessed wind had blown up to refresh their faces, dry the sweat and water, and ruffle their sodden hair. Had this really been the same sea and sky and wind that only a few hours earlier had threatened to extinguish their lives at any moment? Had this really been the same creation of the same God who had toyed with their safety and their state of mind, throwing them into a panic as though they were drawing their last breath? Flora shook her head in wonder, and thought what a life they were leading.

As the sun grew warmer, the trio roused themselves at almost the same moment, their spirits ecstatic, having come through the "valley of the shadow of death" together and survived. The three sat up in the boat and surveyed the early morning ocean. It was, as far as they could see, empty of any other boats. Flora looked at the prince and Neil and burst out laughing.

"Merciful Lord in heaven, but you both look like drowned rats. I must look the same."

"Not at all, Miss Macdonald. You look very pretty and . . . and . . . wet."

Neil grasped the oars, looked toward the direction of the sun, and with a grunt of resignation, knowing that he still had more than enough work for ten men, rowed eastward to Skye.

"Charlie, you'd better take off your cloak and dress because they'll dry much better if we suspend them from the wee mast on the prow. A good wind, and they'll be dry in an hour. If you gentlemen don't mind, I'll do the same, though I'm not looking forward to exposing my body after the freezing and soaking it received last night. But first thing we have to do is to renew our strength by having something to eat and drink."

As Charlie removed his garments to sit in the boat in his sodden petticoats and stays, Flora opened her bag and took out the food and drink she'd brought for the journey. Much had been soaked by the rain, and she threw the sodden loaf of bread overboard for the benefit of the fish. But the cheese and meat were wrapped in oilskin and the ale was bottled, and all were still good and wholesome. She cut off thick chunks that, along with bottles of ale, she gave to the men. When they were eating, she removed her own dress, without any embarrassment, and took hers and her seamstresses' to the prow where she threaded a rope through the armholes and secured them. They fluttered like flags.

Neither Neil nor Charlie looked at her; they were too interested in their food. As she sat, she mused on her circumstances. It was interesting that she was in a tiny rowboat, in the midst of a vast ocean, alone with two men more enamored of their food and drink than on the fact that they were alone with a lady dressed in nothing but her petticoats. Well, two ladies, if you included Betty Burke.

Dressed, fed, somewhat refreshed although still aching and horribly bruised from the buffeting they'd received from the storm, the three took turns in rowing the boat as it plied its way eastwards toward Skye. Having seen the prince hard at work bailing the water, Neil reluctantly agreed to allow the young man a spell on the oars in order to allow him to rest a while; and he had to admit that, except for the beginning when he'd rowed like a drunk after a wedding, the lad had gotten into the rhythm and was now plying the waves manfully, quickly learning how to ride the crests and take advantage of the troughs. Flora also insisted on doing her share of rowing, but although she was strong, she tired easily and could only manage a half of what her prince was able.

As the sun rose, the clothes and their bodies dried and warmed, and the food and ale began to replenish the energy they'd lost during the storm, their lives returned to a semblance of what it had been when they left South Uist. Their spirits were lifting by the hour, especially when Neil pointed up, wordlessly and somewhat laconically, to the sky. Flora glanced up and smiled back. The prince looked upwards and saw nothing.

"Gulls. It means that land is over the horizon," Flora told him.

"But there are always gulls at sea," he said.

"Aye, but not this many. Some gulls fly far out in search of food for themselves and their hatchlings, but most nest in rocks or in the scree and only fly over the shallow waters near to the coast. The more gulls you see in the sky, the more likely it is that land is close by."

Risking seeming ungainly and being tossed around even in the more gentle morning sea, Flora stood in the boat, holding onto the prince's hand to prevent herself from falling. She looked eastward into the morning sky. There was a sea mist that prevented her from seeing properly, but she fancied that along the horizon she could perceive a line that might be land.

It took a further half an hour of Neil's strong arms to row them so that Flora could say for certain that land lay in front of the horizon. She tried to recognize what part of Skye they had rowed to, but from this distance, it was too difficult to distinguish.

"Look out for any boats," said Neil. "It's more likely than not that the English have put out coastal patrols in order to find you."

Both Flora and the prince peered out from port and starboard, but the coast and the sea appeared to be completely empty except for themselves and an increasing number of sea birds wheeling and swooping over the ocean. Now the land loomed large and Neil stopped his rowing to look and try to ascertain just where they were on the western coast of the Island.

After looking carefully and scratching his chin a few times he smiled and turned to the others. "You're lucky, Charlie. I think we've been blown far north. Tell me if you disagree, Flora, but isn't that Waternish Point," he said.

"Waternish? Where's that on Skye?" asked Prince Charles.

"It's a northerly point, the tip of a peninsular, and well to the north-west of the main body of the Island," Neil said.

But Flora was barely listening. Instead, she was looking cautiously at the cliff face and the mountain beyond and realized that Neil was right. "Lucky, you lame brained hog foot? If that's Waternish Point, and I think you're right, then that's MacLeod land, and Betty Burke and I are wearing scarves of the Macdonald tartan. If they see us, they'll shoot at us for certain. I'd rather face the English than the MacLeod."

Being a man of South Uist, he wasn't empathetic to the eternal disputes between the two major clans that shared ownership of Skye, but he was well aware of the hatred they felt for each other. "Shall I row further south to Macdonald country?"

"No," said the prince. "It's safer that we remove our scarves and travel on foot. We can hide more easily on land than on the sea."

Flora turned to him in sudden anger. "Remove my tartan. Are you mad? I'll not deny my clan."

"You have to, if only for a day or two, otherwise the MacLeods will know you instantly," said Neil. He turned to the prince and said, "You're right. If the MacLeod catch sight of you, you'll be dead. Both of you. And they won't spare me for being with you. Don't be so stubborn, Flora. Do as your man says."

Flora sighed, knowing that they were right. But the idea of being without her tartan made her feel as though she would be walking around naked. Which was funny because here she sat in an open rowboat in her petticoats, without a dress or bonnet, and almost naked. Still, she had to acknowledge that if they were caught on MacLeod land, it would be a catastrophe. After all the dangers of the sea, she didn't want to come to her end by suddenly meeting a band of marauding MacLeods. And then she realized what Neil had said to her. "*Your man!*" She thought of correcting him, but just for a guilty moment, she rather liked the sound of that. Flora and Charlie. Her man.

# Chapter Nine

JUNE 29, 1746

The solidity of land felt oddly discomforting as they dragged the boat away from the water and the grasping waves, up onto the shingles to hide it above the high water mark in shrub and bushes. Neil found his land legs almost immediately, having been a sea dweller all his life; but the prince and Flora felt the solid land still roiling and undulating beneath their feet and their bodies swayed as though the waves that had been their driving force for many desperate hours were still pulling and pushing their bodies even on day land.

They heaved the heavy rowboat up the sand and scree and hid it in vegetation at the foot of the cliff until it was invisible from the sea. Neil then kicked sand into the furrow line the keel had made and walking backward, brushing out their footprints with a driftwood branch and leaves, eliminated any sign they had been there. Whether or not they uncovered the boat again depended on what they found when they climbed the cliff and spied out the land; for his part Prince Charles would have been ecstatic never to see the damnable vessel again.

The reception they received also depended upon whether they had been spotted from the shore as Neil had rowed toward the northern part of the Island of Skye. As they drew closer and closer to the cliff face, Flora scanned the escarpment with the eyes of an eagle but saw neither hide nor hair of anybody.

Now they stood on the sandy beach, and Prince Charles adjusted his petticoat, dress, and bonnet. God knew that he'd never tell a living soul, but he was becoming used to women's clothing. Dresses were comfortable, petticoats sensible, and had it not been for the wet straw in his bosoms, he might even have been happy wearing the bodice and stays. Certainly they were far more amenable to movement and the shape of the body than the trews he wore or the uniforms he was forced to don or the silk cuffs and tight shirts with their strangulating neck ruffs and pinching cummerbunds and buckled shoes and stifling itching wigs, all of which constricted his body and made sitting in dining chairs into a nightmare.

"We have to climb up there," said Flora, pointing to the top edge of the cliff high above them. "You're going to find it cumbersome in your dress and petticoats. You might be better to remove them and dress again when you're aloft."

"And if we scale the cliff, and come face to face with an English regiment? How am I going to explain my state of undress? No, Flora dear, if you climb as a woman, I'll climb as a woman."

Neil put the finishing touches to hiding the rowboat and ensured that their bags and other possession were removed. He divided them between the three and then nodded toward the cliff. "Sooner we're started, the sooner we'll be up," he said.

He led the way. From the base, the cliff looked impossibly high, and Charlie wondered about his decision to climb in such unfamiliar clothes. But by the time they'd negotiated the mass of loose scree and were ascending the sheer face, they were soon well above the beach and on their way to reaching the top. He soon came to understand that climbing in a heavy woolen dress wasn't nearly as easy as doing it in trews, but the prince knew that if he were to survive the next few days or weeks before boarding the French boat that would take him to safety, he had both to dress and to think like a woman.

Neil was the leader of the party, and he was already more than halfway up the cliff, scaling it from handhold to handhold, pulling himself upwards easily from ledge to ledge. It was as though the exhaustion he'd suffered from a fifty-mile nightmare crossing only hours previously had been nothing more than a seafarer's yarn; but the bruising on his body was a constant reminder of how real and dangerous the crossing had been.

Next came Flora, who was obviously suffering more than Neil, because her movements were stiffer and more painful. And finally, Prince Charles followed in her footsteps, spluttering from the occasional debris falling onto his face as the leaders of the climb ascended.

It only took six or seven minutes for the three of them to reach the top of the cliff and sit on the level sward of grassland and bushes that stretched into the distance. They were alone, and as they lay on the soft grass and looked up into the blue sky and then around the horizon, they saw with relief that there was neither a murderous party of MacLeods intent on revenge, nor a regiment of English troopers intent on capture. All they could see was a crofter's hut in the distance and a track that led from a ruined dry stone tower toward the inland.

"What's that ruin?" asked Charles.

Flora told him, "It's what we call a broch. It's a building that we think that the ancient Picts put up. You'll find them all over Skye. Some of them are very tall, and there are stairways within them. Nobody knows what they were used for, but probably to climb and look outwards to sea in case of invaders. But what interests me more than some old broch is the crofter's house over there. I've been watching it since we got here, and there's no sign of life. No smoke, no animals, no people walking about. I think it might have been abandoned."

Neil shook his head, saying, "No crofter would abandon a good house like that." He said that it was more likely a winter's cottage for a farming family, vacated for the summer, and suggested that now they were rested, they walk cautiously toward the hut and see whether it could provide them with shelter while they pondered their next move.

Flora cautiously knocked on the door while the two men hid behind the wall. They believed that a lone woman would present less of a threat if the house was occupied, but when there was no answer, she turned around and shook her head. "There's nobody here," she said. She tried the latch, but it was locked firmly.

The other two walked down the path, and both tried the door, but it was solid and would require a strong shoulder to open it. Neil looked to the right and left of the door, and quickly found a washing bucket in the shrubbery beneath a window. He lifted it up, and beneath it found the key to the house.

Flora and the Prince looked at him in amazement. "Think about it. Like I said before, this is most likely a hut used for a few months of the year by a farmer or a fisherman who probably lives in Dunvegan or some other village. He'll not want to take the key with him in case he loses it, so he keeps it here, knowing that nobody in their right minds would willingly visit this godforsaken area."

He opened the door, and they walked inside. It was dank and there was a layer of dust on the table and floor, but it was tidy. Flora immediately opened the curtains and the two windows and they looked around. It was a comfortable home, though with minimal furnishings.

"Here's what I think we should do," said Neil. "I'll go and see what's afoot in the nearest town, which shouldn't be more than ten miles away. I'll ask questions, maybe stay in an inn overnight, and find out where the English army is stationed. There's no purpose in risking all our lives by blundering along roads if not five miles hence we come across a regiment of the duke's men, and then we'll all be hanged."

"But surely it'd be better if I went, because being a woman . . ."

"No, lass. A woman on her own would be cause for gossip and would come to the attention of the English. But I could say I'm a fisherman from Uist blown horribly off course by the storm and needing food and rest before rowing back. I'll be a local hero to have survived such a sea, and they'll buy me drinks, whereas you'll be questioned and under suspicion."

After he'd rested for half an hour, and judging the time to be approaching mid-morning, Neil bade the prince and Flora a farewell and set off down the path toward the rutted track and on to whatever village was nearby.

They stood in the doorway of the house and watched him leave. Then Flora turned back and said, "If this were my house, I'd offer you a glass of ale or whiskey and some oatcakes. But all I can offer you is whatever meager provisions we've brought with us. But you can sit yourself down, Charlie, and rest your bones while I look through the cupboards and try to find anything that resembles food."

Prince Charles looked at Flora, and could barely prevent himself from laughing. "This is absurd. Here we are in a deserted crofter's house acting like thieves in the night; me dressed as a woman, and you're worried about entertaining me. Flora dear, you've suffered as much as have I. Might I strongly suggest that you come and sit down, and we wait for Neil's return."

"But he won't be back till tomorrow, and we'll both be fiercely hungry and thirsty unless we find some food. There's barely enough roast meat and cheese left to last us the day, let alone the night, so we'll need to find food."

He removed his bonnet intent on helping her, but when she looked at his face, she said, "And you, Your Royal Highness, are in dire need of another shave. Your manliness is showing much too readily."

In one of the cupboards, they found some potted beef, dried venison and some smoke-dried haddock and dried oats. After she'd been to the well, Flora immediately put the oats into a bowl of water to refresh them so that they could have oatcakes and perhaps she could make some oat bread. In the garden, they found wild fruits and herbs. They collected additional water from the well, and wood to light the fireplace.

Within an hour, there was the smell of a banquet. Flora had created a delicious herb soup, some oatmeal cakes and warmed some slices of venison and fish on a griddle plate. The prince watched her fussing around the tiny kitchen and enjoyed the sight of her slender yet strong body bending and stirring. He couldn't help but think how refreshingly different she was to the bewigged, perfumed, and powdered ladies who inhabited the courts where he had spent most of his life. These women, all of whom knew how to play cards and sing and make music and conversation, would have been helpless babes in the situation he found himself.

Yet Flora had set to with a delightful and very feminine vengeance and was making order out of the chaos in which they found themselves.

He'd offered to help several times, but she'd told him very firmly that the last thing she needed was a man getting in her way while she was making a meal, even if the man looked more like her sister than her brother.

They sat at the crude table and ate and drank. The meal was delicious, and the prince kept on commenting on how such a miracle had been produced by her in such meager circumstances. But Flora told him firmly, "Charlie, I thank you for your compliments, but the reason the food tastes like nectar is because we're both hungry and exhausted. If you were in one of your palaces, this would taste like what your servants eat." But she could barely contain her mischievous nature and added, "Of course, dressed like a woman, I'm wondering where you'd have eaten such a meal, upstairs or below stairs. Looking at you now, I'm wondering whether the royal personages in Europe would have treated you like a prince, a princess, or a serving wench?"

Charles burst out laughing. He was feeling more relaxed and at ease than at any time in the past six months. Being on a delightful island, in a charming cottage, with a comely and attentive young woman, was every red-blooded man's dream, and it was something on which he'd pondered ever since he began his long and lonely escape from the Butcher of Cumberland. But she was about to be married and was unavailable. Under his normal circumstances, he could have raised his eyebrows, and his servants would have procured a dozen women like Flora for his pleasure. But these were not his normal circumstances, and he could only rely on his own devices. Even so, every time he looked at Flora, he couldn't fail but see her as a married woman with lots of children. And he would do nothing to mar the future of such a marvelous and spirited girl.

They finished the meal and took the dishes outside to where the wash bucket was to be found. Flora tipped hot water from the kettle into the bucket and scraped the food from the plates.

"I think it's time that we used the rest of the hot water for your shave, Charlie. God knows you need one."

The prince nodded, and they went back into the house.

"Take off your dress, and I'll shave you," she said.

Without thinking, he removed his dress, bodice, and petticoats, which he placed carefully on a nearby seat. He stood before her, unashamed, in his linen undergarments. Flora tried not to look at his fine body, at the muscularity of his chest and arms, at his firm stomach but deliberately fussed with the bowl and lather. She looked away from him as she stropped the razor, but by the time everything was ready, she was forced to turn and face him. She realized that she was flushing and worried that he might see. And he did.

"Do I embarrass you, Flora?" he asked.

"No, not at all. Why do you ask?"

"Because you've turned as purple as a beet. I'm wondering if you're discomforted by being so close to a man who's almost naked."

"Och and away with you, you common-kissing coxcomb. I have a brother whom I've seen naked and they say that I was a wild girl while I was growing up. No, Charlie, to me you're just a man in dire need of a shave."

She stood close to him and worked the brush over his cheeks and neck. Then she carefully scraped the razor over the contours of his face, until all the hair of his beard had been removed. Now she had to shave under his nose, which required her to look and stand closer at him to ensure that she did him no damage. She moved a step forward and placed a hand on his forehead.

"You have such smooth and warm hands, Flora dear," said the prince.

"Hush now, Charlie, or I'll cut off your nose."

She shaved his mustache, and then used a wet and warm towel to remove the remnants of soap from his face. She ran her hands across his cheek, ensuring that all the growth had been removed.

"Could you do that again, Flora," he said softly. "Could you stroke my cheeks again? It felt wonderfully gentle and kind."

If she were the color of beet before, she wondered whether there was a color of deepest red able to describe the look of her face now. She felt hot and flushed and found her shallow breathing to be coming in short, difficult gasps. She was feeling and behaving like a lovesick teenager and was mortified by her response. She bit the inside of her lip to try to control her impulses.

Prince Charles put his hands around her waist and drew her to him. She sat on his lap. "Feel my cheeks again, Flora. It felt so very comforting."

She should have stood immediately and chastised him, but she didn't. After the deadly experiences she'd suffered in the storm, the feel of his lithe body, his strong and young legs, his potent arms, pulling her into his naked chest, brought her close to fainting. She wanted to say something, to resist, to stop this silliness, but words had left her brain. She was incapable of moving; she couldn't, she wouldn't fight him.

Feeling her submit, the prince clasped her tighter and held her waist to his. She put her arms around his neck and hugged him. Then reason and memory suddenly took charge of them both, and he said, "Dear God, Flora, I'm sorry."

She sighed and said softly into his ear, "Charlie, I'm engaged to Mr. Alan Macdonald. I cannot be in this situation. Please understand . . ."

He immediately let her go. But she remained seated on his lap, her arms still around his neck. Through her bodice, she could feel the shape of his mouth. It was smiling. "Flora? Do you want to stand, or are you content to remain like this forever?"

"Beloved Christ and Lord God in heaven, Charlie, I don't know. I'm powerfully drawn to staying here and not moving. I haven't been this close to a man, a naked man, in years, and I'm overwhelmed. But . . ."

"But?"

"But I'm committed to another."

"As am I. I'm committed to marrying a member of a royal family. That's my curse and my blessing in life."

"Then don't you think that it would be better for us to separate."

"You're the one who's holding on to me, Flora."

"I know, Charlie, and for the life of me, I don't understand why I can't let go."

He put his arms around her neck and drew her face to his. They kissed, at first on the cheeks, but then on the lips. And continued to kiss until Flora felt as though she would burst from the passion welling up inside her.

She pushed herself away from him, gasping, "Oh dear God, man, I must put an end to this. It can't be. I can't give myself to you when I'm to be the bride of Alan Macdonald. It would be so very wrong."

She stood, but her legs were as unsteady as when she'd first stepped out of the rowboat. She teetered to the door and took the shaving bowl out of the house, tipping the soapy contents over the garden. As she re-entered the house, she had to grasp the door's frame to prevent herself from falling, so overpowered was she by the blood coursing through her body and the roaring sound in her ears. The prince looked at her and stood, his manhood and excitement still obvious.

"You look as though you're going to faint, Flora dearest. Can I get you something?"

"Aye, you can find me somewhere to lie down. I've not been in such a girlish diddle-daddle in years."

He led her to the chair and she sat down heavily. He drew her a glass of water, which she drank greedily. "It could be because you haven't slept all night. Or it could be because your womanhood is rising in you. How long is it since you've known a man?" he asked.

She looked at him strangely. "Is that a question that a gentleman should be asking of a lady?"

He smiled.

"I suppose it depends on what you mean by 'knowing.' I've embraced and been very passionate with many young men while I was in my teenage years. But since I turned into my twenties, I haven't had the opportunity to enjoy the company of many men for fear of spoiling my prospects of marriage. And I've not given myself to anybody. Not fully, if you take my meaning, though the Lord knows I've been close enough. It's remarkable how much enjoyment young people can have without . . . without . . ."

He nodded. He took her meaning well enough.

"And you, Charlie. How long is it since you've known a woman?"

"Touché. To tell the truth, Flora, the last woman I enjoyed was the daughter of a crofter in Lochinver. And that was more than two months ago. She felt sorry for me and the plight I was in. She had no idea I was the Prince Stuart, but thought that I was a Highlander escaping the Butcher of Cumberland's men. It was more encouragement and sympathy than carnal lust, though she was comely enough in a rough and rude kind of way. Oh, we both enjoyed it, but it was closer to companionship than an act of romance."

"And before that?"

"I have always been supplied with women by my servants. They scour the local towns and encourage any woman wanting advancement to meet with me and offer me her comforts. Before that, in the courts, I only had to look and smile at some highborn or noble lady who wanted to ascend to the highest echelons of the courts by way of my boudoir, and they'd be in my bed before I'd blinked. As a prince of the realm, even though our realm was taken from us, I was very high in the hierarchy and that appealed to a lot of women."

Flora smiled. "And is that what I'd be for you, Charlie? Only a woman who offered you comfort or wanted to climb to higher positions on your back? One of the many? A woman who'd sleep with you for advancement? Is that what you think of me, for if so, you're badly mistaken. And being such a woman is hardly the role I'd envisage for myself."

He looked at her softly. "Dearest girl, please don't begin to equate yourself with camp followers or girls of loose morals. For days and days, you've been a model of rectitude, probity, and morality. It's been a pleasure knowing you. I've grown to admire you greatly in the time we've been together. I've admired your strength and your gusto and your love of life. It's me who strongly desires you. These other women, and in that I include most of the women of the courts of Europe who only want to bed a future king of England in the hope that they might one day be queen, are as nothing to me. Yet I've grown strongly and passionately attracted to you. Your beauty, your strength of purpose, and your gentle nature."

"Charlie, you must desist from speaking like this. You must remember my station in life. Your words are . . ."

"Look beyond my words, Flora darling. I'm a passionate man infatuated with you. I see in you the very essence and beauty that is Scotland.

You, Flora, are the reason I'm here. A country is no more than towns and villages; a land is nothing more than soil and rocks. But the very essence of Scotland is you, Flora Macdonald. You're my purpose in fighting to claim what is mine. You are my victory."

"Oh dear God, you're making me feel faint again," she said, listening to his honeyed words and thrilling in the way he stood so close to her. She wanted to reach out and touch his firm and manly body, to caress him and hold him and fondle him and feel his breath upon her neck and his arms touching her breasts and her other womanly parts. And she wanted to grasp his manhood and feel its rigidity. It was years since she'd felt a man's penis, upright and solid. The thought of it nearly made her faint. "Charlie, your words are making me giddy. You forget that I'm only a simple Highland lass, and you're a man of the world . . ."

"I forget everything, Flora, dearest. I know I shouldn't be saying this out of respect for you and Alan and Hugh, but when I'm with you, I forget that I am a prince of the realm, that I'm a man escaping imminent danger, that between me and death, there's only a moment of indecision. I forget who and what I am when I'm close to you. And when I was in your arms just now, I forgot my very existence. It was as though the two of us had become one and we were Adam and Eve in the Garden of Eden."

Flushed, she said, "Stop talking like this. Your words are flooding my mind and I'm losing my ability to resist you. I'm an engaged woman, Charlie. I have a man called Alan Macdonald who loves me and who trusts me. I'll not betray his trust, no matter what my body urges me to do. Desist now, or I'll be forced to leave this house and follow in Neil MacEachan's footsteps. Now back away, Your Royal Highness. Let me recover on my own. Let me fight these silly, girlish feelings that are draining my body of its strength and let us retreat to the lives we were destined to live. Away now, Charlie, and remember who and what we are."

Spending the day walking in the nearby grasslands and looking over the cliffs to watch the gannets and gulls and cormorants wheeling and diving and fishing was precisely what both of them needed. Having spent his life in Rome and Paris, the prince hadn't experienced how awesome Nature was in the wild. He watched in utter fascination as cormorants circled high above the sea, and then suddenly turned into slender spears that plummeted at dazzling speed into the water to emerge minutes later with a fish in their gullets.

The birds, the landscape, and the vastness of the sea were stimuli to their vibrant senses, and every breath was like sipping a heady nectar. The vast horizons, the updrafts of warm air that rose in gusts over the cliffs, the gentle sound of the sea, and the scented aroma of heather were, to their tired and pained bodies, like exotic perfumes from the distant East.

"Dear Lord, but I hadn't realized how much that damnable rowboat across the Minch had exhausted me. Can you feel your battered body? How painful it is to move every muscle? And aren't the gentle sun and breezes refreshing your mind and restoring your body," he said. He realized he was making conversation for the sake of it, but he was concerned about talking in any other way in case she misconstrued his intentions. He had gone much too far in liberties with her earlier and wanted to assure her of his best and most honorable intentions.

But all she did was nod and walk separately from him. The day wore on, and the sun sank below the Western Outer Hebrides islands toward the New World of America. They were seated on a cliff top, their legs dangling over the edge, watching the shadows of the distant sea-rocks elongate to become fingers pointing at them. She had been passively quiet throughout most of the afternoon, as though she was fighting some inner battle. And then, quiet unexpectedly she asked, "Have you ever wondered what it would be like to go and live in America?"

"America is a British colony. It should be a part of my family's empire. When I become king of England and Scotland, I should very much like to visit it. It's a young land, full of opportunity and great wealth. And you, Flora? Would you like to go?"

"One day! I have an urge to travel, to see beyond Skye and the Islands. Last year, I traveled to Edinburgh with Sir Alexander and Lady

Macdonald and saw much that was truly wondrous. But I want to see beyond Scotland. I want to go to London and see the great palaces and the houses and maybe go to a theater. Yes, I want to see America, but first I really want to see London."

He smiled. "As do I."

She turned to him and laughed. The sun's dying rays now cast a reddish glow on the landscape. Looking at him, it appeared as though the prince was bathed in an ethereal light. Again, just as earlier, she found her face flushing and her breath becoming shallow.

Out of instinct, he put his arm around her shoulders. He realized that he shouldn't, because he'd made a vow to respect her engagement to Alan Macdonald, but the intensity of the moment overcame his previous good intentions. Anyway, it was more a gesture of friendship than romance. They were both captured by the beauty of the scenery and the miracle of the sun's rays coloring the world with a kaleidoscope of iridescence and luminosity. And she put her arm around his waist and drew him into her.

As the light turned from reddish to violet, they lay back on the soft bracken and grass and looked up at the indigo sky. Slowly the stars began to emerge, and even though the sun still shone dimly before it sank into the Atlantic, more and more stars glimmered above their heads.

Charlie kissed her gently on the lips. She didn't resist but kissed him back. She put her arms around him and drew him into her. Their gentle kiss grew more and more passionate, until she rolled on top of him, taking control, and allowing her passions a release. She moaned as his hand lifted her skirts and he felt her inner thighs. He gasped as she, too, put her hand inside his dress and petticoats and reached for his manhood. Their mouths never left each other's as they fondled and felt and caressed each other's body, more and more urgently as the night drew on and darkness surrounded them in its embrace of secrecy.

They made love beneath the canopy of the heavens. As he kissed her and entered her body, her thoughts were only of her prince, her lover, her special man. All restraint left her mind and body. She became as one with him. And as he thrust and thrust, and as she received him deeper and deeper, she opened her eyes and cried out to the deity listening, "Oh God, Charlie, oh God. I've been waiting for this all my life."

The following midday, Neil MacEachan returned, and for the first few minutes, Flora could barely look at him for fear of blurting out like a do-laddled girl what she and Charlie had done the previous night. But she restrained herself and remembered the danger they were in.

When Neil had drunk his cool mug of water and eaten his second and then his third griddlecake, he finally was able to tell them what he'd been up to. He was so intent on telling them his intelligence that he didn't notice the sheepish grin on Flora's face, nor the look of studied concentration that belied a guilty secret on the face of Prince Charles Edward Stuart.

Instead, Neil MacEachan said, "I did as I said. I went to the closest town, Locheid, a wee place, but with a good Inn and people who welcomed a fisherman caught far to sea by a horrible gale. I asked for help which they gave freely and willingly. And when I'd eaten and drunk my fill, for which the local councilman took responsibility, I asked what was happening in these parts. And they told me plainly, for I was obviously neither an English spy, nor a loyalist nor a Jacobite, but just a hero of the waters in a rowboat, blown off course, about whom tales would be told for years to come.

"I was informed that those MacLeods who weren't at Culloden are aware that His Highness the Prince of the Stuarts is nearby and trying to get to Skye and they've got patrols along the coast ten miles to the south. They're mighty keen on earning the £30,000-bounty which King George has placed upon your head. Thank God they didn't see us land this far north, or they'd have shot at us for certain, for the terms of the bounty are that you be caught, dead or alive. And they told me that the English are everywhere on Skye. Two and three men patrols are all along the roads, and all the towns have detachments. The large towns like

Portree have regiments stationed there. We're safe if we travel on across fields and hide in barns, but with the bounty on your head and with many of the Clan MacLeod supporting the loyalists of King George, this Island is a hive of bees intent on stinging you. And to be honest, from what I saw and heard, it'd be better if the two of you ladies were alone, and not traveling with me. Much as I hate to leave you, Flora, I think that if you two ladies were seen walking back to your home alone and not in the company of a man, you'd create far less suspicion."

Flora was about to disagree, but Charlie said, "I think Mr. MacEachan is correct. I'm your Irish seamstress, Betty Burke, and you are my mistress, Flora Macdonald. You might command the attention of an Englishman, but once you tell him who we are, reminding him that I speak only Gaelic and so can't converse, they'll allow us past without hindrance. Neil, I cannot tell you what a debt of gratitude I owe to you for your courage and selflessness."

Neil MacEachan stood. Flora packed his bag with sufficient food for the return sea journey to South Uist, confident that there would be no more storms for a month so that his return crossing would be calm and uneventful. This time, returning alone, he could raise a sail and make the journey both shorter and easier.

She embraced him, as did Charles, and watched him leave the house, and stride out to the cliff, at the bottom of which was the boat they'd secreted.

Alone again, Prince Charles and Flora knew instinctively that they had to tidy the house in deference to the owners and leave it as they had found it. Flora was intent on putting the prince into the hands of Jacobites on Skye who would take over responsibility for him and relieve her. The prince intended to travel south toward Borodale that lay on the western coast. He had told nobody, but before he'd left the mainland for the Islands to escape the Duke of Cumberland, he was informed that a French ship would be waiting for him there during the next few weeks to transport him back to Paris.

As they packed their meager possession to leave, the prince noticed that Flora was suddenly quiet and demure. She had been excited by the return of Neil MacEachan, but when he'd left and as they were packing to leave themselves, her mood seemed as though she was suffering some sort of deflation.

"What's the matter?" asked Charles.

She shrugged.

"Come Flora, what's wrong," he insisted.

She walked over and enfolded herself in his arms. "It's coming to an end. I can feel it in my blood. We've had one breathtaking and fantastic night and now there's no more. You're a man of great importance and I'm only a wee Highland Lass and you'll be off with your dukes and duchesses and princesses and all I'll have to remember you by is a secret night of passion and excitement and closeness. In a day or a week, you'll be leaving and you'll return to France and your palaces and I'll go home to a small cottage and a farmer for a husband and I'll never see you again."

He began to say something, but she put her fingers to his lips. "Hush. Don't. Nothing you say can change our situations. I was born to live and die in a croft in Scotland, and you were born to sit upon a great throne. I know that, Charlie. I understand that. But just for a single night, just for a glorious moment in my life, one I'll never forget, I was the Pretender's Lady. I was Princess Flora, wife and mistress and lover and bosom friend to the Prince of the Stuarts. You've opened my eyes to a world I never thought in my whole life that I could become a part of, and now I have to close my eyes and my mind to what happened and get on with my life. But I'll never be able to close my heart."

Tears began to well up in her eyes, and she started to sob.

"Oh Flora, my dearest Scottish girl. How sweet and perfect you are. You understand so well why our friendship has to stay as it is. But just as you'll never close your heart to me, I too will never close my heart to you. I want you to pick me a sprig of heather when we're walking. I want you to kiss it for me and wear it close to your heart. And as we leave each other, as I depart on my ship back to France, I want you to take it out of your bodice and give it to me. And this I swear to you, Flora Macdonald. I will have the finest Italian jeweler fashion the heather and encase it into the most precious metal so that it becomes my golden leaf, and from that moment until the day I die, I shall wear it on a golden chain around my neck with the part your lips touched directly above my heart. The kings of France have a Fleur-de-lis, a lily, as part of their coat of arms. When I become king of England and Scotland, I will make the heather part of my heraldic coat of arms, and for all eternity, you and I will know that my flag and shield and pennant will bear the sprig of heather which my Flora has given to me. This your prince swears to you by the God of all creation."

She kissed him gently. Passionately. And then she said something that surprised her, and utterly stunned the prince.

"Marry me, Prince Charles Stuart. Marry me now. Make me into your wife."

"What? But . . ."

"You said to me only yesterday that being with me was as though the two of us had become one and we were Adam and Eve in the Garden of Eden. I am flesh of your flesh, Charlie. We have been joined as one. Now I want you to marry me."

"Flora, you must understand that . . ."

She smiled and put her finger to his lips. "Not a real marriage, silly boy, not one which the world will know about. Just a ritual that you and I can share and enjoy and make sacred in our hearts. Just to let me hear the words from your lips, words for me alone, which tells me that you're mine, and I'm yours. You're my first lover, Charlie, and when I'm married, I want to remember you, my first true man, forever and ever, amen!

"Right now, Charles Edward Louis John Casimir Sylvester Maria, Prince of the Stuarts, I want you to marry me, not in the eyes of God or the law but just for my eyes and ears. Simply say the words that you'll love and honor me for all your life, and I will say them too, and in our hearts, we'll be as one.

"Don't fear, Charlie, for it will be neither legal nor ordained by the Lord, so in the eyes of the world, it'll be as nothing. But I just want to hear you say 'I will' when I ask you to be my husband. Not for the sake of my mind, but for my heart's sake."

He smiled and held her hand. They stood before the fireplace, cold now with dying embers from the previous night's blaze, and repeated to each other the marriage vows that neither had previously spoken nor had heard said to them before.

"And will you, Charles Edward Louis John Casimir Sylvester Maria of the House of Stuart, take me, Flora Macdonald of the Clan Macdonald of the Island of Skye as your wedded wife."

"I will."

He looked at her in amusement and said softly, "And will you, Flora Macdonald of the Clan Macdonald of the Island of Skye, take me, Charles Edward Louis John Casimir Sylvester Maria Stuart as your lawful and wedded husband?"

"Oh yes, darling. Willingly and whole-heartedly."

They turned to each other and kissed again. "We're wed, Charlie. We're man and wife, and we're the only two in the whole world who knows it. And in a day or so, I'll divorce you, but for this night and the next morning, my darling boy, we'll be laying together as man and wife. And then when you go off and have a proper wedding to a real princess and I marry my farmer, Alan Macdonald, then on our wedding nights, it'll be me making love to you, and you, darling, making love to me. And that will make me very happy."

"And what does a man and his wife do on their wedding night?" he asked, ingenuously.

He started to undo the buttons and bows that kept her dress tied together, as she tore at the bows and sashes on Charlie's dress.

"It'll give us strength for when we begin our journey in the morning," he whispered.

"Oh God, yes, husband, for I have a fierce craving for you and I need to satisfy myself once again." She burst out laughing. "Jesus and all the saints, I'm talking like a sixpenny Edinburgh whore."

"Sixpence? I'll not give you a penny piece. You're my wife now, and you'll make love to me without thought of reward."

She thumped him in the stomach, and they collapsed laughing onto the straw mattress. In her hysterics, she gasped, "What kind of a whore makes love to another woman? Look at us, rutting like stags on the moors, yet both of us in dresses and petticoats. What would people say if they saw us?"

They didn't rise until the sun was setting. And they slept contented all night and began their journey in the morning.

# Chapter Ten

There were twelve altogether, but five of them were barely known out-side of their circles of business and had only been included by the seven famous members because of their wealth and desire to be amongst men of influence. And inquiries for membership were being received from all over London and from the most noble of all the English aristocracy. The club was even being written about in the scandal sheets and by pamphlet-eers, even though it had only been in existence for two months. Imagine its impact when it was mature and its activities became known in the courts of England and Europe!

First to arrive was the founder and the club's patriarch, Sir Francis Dashwood, orphaned by the sudden death of his mother when he was a child and by the unfortunate but timely death of his father when he was only sixteen. Now in his late-thirties, immensely wealthy and gaining a growing reputation as a rake and a rascal, Sir Francis was looking to enjoy every single moment of his life and the club that he'd founded was something of which he was fiercely proud.

He had created the Hellfire Club a few months previously following the dissolution of his previous Dilettante's Club, which tried to promote those aspects of Greco-Roman and European art and culture that the

English were increasingly content to ignore just as they were ignoring the great works of music, theater, and writing being produced in Europe. Oh, certainly the hated Hanoverians had imported Mr. Handel with his oompahs and ponderous and overwhelming *sauerkraut* operas. And with his oratorios and choruses had come his massively bosomed ladies and such, standing on a stage and frightening the audience with their raucous bellowing voices.

And because of Mr. Handel, the music of Mr. Bach and his sons and Mr. Purcell and those like him was more often ignored than performed in the salons. And with the commanding position of Mr. Handel had come the demise of all the other English musicians whose works were rarely played these days? What great works of writing and art and music was England producing, now that the leaden and stultifying hand of George was compressing the nation into a heavy and tasteless sausage, bounded by the impenetrable skin of the German court?

Bored beyond reason by the stifling constraints of life in London under the Hanoverian monarchs and the grave German sausages that the English nobility had become in order to feed George's ego with the sycophancy he relished and fed up with the austerities of church worship, Sir Francis had decided to light a fuse under the backsides of all England and really give the gossips something to talk about.

And still inspired by the wondrous boy king Pretender Charles Edward Stuart, whom he had met and loved some years earlier in Rome, he was increasingly disgusted by the asinine pomposity of German George, his hideous sons and daughters, and all the other awful members of the Hanoverians who had come over and believed they were the aristocracy of England, just because somebody had decided that his father should be king. But worse than Fat George was his murderous son the Duke of Cumberland who had made it his life mission to expose and punish every Jacobite sympathizer and to murder or deport every Scottish Highlander. What the Romans had done to Carthage and the Crusaders to Constantinople and Jerusalem, the duke was happily doing to Scotland, and barely a single English man or woman was speaking out against the carnage.

Which was one of the reasons he'd begun the Hellfire Club—to rouse English men and women, especially the nobility, against the Germanic values imposed upon the Court of St. James's. And even though it was a mere two months old, it looked as if his ploy was going to succeed. Other members of the Hellfire Club he'd inveigled to join were Robert Vansittart, the finest and most brilliant barrister attached to the Inner Temple, William Hogarth, the artist, and a certain Mr. Josiah Hopeful, who said that he would attend meetings whenever he was in London, which was less and less frequently now that he was so involved with the creation of an academy and college in Philadelphia.

But Sir Francis and Mr. Hopeful, secretly and much better known as the American diplomat Mr. Benjamin Franklin, kept up a lively correspondence, and whenever Mr. Franklin was on one of his covert missions in London gathering intelligence for the increasingly temperamental Americans against the government of the awful George from Hanover, he would gleefully attend meetings and have a wonderful time.

Truth to tell, Sir Francis was a source of much information about the mendacity and parsimoniousness of the pumpernickel king, of the inefficiency of the government and of the stupidity of his eldest estranged son who would be king on the death of his father. But Sir Francis was most eloquent when he was writing to Mr. Franklin about the barbarity of King George's second son who was spending all his time killing Scots.

He supplied all of this information gleefully and freely to Mr. Franklin in the hope of embarrassing the Hanoverians, and Mr. Franklin had told him how useful it was to the Americans. Franklin hoped that there wouldn't be a declaration of independence and was certainly working hard to maintain an accommodation with Britain, but he was predicting that in a dozen or so years, Americans would no longer accept that London had a right to rule a colony as far away and as vast as their nation if they weren't allowed to be a part of the governance of the new and lusty country. Being a diplomat, Mr. Franklin was always trying to ameliorate both sides, but it was becoming more and more difficult.

Sir Francis knew that if America did declare its independence of the British crown, as seemed increasingly likely, then he would be sorry to lose such a valuable colony. Many highborn Englishmen were making fortunes out of the trade in African slaves and the growing and sale of tobacco. The advantage of America breaking away from England, though, was that it would be a good stick in the eye to the damnable Hanoverians, and might even see a revolution in England itself against the damned sausage eaters.

As the evening drew on, and the George and Vulture Inn filled with costermongers and fishermen and other tradesmen who had finished their daily chores as well as gentlemen from the business houses of central London who called in for a jar of ale before returning to their homes, Sir Francis reviewed the annals of the first meeting of the club, which was held in this same inn in May in order to discuss the name and purpose of the hellfires. Some of the original members had objected to the name he'd chosen, but he personally liked the idea of Hellfire. Others had voted for it to be called, mockingly, after Sir Francis' country estate and decided upon the Brotherhood of St. Francis of Wycombe or the Order of Knights of West Wycombe, but nobody could agree and it was now becoming generally known as the Hellfire Club and to hell with anybody who thought differently.

It had been decided that the club would discuss politics, indulge in speculation in investments, and purchase stocks in companies or the proposed cargoes of trading clippers when the club met in the coffee houses in Change Alley. But the intended effect of these clever frauds was designed to ruin certain moneymen in London whom everybody detested. And the main purpose, the reason it had been dubbed the Hellfire Club, was to enable its members to enjoy orgies, saturnalia, and celebrate the rites of Bacchus and Ariadne and Venus. For this latter occupation, willing women were needed, and once he'd spread the word in the salons of the Aristocracy, there was no shortage of well-bred ladies who had expressed an overwhelming interest in attending and fully participating in the meetings. Indeed, one, the wife of the Duke of Ashfordbury, had said that she personally would bring along four other titled ladies, their sisters, and, in one case, her ladyship's two married daughters whose husbands were both insufficient and inefficient, as she delicately put it.

First to arrive in the private room atop the Inn was Mr. Paul Whitehead who came with Mr. Edward Thompson. They greeted each other with their secret handshake, alternate winks, and tickling the palm. When their membership had been formally acknowledged, they sat to wait and drink while the others were arriving.

A waiter served the men beer, and as they drank from their pots, each said the motto of the Hellfire Club, *Fay ce que vouldras.* It was a suitable motto, "Do what you will," because in opposition to the German Georges, there were early signs that London was starting to become a city that was willing to devote itself to the pursuit of pleasure. It was some time since the threat to London's safety from the Prince of the Stuarts had been nullified in Derby of all places and not by an English army but by a revolt within his own ranks. The Scots, it seemed, were overwhelmed by the sophistication of England and turned on their tails and retreated to the bogs and caves of the Highlands.

And since that little scare of the previous year, all had been fairly quiet in England. The wars in Europe kept going on and on, of course, with France fighting Austria and with Spain fighting everybody else and the pope issuing demands for obedience and the Scots being deported to America. But Scotland wasn't all death and destruction, because recently some really clever Scots had made a name for themselves, like Mr. Adam Smith and Mr. David Hume who were now the greatest thinkers in all of Europe in the new Enlightenment Movement. So long as King George didn't fund any more European adventures, England could continue to thrive and survive, and damn the rest of the foreigners.

It was so confusing if all you wanted to do was to have fun. And that was the other serious intent of the Hellfire Club—for its members to cause havoc in London and the provinces, to cause scandals, to infuriate the clergy by holding satanic rituals, and to enjoy themselves carnally and gastronomically by guzzling food and quaffing drink and having knowledge of as many women as was humanly possible on the same night.

As they waited and chatted amiably about recent events in politics and society, as well as who had enjoyed a scandal with whom, the door to their private meeting room opened, and a plump gentleman entered.

He was introduced by the waiter, and the party stood to greet the new arrival. He was known and greeted warmly by others, but Sir Francis, surprised at seeing him, walked over and embraced him as though he was a long-lost brother.

"My dear Mr. Josiah Hopeful. How wondrous good to see you, sir. What on earth are you doing in London? Why didn't you write and tell me you were arriving? When did you get in?"

Benjamin Franklin sat down and took the pot of beer offered by the waiter, quaffing a large draft to refresh himself. He had put on weight since the last time they had met and appeared to be suffering from the gout. "I took a packet from New York Harbor last Tuesday and arrived just this morning. I'm here to act as agent for the Hudson Bay Company with a commission to trade beaver furs. I sent a letter to your house by messenger informing you of my arrival this morning, but I assumed that you'd be at some gathering, so when your butler sent back word that you were attending a meeting of the Hellfire Club, and unless you'd unexpectedly changed the venue, I concluded that this must be the time and the place. And so here I am. If I was wrong, I would have enjoyed a quiet pot of ale and retired to my lodgings."

"And right welcome you are, Mr. Hopeful. Sit down, and let me tell you of the club's activities since your last visit in May."

As they talked, more and more of the club's members arrived until the meeting room was crowded and full of amiable chatter and laughter. The group was called to order at a suitable time and communally intoned the solemn oath that Sir Francis had circulated, committing each member to indulge in promiscuity, licentiousness, and unbridled immorality whenever the occasion arose.

They drank, they sang, they connived, they made suggestions, and in the main, their suggestions were rejected with much laughter and the drinking of more beer, and they agreed to meet again in September to further plan the activities. In the meantime, Sir Francis promised that he would arrange a lewd and disgusting sexual orgy at his home in West Wycombe, with numerous willing and able ladies and food and drink aplenty. The date was set for the last week of August, and the members began to drift away as the night watchman called out the hour of eleven o'clock.

By half past the hour, the room was empty, and Sir Francis offered Benjamin Franklin a ride home in his carriage.

"After such an evening of drinking I think I'd prefer to walk so that my mind will be alert in the morning," he said.

"Then let me accompany you and I'll have my carriage follow in our footsteps," Sir Francis said.

They gathered their cloaks, Sir Francis paid the bill for the food and ale, and they left to walk out into the streets of London. Although it was a warm night, those without homes, gangs of children, incapable falling-down drunks, pamphleteers, threepenny whores, and chestnut sellers still inhabited the misty and smoke-filled streets, some huddled around braziers and open fires on the roadside, making the air pungent and heavy with their choking stench. Sir Francis' servant walked a few paces ahead carrying a lantern on a pole so that the two men could negotiate their way around the mud and animal dung that lay in their path, while his horse and carriage clopped over the ruts in the street. They turned right out of Lombard Street into Cornhill, then onto Cheapside walking toward the Old Bailey and Newgate Prison.

As they walked, ensuring that nobody could hear their conversation, Sir Francis said quietly, "Well, Mr. Franklin. What's your real purpose in coming to London? Somehow, I can't envisage you wearing a beaver hat, let alone selling the damn things."

Franklin chuckled. "It was a poor excuse, but the best one I could think up in the time, bearing in mind that I was only here a few months ago, and few in America know that I've left the country. No, Sir Francis, I'm here because of the uprising of Prince Charles Stuart."

"A bit late, if you'll forgive me saying so, my dear Sir. You surely know already that he was soundly defeated by the Duke of Cumberland in the wilds of Scotland. That uprising is no more, I'm afraid."

"Of course I know of his failure. But what interests me is the reaction of King George to the Scottish people. I've come here to find out whether or not the barbarity we've been learning about is as true and indeed as widespread as the informants are saying. We have slave ships filled with Scots men, women, and children arriving at our Boston port, and we're expected to supply them with land without so much as a 'by your leave' from His Royal Highness. It appears that the duke is intending to use America as a penal colony of the Scots and to denude their land in favor of placing these hapless souls in ours. Is that true, to your knowledge?"

"Who knows what's in the heart or the mind of that hideous man. He's commander in chief of the king's army, and if George had his way, the Duke of Cumberland would succeed him to the throne. Unfortunately for the king, his successor, the Prince of Wales, has set up a rival household in Leicester House and is acting like a prince regent. The king is infuriated and regularly wishes his son dead. He says so loudly and often and in public. He calls his son a scoundrel and a wastrel, which augurs well for his reception as our next glorious monarch. Hail and welcome King Whatever your Name, Scoundrel and Wastrel of England.

"Of course, what this means is that King George showers all his love and benefices on his younger son, the Duke of Cumberland, who has proven himself to be a brave and intelligent soldier. He's beloved by his troops and is able to follow almost any adventure, including the annihilation of the Scottish Highlanders. It's nothing short of barbarism, but it's what we have to live with," said Sir Francis.

"How have Londoners taken to the news of the barbarism in Scotland?" asked Mr. Franklin.

"Londoners are barbarians themselves. They most enjoy a public hanging or flogging. But those with Jacobite sympathies are bereft at the failure of the uprising, and not just the Catholics, either. Many eminent people, like Dr. Samuel Johnson for example, although himself no lover of the wild Scotsmen, hate and detest the Hanoverians, and have refused to sign any oaths of loyalty to King George. If you ask my opinion, Londoners were pleased that the Stuart prince's march of conquest failed, for they feared an invader, yet they show no love for the king and his family. But as to how the English have been affected by the news from Scotland, I'd have to say they don't give a twopenny damn."

"And how badly have the Jacobites been affected. Have any been brought to trial?"

"Two Scottish lords who rebelled against the Crown, the Earl of Kilmarnock, and Lord Balmerino have been tried and will face beheading in the Tower next month. No doubt, we'll see many more Scottish lords and nobles brought to trial and their lives extinguished. But the real battle is the hunt for the Young Pretender. The duke and his generals are scouring the Highlands seeking him everywhere. The last report I received was that he had somehow managed to escape from the mainland and was living in caves in the islands on the western coast of Scotland, waiting for a French ship to meet him and transport him back to Paris. God help the poor soul if he's caught. He'll be hung, drawn, and quartered if the duke is given a free hand."

They continued to walk westwards until the cupola of the Old Bailey could be seen in the far distance, outlined in ghostly form against the lights of London illuminating the fog and smoke that rose from the myriad fires in the streets.

Franklin said, "You knew him, didn't you. When you were traveling some years ago in Italy."

"Yes. And I admired him greatly. A keen intelligence, a man of charm and wit, brave to boot, and with a superb understanding of military matters. Had the perfidious French only done what they promised to do, then a French and Scottish army would have defeated the damned Hanoverians and a Stuart would be on the throne of England."

"I also met him once," said Franklin. "In Rome. I spent a couple of hours with him. I found him somewhat vainglorious on matters to do with his place in the hierarchy of royalty, but much more interesting when we got to talk about the rights and privileges of birth. While I disagree with him about the divine rights of kings, I must say that he made his points articulately and passionately. I came away impressed with the young man. Very impressed indeed. I thought then, just as I think now, that one day, when the circumstances are right, great events will circulate around that young man. I thought that his assault on London would be such a great event, but circumstances proved me wrong. However, he's young, and there's a great deal of time for it to happen."

"I don't know," said Sir Frances. "The lad's been kicked in the arse and if he flees England with his tail between his legs, he might find all Europe shuns him. If I were King Louis and he came begging for more money and an army, I'd look at his failures and wonder whether or not I'd invest in him."

Franklin remained silent, listening and judging Sir Francis's words carefully. But the American's thoughts were interrupted by Sir Francis, who suddenly said, a mite too loudly for Franklin's comfort, "So that's what this visit is all about. My God, sir, that's why you're here, isn't it. You espouse the Jacobite cause. You want American colonists to come to the aid of Prince Charles. That's it, isn't it?"

But Franklin simply walked onward, in silence, carefully avoiding the horse droppings in his path. Sir Francis knew not to say anything further. His American friend was much too sharp and intelligent to give away too many details of the purpose of his very secret visit to England.

After a minute, Franklin asked, "Tell me, Sir Francis, what measures will the king and the government take against the Jacobites now that the revolt of the Scots is well and truly over?"

"It's put about in government circles, as well as among the aristocracy, that the king is demanding the enactment of laws which will bring the clans of Scotland to an end forever. A Disarming Act has been introduced into the Parliament that will remove the rights of all Scotsmen to bear arms and forbid military service. They're taking away the right to wear the traditional Highland dress, and no clan chieftain will be able to claim heritable jurisdiction following the introduction of English laws and justices. They're also enacting legislation that will confiscate the estates of many of the rebels who rose with Prince Charles."

"So they're intent on breaking the back of the clans and of Scotland itself," said Franklin.

Sir Francis nodded.

Softly, so softly indeed that Sir Francis had to listen carefully so as not to miss a word, Benjamin Franklin asked, "And in your opinion, do you think that this will be the reaction of the king and his government if America at some point in the future, decides that it cannot abide being ruled from London when the needs of London are to rape our wealth, whereas we are intent upon building a great nation? I ask this not because we are contemplating a revolution, but because the monarchy and the English government are draining America of its lifeblood. What, sir, do you think will happen if America, like Scotland, takes a stance against the rapacity of the monarchy? For if ever it does, Sir Francis, then America must arm itself with more than broadswords and muskets in order to repel such as the Duke of Cumberland. We must begin the training of something more than a regular militia; we must begin thinking of our very own standing army of American patriots to defend ourselves against the rapacity of the Mother Country."

"Matricide?" said Sir Francis, but again, Franklin remained silent. Sir Francis too decided to remain silent, realizing that at this moment, any contribution he might make to Franklin's monologue was unnecessary.

Mr. Franklin continued, "You mustn't misconstrue what I'm saying, Sir Francis. God forbid that I'm advocating independence or revolution. But kick a dog too often, and it'll turn and snap at your heels. I'm a diplomat, sir, and it's my intention to find a negotiated path down which both of our great nations can walk hand in hand. But if that path is wide enough for only one of us, then the other is entitled to take a different course."

Again, Sir Francis wanted to say something, but Mr. Franklin continued, "Don't you get the feeling that there is a change in the air, Sir Francis? That monarchy has become so hidebound, so set in its ways that it is incapable of bending to the will of the people. You had a king beheaded and a commonwealth begun because the monarchy was at loggerheads with the people it was employed to rule . . ."

"Yes," said Sir Francis, "but the Commonwealth didn't last. That scoundrel Cromwell . . ."

"You made the wrong choice of Lord Protector. That's all. Had you chosen somebody else to put paid to the monarchy, then England today would be a republic, just as in the glorious days of Greece and Rome. Had you chosen a Thomas a' Becket or a Thomas More, you'd still be a commonwealth, they'd be no ruling family, Great Britain would enjoy the privileges of a meritocracy instead of an aristocracy, and all England would be a better place."

"But rid England of its aristocracy, and you'll rid the nation of me . . ."

"You are now and will always be, one of the great men of England. But your fellow aristocrats' right to rule is based on birth and not on ability. For a nation to succeed, it must be ruled by men of wisdom, not men who happened to have been born in a silken crib.

"No, Sir Francis, I believe that monarchy and the aristocracy have had their day, and great nations are inclining to breeding Republicans like our ancient forefathers! You might think I'm talking about a revolution, sir, but I think that much can be accomplished by diplomacy and negotiation. Oh, I'm not so fanciful in thinking that any monarch will willingly give up his privileges; but the will of the people, as they did in the time of Oliver Cromwell and the Commonwealth, will soon put an end to the power, if not the presence, of a monarchy.

"The people of France, of Scotland, and perhaps even America are building up a profound inclination to limit the power of those monarchs who wield right of life and death merely because of the fortune of their birth and through no will of the people. I tell you, sir, that the time is rapidly approaching for the people to make a stand against autocracy and in favor of a republic. Maybe today, maybe tomorrow, or maybe in twenty or thirty years' time, but the voice of the people cannot be silenced by such as King George and his nepotistic brood. If they maintain their attitude that they rule by divine right, then they'll soon find that democracy cannot cohabit with monarchy. The two are alien systems. One abolishes the other. And if there is to be an Armageddon, a battle between the Sons of Liberty and the aging Sons of Autocracy, the people shall win. Mark my words, sir. The people will win."

They approached the Old Bailey in silence, but the thoughts flooding through Sir Francis' mind was the extent to which the people of Scotland had been winners in the battle between the Sons of Liberty and the aging Sons of Autocracy. With Scotland awash with Highlander blood and the bones of clansmen bleaching in the meadows, how would other Sons of Liberty fair against those Sons who commanded vast armies and munitions?

THE ROAD SOUTH FROM DUNVEGAN TO DRYNOCH

ISLAND OF SKYE

JULY 7, 1746

The two ladies walked the length of the island avoiding the roads, preferring to travel through the fields and woodlands. But when the trees became too thick and the fields too boggy from the recent drenching they'd received in the storm, they were forced to return to the road and expose themselves to prying eyes.

Both of the ladies were tall and dressed in the costumes of modesty. From a distance, they could easily be identified as the wives or daughters of merchants or prosperous farmers. From close up, it was obvious that one was the mistress, one the servant. The difference between the two women was that the mistress had a dress engaged with attractive bows and embroidery, whereas the servant's dress was somewhat more drab and ordinary as befitted her station in life. The other indication of the difference in status was that the servant trod in the footsteps of the mistress, her head bowed, her eyes cast down in deference.

The guards, who attended the road at the point where it branched left to Portree, saw the women coming from far away. Instructed by General Campbell before he left for the Uist islands to be particularly attentive to any travelers, they moved from their shelter and stood in the middle of the road, their rifles loaded and ready to be fired in case this was some form of ambush.

The two women walked up to the troopers, and the woman leading nodded and said "Good afternoon," as they neared.

"Just a minute, Miss. Where do you think you're going?" asked the Lieutenant.

"I'm going home," she said. She was an attractive lady with gleaming black hair freshly washed in a stream and the open face of a Highlander. The woman behind her, though, was anything but attractive. She was tall and thin and walked with a stoop and an uncommon gait.

"And where's your home" demanded the trooper.

"Why," chuckled the lady. "Do you intend to visit me? Now what would my fiancé, Mr. Alan Macdonald, think about that?" Seductively, she continued, "if it's your intention to search me, I'll have to scream very loud. I hope that somebody will hear the cries of a maiden in distress . . ."

Flora looked at him, winked, and walked onward full of confidence and buoyancy. The two women were walking casually past, when one of the troopers asked, "And who's this?"

The lady stopped and opened her bag, taking out a bottle of water. "This," she said before taking a draft, "is my seamstress. Mistress Betty Burke."

Flora said in Gaelic, "Say hello to the Englishmen, Betty."

Betty looked up and nodded at both the men, saying in high falsetto Gaelic, "Good afternoon, gentlemen."

"She's from Ireland and has worked for me these two years past. She speaks not a word of English, but you'll be pleased to know that she just wished you a good afternoon. Now if you'll excuse us, we have five miles to walk before we reach Roskhill where there's an Inn at which we'll be spending the night."

"Dear God, but she's ugly," said the other trooper.

"Shut your mouth," snapped the Lieutenant. "You know I don't hold with antagonizing the locals. Forgive me, madam, but have you any identification. What's your name? Where do you live?"

She reached back into her purse and took out a Letter of Pass written by her father Hugh before they left South Uist. He had given one to each of them as well as one to Neil MacEachan, who'd used it when he had left them to go to the nearby inn.

"My name is Miss Flora Macdonald. I and my seamstress, Mistress Betty Burke, live in Milton, which is a village far to the south of Skye, which is where we're returning. We've just been to Trumpan where I have been assisting my ailing aunt, who I'm pleased to say is now much recovered. Now, gentlemen, if you'll excuse us, we must be on our way."

The guardsmen put up their rifles and allowed the two women through. As they passed by, the junior trooper whispered to Flora out of the side of his mouth, "If you're spending the night in Roskhill, when I get off duty, would you permit me to buy you a drink?"

"Sir," she whispered back, "three drinks it'll have to be. One for my fiancé, Mr. Alan Macdonald, who's waiting impatiently for my return, one for me and one for Mistress Burke here, who has a terrible thirst. But be assured, trooper, that Mr. Macdonald will greatly appreciate your generosity."

Smiling, she and Betty walked on silently until they were out of earshot, but still they refrained from talking, knowing that the guards would be looking at their retreating backs. It wasn't until they were a good mile away, and after the road curved toward the East, that they felt secure enough to speak to each other, though Betty still walked respectfully in Flora's footsteps.

"You were magnificent. Brilliant. Oh Flora, you are such a treasure of a girl. I'd be lost without you."

She laughed. "You would indeed, for I only barely know these northern roads myself, and I've lived on Skye almost all my life. But I must congratulate you on your Gaelic accent, Charlie darling. You sounded just like a lady. My training worked, for you fooled both the troopers and me. I almost continued to converse with you."

They walked on a further mile or more before Charlie said softly, "Have you decided on an answer to my question?"

She sighed deeply. It was the answer he'd anticipated.

"Why not?" he asked.

"Because I'm not the type of woman who could become a royal mistress. Oh, I know how exciting the life would be, and I really feel extremely grateful that you've asked me, but you must understand my situation, Charlie."

"Is it because of your religious beliefs? Does the Kirk burn that strongly in your heart?"

"No," she said, laughing. "Oh, I go to Church once a month and listen to the preacher and occasionally I try to do as Almighty God demands. But no, that isn't the reason I'll not go with you to France and Italy. I'd give my right arm to spend even a night inside a grand palace and have servants and drudges attend to my every need. And I'm not so naïve that I don't understand the reality of the situation for a woman like me. I'm well aware that I'd only see you once in a month or thereabouts. But there are two solid and unalterable reasons why I have to say no."

She thought for a minute, and then corrected herself. "No, three unalterable reasons. The first is because if I did go, I'd have to accept that you were marrying another woman. Yes, I know that it would be a political marriage, but a marriage nonetheless in the eyes of God and all of Europe, and every night you spent with her in your bed, and not with me, would be like a dirk stabbing into my heart. The second reason is because of respect for my father and mother, who would be shamed by the fact that their daughter is living outside wedlock with a man, albeit that he's a prince of the realm of Scotland."

"And the third reason?"

"I couldn't do it to Alan Macdonald. It would shame him too greatly, shame my clan, and cause an innocent man to be the butt of ridicule and snide glances. He's done nothing to merit such an episode, and I will not be the one who makes him more miserable than he need be," she said. And from her tone, he knew that her decision was final.

"But we've spent two extraordinary nights alone together, Flora and three blissful days. We've behaved as man and wife, and we were even married in the holy altar of the fireplace. Isn't that a betrayal of Mr. Macdonald, even if only in your heart?"

She sighed again. This time, her sigh was deeper than before. "Yes, it is, Charlie. And he'll never find out because neither you nor I will ever hurt the dear man sufficiently by telling him. He will be in ignorance of our transgressions, but all my life, I'll have to bear the burden of my conscience. But do I regret the nights we've spent together? No, not a bit of it. I've loved and relished them, every moment of them. But it's a secret which I shall take with me to my grave. As will you, Charlie. As will you."

And they continued to walk in silence toward Roskhill.

ARMADALE, SKYE

AUGUST 3, 1746

She needed to familiarize herself with her possessions one more time before she realized that the strains of the past two months were finally over and done with, that she was back home in her own room, and that her father Hugh, her mother Anne and now her fiancé Alan had all enveloped her in their embrace and would protect her.

The warmth of their welcome had been overpowering. They had kissed and hugged and kissed and hugged again and again. She hadn't even entered her house and already they were demanding of her and Mistress Betty Burke how things had transpired. It was Hugh who led the demands for answers, followed in short order by Alan. Only Anne had remained silent, looking at her wonderful daughter in admiration and respect.

Hugh demanded to know everything. And his questions tumbled out one after the other until Flora's head was spinning. What dangers did you confront? What routes did you take? Why had it taken so long to travel from the north to the south of Skye? Why was it that Neil MacEachan had returned to South Uist nearly a month earlier and yet it had taken that long for the two of them to reach Armadale? Did they realize how terrified the family had been not to have heard a single word of their fate in all that time?

It took the prince to intervene, and say in a magisterial voice, "Lady, Gentlemen, there's much time for answers, but what Mistress Macdonald needs now is rest. The journey has been long and painful and not the least frightening. We've walked far, but we were forced to travel cross-country because of the English troopers. Sometimes we had to double back because going ahead was impossible and we had to traverse the island just to find a way south.

"But be assured, my friends, that you can be extremely proud of your brave daughter. I tell you, Mr. and Mrs. Macdonald, and you, Alan Macdonald, that Flora Macdonald acquitted herself with incredible gallantry and courage. Now, please let her sit down, for she's probably exhausted."

It wasn't until an hour after they'd returned that Anne declared their dinner was ready. Flora left her room and walked along the narrow but comforting corridor to where the entire family had gathered. As she entered the compact parlor, she was suddenly overwhelmed by its sense of order and cleanliness, of normality and wonderful ordinariness. For so many weeks, her existence had been pressured and pained, life spent in fields and hiding in barns, or sharing a room in an Inn with her lover whom she had to pretend in public was nothing more than her maidservant.

She walked over to her place at the table and saw that it had expanded to include not just her fiancé Alan, but also His Royal Highness the Prince of the Stuarts, now wearing proper men's clothing given to him by Alan and looking lean and tanned and utterly exquisite. She compared the way her prince looked with the way in which Alan looked, and became annoyed at herself for being so gauche as even to consider comparing the two men. Alan was a good, decent, honest, and honorable man. Prince Charles was an ethereal being whose world was in the clouds, and there was no comparison between him and Island men. Yet this ethereal being, this God-chosen man who would be king, had loved her and begged her to return to France with him. And he had forced her to choose chose between a prince and a man of the land, between Bonnie Prince Charlie and Alan Macdonald, farmer of Skye. Flora became faint just thinking about the situation in which she found herself.

But she was brought into a sudden reality as she entered the room when everybody at the table, including Prince Charles, stood as she approached, and raised their glasses in celebration of her. She flushed in embarrassment.

"Flora," said Hugh. "Brave and wonderful girl. We, your parents, your fiancé, and most importantly His Royal Highness, salute you for being a true woman of the Highlands, a true Scotswoman, and a true friend to our cause."

Everybody shouted out Flora's name and drank their ales. She smiled in gratitude and deference at everybody and unsteadily sat down while Anne served her a delicious meal of beef stew, dumplings, freshly baked oat bread, and cakes and a pot of ale. They all waited for her to take the first mouthful, even Prince Charlie, in deference to her courage. Her head was swimming and she didn't know how to react to the sudden and overwhelming praise. But normality returned immediately when she tasted the rich aromatic flavors of Anne's stew. This was food! So different from the dreadful fare they'd been subjected to in the Inns and roadsides of their travels.

She looked up and said softly, "God, but it's good to be home." Which made her mother beam a smile, and Alan to put his arm around his girl and squeeze her.

"You make it a home, darling," he said.

She stole a glance at Prince Charles, but his eyes were downcast, studying his stew.

The following morning, four men came to the house. All appeared at different times so as not to cause suspicion. Each bowed respectfully before the prince and shook his hand. Hugh explained to Flora that these were the men who would lead the prince to where the French ship was expected a month hence. They said that it returned on the third Tuesday of each month at the high tide and stayed for three days, then returned to France until the following month. It was more important than ever that His Highness continued to hide himself in the many friendly houses along the western coast of the Island so as not to be too conspicuous in case of a turncoat and traitor on the Island who might very well alert the troopers. Staying too long in one place would greatly add to their suspicion and increase the danger to the residents of Skye.

His bag packed and three of the four strangers leaving the house at different times, the fourth to accompany the prince, Charlie came looking for Flora. She was in the garden, examining her flowerbed and cutting some blooms.

"Mistress Macdonald," he said.

She looked up in surprise and smiled at him.

"Flora, have you forgotten your promise?"

"Promise?"

"You promised me a sprig of heather which you would wear next to your heart. You promised you'd give it to me when we fared each other well. And my promise to you is that I shall treasure it, and instruct the best jeweler in all of Italy to cover the tender fronds with a patina of gold, which I shall then wear on a chain next to my heart and which I shall never remove, even on the day I die, when it will be buried with me as part of the Stuart coat of arms. Have you forgotten, ma'am?"

"I have not, sir," she said and reached inside her bodice, withdrawing a sprig of the plant that she'd taken from the northern-most fields of the Island of Skye. She handed it to him, but he refused to take it.

"You promised that you'd kiss it for me and that I too would embrace your lips in all eternity."

She kissed the leaf, and he took it from her hands, kissed it himself, and wrapped it in a silk kerchief.

"I shall be going now, my lovely Flora. I shall be returning to France in September, God willing. But I promise you that I shall return at the head of a great army, and when I do, I shall defeat the English. Upon my father's death, I shall be crowned king of England and Scotland, and when I am on my throne, I shall invite you to St. James's where we will dine and remember our wondrous adventure together.

"I can't embrace you, Flora, for it would draw too much suspicion from prying eyes, but in my heart be certain that I am holding you and kissing your lips and your neck and your beautiful breasts. I grieve at leaving you, Flora, but you know as well as me how the world is. So remember me for evermore, dearest Flora and know that you will always hold a special place in my heart."

He bowed, kissed her hand, turned, and walked away.

She stood for many long minutes in her flower garden, looking at the space where he had once stood. Faint, she suddenly felt sick to her stomach, and the emotion of the moment made her want to retch onto the ground.

She felt quite ill, and needed to sit down. She hadn't experienced a feeling of sickness and nausea like this before. It must be because the prince had left her, she thought. After all, what else could it be?

# Chapter Eleven

ARMADALE, THE ISLAND OF SKYE

SEPTEMBER 12, 1746

She knew that it would be the most difficult moment of her life—far harder than the dangers of ensuring the prince's safety. She could no longer lie or prevaricate. She could no longer pretend to those who loved her and sought only her welfare.

Her mother knew, because mothers always know. And she'd given a wry smile and a nod and said that it was all right, because Flora intended to marry the man, and everybody hoped for a bairn to be born out of a wedding, although Anne had added wryly that it was the usual custom for the babe to be born after, not before the marriage.

Hugh, of course, being a man, didn't realize and thought that his stepdaughter's ailments were a result of the danger she'd lived through, or the terrible sea crossing, or the food she'd eaten.

Alan thought of Flora's constant vomiting in much the same way as did Hugh. And it was Alan whom she now had to meet and confess her sins. Alan Macdonald! How he would react would determine the rest of her life. She'd known Alan since she was nothing but a slip of a girl, and they'd been playmates and friends until they were in their teens. And then one day they'd gone for a picnic beside a cove on the sea's shore and even though they were both very young, their conversation had turned to the functions of the body, and as the afternoon had worn on, they had kissed and fondled each other and experimented. It was all innocent play, of course, but it had wakened Flora's body to its own special magic, as though Alan had somehow found a key that opened up the secret door to the joys of adulthood. How little did she realize in those early days of her life that the key not only opened the door of being an adult, but also the door of adultery and ruin. For although she wasn't yet wed, surely having another man's babe whilst engaged was the same as committing the carnal sin of adultery. And didn't the Old Testament say that the punishment for adultery was death by stoning!

But the day had arrived when she could no longer put off telling Alan the truth. Her belly was just beginning to swell and the constant nausea was showing no signs of abating. And before anybody dug Alan in the ribs and called him an old rogue or a dirty dog, it was her duty to inform him. If he walked away from her, as he almost certainly should and would, then the very last thing he'd hear from her lips would be a profound and heartfelt apology. But she would not ask for forgiveness, because in her mind, what she and Charlie had done, under the most adverse circumstances imaginable, was not a sin.

No! When Alan walked away from her as any man undoubtedly deserved to do, Flora would pack her bags, and go to live with Aunt Margaret Macdonald in Glasgow until the bairn was born; she would then determine how the rest of her life would be spent.

She was startled by a knock on the door. Alan walked in and beamed a smile at her.

"Your Ma said that you wanted to see me, darling."

"Come in, Alan. Sit down, for there's something fearful I have to tell you, and you're going to be shocked and saddened, but I can't any longer avoid this moment though God knows I'd prefer to avoid it for the rest of my days."

He looked at her in concern, frowning and suddenly worried. She was sitting on a chair beside the fire, clutching and unclutching a kerchief. He'd never seen his Flora like this.

"Darling," she said softly, fearing that her voice would give out at any moment, "darling, there's something I have to confess to you about myself. I have abused your good nature and kindness."

Alan smiled and laughed. "What? Flora, you're the . . ."

"Let me speak, dearest Alan, for I must tell you without interruption. You're a good man, Alan Macdonald, and I love you very dearly. Since we were children running around naked on the shore, I've always considered you to be my best friend. We grew apart as adults until my mother and father arranged our wedding, and I then realized that I do, indeed, love you. But during the time that we've been engaged to be wed, I have known the body of another man, and I am pregnant with his child. Oh, I'm so very sorry, my love."

She couldn't continue, her lips quivering, her mind racing, her body on the verge of being wracked by tears of shame and sorrow at the hurt she'd done to such a sweet man as Alan.

He shook his head in disbelief. "With bairn? Pregnant? Who's . . . what's . . ."

"It doesn't matter whose babe it is. We both know that it's not yours."

Too shocked to be angry, he said, "I must know whose it is. Flora, tell me . . ."

"It would benefit nobody if I told you."

"It would benefit me," he said angrily. "I can't believe it. You don't look . . . how pregnant are you?"

"Just eight weeks or so."

Alan frowned. "Eight weeks? Two months? July? But that's when . . . dear God. Surely you don't mean that you and . . ."

The look on her face told him who the father was. He breathed deeply and stood from the chair, going over to the window and looking out. She remained silent, desperate to know what thoughts were flooding his mind. She wanted to say something to comfort him, to reassure him, but nothing she could say would make a lot of difference, because she knew with the inevitability of a death sentence that the next thing he said would determine the rest of her life. Her heart was beating so fast she thought she could hear it. When he turned to face her, she couldn't determine from his visage what he was thinking.

"So it's the babe of Prince Stuart?"

She nodded.

"Does anybody else know? That it's his? Your mother or father?"

"My mother knows I'm pregnant. She's assumed that it's yours and is secretly delighted, although never once have I confirmed it, or admitted that it's anybody else's. She came to the conclusion, and I haven't dissuaded her, but I will if you demand it. Hugh, of course, is a typical man and has no idea."

"Did he rape you? Did Bonnie Prince Charlie force you to . . ."

"No!" she said angrily. "Of course he didn't. He was sweet and kind and gentle. We were alone together in a crofter's hut on the north of the island, and Neil had gone overnight to find out what was happening on Skye. We were both frightened and after the terrible storm at sea, we clung to each other for a feeling of security."

"Did you say no? At first, did you resist?"

"Yes. I swear to God I said no. Many times."

"So he did force you."

"No. Not like that. He was persuasive, but if I'd said no more firmly, he'd have desisted. I did say no and he did desist, but in the late afternoon, we were on a cliff, and . . . oh, God, I just don't know . . . I said yes because I wanted to. If you'd been there, darling, I'd have said yes to you.

"And to any other man, by the sound of it," said Alan.

"Is that what you think of me?" she asked. "You think that I would be anybody's? Charlie was the first man I've ever been with."

Again, he remained silent, thinking about the enormity of the news she'd just presented to him.

"Flora, I apologize for saying that. I know what a decent and moral woman you are. But I just can't get my mind off what the two of you have done. Did he use his manly ways to seduce you? On the cliff top where you and he . . . did he use honeyed words and seduction to cloud your mind to what's right?"

"No, darling. It would be so easy for me to say he forced me, or that I was swept up by his talk, but that would be to lie to you, and I've already harmed you sufficiently. You deserve to know the whole truth. No, he didn't seduce me. I was alone and frightened and I clung to him for safety, and as we were clinging to each other, my bodily passions overcame my mind, and suddenly it all went too far and without my real-izing properly what was happening, I found that we were making love."

He remained quiet for some time, and Flora realized that she was barely breathing.

"Did you . . . when he was . . . when you were making love to him, did you see my face or his? Did you close your eyes, and dream of me, or did you only see him?"

She knew that she couldn't lie to him anymore. "No, darling. I didn't think of either you or him, and I didn't think of myself and I didn't think of God Almighty. I was overwhelmed by my body, and I thought of nothing and nobody. I don't even remember the thoughts I had, darling man. I only remember the feeling of being carried upwards in a swirl of passion. It was like suffering from the most intense thirst and I knew I had to drink of the fountain of zeal if ever I was to be satisfied."

"And were you?" he asked softly.

She left the question unanswered. Instead, she said in a whisper, "Oh Alan, I can't tell you how sorry and horrible I feel for you. Not for me, but for you, my sweet. If you walk away from me, everybody will understand. And so will I, for I've sinned in the eyes of God, and in your eyes."

"And do you want me to walk away, Flora? Do you want our engage-ment to be at an end?"

She wanted to say "no," but she knew that in fairness to a wronged man, she must leave that decision to him.

"Darling Alan, whether we continue our engagement is something which only you can decide. Whatever you say, I shall abide by your deci-sion and support it when it becomes known. When anybody asks why we're not to be married, I shall say it's because I have sinned and have released you from your vows. I shall wear all the guilt. No shame will attach to your name or your reputation."

He turned back to look out of the window and remained silent. For too long! Again, her heart was beating wildly, but somehow she felt better now that she'd confessed.

"You realize that if it becomes known that you're carrying the bairn of the Prince of the Stuarts, your life will be in danger. The Butcher of Cumberland will come looking for you, and God help you then."

It was something she hadn't even considered, but a cold shudder went through her body when she thought about his words and realized that he was correct. He turned, and walked back to the seat next to hers. He held her hand. She was surprised. The look in his eyes was one of compassion, instead of the hatred she'd expected. It was so much more than she deserved.

"Listen to me carefully, Flora. What you and the prince have done is a sin; against God and your parents and me. But it is also something which will endanger your life and those around you. For carrying a Stuart child is a death sentence. So you will tell nobody about your night with the prince. This will be my bairn. We'll tell folks that you and I enjoyed passion when we were in your brother's house on Uist. I made you pregnant just before you rowed off with the prince and Neil MacEachan. I will take responsibility for the child and will treat it as my own, just as Hugh treated you as his very own daughter when he married your mother."

She opened her mouth but no words came out. Instead, Flora looked at Alan Macdonald and saw an altogether different man from the one to whom she was engaged. She was holding the hand of a man better and wiser and more wonderful than any she deserved. Tears welled up and ran down her cheeks.

He wiped them with his finger and told her as gently as he could, "The world must know this bairn as Alan Macdonald's. For if the world even suspects that it's a Stuart, you, and it, and very probably I will be hanged."

Flora nodded. "How can I ever . . ."

"By marrying me. And staying faithful for the rest of your life. We come to the altar, all of us, in a state of sin, Flora. But when we walk away as man and wife having made our vows before God, then let the rest of our lives be free of any further transgressions. If you swear that to me, then we shall be wed and live as man and wife with a growing family."

He stood, and kissed her on the forehead. "Now I have to go out and face the wrath of your father for having made his beloved daughter pregnant. And knowing Hugh, I might very well be in for a horse-whipping."

Her morning sickness had now virtually disappeared, and she was looking forward with great eagerness to her wedding just a week hence. Her mother could quite clearly see the bulge in her belly, but by wearing loose clothes and forgoing her bodice, Flora was certain that she could enter the church in her sky blue wedding dress emblazoned with the green, black, and blue stripes of the Island Clan Macdonald tartan. Alan would naturally wear his formal clan dress, buckles, and hat.

They had sent word to family and friends that the wedding was to be brought hastily forward, but without explanation, though everybody receiving it would have immediately understood Flora's delicate condition. For the past week, neighbors and friends had greeted Flora and her mother with knowing grins and nods and wishing them well and inquiring after Flora's health.

But all that came to an end on a Monday morning, at half past nine, just a week before the wedding, when Flora and her mother were about to leave their house to walk the half mile to the Kirk and discuss the flowers for the Altar, when they heard the menacing sound of many feet marching toward their house. Soldiers were common in the area and no longer caused comment, but normally they came in two's and three's.

Concerned, Flora went to the window and saw a troop of twenty English soldiers standing outside in the roadway. She gasped as two officers broke away and walked down the path to her house.

"Dear God, mother . . ."

There was a loud and imperious rapping on the front door. "Open up in the name of the king," said an English voice.

"Don't worry, child," said Anne, and went out of the front parlor to the entrance door.

As she opened it, a tall officer demanded, "Flora Macdonald?"

Flora left the parlor and stood facing the two English officers. "I'm Flora Macdonald."

"Come with me, ma'am. You're wanted for questioning."

"For what reason do you want my daughter?" asked Anne.

"Come with me, Mistress Macdonald," he repeated.

"Why do you want me?" Flora demanded, suddenly angry at the way they ignored her mother.

"I'm not here to answer your questions. I have a warrant signed by General Campbell for your arrest. Now come with me, or I'll have you bound and gagged and carried."

"Arrest? On what charge am I arrested," asked Flora, her confidence suddenly disappearing.

"The girl's pregnant. Can't you see that? You can't arrest a pregnant woman. She's to be wed in a few days' time. Don't you understand?" pleaded Anne.

"That's none of my concern, ma'am. Now please. Don't make this any more difficult for yourself. Come with me, without fuss, or I'll give orders to drag you out. I've got twenty men with me."

Flora turned to her mother and said urgently in Gaelic, "Get Hugh and Alan immediately. Tell them to follow wherever they take me. Do it now, mother, before I'm lost."

She turned to the captain of the troopers and asked, "May I pack some things for the journey?"

"No. You'll come with me immediately. No parcels or bags or anything. Now, miss, out of the door and quick smart."

She was hustled outside by the two officers, who shoved her along the path into the midst of the soldiers.

"On what grounds am I being arrested," she called out to the leading officer as she fell into step with the troopers who surrounded her. "Why are you arresting me? What crime am I supposed to have committed? I demand that you tell me, or I'll lay a complaint against you with your Commanding Officer."

But the officer burst out laughing and said not a single word. Flora marched with the troopers through the village and felt shamed as many of the men and women who were due to attend her wedding came out of their houses and looked as she was escorted away by the English. Some of the men shook their heads in disgust; some of the women held their fists to their mouths to prevent themselves from crying out. And some just looked at the English in utter hatred.

The sign on the side of the ship told her that it was called the *HMS Furnace*. Did that refer to heat from a brazier, or was that the name of the man after whom it had been commissioned? She sat on the dockside waiting for the officer in charge of the troopers to present his compliments and his papers to the captain. There were salutes all around, and when the captain took the papers, he read them, looked at the dock and examined Flora, then looked back down at the papers, said a few words to the officer, and nodded.

The officer barked an order for Flora to be brought to the gangplank and escorted up onto the deck. She had only been seated for a few minutes and was glad for the rest, for they'd been walking for the better part of four hours almost without a break and now that she was pregnant, her legs were swollen, throbbing, and exhausted. They'd only allowed her a few minutes respite on the way, a drink of water, and a hard tack biscuit to refresh her, and then they continued the march to the port.

They pulled and pushed her up the gangplank, and she tripped on a rope near to the top of the rungs. Righting herself, she stepped onto the deck and stood before the captain. He studiously ignored her as he finished his paper transactions with the Officer, who then wished him luck on the voyage with the prisoner and departed.

Suddenly, she was alone on an English ship with a captain surrounded by four midshipmen, all looking at her as though she was some exotic beast from an African jungle.

"Well, Mistress Macdonald. What's to do, eh? You've been a very naughty girl, from what I'm told."

"Captain, I'm nearly three months gone in my pregnancy and I'm very tired from a long march. I've had neither food nor drink of anything worth mentioning. I wonder, in the name of common decency, whether I might sit down and rest."

The ship's captain looked at her belly and frowned. "Dear God, ma'am, did the officer of the guard not know of your delicacy?"

"He did. And it was of no concern to him."

The captain turned to an elderly midshipman and said, "Escort the prisoner to a cabin below and make her comfortable. Get the galley to provide her with good food and ale. Get to it, man."

Flora made herself as comfortable as possible and was grateful for the food and drink. It had refreshed her, but her legs still ached. Carrying a bairn in her belly caused her legs to swell up at the slightest thing, and a long forced walk had made them ache and throb unbearably.

There was a knock on the door. The captain walked in and said, "Ma'am, my name is Captain Squires. You are aboard the *HMS Furnace*, and we are charged with taking you to Dunstaffnage Castle in Oban. It's a short journey and we leave on the evening tide. Our route will take us due south and we'll pass between Ardnamurchan and the Isle of Coll before shifting course westwards to round the Isle of Mull and then into the Firth of Lorn, where I'll hand you over to the Governor of Oban who will escort you to Dunstaffnage. We'll arrive by mid-morning Thursday, God willing."

"But why am I arrested, Captain Squires? I have been told nothing and I am in a delicate condition and greatly afraid for my safety and that of my baby."

He shouldn't discuss it with her, but she was so young and attractive and in her condition, bearing in mind that she'd soon be examined by an English tribunal, he couldn't see the harm in telling her what the indictment sheet said. "They say that you've aided and abetted the escape of the Pretender, Charles Stuart. Two fishermen from Skye apparently overheard talk that you had guided the traitor prince and helped him evade capture. He has now left Skye on a French cutter and escaped punishment, much to the consternation of His Royal Highness, the Duke of Cumberland. Anybody who assisted the traitor in evading capture and punishment is treated as a traitor him . . . or herself. That's all I can tell you, Mistress Macdonald. That's all I know."

And it was all that Flora needed to know. For from this moment onward, she knew that her life was forfeit to the whim of the Butcher of Cumberland, and judging by the way in which he was murdering Scots men and women, her neck would soon be stretched to breaking point.

She burst into tears and buried her head in her hands. Suddenly she felt horribly nauseous. But this time, it wasn't morning sickness.

DUNSTAFFNAGE CASTLE
NEAR OBAN, NORTH WEST SCOTLAND

SEPTEMBER 17, 1746

"You, ma'am, have aided and abetted the escape of the rascal Charles, a man who murdered hundreds of English and Scotsmen, a man who waged unprovoked and unpremeditated war against us. You, ma'am, have acted in a traitorous fashion to King George and the English crown. You, Mistress Macdonald, will be taken to the Tower of London to await your trial, and once found guilty as you undoubtedly will be, then you will be hanged, drawn, and quartered. Is that clear to you, Mistress Macdonald?"

Her hands were tied roughly behind her back and the harsh wooden chair was causing her backside to become numb. She had been listening to General Campbell threaten and demand incessantly for the past two days, letting up only to allow her to eat and sleep and attend to her ablutions in her filthy cell. But all she'd ever said to him and the officers who relieved him to ask her precisely the same questions, was that she had never met Prince Charles, that her father and fiancé were loyal members of the militia of Skye who supported the king of England, and that the two fishermen who had implicated her had made a mistake.

"A mistake, eh, Mistress Macdonald? A mistake? But this mistake was made by two sober gentlemen who observed you in a field with another person who walked like a man. These two loyal gentlemen then followed you and your so-called female companion to your home in Armadale on the southern part of Skye, where your female companion suddenly disappeared. Never to be seen again. And these two loyal gentlemen, alerted no doubt by the very considerable bounty on the head of the traitor prince, wondered whether this so-called lady might very well be a certain gentleman in disguise. Eh, Miss Macdonald. What do you have to say to that?" demanded General Campbell.

"As I've told you, sir, a hundred times, that lady was my maid and seamstress, Betty Burke, who left my house after we returned safely, and took ship to Ireland where she lives. It's no wonder that she walks in a mannish way, because she's elderly and has lost her youthful agility. She's also stricken with an arthritic leg which makes her ungainly. And she's an ugly person as well. But she's a marvelous seamstress and makes wonderful dresses. She will return to my service from her visit to Ireland in a month or so, when you can speak to her and examine her yourself. Why in God's name don't you believe me?"

"And why," he screamed, standing and tipping over his desk and the carafe of wine, "do you persist in your lies and falsehoods. Admit the truth, suffer a year or two in prison, and return to your home. Continue to lie and prevaricate, and I'll have no alternative but to ship you to London and have you incarcerated in the Tower which, for a lady in your condition, is a fate worse than death itself.

"What can I say, General Campbell, which will make you believe me?"

But he didn't answer. He stormed out of the room and barked an instruction. Having failed to break her spirit, he relished the thought of what the torturers in the Tower of London could do to her.

He smiled when he saw her approaching, walking in the middle of two bodies of troopers, but the closer she came to him, the less pleased he was by the look of her. She was wan, exceedingly drawn and looked exhausted. Captain Squires immediately ordered her to be assisted up the gangplank and a barrel to be unlashed and moved to the foredeck to make a seat for her to rest.

"Good God, Miss Macdonald. What did they do to you?"

She sat and smiled at Captain Squires. Although she was on her way to the Tower of London, it would be a good many days before they reached the Thames and she hoped that the sea voyage would do her good. "They treated me as though I were a traitor, Captain, whereas all I am is a woman of the Highlands who is loyal to the king. A terrible mistake has been made, sir, and I am the victim of a great miscarriage of justice."

He shook his head in concern. "If you continue like this, ma'am, I fear that will not be the only miscarriage for which you'll be the victim. For God's sake, does nobody care that you're a lady carrying a child? Has everybody gone mad in this action against the Prince Stuart? Have we lost our common decency?"

He ordered Flora to be brought food and drink. "I shall have a cabin prepared for you, ma'am. I'm ordered by General Campbell to keep you in the brig under lock and key, but I'm the captain of this ship, and once we put to sea, not even a general can order me to do something with which I disagree. You will be given free range while you are on board, ma'am, provided I have your word as a lady that you'll not attempt to escape."

She smiled. "If you think in my condition I can escape from a ship ten miles offshore, you have a greatly exaggerated opinion of my abilities, Captain Squires. No, sir, there will be no attempts by me. Indeed, when I get to the Tower and I'm put on trial, I shall appeal to the sense of fairness of the British judiciary and pray for a just hearing."

"God grant you that, ma'am. Now, if you'll excuse me, I have a ship to prepare for the long haul south to the Thames. We'll be rounding Land's End and the English Channel in six days, as we have to call in at Liverpool and Bristol. Then it's into the English Channel, round at Margate and into the Thames Estuary beyond the Isle of Sheppey. With a good morning tide, I'll deliver you to the gates of the Tower of London and to the mercy of His Royal Highness, the Duke of Cumberland."

"Captain Squires. I wonder, sir, if I might impose upon your good nature. Since I was arrested and incarcerated in Dunstaffnage Castle, my family has heard nothing of my fate. There could be few things more vexing for a family than not knowing if their beloved is alive or dead. I have a fiancé and I'm bearing his child. Would it be possible, sir, for a message to be delivered to them, telling that I'm on my way to the Tower and that they mustn't worry about me?"

He looked at her and said loudly for everybody to hear, "Don't be absurd, woman. Of course, I won't deliver your message. You're a traitor and a scoundrel."

Taken aback, she stared in incomprehension at the captain, who took something out of his pocket and accidentally dropped it on the deck. As he bent to pick it up, he whispered into her ear, "Forgive me, ma'am. There are tattletales everywhere these days. Write your message quickly before the high tide, and I'll give it to a messenger before we sail. But know that it's worth more than my life if I'm discovered."

She breathed a sigh of relief and avoided the captain's eyes, knowing that smiling at him or offering him thanks would garner suspicion. A moment ago, nobody in the entire world knew of Flora's fate or where she was being taken, other than her enemies.

Since her sudden arrest, she had become a woman without a name, a prisoner without an identity, like one of the masses who lay in the wastes of the Highlands, dead from the Butcher's sword and whose existence would disappear forever from the annals of mankind, remembered by nobody as though he had never existed.

It was not the fate for which Flora believed she had been born. But it was the fate that she now accepted would be her death. Still, now at least, thanks to the kindness of an English sea captain, even though her life would pass unnoticed by everybody but her family, at least her mother and father, her brother and his family, and dearest Alan Macdonald, would know about her fate.

Leicester House, London

September 24, 1746

Frederick, the Prince of Wales, heir to the thrones of King George II of England and Hanover, listened carefully to what was being said to him. He asked Lord Milius to repeat the narration again so that he could savor every word. He could barely resist smiling and clapping his hands. It was just too, too delicious.

A pregnant Scottish woman had helped the young Prince Charles to escape and now she was being bundled into the dank and drear Tower of London to await her fate at the hands of his young, impetuous, and brutal brother, the Duke of Cumberland. The very thought of it delighted him so completely that his wife Augusta of Saxe-Gotha whispered to him "*Liebchen,* you're shouting."

"And do we know any details about this young woman?" asked the Prince of Wales.

"Only, sir, that she is a resident of Skye and an honorable young lady. She is said to be very handsome in that crude and rural Scottish Highlands sort of a way; you know what I mean, sir—windblown hair, ruddy cheeks, watery eyes, no perfume or cosmetics to defeat her natural body odors. Yet from accounts which my spies in your brother's service have told me, she's comely and strikingly good looking with a healthy glow from a sea voyage and her time sitting on the god-forsaken rocks of that outpost of civilization.

"But her treatment following her arrest by General Campbell caused great consternation when the news reached the island of Skye, both because she is a woman of impeccable character, well beloved on the Island, who was summarily arrested on the advice of two scoundrels without recourse to her family or her fiancé just days before her wedding, and because she is carrying a child. Now the fury of the Islanders has spread well beyond Skye, and her case has become a cause of great importance in the rest of Scotland.

"Your brother's assaults against the people and your father's demands for a Disarming Act and forbidding the Scots to wear their traditional tartans and plaids, has infuriated them; but this act of arresting a young woman and torturing her for helping the prince to escape has been the spark which has lit the tinder. The men and women of the Scottish towns cowered since their prince's defeat and said little against your brother's assault when he slaughtered the clans. But this assail against a young woman of impeccable character has made them furious. There are voices of important and educated people in Edinburgh and other cities such as Inverness, demanding that she be released immediately and returned to her family. It seems that for the Scots, imperiling the life of a proud Island woman is akin to threatening the continuation of the Scottish race."

The prince turned to Augusta and said, "As it will seem to the English, m'dear. And not just the Jacobites but to the rest of England as well. Oh, Augusta, this is marvelous news, my dearest. Arresting a pregnant woman. The Tower. Could anything be better? I must meet this woman. I must go to the Tower and pay her my respects."

Lord Milius looked at the prince as though he was deranged. "Go to the Tower? No, sir, you can't and must not. Your father would view that as an act of treason."

"Precisely."

"But in his current frame of mind, he'd have you arrested. You know he's trying to ship you off to Hanover and give England to the Duke of Cumberland. For God's sake, Your Highness, don't give the king the excuse he's been seeking to get you out of England."

"Milius is correct, *Liebchen*. The insult to your father would be too great. Such open treason will not be something he can tolerate," said Augusta. "For him to do so would be to abdicate his throne to you before he's in his grave, wonderful as that might be."

"Why shouldn't I cause him apoplexy? Look what he's done to me," said Frederick. "His damnable poodle Mr. Prime Minister Pelham has given important government jobs to all my friends and my supporters and now they've all left me. I've only got devoted Milius and a few other loyal supporters. Just wait until I'm the king. I'll show my one-time friends what it means to remain steadfast. I'll make them all Governors of tiny islands in the Great Southern Ocean. Oh Augusta, surely you can see that this woman, this . . ."

"Flora Macdonald," Lord Milius reminded him.

"Flora from the Highlands can be a rallying point to stick a dagger in the king's heart. Londoners are beginning to hate what's happening in the Highlands. You just have to read it in the pamphlets and posters. They say that we've gone too far and that they don't like the killings. They're calling my damnable brother the Butcher. He was a hero when he won the battle at Culloden, but now he's a butcher. The English have lost all sympathy for what William and my father are doing. They hear the wailing of widows and orphans all the way down here, and it's making them feel mournful. But now that they've arrested this beautiful and pregnant Scottish girl . . ."

"Flora Macdonald," Milius repeated.

"Flora Macdonald, we can make it a rallying point to attack my father. We can cite his brutality, his offense against his own people. We may even be able to use it to force his abdication. Tell people he's gone mad. Get Parliament to appoint me as Prince Regent, as protector of the realm. Oh, there's so much we can do now that Flora has come to town," said Frederick.

"But you must not go to the Tower," insisted Milius.

"No, you're right. I see that now. But I can write a pamphlet and have it distributed in the coffee houses. I'll sign it 'Mr. Leicester' so that everybody will know I've written it, and then, if the king accuses me, I'll deny all knowledge. And I shall call an audience of all the members of Parliament in Leicester House, or maybe we should hold it in Carlton Gardens, and we'll tell the Members of Parliament how concerned we are for England's relationship with our Scottish citizens. That will put the cat amongst the pigeons."

Milius smiled and stood, bowing to the Prince of Wales and to the Princess Augusta. But before he'd reached the door, the prince called out, "Wait, I want you to take a note to the Governor of the Tower. Deliver it personally. Tell him that it's from the Prince of Wales and for his eyes only. Tell him to pass its contents on to nobody, especially Mr. Pelham or any of his government. Give him a big enough purse, and he'll realize which way the wind is blowing. He can be trusted. Tell him that once I'm king, he can expect a high office."

The prince stood, walked over to his escritoire, and scribbled a letter that he handed to Lord Milius.

It took Milius just fifteen minutes to travel by carriage from Leicester House to the gates of the Tower of London. As the carriage rattled over the cobblestones and through the portcullis, he looked up and shuddered at the fearsome towers. He wondered how many prisoners had tried to gaze out of those barred slits of windows, and what they thought as they were dragged away to be beheaded in the courtyard.

The carriage came to a stop at the Eastern entry, and he was shown by a Yeoman Warder to the top of the tower where the Governor's residence and offices were kept. Another Yeoman saluted and opened the door. The Governor looked up in surprise and stood when he saw who it was.

"Good afternoon, my Lord Milius. This is an unexpected pleasure."

"And good afternoon to you, Mr. Governor. I have a private letter for you, the contents of which are for your eyes alone. Neither the substance of the letter nor my visit, are to be reported to the king or the prime minister, or anybody. And once you've read the contents of this letter, you'll return it to me. Is that quite understood?"

"Completely understood, m'Lord."

He handed the letter to the Governor, who broke the seal and read it quickly. "This is from . . ."

"Mr. Leicester," said Lord Milius quickly.

"Exactly. Mr. Leicester. Indeed, m'Lord. The lady in question is currently a guest in one of the smaller cells. Mr. Leicester requests that I offer her the very best of accommodation that the Tower has to offer, as he assures me that during the time of her incarceration, he will ensure that she is visited by many influential and titled people. She is, according to Mr. Leicester, a hero of her people, and will be treated by me accordingly."

He looked up at Lord Milius, handed back the letter and smiled, saying, "Please inform Mr. Leicester that the lady in question will be given the very best treatment and accommodation that I can offer."

Lord Milius took out a purse of gold and gave it to the Governor, who smiled even broader and said, "It's a pleasure doing business with Mr. Leicester. And when his father has gone to a better place and Mr. Leicester ascends to a more important position, I hope that he will remember a certain Governor of a certain Tower, who is now and has always been his devoted servant. And kindly tell Mr. Leicester that this same Governor would dearly like to support him by election to the Houses of Parliament were this certain Mr. Leicester to appoint him as a representative of some rotten borough."

Milius smiled. There was no need to pass on the prince's offer . . . the Governor already had his reward in mind.

When they first came to her cell, she thought it was for some dire purpose. When she'd arrived at the Tower the previous afternoon, the guards had been crude and menacing, taunting her, ridiculing her, forcing her to fetch and carry the cot and chairs from the hallway into her chamber. When they'd closed and bolted the huge wooden door, she felt utterly bereft and intimidated. In the semi-darkness, she had been forced to put her cot together and find straw to fill the filthy mattress. The room stank of urine and vomit, and even breathing the air made her retch. She rubbed her stomach, which was now beginning to show signs of straining against her skin, and sought a place to sit down that wasn't dank and festering.

That night had been hideous, with the screams of other inmates making her fear for her sanity. She cried herself into a state of despair, and for the sake of her mind, she repeated the words to songs she had learned as a child. She found that she was curled up on the floor, arms grasping her knees to her chest, as she had slept when she was a frightened little girl.

The morning had brought some relief, but she really began to question how long she could remain like this and still stay sane. A baby should be born in the clean and fresh air of the Highlands, not in the fetid decaying squalor of the Tower of London.

During the rest of the day, Flora tried to concentrate her mind on what she would tell her torturers when her time came. How long before she could restrain herself under the pain of the torture instruments from admitting that she had aided Prince Charles? How long before they inquired about the baby in her belly? And how long before she admitted that it was of royal blood? That would mean its life would be reported to the Butcher Duke of Cumberland, and only God could foretell her fate when the news became known.

And then the door suddenly opened. In shock, realizing that she was now about to suffer the agonies of the rack and the casket and the fires of the torture chamber, she drew back in terror and stifled a scream. But the man who walked in was fat and beaming a smile and looking unctuous.

"And good afternoon to you my dear Miss Macdonald. I'm Mr. Winters, the Governor of the Tower of London, and I've come to offer you my most sincere and humble apologies for inadvertently placing you in this most disgusting of accommodation rooms. This was done without my knowledge, and be assured, Miss, that I shall seek out the miscreant who placed you here and deal with him very determinedly.

"You will kindly accompany me to another wing of the Tower, where a much more suitable accommodation has been arranged for your pleasure."

He stepped aside, bowed, and pointed the way to the door.

Was this a joke, she wondered. Was this the way in which prisoners were led to the torture chamber or to the execution block, first giving them a glimmer of hope and thereby making their descent from hope into hell all the more painful? If it was, there was nothing she could do about it. The Governor had brought four Yeomen Warders with him, who were all smiling as though she were royalty.

She walked out of the cell and was accompanied along the corridor, up some stairs, down others, through vast halls full of pikestaffs and rondelles of swords, suits of Elizabethan armor and much more that flew by too quickly for her to determine. Up more steps and eventually to a corridor in which there was more light, and she could look down and see the River Thames flowing past. If this was the way to the torture chamber, she thought, then it was very different from her nightmares of dungeons and hooded figures.

One of the Yeomen Warders strode ahead of her and opened a door to a large chamber. There were four rooms. On the floor were rugs and carpets and the furniture was both elegant and comfortable. A spinet had been set up by the window, there was a harpsichord and a lute close by, and she could even see a four-poster bed in a far chamber. There were pots and pans near to an open fire, a table and chairs for dining, and tapestries on the walls.

Had she not known better, she would have thought that she was entering the private chamber of the ruler of England.

"Is this a joke?" she asked the Governor, as he entered and proudly invited her to look around the room.

"Joke? Of course not. This is your chamber as long as you are a guest of His Majesty King George II."

"But he's imprisoned me and calls me traitor."

The Governor smiled and winked, saying, "He might, ma'am, but others call you heroine."

She looked at him in amazement. "Charles?"

The Governor frowned. "Frederick!"

"Who's Frederick?" she asked ingenuously.

The Governor burst out laughing, wished her a good afternoon, and he and the Yeomen retired. And they left the door to her cell open and unlocked.

She sat in amazement and repeated the question, "Frederick? Who's Frederick?"

# Chapter Twelve

SEPTEMBER 25, 1746

His Royal Highness Charles Edward Louis John Casimir Sylvester Maria Stuart, heir presumptive to the thrones of England and Scotland, Wales, and Ireland, son of the Pretender to a lost crown, grandson of the deposed King James II of England, Scotland and Ireland, and great grandson of James I of England and VI of Scotland who was chosen heir to Queen Elizabeth I at the moment of the great monarch's demise, walked out of the northern Salon de la Guerre toward the Salon de la Paix at the southern end of the Great Hall of Mirrors.

Lined up along the entire room, all two hundred feet of it, were the hundreds and hundreds of people who attached themselves to the French monarchy like limpets to the bottom of a ship. Here, resplendent in their uniforms of office, were the princes and princesses, the ducs and duchesses, the marquises and marchionesses, the maréchals and the generals of the French Army, the prelates of the Holy Roman Church and their mistresses, sycophants and influence peddlers, deposed members of foreign royalty, aged courtiers of Louis the Sun King, current and past court officials, members of the Académie Royale, scientists, philosophers, artists, courtesans, past and present mistresses of the king as well as lesser family and irrelevant nobility from the provinces, all assembled at the glittering court of King Louis XV like overlooked and faded *objets d'art* in an storeroom.

And as the prince walked along the Hall of Mirrors in almost complete silence, King Louis sat motionless on his throne at the southern end, scrutinizing him and his every movement. The young prince walked in homage toward the great majesty and victor of the previous year's Battle of Fontenoy, his heart pounding in anticipation of how he would be received; whether as victor, vanquished, lunatic, or savior? His heart was in his throat, but he walked as tall and proud as his tremulous legs would allow.

And then Louis suddenly and unexpectedly stunned everybody by standing, and beginning to applaud his advance. The entire court, whose eyes had been trained on the Young Pretender, turned and looked at their great king. As one, they began to applaud and cheer, though none but a handful understood why. When the young man was halfway down the vast auditorium, the king of France ceased clapping and sat down to receive his guest. Slowly, and then all at once, the courtiers realized that they too must desist from applause, and silence again ruled, except for the footsteps of the prince.

Coming to the edge of the plinth, Prince Charles Edward Stuart bowed low and continued his obeisance to the king of France, saying, "The heir to the throne of England and Scotland greets Louis, by the grace of God, King of France and all of its territories."

"Rise, my dear son. Rise. You return to us a hero. All of France has followed your remarkable odyssey. We have thrilled and celebrated your early victories; we were bereft when tragedy befell you in the inhospitable fields of the north of Scotland; we marveled at your subterfuge in evading capture for all those many months, and we are delighted that our holy France has been instrumental in your rescue to return you to your home, and your mother church."

The king addressed the court. "My lords and ladies, our son Charles left us an adventurer and has returned to us as a true soldier of the Cross, a man of valor."

Again, there was thunderous applause. It was the sign for Prince
Charles to rise from his bow and kiss the ring of the monarch.

"Are you recovered from your ordeal?" asked the king.

"Majesty, it was as nothing. A trifle. Always in my heart, the glory
of France burned bright and warmed me on the cold winter evenings. I
return to you and express my most sincere gratitude that the ship which
you sent has born me back so that I can rest and recover under Your
Majesty's aegis," he said.

The king nodded. He liked the young man's words. "So tell me,
Prince Charles, is it true what my ambassadors and spies at the Court
of St. James's have told me about the Duke of Cumberland? Is he really
intent on emptying the entire land of the Scots and filling it with
English people and with sheep? If so, it seems incredible. One would
have to look to the Ottomans assault against Austria and Hungary, or
the Muslim's Prophet Mohammed as he swept out of the desert, or the
ancient Egyptians of the bible to find a slaughter of innocents of such
epic magnitude. Armies are paid to be killed, but to kill innocent women
and children is barbarism at its very worst."

"Majesty, I don't know what your ambassador has reported, but it
can't possibly have conveyed the full horror of what the younger son of
King George is doing to the Scottish people. Your Majesty defeated him
last year at the Battle of Fontenoy. It is a tragedy that he remained alive
at the end of the battle to wreak havoc and misery barely a year later
against his own people. You say that we must look to the bible for such
an event. Indeed, for the duke is replicating the plague of locust in Egypt
by denuded his Scottish lands of its people, its clans, its government, its
system of laws, and even its animals. Scotland will cease to be, unless
the Butcher of Cumberland is stopped. I have returned, Majesty, to join
almighty Catholic France in my great endeavor. Since the time of King
Henry VIII, his daughter Elizabeth, King James, down to this present
Protestant usurper from Hanover, the people of England have been cut
off from the blood and the body of Christ through their severing of the
bonds which tie them to the throne of St. Peter in Rome. Surely no price,

Majesty, is too great to pay to bring back the people of Great Britain to the Holy Roman See?"

Charles stole a glance at the king and then looked surreptitiously at his elderly Imperial Chancellor, Henri François d'Aguesseau. If the aged treasurer, a virtuous man who was the comptroller of the king's purse, gave a slight shake of the head, it meant that the request would cause further problems between the king and the Parliament, and then Louis would find an excuse to decline the request for help. But if he gave a small and unnoticeable nod, it indicated that the request could be funded and that the decision was the king's. Charles' heart fell when he saw the treasurer shake his head. The movement was so slight that it looked like the palsy of an elderly man, yet Charles instantly recognized it as the seal of death for his future campaign against the Hanoverians.

Louis said, "Indeed he must be stopped, my dear son, but it is surely the responsibility of the British people to realize what the younger son of the king is doing, and to tell him to desist. While we have promised you help in the past, France's eyes must only be opened to the danger posed to us by our real enemies, the Austrians and the Dutch and of course the English when they dare to interfere in our lands. Our only interest, now that we control the Austrian Netherlands, is to establish our border at the River Rhine. These, dear son, are our greatest concerns. Much as we would love to make good our promise to help you restore the Catholic Stuarts to the throne, and force the Protestant Hanoverians to quit our northern neighbor and return to the land of their birth, our funds must be conserved for our own immediate and pressing enemies. My treasury is in debt to an amount of 100 million livres, and I must now increase taxes in order to pay for my armies, my palaces and more."

He raised his voice so that the entire audience chamber in the Hall of Mirrors would hear him quite clearly, "And these taxes will fall upon the heads of the rich and powerful, the aristocrats who live in the comfort and security of our largess, nobility of my court who give no thought of their indebtedness to how they have prospered by their close association with the throne of France and its people."

The entire Hall shuddered at the king's words. Rumors had been circulating for a long time about the king's discontent with the cost of keeping his court and the appallingly low contributions that his courtiers were making. There had been growing indications that all the nobility would soon be taxed for their wealth.

The king continued, "But one day, my dearest prince, I promise you that France's eyes will again turn northward to restore your father and yourself to your rightful throne and hence restore the one true religion, and then let King George beware of our wrath."

When the audience was over, the petitions had been dealt with, the ambassadors received and the business of the day finalized, the courtiers dispersed from the Hall of Mirrors to refresh themselves with coffee and petit fours and patisseries, to huddle in corners and connive about with whom they should meet, who would join whose hunt, who was sleeping with whom, and whether the king might take an afternoon walk in Le Nôtre's gardens, enabling them to carefully position themselves so that they intersected his path to bid him good afternoon. Gifts and contributions about to be delivered to the royal throne were scrutinized by the courtiers in an attempt to see who was trying to purchase influence, dresses were compared for their opulence, and fierce competition was begun with the object of snaring important guests for the many dinner engagements that night in the different apartments.

Charles, on the other hand, had a number of people whom he needed to speak with and could waste no time with the nonsense and frivolities that went with courtly life. Since he'd been gone from the French Court, the king had taken up with a new mistress, a certain Madame de Pompadour. The affair had begun in February of the previous year at a ball to mark the sixteen-year-old Dauphin Louis' marriage to his father's first cousin, the nineteen-year-old infanta of Spain, Maria-Teresa.

Charles had seen Madame de Pompadour briefly in the court, but paid her little attention, as he believed that King Louis was still enamored of his previous mistress; but the beauty and charm and intellect of the Marquise de Pompadour had turned the king's head and now her power was in the ascendancy. It was important that he meet with her, as, even though she was born a commoner, she had access to the king's ear, as well as those other parts of his body that might govern his mind.

He contrived to cross her path when the king had left the audience hall and was in high council with his prelates and ministers. It was a moment in the court when the king's eyes were turned to State business, and people could relax as they went around plotting and conniving.

Charles noticed that a group of ladies had gathered around Madame de Pompadour, who was sitting in her salon in a nearby antechamber. Outside the door was a group of men standing in silence, each awaiting permission to enter the salon in the hope of gaining the Madame's attention as their direct route to the king's ear.

Prepared for his onslaught, Charles walked toward the male courtiers outside the doors to the salon. As a prince and the son of a king, he held far higher status than any of the lesser nobles and courtiers who were awaiting a nod from Madame de Pompadour signaling their right to admission. So the others stood aside as the prince positioned himself immobile in the doorway, waiting for her to look up from her gaggle of ladies and see him.

When she noticed a tall young man standing in the doorway to her salon, she was suddenly taken aback by his imperiousness. Then she recognized that it was the Prince Pretender of the Stuarts, a future king of England.

She stood, and curtsied. "Your Royal Highness. You honor me with your presence."

"No, ma'am, you honor me by your recognition. I have come to pay my respects to the king's particular friend."

She smiled and invited him inside. As he entered the room, he pointedly closed the doors, infuriating the men outside and adding a frisson of excitement to the life of the ladies in the salon. Rarely was a door closed as those inside had to know what was happening outside, and vice versa; but when important matters of state or great secrets were being divulged, the shutting of the door added greatly to the sudden importance of the occasion. It would guarantee an afternoon of gossip, innuendo, and intrigue.

He walked over and took her hand, kissing it. The ladies of Madame de Pompadour's salon suppressed their gasps. For a commoner, even one who was mistress to the king of France, to be kissed by a prince of the realm, was unprecedented. It indicated an acknowledgment of her status. Madame de Pompadour understood precisely what Prince Charles' gesture signified and beamed at him in gratitude. His regard for her would spread immediately around the court and would soon come to the favorable notice of the king.

"Please, Highness, sit down and take coffee with me. Are you still exhausted from your battles in Scotland? I'm told that you came so close to conquering the whole of England. Why did you turn back?"

"In a war, ma'am, supply lines are as important as are front lines. My army had a surfeit of courage, but a deficit of arms, ammunition, artillery, and manpower. We were within thirty leagues of entering London, but there were powerful and well-armed military forces to our right, left, and front, and I would not countenance the slaughter of my many supporters. Sometime, ma'am, retreat and regrouping takes more courage than advance and attack."

She smiled and immediately began to enjoy the company of the young man who sat opposite her. He cut a dashing figure and no doubt would win the hearts of many young ladies in the court.

"And are these the end of your adventures in England and Scotland, sir?" she asked.

"My quest for the return of my family's rightful throne will never end. While ever I have strength and purpose, I will continue to oppose the Hanoverians and propound the Stuart cause."

He sipped his coffee and looked closely at her. She was indeed very beautiful. Her voluminous white wig and white painted face were like a sculpture and her eyes were an intense green that seemed to seek out and comprehend the very heart and soul of a man.

But sitting in her presence in the confectionary court and perfumed atmosphere of Versailles caused his mind to fly back a thousand miles to the north of Scotland to a crofter's hut, to a woman whose beauty didn't come from powder and rouge and wigs.

He looked at Madame de Pompadour and realized that there was an absolute artificiality about her compared with Flora Macdonald. Flora had the skin and eyes and face and freshness of a mountain stream, whereas the marquise seemed more like one of the delicately constructed pastries to which the court's chefs devoted so much time and energy but in the end were little but air and sweetness with almost no substance, quickly consumed and just as quickly forgotten.

When he'd finished his coffee, Madame de Pompadour said discretely, "And what of the Scotland to which you returned. Was there much which you found beautiful?"

"The lochs, the hillsides, the valleys are all very beautiful. But it's the people who I found most appealing. They aren't the sort of people you find in the cities and towns of France. They are wild and rugged as they must be to survive the inclement weather which afflicts the north of the country. But there is an openness and an honesty, a friendship and an intelligence which makes one feel welcomed. They say what they mean, and they mean what they say," he told her.

"And the ladies? Tell me about the ladies?"

He smiled. "The ladies suffer from the rigors of the landscape and the privations of life in the Highlands. There are castles and manor houses, but most of the populace lives in crofts which are usually of wood and straw, although sometimes they are constructed of a mud they call peat. There is neither time nor money to spare for the ladies to adorn themselves with fine clothes or perfumes or jewelry. Every day is spent in tending to the needs of the family, in feeding and clothing them, and in helping the man of the house in farming and with the livestock."

"But how is that different from the rustic men and women of France?"

The prince laughed. "And how much does Your Ladyship know of the rustic men and women of France?"

She burst out laughing. "My family are financiers in Paris. The closest I have been to the rural parts of our nation is along the road from Paris to Versailles. But more than the economy of Scotland, Your Highness, I was particularly interested in any young ladies who might have taken your attention. Were there any?"

"One. A charming and gentle and sweet lady, who is as brave as she is beautiful. But with the very greatest of respect, my lady, her name is a secret which will remain with me."

"Ah. Then you're in love."

"Men born of my station in life can't afford the luxury of love. Only one as lucky as yourself can sanction that state of being."

"But even creatures as fortunate as me, to be friends with a king of France, must accept the status which that brings. You have been away from France for a year, sir, and so you cannot have heard the cruel things the peasants are saying about me. Have you heard of the *poissonnades* which have been written about me?"

"Fish stew? I don't understand."

"It is a ridiculous game of words, played against me because my family name is Poisson. These poisonous posters and pamphlets appear all around Paris. And now they've begun to appear in provincial towns as well."

Mystified, the prince asked, "But I don't understand. Why are the people against you?"

"They call me daughter of a leech and a leech myself. It's because I'm a commoner, not born of royal stock, and the people think I'm flaunting myself and that I'm arrogant, and they think that it's immoral for the royal member to find its way into the body of somebody without royal blood."

The prince shook his head in amazement. "Ma'am. The woman I met in Scotland was the daughter of a simple farmer. Yet she was educated, charming, uncommonly attractive and above all moral and brave and God-fearing. She was worth a hundred times the value of any woman in the English court, yet through her birth she was tied to her simple home, her family, and the status to which she was born. A woman such as her will never see the inside of a great palace, yet a woman such as her, and dare I say yourself, would bring great benefits to those of us who are born to rule."

## THE TOWER OF LONDON

### SEPTEMBER 27, 1746

Having lived in a simple croft all her life, Flora Macdonald didn't believe that she'd ever become used to the sheer opulence of her surroundings. She had to remind herself time and again that this was a prison and not a palace. Occasionally, in the stillness of the night, welling up from the bowels of the dungeons, she heard the excruciating screams and pleas of men and women being tortured. But whenever she looked around at the rugs, the sumptuous furniture, the kitchen and its banquet of food, and her bedroom with a bed and mattress thick enough to envelop a field of straw, she couldn't help but believe that this was nothing but a dream in which she was a princess and that at any moment she'd awaken and find herself in the hideous reality of a normal prisoner.

But she pinched herself, knocked her head against the hard stone wall, paced the floor, looked out of the windows at the rest of London, and despite her best efforts soon realized that she wasn't asleep, this wasn't a dream, but she was living the life of royalty.

Absurd. Impossible. True.

How had it happened? How was it possible that she had left Scotland as a despised prisoner of King George and was suddenly ensconced in one of his palaces like a guest of honor? The guards were of no earthly use. Every time she left her apartment and went for a walk in the corridors, or outside on the balustrades, they would smile and greet her in admiration and respect, calling her Madame and Your Grace. But when it came to answering her inquiries, they smiled, shrugged their shoulders, and told her that they didn't know the answer.

She asked to see the Governor of the Tower, and he was by her side within minutes. She invited him inside for ale and coffee and cakes, served by the maid she'd been given to look after her, and they chatted amiably about the weather and social events and what she simply must do in the entertainment gardens at Hyde Park and Vauxhall Gardens when she was released from her temporary custodial confinement. He inquired about how her pregnancy was progressing and whether she would like to see a physician. She told him that she had no money to pay for such an expense, and he laughed, telling her that her friend Frederick would ensure that she suffered no financial distress at all and would receive no accounting from a learned doctor.

"But who is this Frederick that I'm supposed to know and in whose gratitude I find myself?" she asked.

Again, he burst out laughing. "While I find your discretion admirable, ma'am, be assured that I am a soul of discretion myself, and I have been very well rewarded by Mr. Leicester to ensure your convenience."

"Mr. Leicester?"

"Yes," the Governor said with a knowing wink, "Mr. Leicester."

"Who's Mr. Leicester?"

Again, the governor burst out laughing. "I didn't realize that the Scots had such a ribald sense of humor. Anyway, I must be away, for I've been informed that Lord Milius wishes to visit you and will be here within the hour. Is there anything I can do for you, Mistress Macdonald, to facilitate your interview with his lordship?"

The stunned look on her face told the Governor that she had everything she required. And the last thing she wanted was more laughter from the Governor of the Tower when she asked, "who's Lord Milius?"

He was attractive in an effeminate way, though his voice was deep and he enjoyed a good height and had strong shoulders. He'd bowed as he'd walked in and then strode across the room to shake her hand.

Now they were seated, and her maidservant had served them coffee and cakes from the kitchen. She sipped the coffee but still found it as bitter as her taste of it the previous year when she met Mr. David Hume and Mr. Adam Smith in the Coffee House in Edinburgh. This time, however, she was ready for its taste and tried not to wrinkle her nose.

"It's an honor and a privilege to meet with the illustrious Flora Macdonald," he said, sitting opposite her and scrutinizing her movements. She remained silent and passive, waiting for him to open up.

"I'm sure that you're wondering what you might have done to merit such advantageous circumstances."

She nodded. "It did occur to me that if this is the way in which King George treats all his prisoners, there would be a lot more footpads and murderers on our streets trying desperately to get caught."

Milius burst out laughing. She was an amiable woman, far from attractive for she didn't have the grace or the sophistication that he found desirable in a woman; but for all her rustic looks and dress, she was alert and striking and could, under some circumstances, be called pleasing.

"So, Lord Milius, I assume that you are my protector, though for the life of me I can't understand why. But I would prefer to know sooner rather than later precisely what service must I perform to show my gratitude for your generosity? I assume that you are this Frederick gentleman or this Mr. Leicester that the Governor continues to mention. You do realize that I am three months gone with child, don't you."

He looked at her dumbfounded. "Service? You're surely not talking about services of an intimate nature, are you?" Again, he laughed. "Mistress Macdonald, in London today, a woman's body is the cheapest form of currency. The very last thing that interests me, or my particular friend, is service of that nature. No, ma'am, you are far more valuable to me and my friend as a pregnant heroine than for any seduction which your body might provide. More valuable than you could ever possibly imagine. Indeed, the weight of a crown could hang upon your shoulders."

She reeled in shock. How could he possibly know that the bairn inside her belly was the child of the Prince Stuart? Unless Alan had told somebody, or he'd been tortured and she couldn't countenance that prospect. But she had to find out more, and so she calmed herself and continued with the interview.

"The weight of a crown? Whatever could you mean?" she asked nervously.

"That is something which I will tell you shortly. But in the meantime, be assured that whatever it is you want will be supplied to you. Our only regret, my friend and me, is that you have to survive such miserable surroundings. However, we've made an effort to make life as comfortable for you as these unfortunate circumstances allow."

"Are you able to tell me, then, exactly who you are, and who is your friend?"

"You are in the protection of His Royal Highness, the Heir Apparent to the Throne of England and Scotland, Frederick, Prince of Wales. I am his friend, the Lord Milius."

"The Prince of Wales? The prince? The next king of England?"

Now it was her turn to burst out laughing, for a terrible error had been made. "Forgive me, sir, but if the Prince of Wales knew who I was and of what I've been accused, he'd lock me in a dungeon himself and throw away the key."

Smiling, Milius said softly, "You are Flora Macdonald. You are the stepdaughter of Hugh, who is master of the English Militia on the Island of Skye. Your mother is Anne, whose first husband died when you were two years of age. You are engaged and are pregnant to a farmer of Skye named Alan Macdonald of your clan, and he, too, is a member of the Loyal English Militia.

"Against your father's and fiancé's permission, you have recently guided Charles Edward, Prince of the House of Stuart, from the Island of Uist to the Island of Skye following which he was able to escape the clutches of the king's second son, the Duke of Cumberland and is now in France where he is entertained by the king of France's new mistress, Madame de Pompadour in an attempt to persuade the king to fund another expedition to England in order to recapture the Stuart family's throne."

She sat back in her chair and realized that her mouth was open.

Again smiling, he said gently, "So, Flora, is there anything I've omitted?"

She shook her head.

"More coffee? For a prison, it's really very good," he said and brought another cup over to her seat. She took it and drank it, not tasting its bitterness.

After a moment in which he allowed Flora to digest both his knowledge of her and the coffee he'd supplied to the prison, he said, "Of course, the question uppermost in your mind is 'why is the heir to the throne of England protecting a rebel and a criminal and a traitorous Jacobite?'"

Again, she nodded. She couldn't participate in the conversation, because she had lost her power of speech.

"The answer is simple, Flora. It's all to do with the relationship between the king and the heir to the throne. You see, the Prince of Wales detests his father. He hates him and wishes him dead, and the same is true in reverse. Please don't be shocked, for it's a curse of the Hanoverians that the father hates the son with the same intensity as the son hates the father. George I hated the present king and vice versa, just as George II hates the future George III and vice versa. And no doubt Georges V and VI and if, God wills it, there's a George VII, then all will each hate the other. Don't ask me why, but that's the way it is.

"What you have to keep in mind during your adventure in London is that the king wants to replace his heir, my friend the Prince of Wales, as heir to the throne of England. He wants his younger son, the Duke of Cumberland, to be king of England and your protector, Frederick the heir presumptive, to sit on the throne of Hanover. But he is finding little support because of the law of primogeniture. Hence, he wants to find an excuse to send the prince away to Hanover in order for him to leave England and his sight forever.

"The prince and the princess of Wales have established a rival court in Leicester House. This has infuriated the king, but the Prime Minister, Mr. Pelham, has used subtle and devious means to rob the prince of many of his supporters by offering them preferment in government positions. So the prince has to gain back public support to his side and against the king and his younger brother, the duke. Unfortunately, the duke is a hero following his defeat of the Prince Charles Edward in Scotland. But there is the beginning of a move in London against the duke, now that the news of the barbarity he's exhibiting to the Scottish people is becoming known.

"The arrest of Flora Macdonald, a heroine to the Scots, and especially a pregnant heroine, is a Godsend to the cause of the Prince of Wales. His Highness will ensure that you enjoy a constant stream of influential visitors to these rooms so that a groundswell will build against the duke and his father for keeping you in prison. You and your cause will become a talking point in London society, the only society in England which matters. This will cause severe problems for the government. And if your plans come to fruition, then your presence will rein in the ambitions of the duke, severely embarrass the king, and show that the Prince of Wales loves all of his people, especially the Scots, and not just those of England. There is a chance that the groundswell will be so great that it might force the king to abdicate in favor of his heir presumptive, my particular friend. This, my dear, is why you are carrying the weight of the Crown upon your shoulders."

Again, she stared at him, dumbstruck. "Me? But I'm not known. I'm nobody."

Lord Milius smiled in approval at her naivety. "My dear, with the prince's connections to high society, London will soon be close to revolution and the declaring of a republic when it learns of the treatment by the royal household of a pregnant heroine. Once London rallies behind a young, pregnant and pretty Scottish lass, brutally treated by the Butcher Duke of Cumberland . . . why, there's no telling to what lengths London will go."

She nodded. Her mind was still reeling with the extraordinary turn of events.

"Does that answer all your questions?" asked Lord Milius. "The Prince of Wales' preferment comes without cost to you, but you must act the part of the aggrieved heroine on his behalf. Of course, you must say nothing about the prince or his preferment, nor in any way imply that he instigated your cause. In time, he will speak on your behalf, but when he does, it will be to take up the cudgels of justice against his dastardly father and brother.

"Now, m'dear, understand clearly what I am going to say to you. Refuse the Prince of Wales this simple service, and you will immediately become anonymous, buried in the pits of this prison's dungeons, and almost certainly die a slow and agonizing death, along with your unborn child. But act the role of a pregnant heroine of Scotland, poorly done by the Butcher Duke, and you'll spend your pregnancy and confinement in the lap of luxury, treated by the very best physicians and barber surgeons, meeting the most brilliant and intelligent members of London society, and promoting the cause of your beloved Scottish people. The choice is entirely yours."

He sipped his coffee, while she remained silent, simply staring at him. For the first time since her early childhood, she was utterly lost for words. They remained looking at each other for many long moments, until she inclined her head with a slight nod. She had no other choice, both for herself and for her babe and because what Milius wanted her to do was tell the truth. Her nod was the acknowledgment, the agreement that Lord Milius knew for certain she'd give.

He stood to leave, shaking her hand with a studied formality. As he walked to the door, he said as an afterthought, "On the assumption you would agree with our little masquerade, I have sent a purse of gold to your parents and your fiancé with a letter explaining what has happened to you and where you are. The letter assures them that you are well and comfortable. The purse is to defray their traveling expenses to London. I assume that they'll all be here with you within the month."

"And if I had said 'no'?"

He smiled and said softly, "They would still have joined you. But none of you would have been nearly as comfortable."

He left. Flora continued to look at the door for half an hour, trying to come to terms with the wondrous enormity of what had befallen her. And the danger!

Le Château de Versailles, Paris

October 22, 1746

The previous month, there had been eight invitations every day, begging His Royal Highness the Prince Charles to grace the host with his glorious presence and attend luncheon or dinner or supper or a hunt. They were all delivered by white-gloved servants with respectful bows. Today, there was only one invitation, delivered in person by Madame de Pompadour's private secretary, M. Chamblaine, who placed it into the prince's anesthetized hand, saying without any formality or respect, "Young man. If you deign to accept Madame's particularly generous invitation, bearing in mind your recent activities, might I suggest that you shave and bathe and powder your wig. It will embarrass Madame greatly if appear as you are."

With that, the secretary walked away, and Prince Charles Edward grunted, closed his eyes, rolled over, and went back to sleep. He remained asleep for the entire day, while King Louis XV received petitioners and ministers and clerics and ambassadors. He snored when the court retired for luncheon at tables set up in the Salon de la Paix, as the weather was inclement and there was an October breeze that was judged too cold for the ladies. He slept when the court resumed for the afternoon and was presented with a one-act performance of a new play by M. Pierre Claude de la Chaussée that caused many of the ladies in the court to cry, and many of the men to burst into hysterical laughter. And he fell out of his bed and onto a rug on the floor while at that moment, in the Hall of Mirrors, a young man of great passion and intelligence called Denis Diderot, who wanted the king to subscribe to and support an encyclopedia that he was in the process of writing, gave a presentation of his views of the new Enlightenment. The king was less impressed with the concept of the Encyclopedia than was Madame de Pompadour, for he said that its assumption that the aristocracy must consider the welfare of the common classes as their greatest cause, would undermine the good order of France. But Madame de Pompadour had privately invited the philosopher to her chamber for dinner that night and particularly wanted the young Prince Charles to attend. Having most recently been in Scotland, which was the epicenter of the new Enlightenment movement, she thought that the prince and the philosopher might enjoy each other's company.

When they heard the thump, the prince's servants cautiously entered his bedchamber and lifted their prostrate master back into his bed. They reckoned that by the look and smell of him, he'd be sleeping for at least another four or five hours.

The heir to the Stuart throne awoke with a grunt and a snore, coughed, squinted at a clock on the mantle, and tried to determine the time of day. From the look of the dull light beyond the shutters, it was approaching evening, and in his addled state of mind, he tried to remember whether it was the evening of the day he had drunk to excess, or the following evening, meaning that he'd slept through another entire night and day, and his absence from the court would be cruelly discussed.

He sighed, and tried to stand up from his bed, but his legs were weak and his head felt as though it was full of liquid, and all he could do was to sit on the edge and hold his aching head in his hands.

"Pierre," he shouted. There was no response. He screamed for his servant again and heard the door to his chamber opening cautiously. The little man walked in.

"Majesty," he said. "How are you feeling now?"

"Have I been sick?" asked the prince.

"Drunk," said his servant. "Dead drunk. You've been asleep the entire day. I tried to wake you this morning, but you told me to go away. So I did. I brought you some meats and bread for luncheon, but I still couldn't rouse you. Dear God, Master, but you must have put some away last night. It took three of us to carry you back from the duchess' salon."

The prince tried to stop his head from spinning as he sought desperately to remember where he had been the previous night, and in whose salon he had become drunk. But for the life of him, he couldn't remember a single thing, and his pride wouldn't allow him to ask his servant, for such a question would be another tidbit of gossip that would get back to those ears that were aching to participate in his downfall because of his special relationship with the king's mistress.

"Get me a drink," he ordered.

"Coffee? Water?"

"Wine, you fool."

The servant walked over to the buffet and poured a glass of wine from the carafe. Charles drank it in one gulp. It made him feel better almost straight away. With restored strength, he stood, and ordered Pierre to fill the washtub with water so he could wash his face and the foul taste from his mouth.

As he walked unsteadily from his bed, he saw an invitation on the floor. Normally he'd have left it there, but he noticed that this invitation bore the crest of Madame de Pompadour. As he bent to pick it up, Pierre said, "Monsieur Chamblaine brought it after lunch. I tried to stop him coming into your bedchamber, but he brushed me aside. He's very rude and presumptuous, isn't he! Anyway, as he left, he ordered me to ensure that when you returned from the dead, you were to read it so that a reply could be sent before the evening."

Prince Charles squinted to try to read the words that floated on the card. He was invited to supper after ten o'clock to be entertained by some man called Diderot. But the important thing wasn't who was coming to the salon but that he had received the invitation from the king's mistress. His mood quickly brightened. Memory of the previous night was beginning to return to his addled brain. It had been a gathering in the chambers of the Duc de Vérone, one of the minor dignitaries of the court, a man who didn't even rank as worthy of the king's eyesight. He and his young and attractive wife were positioned in the ranks of the audience chamber furthest from the Crown. The prince normally wouldn't have noticed one such as him, except that his wife, the duchess, had approached him when he was sitting in the gardens beside a fountain, trying to clear his head from the previous night's spectacular drinking session. She had inveigled him to attend a gathering that night in her husband's apartments and as she bent over his prostrate form, one of her breasts had accidentally slipped out of her bodice. It was a beautiful breast, round and ripe, and when the prince had stared hard enough at it, she had giggled, placed his hand upon her nipple, and assured him that there would be much more if he were to grace their presence that night.

The evening had begun boisterously, with a dozen or more very minor couples invited especially to meet and entertain His Highness the Prince of the House of Stuart, knowing full well that the prince was the special friend of the king's particular friend, Madame de Pompadour. And as the night progressed, the other couples were ushered away by the duc until there was only the three of them in his chamber. By then the prince had consumed two liters of wine, half a flask of brandy, and eaten six courses of food. The duc, apologizing sincerely and profusely for having to retire early, citing urgent court business the following morning, had left the prince alone with his wife, the duchess.

He blanched as he tried to remember what had happened next. He clearly remembered her feeding him grapes, then exposing her breasts and using one of them as a napkin to wipe his mouth. Then he remembered her skillful hands and how they had removed his trousers and coat and exposed him to the flickering candles. He remembered her delicate body, full yet lithe. And he remembered exploding and crying and something else. And then he recalled that he'd mistaken her name. She told him that it was Clodine, not Flora. And he had burst into paroxysms of tears, forcing her to dress quickly and call for his servants. The rest of the evening, if there was a rest, was a blur of corridors and struggles and assurances from his manservant Pierre that everything would be all right.

The prince splashed water over his face and looked at himself in the mirror. He was gray with exhaustion, his eyes were red-rimmed with frustration, and he bore the unkempt uniform of a wastrel. He sat down hard on a chair and wondered how it had all come to this. In only a month, he had returned to France a failed hero; he had been feted by the king; he had been taken up as a favorite by the king's mistress giving him access to the king's private ear; yet despite his entreaties, the king continued to refuse to finance another army and expedition to England to enable him to attempt again to take the throne back from the Hanoverians.

And for the past month, he had drunk, eaten, and cavorted around Versailles like a buffoon, causing offense to the king and his chamberlains and ministers and especially to the cardinal and the other churchmen who had the ear of the pope.

Yet he seemed to be driven to excess and knew that he was becoming a scandal in the court. Even though he knew he should control his behavior, the drink, and the food and the women were taking control of his life.

But the invitation from Madame de Pompadour to meet this person Diderot was a lifeline. If he could moderate his drinking, clean himself up, refrain from eating everything presented to him, and speak as a prince and not as an inebriated coxcomb, then perhaps Madame de Pompadour's largess might grow and he could find his way back into the glittering circle a man of his rank should occupy.

Determined, he stood and saw that Pierre was cleaning and airing the bed. He fussed around picking up this and putting away that. It was of no concern to the prince, who had to decide what outfit he would wear for the madame's soiree that evening. He entered his closet and began to choose.

In the bedroom, Pierre was putting the night's rubbish into a sack. On the floor, under the bed, was a strangely shaped leaf. No, not a leaf, so much as a frond. He picked it up and smelled it. There was the faintest aroma of a long-departed perfume, a delicate and gentle scent of fields and honey and summertime. It was pleasant. Perhaps it was something that the prince had brought back with him from Scotland.

He put it into his rubbish sack and left the room.

# Chapter Thirteen

THE TOWER OF LONDON

OCTOBER 17, 1746

Her maid, who had been loaned to Flora by the wife of Lord Milius, told her that she looked very charming for the coming meeting. But when Flora looked in the mirror and took particular note of the woman staring back at her, well, there was no word for it but stunning. Without the benefit of more than a small and pitted mirror of burnished bronze in the entire household at Armadale in Skye, she was rarely ever able to catch a glimpse of anything other than her face unless she looked down at her reflection in a very still loch. But to have a large mirror standing on a side dresser, and able to see her hair and her bosom and all the way down to her waist, was something she found vicariously shocking and particularly exciting. It was an amazing device, pure glass coated with a silver substance that she'd been told was called Mercury. And in it, she could see her reflection perfectly.

Had it not been for the growing bulge in her stomach, she would have been presentable at a royal ball. Her hair was immaculately dressed with bows and ribbons of green and gold, her neck was adorned by a sumptuous necklace of rubies and sapphires loaned to her by Milius, her dress, also loaned from Milius' home, was lilac and white and low cut so that the upper bulge of her breasts became both visible and rounded in the fashion of London society.

Her mother Anne entered the chamber and looked at her daughter. She beamed a smile and gave a mock curtsy. But when she ascended from her genuflection, she said to Flora, "If Hugh sees you with half your bosom exposed to the world, lass, he'll have apoplexy. Don't you think it's immodest to be seen in that fashion?"

"Yes," said Flora, "but all the society ladies dress in this way. Anyway, mother, I'm a prisoner in the Tower of London and hardly likely to step out in style on the streets of Maida Vale or Kensington Green, now am I?"

"It's not where you go, Flora darling, but how you think of yourself that matters. Dress like a loose woman and you'll think and act like a loose woman."

Flora smiled. "But in the eyes of the world, mother, I am a loose woman. I'm pregnant and not married."

"And does that make you the first unmarried mother since Adam and Eve were expelled from the Garden of Eden? No, lass, so long as you're pregnant with the child of your beloved, everybody will understand. Even Hugh has accepted that his wonderful stepdaughter won't be a maid at her wedding.

"But who is calling on you this afternoon? So many people! And I still don't understand why they're all coming to see you and pay you court, when you're imprisoned for treason against their king. Surely they'd be avoiding one such as you as though you were carrying the plague."

"It's complicated, mother, but suffice to say that those who are visiting me and paying their respects are no friends of the king of England. Rather, they're friends of his son, the heir to the throne, the Prince of Wales," she explained. "The Prince of Wales hates his father, and I am being used to promote the prince's cause. Does that make it clear?"

But from the look on her face, it was apparent that it didn't. It was the third or fourth time she'd held this conversation, but still her mother couldn't understand why she was living in such luxurious circumstances when she was a prisoner. Nothing in London made sense to Anne, and what she knew she should do was to take her husband back to Skye and return to her life as a farmer's wife. But with a maid serving her tea and cakes whenever she wanted, with all her meals prepared by the cooks that came early in the morning just to spend all day cooking for whoever entered, with a large four-poster bed with a huge and capacious mattress in which she and Hugh had enjoyed some rare and vicarious moments of pleasures, and now that she was meeting lords and ladies and important people, she had delayed her return several times and was coming to terms with being here for a number of months more.

Scotland, after all, was not a very pleasant place in the dead and dark of mid-winter, whereas London's streets were ablaze with lights and the shops were full of dresses and bolts of cloth and bows and ribbons and wondrous things from over the seas in America or on the continent or silk from as far as China, and she could wander along any road and purchase a bag full of delicious hot chestnuts or a bag of warm pork crackling or a roasted potato and just about anything else. And every time her purse was empty, Flora filled it again from her bedside cabinet that seemed to be continually full of money. It was all too mysterious, and she preferred to close her mind. It was enough that Hugh understood.

Flora's maid put the finishing touches to painting her mistress' face from the pot of rouge, ensured that her dress was sufficiently revealing but delicately demur to satisfy all inspection, and retired to her salon to await Mr. Samuel Richardson. She had been told that he was a respectable printer, and had written a very well received book some years earlier called *Pamela* that had caused a sensation among the intelligent people of London. She had not, of course, read it but was told that it dealt with a serving wench who spent the entire book defending her honor and chastity against an evil employer.

Lord Milius had told her that the sensation was continuing and that all London was now divided between Pamelists and Anti-Pamelists. The first believed in honor and sanctity and virtue above all else; the second believed in lasciviousness and free-thought and were against religion and felt that Mr. Richardson was a hypocrite and a bigot, and had written a cheap work of lewdness and impiety to scandalize all London. If that was the case, then he was also scandalizing all of Europe, because his book had been translated and published in France and Italy and even Russia.

Quite why Mr. Richardson wanted to attend her, neither she nor Lord Milius knew, but he assured her that a visit from a writer as famous as Mr. Richardson would quickly become a talking point in London society and would mitigate strongly in her favor. So important was Mr. Richardson's visit that within moments of it happening, news would spread to the coffee houses. The reporters who worked for *The Tattler* would hear of the news and report it so that it would be printed in one of the thrice-weekly editions. This would then be further printed in pamphlets and picked up by polite society during their evening soirees. It would take a mere few days before news of the visit reached the royal court, which would place further and intolerable pressure upon the king. Milius had kissed her hand and then embraced her on both cheeks and seemed to be in a genuine state of excitement before leaving her and returning to report the events to the Prince of Wales.

When they had first connived, and she had become part of his great scheme to embarrass the king, he had treated her as though she were a servant; but he had watched carefully the way she had held court with the many great men and women who had come to see her in her prison chambers and met them with openness, honesty, and wit. He recognized in her an innocence and ingenuousness that he found appealing, and he now treated her both as a co-conspirator and as a genuine friend. Flora was so unlike the many women who graced London society, from the palace down to the humbler households of minor nobility. In her, there was none of a society woman's artifice that so delighted their men folk; Flora had none of the skill of verbal thrust and parry in which these women were so skilled, but when she spoke, it was always sensible, insightful, intelligent, and precise. She concerned herself more with what her thoughts conveyed than the wit with which they were spoken. She thought what she should say and then said it, telling people who didn't necessarily want to hear it what she considered the truth. More often than not, the intelligent men and women of London walked away from

Flora's prison apartment with a feeling of refreshment and delight at having been in her company. Milius spoke about this simple Scottish lady so often that his wife had quipped he should perhaps move into her prison cell.

And for her part, Flora had met so many important and interesting people, that she eagerly anticipated Mr. Richardson's arrival. He was expected at any moment, and so she rearranged her dress and sat staring at the door to her salon. She had barely been seated for more than ten minutes, when she heard footsteps in the corridor. There was a knock on the door, and her maid walked in, introducing Mr. Richardson. He was much older and portlier than she'd expected. The writers who had come to meet her on previous occasions were generally young and raffish, full of their own self-importance, and talking at her rather than listening to what she had to say.

She had no way of knowing whether or not this was part of the writers' trade, for Flora had never before met with anyone who had written anything, and she found their way of talking particularly exciting, especially writers who imagined stories about events that hadn't happened. So when Mr. Richardson walked into the salon, puffing from the exertion of climbing the stairs, he really wasn't what she expected. Indeed, he was of a very much more mature tendency than she could have imagined.

She stood as he entered, and her maid introduced them. He bowed; she bowed. They sat opposite each other, and the maid brought both of them tea while Mr. Richardson tried to compose himself from the long climb to the top of the tower, wheezing like an elderly ailing dog and constantly mopping his brow with a very large green kerchief.

"Forgive me, ma'am, but I'm not as young as once I was, and the steps were really very steep. I am no longer a well man, and my exertions afflict me. I am suffering from the gout and also from phlegmatic congestion of the lungs."

He struggled to a seat, waved around his large kerchief, and wiped his forehead and face before saying, "How do you do, Mistress Macdonald. I've been looking forward to our meeting. You may or may not know this, but although I am not by any means a Jacobite, I have followed your trials and tribulations with a great deal of sympathy and believe that your incarceration in this nether region of Hades is a national disgrace. I have said so in a letter I wrote to Mr. Pelham, and I have also sent a copy of this same letter to the editor of the Daily Courant. In time, I hope to write also to Mr. Benjamin Franklin who has just begun to publish magazines in America, for our colonies should be informed about what their king is doing in their name to his citizens."

"I thank you, sir, for your consideration," she said.

He waved his hand in the air, as though it was a mere trifle. "To think of a lady in a delicate condition being incarcerated in a prison is unconscionable. It will not do!" he said, sipping his tea.

"Mr. Richardson, I am very grateful for your concern, but my plight is as nothing compared with the plight of other Scottish men and women who are daily being butchered by the Duke of Cumberland."

"Yes, ma'am. I know all about the damnable duke and his nefarious activities. I'm not sure whether you're familiar with the greatest voice of the English language, Mr. Shakespeare, but in one of his marvelous and profound speeches from his play concerning a certain Merchant of Venice, the person who portrays a judge says that mercy becomes the throne'd monarch better than his crown, the attribute of awe and majesty, wherein doth sit the dread and fear of kings. But then, ma'am, he goes on to say that mercy is above the sceptre'd sway, it is enthroned in the hearts of kings, it is an attribute of God himself, and earthly power doth then show likest God's when mercy seasons justice.

"Do you understand the import of that, Mistress Macdonald? Mercy must season and temper justice for we cannot live in a land which is devoid of morality. Further, ma'am, in a land with no justice, there shall be no peace for its citizenry. And that's precisely why so many of us in England detest the Duke of Cumberland and what he and the king are doing. For having won such a monumental victory over the Scots, mercy should have tempered their desire for revenge. The Jacobites had to be turned back at Derby. It was wrong for them to attempt to capture England. But the Duke of Cumberland, having killed so many, driven so many from their homes, salted their lands like some conquering Pharaoh from the Book of Exodus, should have shown your people mercy and beneficence. But what have he and his German father done? They have created hatred of the English people by the Scots, and more trouble will ensue. Mark my words, ma'am. More trouble will ensue."

"But forgive me, sir, I don't understand how you as an Englishman can oppose your king? Much as I'm gratified by your comments and appreciate them, surely that is as treasonous as the crime of which I've been accused? I'm only a simple woman, Mr. Richardson and even though I have met some wondrously clever people since my incarceration, it still mystifies me that so many are against the king, yet are still able to speak their minds freely."

Richardson smiled. "A simple woman, perhaps, but an honorable woman. You fought valiantly for your ruler of the House of Stuart and you risked everything, including your life in an open rowboat around the islands of Scotland in a fierce storm. I shall write about you, just as I wrote some years ago about another woman of honor called Pamela.

"As to your question concerning treason and our opposition to the Crown, I'm delighted to say, ma'am, that we in England elect our leaders, if not our rulers. When our rulers become too autocratic, like Charles I, we chop off their heads. That soon brings aristocracy to its senses. Unfortunately, because Queen Anne died without live issue, we have had to import these Germans from Hanover and they've brought their Hanoverian habits with them, habits of brutality, ignorance, greed, mendacity, internecine hatreds, utter humorlessness, and distressing fecundity. With the number of children they seem to produce, there'll be no getting rid of them."

He burst out laughing at his own comments, mopped his face again, and continued, "That's why you are such a celebrity among the intelligentsia and those of us who lead the movement to enlighten our nation. Because we view you as a courageous woman, honest and moral and honorable."

She smiled and nodded in gratitude. "Like your Pamela?"

"Like my Pamela."

She decided to be very wicked. Lord Milius told her that she must behave like a London lady, to smile and nod and acknowledge, but the Hebridean Flora was itching to get out. He'd told her, "People come to see you, m'dear, because you are a heroine, and not a philosopher. Let them walk away from your salon thinking of you as a woman driven to destitution by the cruelty of the king and his son. I don't want them walking away regarding you as a free thinker or a radical."

And she had played her part with consummate ease. In many cases, when men and women of great education had visited her, she had nodded and smiled and remained as silent and grateful as she could until they began to treat her as though she were a favorite lap dog. It was then that her Scottish upbringing wouldn't be silenced, and she said those things that were in her heart. In other cases, when the gentlemen had talked to her of literature or philosophy, she had wanted to contribute and did so with gusto.

But Mr. Richardson was just too tempting a target for her wickedness. She said to him, "You know, Mr. Richardson, I was visited by a gentleman writer just the other week. He was a certain Mr. Henry Fielding. His book *Shamela* is said to be very popular. Did you write about your Pamela as a result of reading his?"

Richardson grew red-faced. "The contrary, ma'am. Mr. Fielding is a hypocrite and a satirist. My book *Pamela, a Virtue Rewarded* is as fine a work of morality as has ever been written and was printed a year before Fielding's disgraceful work. My book is a sincere inquiry through the medium of letters of the woes of an honest and industrious young servant girl who fights for her honor against the immorality of her master. Fielding read it and accused me openly of hypocrisy and of pandering to base instincts."

She showed that she was startled by his sudden vehemence but had to bite the inside of her cheek to prevent herself from bursting out laughing. Mr. Richardson was so pompous and easy to mock.

Without pausing for breath, he continued, "Yet I tell you ma'am, it is his Shamela, not my Pamela, which is the work of utter depravity, for in it, he depicts a promiscuous servant girl using the pretense of coyness and mock modesty to ensnare some poor young man into marriage. I beg you, Mistress Macdonald, if you are to be my particular friend, not to mention that disgraceful book nor Mr. Fielding's name in my presence, ever again."

He took out his kerchief yet again and wiped his brow. She didn't know whether to apologize or refute his argument but remembered Lord Milius' instructions, and nodded sagely and remained quiet. But she was rapidly coming to the conclusion that the wars between writers in London was of a severity with the war between armies on the battlefields of Scotland.

VERSAILLES, PARIS

FEBRUARY 17, 1747

The private secretary to Madame de Pompadour, M. Henri-Marie Chamblaine, sighed and said to his Mistress, "Madame, you cannot."

Madame de Pompadour repeated, for the fifth time, "Why not?"

"Because Madame, he is a drunkard and a wastrel and filthy and a sot and lascivious and a womanizer. He was rude and imperious with your guest M. Denis Diderot, following which you banned him from your salon, yet now you are considering inviting him yet again, just so that he can make a fool of himself with his drunken revels and cause a sensation around your person.

"He is a disgrace to the House of Stuart, an embarrassment to your particular friend, Louis, the talk of the court, and a scandalizer. He has turned his back on the Holy Catholic Church, he walks the corridors and salons of the palace trying to seduce anything in a dress, from the lowest serving wench to the highest ranks of the nobility. The ladies of the court now send their servants on ahead to ensure that they don't suddenly come upon the prince in a corridor. His behavior is both unpredictable and appalling. He is dishonorable, wicked, cruel. Madame, I could go on and on about his affairs, his fights with members of the Cabinet and the Ministry, but to do so would be to soil your ears. In short, Madame, you cannot receive him."

Madame de Pompadour nodded and said softly, "He is a prince of the realm. He is a future king of England. Yes, he has been drunk and rude in my presence, but I believe he has become so because of the treatment he has received in our Court and that given the proper circumstances, his soul can be redeemed and then he will become again as he was. All he needs is some of Louis' money and an army, and he will repeat the victories he enjoyed in Scotland and England, but this time, he will win. He will fight the Germans and he will oust them, and Charles will be crowned king of England. Of this, I'm certain.

"Don't you remember him when he first came to our courts, Chamblaine? He was magnificent. He was a most impressive young man. The man you see today is a creation of the frustration of Louis' refusal to assist him in winning back his throne. He is shunned by the entire court and spends night after night in his own chambers, alone with his one remaining servant, drinking himself into a stupor. So I ask again, why can I not invite a prince of the House of Stuart into my salon to meet with Voltaire and my other gentlemen. I've also invited M. Jean-Jacques Rousseau,"

Chamblaine looked at her in astonishment. "Rousseau? But Voltaire and Rousseau detest each other."

Madame de Pompadour smiled. "Yes, I know. It'll make a great scandal. It'll keep the court occupied for days."

Chamblaine shook his head. "Rousseau will never come if he knows Voltaire will be here."

"We shall see. I have my ways."

"I know, Madame, but even if he does come, do you really expect M. Voltaire and M. Rousseau to sit at the same table as the Prince Charles? The young man's reputation has spread throughout France."

She was about to answer him, when he spoke over her and continued, "And it also concerns me that you are inviting M. Voltaire to the palace when he is living in a certain situation with the Marquise du Chatelet in Luneville? It's a scandal, Madame, and the friend of the king of France should not become involved."

Madame de Pompadour struck him on the arm with her fan and laughed. "You're such a prig, Chamblaine. The Court eats and breathes scandals. It's the blood which flows through the body of Versailles. Nobody cares about M. Voltaire's romance with a certain lady. Not today, anyway. And as to the prince, his servant assures my maid that Charles will be completely sober and that he will bathe, shave, wear clean and fresh garments and a powdered wig, and appear respectable. Don't you see, my dear, if I offer him this lifeline, it might turn him around and make him respectable again. Surely it's the very least I can offer to a man of royal blood?"

Her secretary sighed and said, "And what will your particular friend think if he knows you're entertaining Prince Charles? It's well known that the king is horrified by the way in which the prince has become a drunkard in so short a space of time. If there was little chance of French help for his plans to conquer England when he first returned from Scotland, when he was sober and respectable, then surely you must appreciate that there's no chance at all of any help being given today to a man who sleeps the entire day and drinks the entire night.

"Madame, I know you think I'm old fashioned and conventional, but be assured of my love and devotion to you, and my fear for your reputation should this young man be invited into your salon."

As the evening drew on, Henri-Marie Chamblaine felt an increased sense of trepidation. He could cope with a verbal tussle between two philosophers of the intellectual standing of the middle-aged colossus Voltaire and the young and zealous Rousseau; but to have the mistress to the king of France involved in an ugly scene with a rake and philanderer and drunkard was too dangerous. The French court relished a scandal, but not one involving either the king or his particular friend. If Madame suddenly found herself excluded from the king's bedroom because she was the epicenter of too-great a scandal for the king to ignore, then he too would find himself excluded from the highest echelons of power, and the position of power he now held courtesy of the

Marquise de Pompadour was something for which he'd worked and connived all his grown life.

There was enough scandal already because of the king of France having an affair with a commoner. But a scandal involving the commoner was too dangerous and her position in the king's boudoir still too precarious.

She had to remain the king's favorite for the next several years if his plans were to come to fruition. The chateau on the Loire was almost his, but he still had to earn enough to purchase a noble title. Then he had to guarantee that his money would last his own and his children's lifetimes—following that Madame de Pompadour could do whatever she wanted.

His family had, except for the interruption of his father, tied their fortunes to the kings of France. His grandfather had been secretary to the Sun King's mistress, Madame de Maintenon, and had acquired great wealth and status. His father had drunk and gambled away the fortune, but when the Sun King's great grandson became Louis XV, M. Chamblaine seized his chance and petitioned for a position in the court.

He had first worked as undersecretary to a minor functionary and minister and had been a drudge and amanuensis, but his chance came when he met and befriended Madame de Pompadour. Lowborn as Jeanne-Antoinette Poisson, nonetheless, she was blessed with a father who was steward to the most powerful moneymen in France. Somehow, the adorable woman had connived to meet Voltaire, who was fascinated and entranced by her. And when Voltaire brought her to Court, it was Henri-Marie Chamblaine, a man who stood at the back of the room, who instantly recognized a beauty that would capture the heart of the king.

Connivance was everything in France, and so he contrived to have her positioned in the most visible place possible for the engagement ceremony of the Dauphin. His scheme had worked, and Jeanne-Antoinette began her meteoric rise into the French court's firmament. And as promised, she took him with her. Yes, he was merely a secretary, but he had the ear of the woman who had the ear of the king, and he was earning a fortune from those who wanted access.

But one false move on Madame de Pompadour's part, one whiff of scandal, one momentary cause for the king to look at her and question her motives or judgment, and the entire edifice he'd created would come tumbling down on their heads. And Prince Charles Edward Stuart was just such a cause.

But there was no changing her mind, and so he was forced to accept the dangers of the evening and determine ways of limiting its damage.

In the beginning, the evening was relatively pleasant. To Chamblaine's surprise, the Prince Charles Edward Stuart had arrived looking smart, confident, clean, and most importantly, sober. Whoever had whispered words into his ear had obviously had a good effect. The prince arrived first, ten minutes too early at just past a quarter to ten o'clock. The Madam was still entertaining the king in his suite of rooms, and so the prince sat alone drinking a light Chablis that Chamblaine didn't think could do him much harm. He picked delicately at the *petit fours* for several minutes, but when the waiters entered carrying trays of poached fish, capons, duck, chicken legs, *foie gras, canapés*, and veal stuffed with herbs and spices, he took a dinner plate over to the buffet without waiting for any other guests to arrive, and most rudely, without waiting for the hostess' permission, filled it to capacity. The prince saw no reason why he should offer an explanation for his hunger to a mere secretary, and so he sat in a corner of the salon and ate.

At five minutes past the hour of ten, François-Marie Arouet de Voltaire was introduced by the master of ceremonies, and as he entered the salon, looked around in surprise that apart from a young man gorging himself on a plate piled with food, he was the only one present. He beamed a smile at Chamblaine who nodded toward the corner where the prince had seated himself, and shrugged. Voltaire looked carefully once again at the young man whom he'd already noticed and saw that he was tall, drawn, and somewhat haggard. He was eating as though he'd never seen food before. Yet from his dress, he was obviously rich and well appointed.

He walked over to the young man and bowed, saying, "Voltaire."

The prince wiped his face and his hands on a napkin and remained seated, according to the hierarchy of his rank. "Charles Edward, Prince of the House of Stuart."

"Ah!" beamed Voltaire, "conqueror and conquered in one body. I've looked forward to meeting you, young man. I'd heard that you were an undertaking of Madame de Pompadour, but voices told me that you were more in need of an undertaker than a patron. I'm surprised to see you in Madame's salon, but I shall look forward to talking to you about your adventures."

Before the prince had a chance to respond, Voltaire had turned and was walking over to speak with Chamblaine when the master of ceremonies threw open the door, and introduced a tall and wan young man, shouting out to the nearly empty room, "Monsieur Jean-Jacques Rousseau."

Voltaire turned and looked in shock at the young man who entered the salon.

"Rousseau," he spat in horror.

"Voltaire," said Rousseau, equally appalled at the presence of his *bête-noir*.

"You were invited?" said Voltaire. "Madame de Pompadour asked you to be present?"

The young man walked into the center of the large room and stood face to face with Voltaire. "I was asked to attend in order to expound upon my philosophy of the responsibility of the State to its citizens. I certainly didn't expect to see you here. But in retrospect, it's logical that Madame de Pompadour would want to have by her side a man with the skill to lick her feet at the same time as he's eating her food."

"And now I can understand the reason for your presence, Rousseau," snapped Voltaire, "for who else in France but you can compare the glory of our surroundings with the savagery of the jungle which seems to attract you so much. Tell me, have you brought any of your savages with you today?"

"Why bring savages when this room is full of them?" Rousseau responded.

"You would bite the hand that feeds you?"

"There is enough food here to feed half of Paris. We gorge ourselves while citizens starve. If the king is the state, and Madame de Pompadour is the comfort of the state, what responsibility does the state have for those who are the foundations of its buildings? Treat badly the props which hold up the state, and the state will collapse."

Chamblaine walked over to separate the two men, but before he could say anything, the master of ceremonies again threw open the door of the salon, and announced Madame de Pompadour. She was ushered into the chamber and walked over to the two philosophers, shaking their hands and making them both welcome. Then she walked over to Prince Charles, who stood and bowed. She extended her hand, and he kissed her enormous diamond ring.

"I'm so very pleased that you accepted my invitation to supper, my dear Prince. It's been too long since we've met," she said.

"I am greatly honored that you remembered me, ma'am. I am aware of how difficult this invitation must have been for you to extend, and I assure you of my very best intentions," he said.

Chamblaine breathed a sigh of relief and introduced Rousseau to the prince. Having just returned from Switzerland, Rousseau had not heard about the scandals surrounding the prince's recent history at Versailles, but he knew of him as the man who had tried to regain his family throne from the Hanoverians. He bowed, and Madame de Pompadour invited everybody to sit and eat so that after their supper, they could begin their discussions.

"Is nobody else coming?" asked Rousseau.

Madame de Pompadour smiled and shook her head. "A soiree should have a large measure of both genius and courage to keep all of the guests entertained. There is enough genius in the minds of the philosophers in this room for a dozen salons, and His Royal Highness has exhibited enough bravery for an entire army of men."

As they took their food, the prince returned to his place and continued eating. Chamblaine noticed with increasing concern that the prince had already finished his glass of Chablis and was now pouring himself a glass of Madeira. He also noticed a bottle of Burgundy had been seconded and was on the floor beside the prince's seat. For a reason that worried Chamblaine, the prince looked as though he was beginning to feel uncomfortable with present company. It might be necessary for him to find a reason to distract the prince, suggest he leaves the salon, and have him escorted back to his suite of rooms. It would cause much gossip, but at least it would remove any scandal from Madame's door.

Madame de Pompadour turned to the prince and asked, "Highness, why are you removing yourself from our presence? Why sit on your own, when you could be sitting with the two greatest minds in all of France?"

"I feel myself unequal to sit in the presence of your friends, ma'am. Though I am highborn, your friends are known to me and tower over my stature in their genius. I am a mere prince. How can a mere prince compete with intellectual kings such as Voltaire and Rousseau?"

Voltaire sought permission from the hostess to answer. "Sir, to act in a truly modest fashion, a man must first be very arrogant. Neither Rousseau nor I would separate ourselves from the light which illumines in the court of France, for anywhere else and we would be diminished. We, my philosopher opponent and I, think very differently about the world, yet no matter how different our paths, we accept that we have the same end in sight, which is the betterment of our society. Yet while we think, we do not act. We see our worlds in our minds. You, on the other hand, my dear Prince, are a man of action. A man who does, rather than a man who speaks. You see your world in the stark reality of a battlefield, where life and death, victory and defeat are of the same coin but just the thickness of a sword apart.

"You, Highness, are a soldier, and while we philosophers connive and cogitate and consider, you are in the field of battle, facing the sword and

256 • Alan Gold

the dagger and the gun. So put away this false modesty, young man; have done with it; join us and tell us about your adventures. Her Grace has no doubt heard our philosophical arguments many times, and we can gain little from further explanation, except to add incrementally to the scales in which our arguments are balanced. But you have tales of gunpowder and shot and tactics which will fill an entire night with vicarious adventure."

The prince stood, and brought his plate across to the table at which the others were seated. He also carried the bottle of wine, which he poured into a new glass and drank in one mouthful, filling it a second time.

"You want to hear about life on the battlefield, do you Voltaire? Do you, as well, Rousseau? What do you want to hear? That it's all flutter-ing flags and gallant men marching and singing patriotic songs, and in an hour, we're victorious and have gained all of our objectives? I could have gained all my objectives and had my flag fluttering above St. James's Palace in London right at this moment if King Louis had come to my aid.

"So is that what you want to hear, Philosopher? About my failures. For they're well enough known. In the end, does it matter how many soldiers on either side die, just so long as one side is victorious? Does it matter how many women are widowed, how many parents will never see their sons again? Is that what you want me to tell you?

"For if it is, then it's obvious that you've never set foot near a battlefield, because if you had, you'd never want to talk about it. You'd have seen the bloodied corpses and twisted limbs and headless bodies and men scream-ing in agony and begging for death to relieve them of their pain," he said.

The prince drank another full glass of wine and refilled it from the bottle. Chamblaine looked in concern at what he was doing, and indicated his concern to Madame de Pompadour, who nodded in reassurance, though he knew her well enough to know that she was becoming concerned.

"My dear Prince," said Rousseau, "Voltaire and I may not have . . ."

"Silence Philosopher, and listen to a soldier prince tell you about the realities of life in a war . . ."

And for the next many minutes, to the increasing discomfort of the Hostess and the two other guests, Prince Charles Edward Stuart drank and told them about his glorious victory at Prestonpans, of reaching Derby in England and being forced to turn back because of the cowardice of his commanders, of his betrayal by King Louis of France who needed to send only ten thousand men and England could have been Charles', and of the ignominious defeat at Culloden Moor. And as he reached the climax of his story, he finished another bottle of wine and indicated to the waiter to fetch another.

By the time he'd completed his journey from enthusiasm to victory to defeat to frustration, he had already consumed two entire bottles, as well as half of another one. It was time to put the diatribe to an end.

Madame de Pompadour looked at Chamblaine and indicated her apology. He had been right all along. It was silly to think that the prince could be redeemed. She put her hand on his arm and said gently, "Highness, don't you think that it's time to stop drinking. After all . . ."

He turned to her and sneered. "You dare touch me? You, a commoner, the daughter of clerk, dare touch the heir to the thrones of England and Scotland. You dare tell me to stop drinking . . ."

Voltaire and Rousseau reeled back in shock. Both were about to berate him for his extraordinary offensiveness, but they didn't have an opportunity. Chamblaine stepped forward and grasped the prince by the arms, hauling him out of the chair. "Her Grace dares do whatever she wants, young man, for she is the particular friend of the world's most powerful man, and you patently are not. It's time for you to leave her apartments. And if you know what's good for you, you'll leave Versailles this evening and never consider returning, for if you do, you will be shunned by everybody in the court. Return to Italy, Prince Charles and don't ever seek our companionship again."

THE TOWER OF LONDON

MARCH 21, 1747

Flora Macdonald screamed in agony and looked at the man who was holding the evil instruments of torture. Her face was contorted in pain, her hands white and she was near to drawing blood from where her nails were biting into her flesh. She swore at her torturer and said to him, "Dear God in heaven, for if I survive this, I'll kill you with my own bare hands, you spur-galled scut. Have you no mercy. Put an end to this. I'll do anything."

He bent over her and turned to the woman standing beside him. "Soon," he said. Then he lifted her skirts and felt between her legs, but Flora didn't know what he was doing for the pain was too great.

The woman standing beside him looked into the most private regions of Flora's body and could see the advance of the babe's head. She washed the vagina with vinegar and peppermint water and soaked her hands in the solution. Then she gently grasped the baby's head as Flora screamed in the agony of the contraction. The doctor offered the midwife the instrument he used for pulling the head of a large baby out of the womb, but she knew from looking that the babe would come out with the next contraction and refused the offer.

A twist, a tug, another twist, and as Flora screamed, she eased the babe's head, then shoulders, and then his entire body out of Flora and into a swaddling cloth.

Flora stopped screaming, and her entire body deflated like a winded bagpipe. She lay back and closed her eyes in the blessed relief, hearing the midwife smack the babe's bottom. There was an echoing yell that reverberated off the walls of the chamber, and the door suddenly burst open and Flora's mother, father, and fiancé rushed in.

"A boy," said the midwife. "A very fine boy."

Softly, as she received the babe from the midwife's arms, her voice harsh and raw from yelling in pain during the birth, Flora whispered, "He shall be called James Charles Stuart Macdonald."

There was to be no argument.

# Part Three

# Chapter Fourteen

HALIFAX, IN THE ROYAL COLONY OF NORTH CAROLINA
THE DOMINION OF AMERICA

JULY 23, 1772

The air she breathed from the rowboat was different, subtly, yet unmistakably different. After day upon day cramped inside an ocean-going vessel smelling nothing but the salt-tang aroma of the ocean mixed with the stench of dank wood and rotting ropes, she'd thought that this trip in the rowboat up the river would refresh only her eyes and her heart. She did not expect it to enliven her sense of smell, but she was wrong. For while the air was warm and perfumed, full of fluttering leaves and floating pollen that drifted past her boat to the accompaniment of an orchestral drone of bees and the incessant tympany of insects, it was the fragrance of the air that captured her interest. In Scotland, the air didn't smell of anything other than when the heather was in season. The air of North America, though, exuded perfume from its trees and flowers and grasses. The sweet smell of freedom was everywhere.

The undulating land through which the river ran was replete with potential, as it should be. It was a new land, full of promise and excitement, and although she was beyond her fiftieth year and at a time of her life when she should be sitting in a rocking chair covered by a blanket, with her gray hair pinned up instead of fluttering in the breeze, she was eagerly viewing a strange and unfamiliar landscape with trees and leaves of a different shape and quality to those she'd lived with all her life. There were sights she'd never seen before, smells she'd never experienced and the excitement of tastes and touches that were to come.

If she were like the other women of the Highlands, those few who remained after the mass murders and evictions by the late and unlamented Duke of Cumberland, she would have been playing with her grandchildren in some Highland garden and supervising her sons and daughters living their own lives. So few remained in Scotland, and all the talk was of further emigrations, whether voluntary or enforced. The English were populating all Scotland with their flocks and herds, and since the policy of *Fuadach nan Gàidheal*, the expulsion of all people who were Gaelic, nobody looked at the Scottish hills and lochs and saw their ancestral land anymore, only land that the English would now claim as their own.

But for Flora, these were issues of the past. In her heart, she was singing as though she was a twenty-year-old. And this was the way it had been since her feet left English soil for the last time. Others on the ship had travelled in trepidation, fearful of sinking or drowning or being victims to piracy or some foreign navy, but Flora found every moment of the sea journey a thrilling experience, from the disappearance of the Liverpool coastline to the vastness of the Atlantic Ocean, to the strange fish that the sailors pulled from the sea, to the huge beasts called dolphin that swam beside their ship ducking and weaving as though playing a game and whose eyes she looked into and truly believed that they could tell what she was thinking.

The air was redolent with the scents of pine and birch and elm and oak, as well as the bouquet of other foliage that she had yet to identify. She trailed her hand in the warm water. She had been gazing dreamily at the riverbank as it flowed past the huge rowing boat, pulled by six burly sailors since they'd transferred from the ship. The crossing from the North of England to the North of America had been uneventful, thank God, better than for those other poor devils on the *HMS Gordon*, which had sunk the previous month with no trace of the 234 souls on board.

Flora had smelled the land long before the sailor up high above the deck in the crow's nest had shouted out "land hoy." Of course, everybody had known that the land was just over the horizon, as the sea birds had suddenly appeared to accompany them into port, and the huge white albatross and gulls had spent the day wheeling in circles around the masts. A tear had run down her cheek as the gulls accompanied her boat to land. She'd been cast back more than a quarter of a century to another time, another boat, and the horrific dangers of a summer storm.

Flora was the only one on board who fancied that she could actually smell the blossoms and the flowers, the trees and the musk of bison and beaver and all the other exotic fauna that she'd spent the past year reading about.

They'd pulled into Columbia on the coast of North Carolina and transferred into a shallow bottom boat, but they'd hardly begun their journey upriver when the captain determined that because of the lack of rainfall, the river was too low even for a craft that drew as little water as his. So they'd moored and transferred all the passengers bound for Halifax onto rowboats and now they were being taken up the Roanoke River to where they would spend the rest of their lives. They rounded bends and each pull on the oars delivered a new and extraordinary vista, both of gentle plains that formed the Roanoke Valley and beyond the vast grasslands and forests in the distance to the huge mountains that seemed to form a barrier to what might be beyond.

She looked at Alan and felt saddened that they couldn't have traveled to this new land while he was still a young and strong man. He retained much of the vigor and vitality that she'd always known, but during the past five years or so, he'd aged in mind as well as in body, and now perhaps he was too old to accommodate to the vitality and youth of America. Then her gaze shifted to Jamie and Angus and Lachlan and John, then over the other side of the boat to Ruth and Esther, all of her beautiful, wonderful children. Each of them welcomed . . . no . . . each of them was ecstatic about the move to America. All of her children loved Scotland and swore they'd never forget the islands and the highlands, but the thought of going to America and being able to hunt and fish and run free without some English lord telling them what they could and couldn't do was so liberating that Flora thought they'd all burst with excitement before they even set foot on the ship in Liverpool.

Flora could barely quell her own excitement. She and Alan had made the decision that at some stage in the future, they would take their six children to America and follow in the general migration that the Scots had begun many years earlier. The question was all about timing. He wanted to leave immediately, but he couldn't persuade his wife to go. She refused to leave Skye, despite the difficulties created by the damnable English until her mother Anne had passed away. Exhausted, sick, and bed-ridden these past seven months, Anne had not been the same since her beloved Hugh had died of a fever three years earlier. As he was lowered into his grave, Flora was certain that she had seen Anne's spirit and will to live disappear into the cold earth with him. Since his passing, Anne had barely smiled, and her grandchildren, for whom she lived, no longer gave her the pleasure they once did. It was only a matter of time, and Anne's spirit was finally exhausted, and her body had passed away the previous month. After a suitable mourning period, Alan and Flora announced their decision to abandon their house in Armadale and leave for the New World.

As Skye and the Highlands were being denuded of Scots and replaced by Englishmen and sheep, America was filling up with expatriate Scotsmen and women. Tens of thousands had migrated across the water to seek freedom from the oppression of the Lord North, a penny-pinching madman who had been appointed prime minister by King George III in England. He and the English Parliament were oblivious to the privations they were causing in Scottish life. Industry and commerce had come to Scotland thanks to the English, but it was the English in Scotland who were enjoying the benefits, and not the Highlanders, who were becoming a poor servant class, little more than slaves to their English overlords.

The sailors heaved again in unison and the rowing boat surged forward further up the river and against its seaward flow. The banks were so fertile, the trees and the grass so green, the sky so luscious and blue, that Flora was nearly overcome by her senses. In the distance there was a field, planted with a tall crop that she'd read about in the pamphlet on vegetation and agriculture in America; she looked at them as carefully as her aging eyes would allow; they could be tall wheat or even taller corn, or maize or . . . or . . . she would have to wait and become more experienced in the nature of the farmland of North Carolina rather than make wild assumptions.

Again, her body was pulled and pushed by invisible forces as the oarsmen rowed up the river. She'd been assured that it wouldn't be much longer before they would sight Halifax, which was only another three miles away.

She enjoyed being in a rowing boat. And although the circumstances were vastly different, she remembered how she and Prince Charles escaped the English in a rowing boat from South Uist to Skye all those years before. What an irony! She was still escaping the English. What was it about the English that made them so rapacious? Colonies that didn't share in the wealth of the mother country but were treated as a treasure store to be robbed at will, would soon rebel against the exploitation. She'd wanted to see it happen in Scotland; please God that it didn't happen in her new home, she prayed

As the rowboat took Flora and her family deeper and deeper into America, she mused on the past quarter of a century of her life. No! Twenty-six years. Almost to the day. She couldn't remember the month, but the year was 1746. It was a sunny month, so it must have been June or July. They'd been lucky to remain afloat in the storm and not all be drowned. She remembered climbing a cliff. She remembered the crofter's hut. She remembered oh so clearly the night the boatman, Neil MacEachan, had gone into town leaving them alone, not even suspecting for a moment that there was anything that would happen between the Prince of Scotland and the daughter of a farmer.

But it had, and she looked lovingly at her son Jamie. Was it just a coincidence that Jamie was exactly the same age today traveling by ship to conquer the kingdom of the New World, as was his father Prince Charles when he'd come from France by ship and landed on Eriskay in the Outer Hebrides to claim his kingdom? She looked at him long and lovingly. He was so very different to her other children. He was taller and fairer and with prouder features. Her other children, by Alan Macdonald, were stockier and more like Highlanders. But only Alan Macdonald knew the truth. And just like Hugh had treated Flora as his own child when she came to him at the age of two after the death of her natural father, Alan, God bless him, had treated Jamie as his very own bairn since the moment he was born.

And in all that time, Flora had not heard a single word from Prince Charles. Not a letter, not a messenger, not a greeting. Nothing. She didn't know whether he was alive or dead, whether he was going to return and claim his land as he'd promised, or whether he'd accepted the reality that King George III, the first of the Hanoverians to be born in England, would be king for many years to come, and his son would take over the throne from him. Yet when she'd left Scotland to travel to Liverpool in order to catch the boat to the New World, the last thing she'd done was to pick a sprig of heather that she'd encased into a piece of parchment and wore on a chain between her breasts. She'd told Alan it was a memento of Skye, but the truth was it was to remind her of her time as the lover and wife of the handsome prince who one day would use it as part of his coat of arms.

Or would he? She'd heard neither hide nor hair of him since the day he'd left Skye. Was it an end to all the hopes of a Stuart line of kingship? Had all those good Highlands people died in vain? Or did Charlie have other sons who, like their father, would sail to England and try to claim the English and Scottish thrones for the Stuarts? Would Charlie, or one of his sons, one day sit upon the Stone of Scone in London's Westminster Abbey, the ancient throne on which the kings of Scotland were crowned, and claim the kingdom for his own. If only she knew what had happened to her bonnie prince, Charlie.

Flora realized now that she'd never loved him. She'd been infatuated, certainly, but it was different from the love she bore her Alan. It had been a girlish fantasy, a night of carnal lust in a lonely hut on a deserted part of Skye; she'd been alone with a lovely and elegant man who lived in another world, a world that had always fascinated her. But that world had entered her body and then withdrawn completely, and she realized that he'd treated her like he treated all the many servant girls and strumpets who'd willingly allow him their bodies, in the hope of a reward, or just to say that they'd bedded a prince.

As she sat in the boat being pulled upriver, Flora was amazed by the rawness of her emotions. After all these decades, she still felt hurt and angry and embarrassed and was mortified that her face flushed in humiliation before her husband and children. Thank God they were looking at the scenery and not their stupid mother. For she was the one who had kept the flame of that night alive all these years. She, reminded every day when she looked at her beautiful son Jamie who was the very image of the Bonnie Charlie who had fathered him, but who, unlike the father, was a quiet and reserved and demure lad who rarely spoke unless he had something important to say. In that way, God bless him, he was the very image of his adoptive father Alan. Flora mused on how funny the world has turned out.

As they rounded a bend in the river, the sixty houses that made up Halifax, North Carolina, came into view. Smoke was coming out of some of the chimneys. Horses and wagons were plying the streets. Her new home looked very pleasant. She smiled at Alan and blew him a kiss. She hoped he'd think her flushed with excitement and not for any other reason.

All the children looked keenly at the settlement. It was a very attractive settlement, built on a bend in the river. The township was neat and there was a strong wooden stockade protecting it from attack by the native Indians. But the gates had been thrown wide open and there was nobody appearing to guard the community. Jamie, immediately understanding his mother's concern, put his arm around her and said softly, "I've been reading all about the natives, Mother. Around here, they're called the Iroquois which is a confederation of five Indian nations, the Mohawk, the Onondaga, the Oneida, the Seneca, and the Cayuga. The English are on very good terms with them, and there's much trade between the peoples. There hasn't been an Indian attack in Halifax or the farmland around here in years. It's perfectly safe."

She smiled and put her hand on his shoulder and thanked him. Of all her children, he was the only one who had mastered the art of reading, and he would devour any book that Flora or Alan happened to acquire in their journeys around Skye or on the occasion when they went to Edinburgh. He was a quiet and a studious lad, and sometimes he was embarrassingly shy when in the company of people. He only ever spoke when he was spoken to, and sometimes Alan and Flora would be in bed, realizing that Jamie had not spoken one word in their presence in all the long day. Even when he was with his less taciturn brothers and sisters, he was always the one who stood on the sidelines and watched their interchange. Yet for all that, he was the voice of moderation, the calm and mature influence on his wilder and more irascible siblings. Although he wasn't Alan's flesh and blood, he had somehow inherited Alan's reserve. There were times even when Flora was alone in the house and would turn around and find that Jamie had been there for some time without making himself known.

Did that mean he didn't contribute to his family? Not at all. He was determined and made his viewpoints well enough known. But unlike her other more garrulous children who had to be told to shut up, Jamie had to be asked to voice his opinion.

The boat pulled into the riverside dock and tied up at a jetty. The other boats from the ship were still half a mile or more behind, so their bags and packages and possessions were taken quickly to the boat shed, and Alan, Flora, and their six children were helped up from the boat to climb the river slimed steps onto firm land.

A florid man dressed in an oddly shaped round hat, wearing a battered brown jacket and violent yellow waistcoat with faded blue trousers, came out of the shed and opened his arms.

"Welcome, welcome ladies and gentlemen. Welcome to Halifax, your new home. Welcome one and welcome all. You must be the Macdonalds," he said, consulting a list that he held in his hands; it fluttered in the gentle breeze. He had a strong accent that wasn't Scottish, but sounded much like the accent of some of the people she had met who now lived in Edinburgh, yet who had been born in Portsmouth and other parts of the south of England.

Alan smiled and shook his hand warmly. "We're all Macdonalds, sir, and there's many more to come on the next boats. They're from our clan, but they're Macdonalds from a different part of Scotland and are no part of my family. Here you see the family of Mr. Alan Macdonald of Armadale in the island of Skye. My wife Flora and our six children. And who do I have the pleasure of addressing?"

"I'm the Mayor of Halifax. I'm Mr. Gabriel Sheldon. I was born in this country and have lived here in Halifax all my life. And let me tell you, sir, and you, ma'am, that it's God's own country. Plant an acorn and you'll have an oak tree by morning. The ground is so fertile, the weather so clement that you'll curse yourself for not arriving here earlier. Now, let me have your bags taken from the shed to where I've arranged temporary accommodation for you. It's commodious but not fancy. If you want fancy, you'll have to build it yourselves.

"You'll find building materials have been laid out on your land by the residents' committee. There's a charge, but you can pay that after your first year's income from your crops. There's men who'll help you build if you need assistance and if you have the money to pay, but looking at your sturdy children, it's not likely that you'll need the help of strangers to build your home. And there are traders who'll sell you Negro slaves who'll work for you. They come here once every three months when a new shipment is just in from Africa," he said.

Flora reacted in horror. "There'll be no slaves in my household, thank you very much, Mr. Sheldon. We didn't escape the slavery of the English to become slave owners ourselves."

Sheldon noted her vehemence and said, "That's entirely your decision, Mistress Macdonald, but there's many folk here that do own slaves and they find the arrangement very profitable. Anyway, how and when you build your house is your affair, but if you'll take my advice, you'll build it sooner rather than later, for although the weather is temperate now, winter is only a few months away, and the nights here get powerful cold. While you're building your dwelling, if you so desire you can come back to Halifax Township and remain in paid accommodation each night for protection. The costs are minimal and the committee can even subsidize you until your home is built, though you'll have to repay the amount plus interest once your farm is on its feet. Not many folks do return once they get to their land, for they prefer to sleep under canvas while the building is taking shape. On average, it should take you not more than a week to build a habitable shelter, which you can extend into a home while you're under a roof. You'll find a stream for pure fresh water on your land, and in time, you'll dig a well down to the water table, which'll keep you in drinking water during droughts so that you'll never run dry. Then that will be that."

They followed him along the jetty, and before he reached the boat shed, he stopped, and pointed to the far horizon. "Folks, you can't see it from here, but five miles down that road is your very own twenty acres of some of the best farming country in all of America. It's the king of England's land, but we lease it from him, and you lease it from us. You pay us rent, you clear the trees from the land and then you grow crops or sell the wood, and you earn what you can from the land. As farmers, you know you'll never starve, and if you're real smart, you'll run twenty, thirty head of cattle or sheep and that'll give you extra money come slaughter-time. We'll set you up to meet the traders who'll buy the hide off the cows or the wool from the sheep if that's your fancy and whether you sell the meat or salt it and eat it is up to you. Point I'm making, folks, is that hard work will reward you handsome."

He moved his extended arm to another part of the horizon. "Ten years ago, another fella, man by the name of Josiah Marchment, took lease over twenty acres, just like you're doing. Right smart fella he is, too. Within two years, he'd bought those twenty acres outright. Five years ago, he bought another twenty acres, and just last year, he bought a whole hundred acres toward the foothills of the mountains. He's running a thousand head of cattle and only the Lord God knows how much he's worth. He's built himself a fine six-room house over yonder with a dining room and a room where you can dance. And in two months' time, he'll have completed the purchase of another fifty acres to grow tobacco and corn which he'll sell all over Carolina. I tell you, sir, that's the sort of man we want in America. A real go-getter."

Mr. Sheldon looked at Alan, then at Flora, and then at the children and asked quietly, "Tell me, sir, are you a real go-getter?"

Alan smiled and said softly, "That depends, Mr. Sheldon, on what I decide to go and get."

THE APARTMENTS OF PRINCESS LOUISE OF STOLBERG-GEDERN

HOTEL MONDIAL

ROME, ITALY

JULY 23, 1772

Her maid, a private gift of M. René Augustin de Maupeou, Chancellor of France, finished combing the princess' hair and arranging the bodice of her dress. She picked up an enamel and ceramic pin with its depiction of a hunting scene, and carefully threaded it through the curls, avoiding touching the princess' scalp. Then she wound and tied different colored ribbons over the pin so that they hung down through her hair. A further touch with the comb to hide the pin and the princess was ready to make her appearance.

"Madame looks very beautiful," the maid told her. But her mistress remained seated, looking at herself in the mirror while the maid fussed around the boudoir, picking up the previous night's bedclothes, paper wrappings from chocolates, and documents scattered over the bed.

She had finished tidying the room, and yet the Madame remained seated. "Will Your Highness not come to breakfast?" she asked. It was nearly eleven o'clock in the morning, and the food prepared by the chefs, another gift of the generous Chancellor of France, would already be turning cold and spoiling.

"I will eat when my husband rises," she said, barely audibly.

The maid curtsied and left the room. Princess Louise repeated the word to herself, looking into the mirror to see how ugly her mouth became when she pronounced the word.

"Husband!"

From the shape of her face and the sound her lips made as she spat out Charles' status in their marriage, the name sounded more like a curse than a title. It was so false, so artificial. But what else could she call him? Majesty? King? Prince? Drunkard and sot and womanizer and wife-beater. Failure? Demi-man?

They all applied. Every title and every name he used for himself and which in the privacy of her boudoir she used for him, was equally valid, especially for a man who didn't know who he was today and had not known who he had been for thirty or more years. He called himself king, yet he was living in a distressed apartment, paid for by M. de Maupeou and only because of the Chancellor's certainty that the French monarchy was doomed and that support for the Stuarts might benefit both France and himself.

Now that his father was dead, he called himself king. But he had no lands, no people, no palaces. Others to this day called him Prince, for to call him king was a false assumption. Kingdoms had to be earned, and in his more lucid moments, he recognized that, and he styled himself Prince in Exile.

He was the son of a king and yet he would never be a king in his own right. He called himself Majesty, yet his own Scottish people hated and despised him for his drunkenness and violence, for the loss of human life they'd sustained through his adventures, but mostly for the loss of their land and their ancient clan hierarchy because of his presumption in trying to gain control of the English throne without a French army to back him up. Twice he'd returned to England and Scotland to rouse what remained of the clans, once in 1750 and again four years later, but on both occasions, he'd been rebuffed even by those who had been his most ardent supporters. His friends, those who remained by his side, had told her that he'd returned to Italy in a state of humiliation and deep despair and had consoled himself with copious quantities of wine, brandy, and women.

When they met for the first time a month after their wedding, she had felt sorry for him and understood his drunken rages. She thought that she could pull him back from the precipice of despair—that by her ministrations she could save him from himself. She'd tried to pacify him, to offer him her lap for a pillow, but when he turned his fists against her, not once but a dozen times, she had demanded a separate bedroom and had not been a wife to him since. And nor would her body be his until he stopped drinking and controlled his fury.

So what title did she use when they were together? How did a wife view her husband when he was neither king nor prince nor Italian nor Scot nor Englishman nor anything? Yet he demanded deference from everybody he met. And worse, most blasphemous, most evil of all above the temporal titles he awarded himself . . . he dared call himself Catholic, yet he cursed God and Jesus for being the instruments of his failure rather than accepting his rightful fate; and while he was cursing the names of the most holy, Charles drank himself into unconsciousness every night, and when he was sober, he would attempt to seduce any woman who came upon his path—any woman except his young and terrified wife, whose virtue and modesty infuriated him and whose boudoir door was bolted against him when he returned home in his drunken state!

Was it any wonder that His Holiness Pope Clement XIV wouldn't change the decision of his predecessor in refusing to recognize Charles as King Charles III of England and Scotland? Why would such a holy man as Giovanni Vincenzo Ganganelli offer the blessings of the papacy to a man who could control neither his rages nor his drinking? Why would the papacy support such a disreputable pretender to the throne of England, even if it had the advantages to the Catholic universe of replacing the Protestant Hanoverians with a Catholic Stuart?

Princess Louise gripped her comb tightly as she contemplated rising from her dressing table, opening the door to her bedroom and treading the creaking corridor past Charles' quarters to descend into the breakfasting salon where their table had been set. For she knew that today would be no different from yesterday or the day before. She would creep past his room, and he would awaken to the creaking noise that the wooden floorboards made. He would call out and demand her presence in his bedroom. If she pretended not to hear him and ran downstairs, he would appear moments later at the dining table in his nightshirt, still drunk from the excesses of the previous night, and ridicule her in front of the servants. If she entered his room and closed the door, she risked a beating for daring to reject his sexual advances.

He called himself husband, yet he was a brute who thrashed her in his continuous drunken wrath, and she wore the bruises and scars of his evil ways when she walked the streets of Rome and people looked at her in pity and knew what she suffered.

She felt herself on the verge of tears. It was a common enough occurrence since she'd been married to the brute. They'd been wed by proxy in March, she in Austria and he in Paris. They had met for the first time in April, and although he was older and much fatter than she'd been told by her protectress, Princess Maria Theresa, she knew that as the daughter of an impoverished noble family, marrying a king in exile, was the very best she could hope for.

But in the intervening months between April and July, as they'd traveled around Italy on a honeymoon, her worst fears about the rumors she'd heard of him became more and more pronounced in her mind. A honeymoon should have been a period of joy and delight for a young couple getting to know each other. He was older than her by thirty years and treated her as a dullard and a child, demeaning her in front of hoteliers and visitors and clerics and even the Cardinal Archbishop of Krakow alone and without her.

And when she complained, he had sulked off to his rooms and stayed there for hours, only emerging looking like a disheveled footpad demanding more wine. The first time she'd tried to stand up to him, he'd hit her brutally and she had been forced to run to her room and close the door. The other guests in the hotel complained to the manager who deferentially took her husband's side. Yet the second and third time it happened, they had been asked to leave the hotel, and from that moment onward, her husband's mood had become increasingly terse.

Now his entire life was a state of drunkenness or recovery and with drunkenness came more and more violence. He'd been thrown out of inns to sleep in the filth of the roadway until he was carried home on a cart by his servant to sleep until evening when the whole thing would begin again.

She'd hoped that their return to Rome might calm him down—that the pressures of mixing with elegant Roman society would have a positive influence on him. It was, after all, his home—the city where he'd been born, the society that had accepted him and encouraged him in his endeavors to reclaim the Stuart dynasty and to rid England of the hated Hanoverians. It was the city he'd left as a young man full of ambition and promise, but it was also the city to which he'd returned when he'd been defeated in England and spurned in France—a city that looked on his growing inebriation and violence and intemperate moods as increasingly unacceptable, and which, like France, spurned him from its society.

No, returning to Italy with a new young bride hadn't been a positive influence on him. Instead, it exacerbated his drinking and his continuous rages as he walked the outer corridors of the elegant houses and palaces to which they were invited as a couple, complaining how dowdy and run-down Roman society was these days under the Holy Roman Empire, and how London's palaces were so elegant and rich and beautifully designed. In the first week of their return, they had received numerous invitations; but as time wore on and the rumors about him transmuted to known facts, they were lucky if they went out to a party or soiree once a month.

She sighed heavily and plucked up the courage to leave her room. She opened the door and saw to her horror that Charles' bedroom door along the corridor was open. His servant must have entered to see if his master was still alive, and failed to close it properly. Princess Louise tiptoed past, but she saw Charles through the open doorway sitting in bed, sipping a cup of coffee and reading a letter.

He saw the motion in the hallway and called his wife into his room. She entered, and curtsied.

"Good morning," she said, her throat dry with dread.

"Good morning, Louise. How are you today? Did you sleep well?"

She smiled and nodded, unsure why he wasn't screaming at her.

"I thought that this morning, we could take the carriage and visit the Gardens beside the Tiber. It's a beautiful day and we should both get out more," he said.

She continued to look at him, mute, wondering what was going to happen next.

"Is that agreeable to you, my dear?" he asked.

She nodded.

"You're very quiet. Is something wrong?"

"You seem in an unusually calm mood, Charles. Normally nobody can speak with you until well into the afternoon and you've recovered from the previous night's entertainment. But it's not yet midday and you seem . . ." she searched for the word . . . "composed."

"As would you be had you received this," he said, struggling to rise from his bed and handing her the letter. She looked at the crest, seal, and stamp and saw that it was written by none other than His Holiness, Pope Clement XIV. He moved his legs from the bed onto the floor and supported his weight on a wooden upright, standing there while he gained both balance and posture. He was lightheaded from the exertion and moved slowly, cautiously toward the chair of the dresser.

"I don't understand. Why would the pope write to you?"

"Because I am the king in exile to the throne of England. Because by rights, England should be a Catholic nation and the pope obviously wants me to make it so."

"But his predecessor said . . ."

"I wrote to His Holiness last week, requiring an audience in order to present new grounds for his support of my claim to the throne of England. His secretary has written back, asking me to attend an audience with His Holiness next Tuesday."

He grasped the chair, and pulled it away from his dresser and sat down heavily. Looking at him in the mirror, she was shocked to see that his eyes were red, the rims dark from lack of sunlight. He was a denizen of the night and his face suffered from the way he led his life.

"Charles," she said softly, "should you build up your hopes when His Holiness is so busy with the problem of the Jesuits? The French,

Neapolitans, Portuguese, and Spanish ambassadors are continually peti-
tioning the pope to ban the Jesuits. As the king of France has withdrawn
support from you, is it likely that His Holiness will offend King Louis by
supporting your claim? Forgive me, husband, for commenting on your
affairs, but I don't want you to be disappointed should your audience not
proceed as you would like."

He turned and smiled. She hated his smile. She compared it to the
smile of a reptile. What teeth he still had left were stained the color of
mustard. "Child," he said, "these matters of international politics are very
complex, and you are looking at them with a simple eye. I've involved
myself in the politics of the world for my entire life. Trust your husband
when he says that there is more which is hidden in a letter, than that
which is written."

His servant entered the room without knocking, moved toward the
dressing room, and took down his clothes for the day. Moving to where
the pretender king was sitting and without a by-your-leave from Princess
Louise, the servant dressed him quickly, paying far less attention to his
clothes, powders, and wig than her maid paid her. They left his bedroom
to descend to the dining salon, where they would eat breakfast, and then
they would order their carriage be brought to the front of the Hotel,
where they would ride in the open to the banks of the River Tiber, barely
visible in the distance. The gardens were becoming a fashionable place for
gentlemen and their ladies to walk, and they would be noticed.

Was this a new beginning, she wondered, or merely a brief respite
from the nightmare of the past three months? Only time, His Holiness,
and his next drink would tell.

HALIFAX, IN THE ROYAL COLONY OF NORTH CAROLINA
THE DOMINION OF AMERICA

AUGUST 13, 1772

The house was larger than they had originally intended, and they quickly
ran out of the wood that had been deposited on their land by the local

committee. They'd cut down trees from their property and fashioned them into planks that enabled them to extend the footprint of the house so that there were three bedrooms instead of just two, and the eating and sleeping quarters were separated from each other by a double thickness of timber and Hessian sacking that they'd taken from sacks of flour and sugar they'd purchased and washed clean in the stream.

The long pathway from the road to the house was now cleared of trees, and Luke, always the artist, had fashioned a sign, using fire to etch letters outlined for him by the literate Jamie, which now proudly proclaimed to any passerby that this house belonged to

*The Macdonalds of Halifax NC*
*formerly of Armadale in Skye*
*Anno Domini 1772*

Life was more pleasant than Flora had a right to believe. They lived in a new land with good, decent, honest hard working people. During the week, neighbors came to visit and brought food and drink in case they ran short while building their home. On Sunday mornings, they went to the tiny wooden Catholic Church beside the river and prayed. On Sunday afternoon they visited their new friends, and in the evening the men, and in this she included all of her sons, went to the saloon and sat and drank ale and whisky and played cards and came home at midnight and slept late on Monday morning until mother and daughters hurried them out of bed because chores had to be done.

The girls of the house spent Sunday evening with other young women of the district, planning dances and balls and parties that never seemed to eventuate. And Flora grew to know and like her neighbors, almost all of whom were Scots from the Highlands, as well as English men and women who had come for a better life.

What Flora found to her amazement was that she was renown throughout North Carolina as the woman who rescued Bonnie Prince

Charlie. It was so long ago, so much a part of history, that she'd assumed it would have been long-forgotten. But it appeared to be an important Highland legend, and having lived for so long on Skye, where Flora was so well known but where the outside world never seemed to impinge, it never occurred to her that men and women from Aberdeen, Inverness, and other parts would be singing her praise.

And her fame reached the ears of one who was already very well known in the English Dominion of America. A certain Mr. Benjamin Franklin, who, when he heard that Mistress Flora Macdonald, the heroine of the Highlands and the prisoner in the Tower of London during the reign of George II had come to America, decided to ride to North Carolina and pay his respects to her.

A man of vast bulk, sitting atop a sagging horse, Ben Franklin rode slowly along the banks of the Roanoke River. His imminent arrival had been the talk of the town for more than two hours prior to his exhausted horse plodding through the open wooden gates. He slid down from the saddle and onto the ground in a pall of dust. He was greeted by Gabriel Sheldon, the Mayor of Halifax, supported by an assembly of important townspeople.

"As I live and breathe. Mr. Benjamin Franklin. Why sir, I'd know you anywhere. It's an honor and a privilege to have you come to our town of Halifax. I'm Mr. Gabriel Sheldon, the Mayor. What brings you to Halifax if I might ask, sir?"

"I'm here to visit one Mistress Flora Macdonald, Mr. Sheldon. Are you acquainted of a lady by that name?"

"Sir, we have many Macdonalds in our fair town. But yes, the Mistress Macdonald you speak of arrived here not all that long ago. I visited the family myself just last week, and they're building a fine house five mile out of town. But how long will you be staying in Halifax, Mr. Franklin? A week? More than a week?"

Ben Franklin smiled. "Mr. Mayor, both a fish and visitors tend to stink after three days, which is when I'll be leaving. I have to pay my compliments to Mistress Macdonald."

The Mayor was surprised. "Mistress Macdonald is known to you?"

Franklin looked at the Mayor. "Sir, Mistress Macdonald is known to the whole of England, Scotland, and no doubt France and Italy. She is a heroine, sir, of the Jacobite uprising of 1745. You are honored to have her in your county."

The mayor stared at Franklin. "The heroine . . . but she never said . . . she's just an ordinary woman and I . . . well damn me . . ."

"People that are wrapped up in themselves make small packages, Mr. Mayor. I'm sure that Mistress Macdonald's modesty is an aspect of her heroism. Now, sir, if you could direct me to an inn or a hostelry, I shall avail myself of their facilities and then travel to Mistress Macdonald's homestead in the morning."

The arrival of Benjamin Franklin, the brilliant, acerbic Pennsylvania printer and politician, was known to the entire community of Halifax and by morning, when he mounted his horse and prepared to follow the directions of the Mayor and ride out toward the Macdonald homestead, a crowd of some thirty men and women had gathered outside the Inn to look at him. He greeted everyone as though he was running for office and gave a short speech about the importance of townships like Halifax to the opening up of the hinterland and the growth of America; he was cheered on his way and rode through the open gates of the settlement along the road that serviced ten farms stretching toward the distant lofty hills. The Macdonald's farm was fourth along the narrow and dusty track.

His horse carefully negotiated the wheel ruts, which had inscribed deep grooves in the earth, and clopped at a leisurely pace toward the far-off mountains. After half an hour, he was delighted to see a burnt wooden sign, announcing the Macdonald household.

No fences, no gate, no formal entryway; just a clearance of trees that formed an alley leading toward a pleasant timber shack, newly built with construction material still splayed all over the ground. In the far distance, barely visible from the house's entryway and beside a stream that mean-dered through their land, were an older gray-haired man and several young men engaged in the act of felling timber. They were working so hard that they didn't notice him arriving at their homestead. Beside the house were two young women, little more than girls really, washing clothes in a tub. And sitting on the porch plucking a huge bush turkey was a matron who was obviously the mother of the household.

The girls and the mother looked up as soon as Franklin's horse neared. Initially concerned that they were alone, but knowing that all she had to do was to sound the iron triangle and they'd come running, Flora looked at the man who approached. From his age and girth, she knew that he posed them no threat.

"Do I have the honor of addressing Miss Flora Macdonald?" he asked.

"You do sir. And who are you if I might be so bold as to ask?"

Franklin introduced himself, and Flora said that yes, she had heard of him. He was well known to her as a scientist and writer and philosopher and in other spheres as well.

"You must excuse me, sir, for I was not expecting company, and this bird is our food for the week. Had I known you were coming, I would have accorded you the dignity to which you are entitled."

Franklin smiled. "Ma'am, it is I who come to accord you respect. You are the Flora Macdonald, who assisted the Prince Charles Edward Stuart in his attempt to rid England of the Hanoverians, are you not?"

She burst out laughing. "Mr. Franklin . . . that was a lifetime ago. Surely, a man such as you lives in the present and not the past. Yes, I was the Flora Macdonald who helped him escape. But so did numerous other Scotsmen and women throughout the Highlands who suffered grievously for the aid they gave him because of the Butcher of Cumberland's desire to punish us for supporting the Jacobite cause."

"A damnable man indeed, now thankfully gone to his maker where he will have to atone for his crimes. And as to my past, ma'am, it is your present, for you are renown throughout Europe and America for your bravery. You are the stuff of legend, ma'am."

She stopped plucking the turkey and looked at him in amazement. She burst out laughing. "Legend? Me? I think you have me confused with someone else."

"Not at all, ma'am. The uprising of 1745 is celebrated in Scotland, in England, and in France as a grand and glorious moment in history. It symbolizes an event in which a young man deprived of his inheritance by German usurpers, tried to reclaim it. A glorious defeat is more admired than an inglorious victory. The name of the young Bonnie Prince Charlie is more revered than ever will be the Duke of Cumberland's. A pity that the aging King Charlie does great dishonor to his former self. And you, Flora Macdonald, are very much a part of the legend which is accreting to that event and that moment in history."

She shook her head in wonder. "I'm a simple farmer's wife, Mr. Franklin. But I'm being rude, sitting here and plucking our dinner while you're stuck on top of a horse. Please, sir, dismount and enter our home and take refreshment. Ruth, Esther, take Mr. Franklin's horse and give it hay and water, and then give it a good rub down with straw. This way, sir."

They entered the house, and Franklin looked in admiration at the neat and tidy cottage. It had all the charm he would have expected from a Highland woman who was determined to make a home for herself and her family in a distant and strange land. On the shelf above the fireplace was a sprig of heather encased in glass; on the table was a length of Macdonald tartan; on the floor were ceremonial swords and shields, waiting for the inside of the home to be finished so they could be erected. And in pride of place was a bookcase with dozens of books inside.

"You're a reader, Mistress Macdonald," said Franklin.

"Of course. And my son Jamie is an avid reader as well."

"A house is not a home unless it contains food and fire for the mind as well as the body," he said. "Feed the mind, ma'am, and the body will find more nourishment than it can possibly absorb."

She poured him a glass of ale, and he drank it thirstily. They sat at the table, the door closed against the ears of her children.

"Tell me, Mr. Franklin. What news do you hear of the Prince Charles Edward Stuart? You alluded earlier to his condition, but that's the first I've heard of him in half a lifetime. I ask because we became good friends in adversity, and since that time with him on Skye, I haven't heard hide nor hair of his whereabouts. You move in far more elevated circles than do I. What have you heard of his fortunes?"

"Not good, ma'am. Not good at all. He returned to England twice after the disaster in forty-six, and he was rebuffed by those he wished to lead. It has completely broken his spirit. What once was a colt is now a shambling dray horse. I knew him when he was a young lad in his early twenties. I met with him in Italy, and he was a tall, slim, elegant, lovely boy. Clever and brave. But the Charles Edward today, the man who calls himself Rightful King, is a lumbering and ungainly wreck of a man—a married man who drinks himself into a nightly stupor and who is reputed to raise his fists to his wife. No, Mistress Macdonald, the reports of him are very discouraging," Franklin told her.

He was surprised by her sudden sad demeanor and wondered if there was more to their relationship than a mere friendship under adversity. His interest was spiked even further when she asked, "And do you have any idea whether the prince has any children? Any heirs to whom he'll be passing on his title?"

He looked at her in deepened curiosity. Softly, he said, "As far as I know, ma'am, he has one illegitimate daughter, but no male heirs."

"And his flag and Coat of Arms, Mr. Franklin. Is there anything special to it?" she asked.

Franklin frowned. "Truly ma'am, I don't know the answers to your questions, but your curiosity intrigues me."

She shrugged her shoulders and seemed to return to the present. But without giving any of her thoughts away, Flora suddenly asked him, "So why are you here, Mr. Franklin? I've only just arrived in this country, hoping to start a new life, and suddenly I find I'm visited by one of her most famous and important sons. I'd be grateful if you'd tell me the reason."

He took another mouthful of ale before he answered her. "Many years ago, Flora . . . I may call you Flora?"

She nodded.

"Many years ago, I was secretly in London on behalf of a number of the colonies, determining the way in which the Scots would react to the defeat of Prince Charles. I met with many people, especially Sir Francis

Dashwood who founded the Hellfire Club. You may not have heard of it, but it is a coterie of freethinkers, and a place to meet influential lawyers and politicians without the scrutiny of the government or the civil authorities. It has a scurrilous and libertine exterior, but I joined because it enabled me to meet many in private whom I would not otherwise have been able to without drawing unnecessary attention to myself and my cause.

"I was there in the summer of 1746, just weeks after the defeat of the prince at Culloden Moor. I was sent there as a result of rapine committed by the Duke of Cumberland in your Highlands. It occurred to me then that the treatment of the Scottish people mirrored the treatment which Americans might expect if we refuse to pay the Stamp Tax or any other tax which King George imposes upon us. We are unrepresented in their Parliament, yet they tax us. Is that fair, Flora?"

He didn't wait for an answer, but continued, "Although it was a quarter of a century ago, the seeds of our destruction were being sown by the imperiousness of the Duke of Cumberland and his father. The Hanoverians have a particularly Teutonic mind; they see no shades of light and dark; they're humorless and cruel. And they'll drain their people . . . all their people in whatever part of their empire . . . of lifeblood to ensure that their coffers are full and ripe.

"But many people with whom I'm associated, Flora, believe that the American people will no longer accept the rapaciousness of the British Crown toward its colonies. They ask why they should work hard and accept the privations of life in America, when they are being bled dry by the Crown?" he said. "I am a man who would prefer a negotiated settlement, but my voice is tending toward a minority."

"But what has this to do with me, sir?" she asked.

"When I told my colleagues in the North about your arrival in America, they begged me to seek you out. They want you to speak on behalf of the Scottish people in this nation of ours. You're a symbol of Scottish bravery and resistance, my dear Flora. When the time comes, my colleagues want to know whether or not you and your husband will stand shoulder to shoulder with your American brethren and rally the many thousands of Scots in America to take up arms and throw off the shackles of British rule?"

She looked at him dumbfounded. "Dear God in heaven, Mr. Franklin. I've just traveled three thousand miles to escape fighting the British. And now you want me to rouse the Scots here to form an army?"

He smiled and nodded. "Not necessarily I, ma'am, but my colleagues. Will you rally the people of Scotland to fight on behalf of their new country?"

"But I'm no fighter, Mr. Franklin, be it with a weapon, or with words. Even when I took Prince Charles over the sea from Uist to Skye, I never held a pistol or a dagger. I'm a simple woman, sir."

"But you have in your possession the most potent weapons on God's earth, ma'am. Integrity! And this will shine through in your words. Your presence will rally an army of America's Scots against the English, should there be a revolution. My colleagues want you to gather the clans, remind them of what the English did to the Scots in forty-six, and give them the courage to rise up and defend themselves against English muskets and rifles and swords. Will you do that for America, Flora? Will you rouse the large Scottish community in America to the side of the colonists?"

Before she could answer, she heard footsteps on the wooden porch. The door burst open, and a young, tall, and handsome man with finely carved features walked in.

He looked in surprise at his mother, sitting with a very voluminous gentleman, sipping ale. "Forgive me, mother, I didn't know you had company."

Flora beamed a smile. "Mr. Franklin, may I introduce you to my eldest son, Jamie."

Franklin stood and shook hands with the young man, introducing himself and at the same time scrutinizing him intensely. He stared at his face as though it was a holy relic.

"Father said to let you know that he's just caught two large crayfish in the river, and he's bringing them home. Anyway, I have to go back and help. It was nice meeting you, Mr. Franklin."

Before he left, Franklin asked, "Mr. Macdonald, tell me, sir, in what year were you born?"

Jamie looked at his mother and frowned. "In 1747, sir. I'm twenty-five years old."

He smiled, and the young man left as quickly as he'd entered. Franklin sat down with a thump.

"Do you know what *déjà vu* is, Flora?" he asked.

She shook her head.

"I've just been carried back neigh on thirty years to a time in Rome, when I was introduced to the Young Pretender to the thrones of England and Scotland. Your son, Jamie, Flora, is the very image of the young man I met all those years ago. He's . . ."

He stopped talking and stared at her. Her face was expressionless. They stared at each other for many moments, before Franklin said, "Does your husband know?"

She nodded.

"And he accepts the boy as his own?"

Again, she nodded in silence.

"You have a remarkable husband, Flora. Who else knows?"

"Nobody. Only you."

"Not even the boy . . . the prince's son?"

"We've never told him. There's no reason to," she said softly.

"And not even the father knows? Does Prince Charles not know he has a son?"

"He hasn't been in contact with me. As I said to you, sir, I haven't heard a word from him since he left me on Skye."

Franklin nodded.

"I've remained silent for the sake of my son. Alan, my husband, has been the most perfect of all fathers. It is nobody else's business. Nobody's, Mr. Franklin. Is that understood?"

"And silent is precisely the way it will remain. I shall leave you now, Flora, but I shall be in contact with you by letter post concerning the other matter of which we spoke. I think in the future you and I will get to know each other well. Very well indeed."

# Chapter Fifteen

No matter how many speeches she gave, no matter how often she stood before an audience, her throat always dried up before ascending the stage, and her first few lines were delivered as though by a gray-haired drunken slattern. Her friend, Mr. Benjamin Franklin and her son Jamie, who had been delegated by his father to travel with his mother and protect her, knew the traumas she suffered, but nobody else in the audience had an inkling.

Instead, they knew her by reputation and came out in their droves to see her. And for those who attended the meetings out of curiosity, there was always Benjamin Franklin, or some other man delegated by him, to introduce her and assure the audience of Scots that she was the very self-same Flora Macdonald who had been party to the attempted overthrow of George II, grandfather of their present King George III.

She had not been to Richmond before. She had been to New York and Boston and Philadelphia and Charlottesville and many other large and small towns and hamlets, speaking sometimes to ten people, sometimes to three or four hundred. She tried to get home as often as she could, but Mr. Franklin allowed her very little rest, and so long as she had Jamie with her, she felt a connection to Alan and her children.

Alan! How badly things were going for them now. Their years of happy marriage, their excitement at the prospect of a new life in America, had come to grief because of the difference in how they viewed their new land. Alan objected to Flora speaking against the British. For some reason, he and many other Scotsmen objected to the stance that the Americans were taking toward the Parliament of Great Britain.

It was odd, for in Scotland and even on the way to America, Alan had been a vocal critic of England and everything that it was perpetrating against the Scots. But almost from the moment he'd set foot on American soil and started building up the homestead and the farmland, he'd changed and found fault in the attitude of the American colonists toward London. She had spoken to him about it at great length, but it seemed that Alan, like many other Scotsmen, saw the king of England as a father to his American people, and despite their acknowledgment of the rights of Americans, they did not want to fight against their father.

Flora and Alan had argued about it, discussed it, even raised their voices by the riverside and away from the hearing of their children, but it was all to no avail. Just as she wanted to use the platform she'd been offered by Mr. Franklin to rouse the Scots to action against the English when the time came, so Alan became more and more convinced that he would join with other loyal Scotsmen and oppose the colonists if they tried to wrest America from the English. In exasperation, she demanded to know why he had suddenly changed his loyalties.

He acknowledge the unfairness of the taxes the English were imposing on the colonists to pay off the huge debts incurred during the recent wars with the Spanish and French, but since he'd traveled to the New World, he told Flora that he felt a strong connection to the Old World and that America was not yet ready for self-government. He admitted that when he'd been in Great Britain, he'd detested it and only wanted to leave, but now that his feet were firmly planted in the New World, his eyes looked longingly toward the old and the life he'd known all his days. Flora had left him to travel around the Eastern Seaboard, hoping beyond hope that that one day soon he'd work out where he wanted to be, and more importantly, why.

Today it was Richmond, Virginia's turn to hear her. She waited in the wings of the hall as Mr. Barrie, Benjamin Franklin's local representative,

288 · Alan Gold

spent many minutes telling the large Richmond crowd of Scots about their good fortune in having Flora Macdonald speaking with them. She looked at the audience and tried to spot a familiar face. Sometimes, she recognized somebody from the old country, and then after her address, they would spend many minutes working out whether or not they'd met in Edinburgh or Inverness or somewhere else in the Highlands. When she met a former resident of Skye, they would spend hours talking about the hills and the valleys, the coastline, the people and the wild beauty that they always admitted missing fiercely.

Suddenly she felt a hand on her shoulder. It was her wonderful Jamie, who whispered in his mother's ear, "Almost time, Ma."

She nodded in thanks, and cleared her throat, listening to Mr. Barrie finishing his introduction with the words, "And will you give a warm and Scottish welcome to the heroine of forty-six, the woman who saved Bonnie Prince Charlie from the English at grave peril to her own life, Miss Flora Macdonald . . ."

There was a huge cheer from the audience, as Flora walked up the steps onto the stage and stood in the center while men and women cheered her. She smiled and raised her hands for silence.

"Mistress Macdonald, it's a pleasure to meet you, ma'am," he said. He was tall and young and handsome and rugged. "My name is Patrick Henry. I'm a lawyer and a would-be politician. Ben Franklin told me to come and hear you when you were speaking in Richmond. I have to say that you were inspirational. Understated, yet with tremendous power and authority to your words."

She thanked him. "A lawyer. And interested in politics. You must be a very committed man."

"Committed to an America free of being a colony. Committed to an America not tied to the birth cord of England's womb. Committed to an America which can take its place in the world alongside France and

Scotland and even England in the family of independent nations. Yes, ma'am, I'm committed."

"Such imposing commitments will take much time and effort. And much bloodshed, Mr. Henry," she said. "I left a nation two years ago which had slaughtered thousands of my countrymen and women for daring to stand up and demand freedom. God help Americans if there is a revolution because I've seen with my own eyes what standing up against Great Britain will do. The hills and valleys and streams of Scotland ran red with the blood of Highland martyrs. I'd hate to see this new and beautiful country stained in such a way by suffering the same fate."

He nodded and said, "If we cannot have liberty from England, then I'd rather chose death."

"Chose your own death, Mr. Henry, but how many will you carry with you into the grave?"

"Are you against revolution?" he asked. "Ben Franklin told me that you were a strong supporter of our cause."

"I'm a strong supporter of independence from England. But I'm no supporter of the death and killing and slaughter of innocents. If revolution for the cause of freedom means the deaths of our loved ones, then I'd have to question the wisdom of such a revolution. But if the revolution can be accomplished by peaceful means, by negotiation and goodwill, then I'm all in favor of such a revolt against the English crown."

He laughed. "Surely your experience in Scotland would have taught you that England will never willingly give up what's hers without the bloodiest of fights."

She looked at him. He was an attractive man. In age, he was between her son Jamie and herself. It was difficult to tell, because by the looks of him, he couldn't be much above forty, yet he had the eyes of a man who had seen and thought much.

"Tell me, Mr. Henry, would it be considered a gross breach of propriety as a woman if I asked you to buy me and my son Jamie an ale at a nearby Inn. After my speech, I've a powerful thirst, and I'd like to continue talking to you."

He laughed again. He had a delightful laugh. "It would give me great pleasure. And it would be an honor."

They walked across the street, avoiding horses and wagons and the muddy pools from the recent shower to an Inn where the smoke was so thick that it seemed like a cloud hung beneath the ceiling. She was immediately transported back to her youth, when she'd dared to enter an Edinburgh coffee shop to speak to a philosopher about the implications of Bonnie Prince Charlie invading Scotland.

Her thoughts of Charles had diminished steadily in the many years since the birth of Jamie in the Tower of London until she barely thought of him at all. But in the past two years, since Mr. Franklin had gained knowledge of her deeply held secret, she'd thought about him more and more. Perhaps it was because Jamie was now at the same age as Charlie when he came over to Scotland to take back his family heritage, or perhaps it was because her own marriage to Alan was so stressed because of their different ways of viewing their new home, or perhaps it was because Mr. Franklin had told her about the way in which Charlie had been driven to drink by the frustration of not being supported by the kings of France.

But whatever the reason, she had thought of him with an increasing fondness and affection, even though he'd abandoned her despite his promises to remain in contact.

Mr. Henry found them an empty spot near to a window. He ordered three ales and asked Jamie how much he was enjoying his new life in America.

"Just wonderful," said her son. "I miss Skye, but I don't miss either the weather or the brutality of the English."

"Did you suffer much brutality?" he asked.

"Not personally, but you always knew it was there. English soldiers were often on the Island, and English landlords had taken over the ownership of our lands. When they came to inspect what we were doing and assess how much they'd tax us, they always brought a dozen or more soldiers for protection. It made me feel as though I was in prison."

"And is this the same type of brutality you expect in America if we take a stand against the English?" Flora asked.

Mr. Henry took a long draft of his ale. Slowly he nodded his head. "I'm afraid so. The king, the Parliament, and the East India Company will never allow us to secede without a very serious fight. There will be many deaths and much suffering, but if a cause is worth living for, it's surely worth dying for."

"Dear God in his heaven," she said in exasperation, "I've heard enough battle cries from the mouths of the Scots to last me a lifetime. I never thought I'd hear it in my new country. Surely, there's another way, Mr. Henry. Surely we can talk and negotiate and compromise. Why make widows and orphans when we can all live together in peace."

"Because, Flora, the peace which we want will never be acceptable to the king of England or his Parliament. We want representation in the English Parliament because the king and his prime minister Lord North are taxing us and there's nobody in England to speak on our behalf. Just last year, as you know, Lord North passed the Tea Act, and now the East India Company has complete monopoly powers over our tea and honest businessmen have been put into bankruptcy because of a stroke of the pen. No nation, colony or not, can live under these conditions. The English treasury is empty because of squandering and waste and especially because it's forced to carry a vast army and navy to protect itself from invasion from France or other nations of Europe. Yet much of its army is stationed here, to keep control of us Americans. And we are expected to fill the English treasury from money we've earned so it can be spent on an army controlling us. It's absurd, especially when we need the money here to build schools and roads and everything that a new nation requires if it is to meet the needs of its people. Why should we send our money overseas without having representatives in the English Parliament to determine how much of it is spent on the welfare of its colonies?" he said.

"So there's no way we can avoid war?" Jamie asked.

Patrick Henry laughed. "Only by cutting off the king's head again. Getting rid of the whole damnable monarchy."

"Cut off the king's head?" said Jamie, shocked by the notion. He wasn't a student of history and knew almost nothing about the past.

"It's been done before. Over a century ago, England's King Charles I lost his head on the chopping block because he was an evil autocrat. Following him was a commonwealth, which gave great hopes to all of England and her colonies. Unfortunately the lord protector of the Commonwealth, Oliver Cromwell, was as much of a brute and a tyrant as Charles, and the English couldn't wait to bring back their king."

"What's a commonwealth?" Jamie asked.

"It's a republic. It's a form of government that gives power to the people to rule themselves through properly elected representatives. People rise as a result of ability and not a result of the luck of their birth," he said.

Jamie shook his head, not understanding the term "republic" or the idea that people could rule themselves! Comfortable with the concept of a king ruling a nation, Jamie had never fully understood what was meant by any other kind of government.

While he was coming to terms with the different forms of government, Flora's attention was transfixed by the conversation but from a different perspective. It was as though a key had been turned, a door opened, and an entire vista had suddenly been revealed upon her eyes.

Softly, Flora asked, "But why can't all the colonies join together as a commonwealth? England could be father to the family of Wales and Scotland and Ireland and America and Jamaica and all the other nations of the empire. If each governed itself, had its own parliament, yet looked toward the king for guidance and trade, then it would relieve the king of having to employ such huge armies which are denuding his treasury, and each nation in this commonwealth could pay a levy or tax each year to the king for its membership."

He looked at her strangely. "But if each nation had its own Parliament and independence, what value or reason would there be for continuing our relationship with Britain? Why would we need a king?"

She became increasingly animated as she formulated the idea in her mind. "Don't you see, Mr. Henry. There would be enormous benefits which could accrue if the king of England became the king of a commonwealth of nations, all joined together in brotherly love as is preached by the Quakers. You say that a hundred years ago, England beheaded its king and suddenly became a commonwealth of citizens. But why not a commonwealth of its colonies? Surely, the king could understand that Scotland and Ireland, Wales and America and all the other British possession and territories would prosper if they were independent, yet England would prosper most of all if they all joined together in such a commonwealth. A small and impoverished country like England can't possibly hope to retain its control over all the lands and nations it once did. But if the king and Lord North could be made to see that, can't you see all of our lives would be more prosperous. Surely he could be shown that if he released his grasp and let each of his colonies prosper in its own way, each acknowledging him as their king, yet each independent, it would no longer be force which held his empire together, but it would be the love and friendship which he would merit by setting us free—just like a father frees his sons and daughters to start life on their own when they're old and mature enough."

Patrick Henry looked at her in amazement. "A wonderful Utopian dream, Flora. A commonwealth of nations in the British Empire. And the chances of King George or his prime minister allowing it to happen are precisely nil. Why should Britain give up its possessions and the products and goods, the crops and furs and the taxation they provide? Without the taxes and the trade which come from us, England would be on its knees. Do you think Spain or France or Portugal would give up the vast wealth which flows to them from their possession across the sea? Then why England?"

"Because it's much less costly than finding itself in a war in all parts of the globe, Mr. Henry. Britain is bankrupt because for the past seven and more years, it's been fighting wars in Europe. It can't hope to finance a war against its own colonies. And to avoid bloodshed and expense, maybe the king can be persuaded to create such an association of like-minded colonies, a commonwealth of empire nations. Just maybe?"

Patrick Henry smiled, "But then he would be king of just a small island and not of a large part of the world. And who would rule these nations? America already has its king, and if we lose George, I can't see us crowning one born in this land. Frankly, ma'am, I could never see us as anything other than a colony or a republic. So who are you suggesting would be king of America or the king of Scotland and the king of Ireland?" he asked. "And in this Utopia of yours, Mistress Macdonald, why would you have such an ancient and debased system called monarchy, when you could institute a brave new world by revisiting the republics of ancient Greece or Rome?"

She nodded, having anticipated the question, and looked at her son. She reached over and held Jamie's hand. "America will be a republic if the king agrees. And it can still be a part of a British Empire. But Scotland wants a monarch. We've had monarchs since the beginning of time. King George is filling Scotland full of rich Englishmen and sheep, but there are still enough remaining Scotsmen and women to want their own king. And if the king of England agrees, then Scotland will have a monarch of its very own," she said. She finished her ale in silence and stood.

"Come Jamie. Mr. Henry, if you'll excuse my son and me, we have to leave. I must go back to my rooms and make myself ready for my return to North Carolina tomorrow morning."

"But I thought you had other speeches to give," he said in surprise.

"I had, but I shall be writing to Mr. Franklin, begging him to excuse me. After our talk, I have had an idea which I must discuss with my husband. And my son. In the fullness of time, you will get to hear about it. And you will be both surprised and I hope pleased by what I think I shall do."

They shook hands with Patrick Henry and left the Inn. As they walked in silence along the roadway to their lodgings, Jamie asked his mother, "What's the idea you wish to discuss with me, mother?"

She smiled and reached for his hand. She hadn't held his hand in public since he was a small boy in Scotland, but somehow, when she told him, she wanted to be touching him.

"Jamie, darling. You and I need to go on a very long journey. We need to return to England. This is going to come as a shock to you, my darling boy, and I would never otherwise have told you, but I have an idea which, if properly executed, will prevent bloodshed and countless deaths of Americans and others. I have seen far too much death in my life, darling, to risk causing more deaths when men fight for their cause. If I can prevent those deaths by inconveniencing myself, then it's my duty to do so. But first, I must discuss it with your father, and if he agrees then I shall tell you and ask your permission. If you grant it, then you will become part of what I intend to do."

He looked at her in surprise. "What on earth are you talking about?"

There was a lightness in her step, an energy that had been missing since she'd begun her long trips around the country. "Darling, you and I are returning to England to reclaim your rightful heritage. Your father did the same when he was about your age, and now you're going to do it. And in the process, we're going to convince King George that instead of fighting and killing, a far better way would be to create a commonwealth of nations of the British Empire, a true and proper family of old England and its fledgling sons and daughters. No longer colonies but proper nations in a family of nations, with Father England at the head of the table. The question, Jamie, is whether King George will agree."

"King George? Agree? And what heritage? What in God's name are you saying?" he asked, beginning to think that his mother had suddenly gone quite mad.

*HMS Penelope*

October 24, 1774

The captain of the *Penelope* was well satisfied that the sails were set correctly to take advantage of the breezes that blew strongly at this time of year. While not as efficient as a good wind to push the ship along at full knot, the breeze was sufficient to fill the mizzen, the cross sail, and the crossjack until they were in deeper waters and could benefit from the full force of the gusts that followed the North Atlantic current. Right now, they were still in the grip of the current that came down from Labrador and was trying to push them south into the warm waters that flowed out of the Gulf. But soon, in a hundred or so nautical miles, they'd be released from that current's grip and then the winds of the middle Atlantic Ocean would steal up behind them, fill the ship's sails to billowing, and blow them nicely toward England.

His holds were full of a cargo of tobacco, maize, and sugar, and if the prices on the London Markets of Exchange held good, he should make a handsome profit for his masters and that meant a nice bonus for him that would see him well-endowed for the months leading to Christmas so that he could buy his wife a beautiful new dress and his children all the gifts they desired.

His attention was caught by the middle-aged lady walking the upper deck. She was grasping the railings, obviously not yet in possession of her sea legs. At least she wasn't heaving her guts out over the side, as were many of the occasional travelers who bought passage on board his vessel.

Captain de Villiers had been introduced to her when she and her son, a tall and strapping lad called James, came aboard in New York Harbour. He assumed that she was a newcomer to the colony, discontented with what she found and intent upon returning home. Or perhaps she was a widow of a Britisher murdered by the Indians or the locals, a woman who had decided to return to England now that events in the colony were starting to become unsettled. He'd heard that because of these new taxes and the general unhappiness with what the Parliament in London was doing, there was a militia walking around the streets with guns . . . Redcoats arresting anybody they thought looked suspicious . . . the colony was a disturbed place to be. Not even de Villiers, who had sailed these waters for the past ten years, was confident he'd ever sail into a peaceful American harbor again.

Captain de Villiers smelt the air and looked up at the sails. It would be a good run, provided that no October storms suddenly blew up. The air didn't feel heavy enough for a squall or a storm, but the Atlantic Ocean was a troublesome mistress and he'd often gone to his cabin at night in a lullaby sea to be woken up during the witching hours by a raging tempest.

He looked again at the woman who stood by the railings with her son. He didn't like carrying passengers at the best of times, but she'd paid good money and accepted the meagre accommodation that was offered by the trading packet, rather than wait for a passenger boat due to reach America in four days' time. But something about her told him that she was trouble. He couldn't put his finger on it, but normally when passengers came aboard, they were either very excited about returning to England or heartbroken at leaving America. Yet both she, and her son, had been still and stiff when they'd come on board, hiding any emotions of happiness or sorrow. They mounted the gangplank, nodded politely to him, shook his hand, thanked him, and retired to their cabin. Now that he was twenty miles off the American coast, they had come up on deck, where the woman and her son seemed to be engaged in a serious conversation. Well, he thought. That's their business, so long as they mind it and keep out of his.

"It's time you told me?" Jamie said to her sternly. "I've waited in ignorance long enough. Now, what's this great secret?"

Flora nodded and smiled. "Yes, darling, this is the time. I've delayed cruelly and caused you much anguish, but I had my reasons which I'll explain. I told Alan that I wouldn't reveal the secret until we'd sailed a sufficient distance that we could no longer see the American shore for fear that you'd refuse to come with me to England. He was very angry with me and told me I had a duty to tell you first so that you could refuse to travel with me. But I had enough confidence in you to ensure you'd travel with me, whether you knew or not, and so I made a pledge with myself that I'd reveal all when the coastline disappeared and we were in no man's land between the New World and the Old World."

"Mother, you're frightening me. For God's sake, tell me what this secret is," he demanded. The concern and anger in his voice was lost in the wind. But Flora knew all too well. What she didn't know was the reaction he would suffer.

"Darling boy," she said, "many years ago, nine months before you were born, I ushered to safety the Young Pretender to the Throne of Scotland, Bonnie Prince Charlie."

He laughed. "I know that. Everybody knows that. You're a hero because of . . ."

She put her finger to his lips. "We were thrown together for two weeks of terrible danger and gripping fear. The crossing from Uist to Skye was against a horrifying storm which nearly saw us drown; then we had to dress him in women's clothing and walk the entire length of the Island to Armadale, spied on by men of the MacLeod as well as hundreds of English soldiers. Every step of the way was almost certain death. Yet we arrived having evaded the entire English Army and he managed to escape to France. But someone on the Island told the English of my part in his escape, and I was arrested and locked up in the Tower of London, which is where you were born, my darling boy. Had it not been for the Prince of Wales, the man whose early death tragically prevented him from being the king of England today, God rest his soul, I'd have suffered terribly."

Jamie began to frown. Whenever he'd tried to ask his mother about her experiences, she'd always made an excuse not to tell him. And now she was treating him like one of her audiences.

"Darling, have you ever wondered why you look so different from your brothers?" she asked.

He stared at her for long, agonizing moments. She could barely speak the next few words; yet just as she'd been forced to tell her husband Alan that her unborn child wasn't his, so she would have to tell Jamie the truth.

"Bonnie Prince Charlie is your father, darling. Not Alan Macdonald, although he loves you fiercely and you are, and always will be, his."

She held her breath, waiting. And she continued to wait as he stared first at her, and then beyond her out to the sea.

"When?" he asked. "When did he . . . you and he . . ."

"In a small Crofter's house in the north of Skye. We were alone."

"Did he . . . was he . . ."

"No, darling. He didn't force me or rape me. I was young and not yet married. It was the danger and the excitement of being alone with him. I resisted, but . . ."

"So he did rape you."

"No!" she said. "Don't think that, for then you'll hate him."

"Or I'll hate you!"

It was like a knife cutting into her very flesh. But it was what she deserved. She tried to calm herself and said to him gently, "you may hate me for lying to you all these years. Yes, Jamie, you have a right to hate me. For betraying your father, you have a right to hate me. But you have no right to hate me for loving you and for being a good mother to you. You may hate me for any sins you believe I have committed, but I have never committed the sin of abandoning you, nor refusing to accept you as my very own son. I have never knowingly hurt you or belittled you or treated you any differently from my other children. Hate me if you will, darling, but never hate me for being a good mother who loves her son and would lay down her life for him."

"How could you?" he whispered. She could barely hear him over the seagull's screams and the voice of the wind. "How could you betray father? How could you do such a thing?"

"I offer you no explanation, other than an apology. I was a young woman. I was your age. I was alone with a man in a house in a remote part of the Island, and we were both in great danger. Our lives could have been extinguished at any moment. With all those pressures, my sense of decency and morality left me and the moment overtook and nullified my principles."

She had no idea what reaction to expect. Only once before in her life had she been in a situation where she had not been able to anticipate a loved-one's response. And that was when she told Alan about her pregnancy to Bonnie Prince Charlie. Now, Flora waited to see whether she would be as estranged from her loving son as she had recently become estranged from her loving husband. She sighed and wondered why, at the end of her days, her life had become such an unholy mess. She hoped that one day Alan would understand her reason for returning to England and Scotland and trying to avoid the deaths of thousands of Americans. Now she had to hope and pray that her son, Jamie, forgave her for a youthful indiscretion. She realized that she was barely breathing.

Jamie looked out over the white-capped waves and gazed into the far distant horizon. But he remained silent. Then, without even looking at his mother, he walked away along the main deck and climbed the quarterdeck to be alone in the furthest reaches of the ship. Alone, bereft, knowing that she had ruined the lives of people she loved the most by the one act of unchastity in her life, she turned away from her son and returned to the tiny cabin.

Flora Macdonald waited for much of the afternoon and into the early evening. She just sat on the bed and stared at the door, praying for it to open. It kept sullenly closed. She couldn't read or eat or walk or sleep or even think. All she could do was to wait until her son returned and gave her the verdict with which his mind was wrestling. Would he ever talk to her again? Would he curse her immorality now and forever? Would he . . .

She reacted in shock to a rap on the door. She tried to say 'enter' but her voice failed her. It opened, and Jamie walked in, looking wan and tired and windblown.

They looked at each other, mother and son, neither smiling, neither giving the slightest sign of an emotion. And then Jamie said, "Are you coming to the galley for some supper, Mother?"

She swallowed to try to regain her voice and said softly, "No, darling. I'm not the least bit hungry."

"Neither am I. Will you come for a walk on deck? It's cold and you'll need a scarf and a cape."

She dressed and ascended the steps in the wake of her son, and into the dark early evening October sky. There were half a dozen crewmen in the riggings and on the deck and they paid the two not the slightest attention. Jamie walked over to mid-deck and stood by the railings. Flora followed sheepishly.

"Did you love him?"

"At the time, yes. I was swept over by him. He was intelligent, charming, and very handsome."

"So you don't love father? Not as much as Prince Charles."

"I love your father dearly; I've loved him since we were young. I've borne five of his children and proudly call him husband. I'm devoted to him."

"But how can you love two men?" he asked.

"You loved Sarah McIver who lived with her aunt on Skye, and then you fell out of love with her and fell in love with Jenny Roberts. Love when you're young can be transient, darling. It can seem perpetual, but just as it begins quickly, it can last just as long as the heart flutters. My love for your father, your real father Alan, not the father who made me pregnant with you, has lasted all my life. My love for Charlie lasted weeks, if that."

"Who else knows?" he asked. "Do my brothers and sisters know? Or is it only me that's been made to look like a fool?"

She bridled at the gratuitous insult but fought to restrain her temper. "No, the only people in the entire world who have any knowledge of my sins, are you, me, Alan and Mr. Benjamin Franklin, who guessed."

"And my father? My real father? Prince Charles? Does he know?"

Again, Flora shook her head. "According to Mr. Franklin, Prince Charles returned to France but since then has lived the rest of his life in Italy. He has taken to drinking large volumes of wine. He is no longer the man I met and loved."

"But does he know about me?" he asked, a sternness in his voice.

She shook her head. "Not once did he write to me or ask after my welfare. Not once even though he promised me eternal friendship. So he didn't even know that I was carrying his child."

"So not even he knew that to him had been born a son. And what of my . . . the man I used to call father?"

Now she became angry. "And father is what you'll still call him. He's a blessed man who could have spurned me when I told him that I was pregnant by another man. But instead, because of his love for me, he treated me as wife and accepted you as much his son as though you were his own flesh and blood. He has never once looked upon you with anything other than the eyes of a devoted father. Curse me as you will, Jamie, but never dare damn your father for my sins."

The young man breathed deeply. He looked out to the darkened sea, illuminated in patches by wraith wisps of phosphorescence. Then he turned to Flora and nodded. It was an acknowledgment, an apology. He asked simply, "Why are we going back to Scotland?"

It was the moment Flora knew that her son forgave her and that their relationship would eventually continue on as normal. She smiled, hugged him, and held his arm.

"When Charlie and I were together in the Crofter's house, we made a vow to each other. A vow of marriage. We went through a ceremony. At the time, I thought it was just a piece of nonsense. But when I told Mr. Franklin, he told me of something called the ancient Salic Laws which used to govern much of France and Germany and other countries. He told me that under these ancient laws, I could be deemed to have been lawfully married. And when you were born, your father Alan made me promise to have no more of any other man, which I willingly accepted. That, according to Mr. Franklin, was a divorce in the Salic Laws, and so it made you the legitimate heir of the Prince of the House of Stuart, and the next in line to the throne of Scotland, for you are not Charlie's bastard son, but his real and proper son, born in wedlock according to the Salic Laws. Laugh as much as you want, lad, but you've got royal blood in your body."

And laugh he did. "But I can't be the heir. Bonnie Prince Charlie doesn't even know me . . ."

"But don't you see, darling, that as Charlie has no male children, you have a valid and legitimate claim to be known as the rightful male successor to the throne of Scotland and because of the ceremony we went through in the Crofter's cottage, you're not illegitimate, but his right and proper heir. It's my intention to go first to London and have you crowned as king of Scotland on the Stone of Scone in Westminster Abbey. Then I shall return with you to Scotland and there I shall petition the lairds and noblemen to have you accepted by them as the rightful king of Scotland, assuming that they won't accept Charlie as their monarch. He's tried three times, and I doubt they'll give him another chance. So I will then beg King George III for an audience, present you as the king of Scotland, and ask him to create a commonwealth of Nations of the British Empire."

Jamie looked at his mother Flora and again burst out laughing. She looked at him for an instant, and then she burst out laughing as well. They hugged each other and had to hold on to the railings to prevent themselves from falling in the swell.

"And what hope do you think you'll have of doing all these things?" he asked, hugging her.

"Very little," she said. "But none at all unless I try. And if there's one thing which sets me apart from every other Scottish woman alive, it's my determination. God help any king or prince of England who tries to stop Flora Macdonald in her tracks."

They nearly fell about the deck of the ship in hysterics. Captain de Villiers, who had finished his evening meal and just ascended to the quarterdeck to ensure that all was well, looked at the distant figures of the mother and son passenger hugging each other in uproarious amusement. He nodded in satisfaction, thinking that any tension that might have been between them at the beginning of the voyage had disappeared, as so often happened, in deep water. He never ceased to be amazed at the miracle of the sea for putting all human problems into perspective.

# Chapter Sixteen

November 29, 1774

The funeral procession wound its way from his home in Berkeley Square toward Grosvenor Street. The cortege was preceded by twelve white horses draped in black, pulling a gun carriage on which the coffin was centrally positioned and covered in the flag of England. Following the gun carriage were hundreds upon hundreds of black-clothed mourners, a line that stretched around the corner of Berkeley Square and out of sight.

The huge procession prevented Flora and Jamie from crossing the road and they stood in respectful silence for over fifteen minutes as it passed them by.

"Who was that?" asked Jamie.

The gentleman who accompanied them, James Boswell, said softly, "That, sir, was the late Robert Clive, our man in India, the First Baron Clive of Plassey. A great man, sir. A very great man, done to death by the little men of England. So outraged was he of the abuse of his name and reputation, that he committed suicide some days ago. The whole of England is shocked by his demise. And all on account of the little men of England. I tell you, Mr. Macdonald, that this nation is going to the dogs. The little men will have us one day, sir. You mark my words. We shall be submerged by the petty jealousies and inconsequential thoughts and insignificant posturings of silly little men like politicians and third-rate pamphleteers and the second sons of Peers of the Realm. They'll bury all the great men of England and Scotland with their carping and harping and moaning and envy. You see if they don't."

Eventually, the last of the mourners passed them by and they were able to cross the street toward Mayfair and the house where they would be meeting Dr. Samuel Johnson. Jamie had a dozen questions to ask Mr. Boswell but refrained, for this was a meeting arranged by his mother, and although he was instrumental in her plans, at this stage, he was very much a follower rather than a leader. Mr. Boswell said little as they paced toward the meeting.

"Do you live in London, Mr. Boswell?" Flora asked as they rounded a corner.

"No, ma'am. I live in Edinburgh where I am employed as a lawyer, an execrable profession. It was Shakespeare who thought that before society could improve, first we had to kill all the lawyers, which is why my favored profession is that of a writer. You, I know, have visited Edinburgh, and you will know its provincial charms, but I am able to travel to London regularly on vacation and in the holiday terms of the courts. It gives me a good amount of time to spend in company with my very dear friends here, first-rate minds, men of letters, and also to continue my major goal, which is writing of the life and times of Dr. Samuel Johnson, the gentleman you are about to meet."

"Is he so famous that a book is being written about him whilst he's still alive?" asked Jamie.

Boswell smiled. "Oh yes, young man. Dr. Johnson is our foremost man of letters. He is perhaps the greatest scholar and intellectual in all of England. When I sought your mother out at your lodgings last week, only that very morning, I had just put the finishing touches to the first part of the first section. I intend to write ten sections. Dr. Johnson is an astounding man, as you'll see. And I assure you that when you meet him, he will be very sympathetic to your cause. While he is no longer a supporter of the Jacobites and will not assist you in any endeavor you may harbor to replace King George or his issue, be assured that he has no love for the House of Hanover. Had Bonnie Prince Charlie succeeded, Dr. Johnson would have been the first leading the dancing in the streets.

But sadly, history tells us that it wasn't the case, and now Dr. Johnson considers it too late to replace the Hanoverians. He says that they are ensconced for the duration until they die out from disease, inbreeding like the Egyptians or exhaustion. Unfortunately, with their Germanic fecundity and the amount of children they have already produced, an Egyptian plague seems the only way they'll come to an end."

Flora was about to comment, when Boswell continued, "Of course, that's not to say that Dr. Johnson won't support your very interesting plan to petition for a monarchical commonwealth under the aegis of the king of England. I'm pleased that you explained it to me, for I think that when you tell Dr. Johnson of your reason for seeking an audience with the king, he'll share my reaction and support you fully. Frankly, ma'am, it's a sensible and timely invention, and one which will save countless lives and vast sums of money, provided the king can be made to see sense."

"What are the chances of gaining an audience with the king," asked Flora.

Boswell thought for a moment and said, "None at all without going through the prime minister, and fortunately Dr. Johnson is a friend of that very gentleman."

"And if we get to see the king, what chance do you think there is of his agreeing to my mother's proposal?" asked Jamie.

"Impossible to say," said Boswell, "but at least we're ruled by a man who understands what we're saying and whom we can understand. King George III is the first ruler of this realm since the reign of Good Queen Anne who speaks passable English. His grandfather, George II barely understood a word of what was being said to him. Imagine that, ma'am, a nation ruled by men who don't understand what we're talking about. A paradox which hasn't existed since the time of the early Plantagenets."

He chuckled to himself at the absurdity of monarchy as he walked at a rapid pace. They rounded yet another corner into a street of grand houses, avoiding the mud and puddles from a recent rainstorm and the liquid horse droppings, and after they'd passed by four houses, Boswell suddenly turned into number twenty-two and ascended the steps into the portico. He rapped on the door with the iron handle, and moments later, a liveried servant replete with white gloves and white wig opened it, bowed, and welcomed them inside.

Well known to the household, Boswell invited both Flora and Jamie to follow him as he climbed the sweeping curved staircase, past several rooms filled with bookshelves carrying volumes of books from floor to ceiling, until they came to a room with another liveried servant standing outside.

Without even a nod of acknowledgment, the servant knocked discreetly on the door and opened it to admit the newcomers.

Jamie was stunned by the opulence of the room. It was vast, seeming to be at least as big as his entire house in North Carolina. On all walls except for the wall containing the huge casement windows were books. Books of every shape and size. Leather books, books in red and dark green and black coverings, books standing in military rows in their shelves, books opened at particular pages and strewn around the floor as though tossed aside in a frenzy, books that lay horizontal on shelves and on chairs as though they had been haphazardly discarded in a moment of drunken forgetfulness, and books that teetered against other books at an angle.

And in the middle of the library stood a huge circular globe of the world in its brass spherical stand. The globe was positioned directly beside the gargantuan oaken desk of a heavy middle-aged man who sat there in his long dirty gray wig looking as though he'd only just risen from his bed. Despite their entry into the room, the fussy gentleman remained hunched over his papers, quill in hand, tongue lolling out of the corner of his mouth, mumbling to himself. He was concentrating so intensely that he simply had no idea that anybody had entered the room.

Flora looked at the gentleman in amazement. This was not the London she'd expected, where men and women of society took hours dressing in the very finest of apparel. This man, whom she assumed was the renowned Dr. Johnson, was wearing little but shirtsleeves, trousers, and an open waistcoat. His utter oblivion to their presence was both amusing and annoying. Were it anybody other than a man with his reputation, she'd have viewed it as pretentiousness. But being Dr. Johnson, whose literary and intellectual output was prodigious, she found the situation amusing. A battle could rage in the room between competing armies, guns and cannon could explode, and it didn't seem as though anything would disturb him from his labors.

He was writing furiously with the quill, the inkpot close to his hand, muttering to himself despite the fact that his tongue, which continued to loll at the edges of his mouth, was operating independently of his mind. There was a plate of uneaten bread and meat and cheese beside him, a glass half-full of some purple wine beside a decanter that was nearly empty. Flora looked at the famous literary lion and couldn't help but be amazed both by his appearance and by his total concentration to the defeat of all around him. She wouldn't have been surprised had he been surrounded by a cloud of dust with flies and midges circling his head. She didn't know whether to laugh or cry. Was this the man Mr. Franklin in America had urged her to see in order that he may use his brilliance to advise her concerning making her son into a king? Was this the man who was considered the most brilliant of all brilliant Londoners, a man whose tongue was as sharp as an axe and whose wit was as painful as a wasp's sting?

Boswell coughed respectfully. It made no difference. The vast lumbering man remained hunched over his desk and continued to mumble to himself, laugh at his own joke, make some comment, and continue writing in a fury of speed and concentration.

Boswell coughed again. Louder this time. It caused Dr. Johnson to look up and realize that he had been joined in his study by others. He stood and said apologetically, "Dear God, ma'am. Gentlemen. I apologize. Boswell, how long have you been here. Why didn't you make your presence known? I was engrossed in my writing, and I failed to appreciate your sudden manifestation; where once was solitude, now there is company. Please accept my most sincere and profound apologies."

He came over and extended his hand toward Flora. "And you must be the admirable Mistress Flora Macdonald, the heroine of Scotland. Madame, it's a rare and excellent pleasure to meet you. How do you do."

Before she could tell him how she did, he turned his attention to Jamie and extended his hand to the bemused young man. "You are James, son of the heroine. A pleasure, sir. A pleasure. Some wine? Brandy? But you're Americans now and no longer Scots, so what will you drink?"

"Forgive me, sir, but it's only eleven o'clock in the morning. A cup of tea would be very nice," said Flora.

Johnson burst out laughing and said, "One of the disadvantages of wine is that it makes a man mistake words for thoughts. I have mistaken both the word, the deed, and the time. I have been writing since three in the morning, so for me, it's the end of the day and nearly my bedtime. Forgive me, for I sometimes forget how other mortals live. I shall immediately order you tea."

He picked up a bell from his desk, rang it, and continued to mutter to himself. Jamie looked at him in amazement and couldn't decide whether he was like one of the elderly men in the town of Halifax who stumbled and spoke to themselves as they tried to remember where they lived or one of the drunks in the Inn who laughed at everything. But this Dr. Johnson had been promoted by his mother as a genius. So far, Jamie hadn't heard much genius, but he'd seen much foolery. He looked at Mr. Boswell, who was smiling amiably, as though he was a proud child presenting his extraordinary father to his friends.

"My work and a little too frequent libation has the effect of making me forget the time of day, Mistress Macdonald. Once, only last month, I rose from my bed in the early hours of the morning and for some obscure reason I thought that it was eight or nine o'clock, dressed and shouted for my breakfast. Nobody came, and I went out into the vestibule and cursed all the servants in the house for being lazy and slothful. My manservant came running out wearing his nightcap and carrying a candle to inform me that it was half past three in the morning and asked whether I was ill."

Johnson burst out laughing and ushered them into chairs near to the enormous windows. Flora was about to explain why she had sought an interview with the good doctor, but before she could begin, he said, "My dear friend, Mr. Benjamin Franklin, arguably the only intelligent and certainly the only interesting man in America, although some demand that I include Mr. Thomas Jefferson in my trans-Atlantic pantheon, has written to me and requested that I allow you an interview in order for you to seek my advice concerning grave matters of State, which is why I asked Boswell here to contact you last week. You are known to me, Mistress Macdonald, as doubtless you are known to most English and Scots folk, as the woman who all those years ago saved the life of the Young Pretender. Such a pity about him, eh? What a wasted life. I detest waste of any kind, both time and effort. If an hour is spent in idleness, five productive hours have been wasted. In Prince Charles' case, I'm afraid, it can truly be said that he is an exemplar of a wasted life. You see, Mistress Macdonald, life is not long, and we spend far too much of it in idle deliberation how it shall be spent. This is what Prince Charles is suffering at this moment. All his early zeal and fury could have been spent wisely, but now it is to no avail. Every man suffers defeat, but a true man rises from his defeat like a phoenix and learns from his woes. But Charles has done none of this. He is a pisspot now, a shambling, rambling sot whose reputation throughout Europe is that of a drunkard and a violent womanizer. What a thing to come to pass, eh? What a thing to come to pass!

"But please continue. I'm interrupting. Mr. Franklin informs me that you now live in America, due no doubt to the murderous policies of the unlamented Duke of Cumberland. But my American friend did not tell me the nature of the advice which you seek, so I shall await your condescension."

She had been thinking for days of this moment and how she would begin her request. She'd tried it out the previous day on Mr. Boswell. His reaction had been very positive, but the important discussion was the one she was about to have. And being a straightforward woman, she decided to be straightforward.

"Sir, I am here to stop a war and all the carnage which results. The Stamp Act and now this terrible tax on tea and the monopoly of the East India Company is infuriating my American compatriots to a level of vehemence, and I fear that blood will be spilt unless sense prevails. They are demanding representation in the Parliament, and the government of England is showing no signs of accepting the right of a people who are taxed to determine the laws and procedures by which these taxes are raised. That's the reason for the growing conflict, but I fear that it will result in a war, and I have seen too much of killing for a cause to allow it to happen again in my adopted homeland."

"Very commendable, ma'am," said Boswell, who moved his chair closer to the center of the little circle that had been formed.

"England wants money from the colony to pay its debts. The colonists in America, and no doubt other colonies, want representation and fairness. We'll pay our dues provided we're not taxed to extinction by a rapacious Parliament," she said.

Johnson and Boswell hung on her every word.

"What I want to do is to meet with the prime minister of England, and the king, and propose a new arrangement which will make everybody happy. Nobody will suffer, all will be rewarded, and England will be the strongest nation on the face of the earth."

"Utopia? Estimable, Flora, but what is the shape and substance of this New World which you are suggesting."

She breathed deeply. She'd only ever discussed her idea with Alan and Mr. Franklin before she left. Boswell had been enthusiastic. Alan believed that these matters should be conducted by men, especially men ordained as the proper representatives of the American colonies; Franklin had nodded his agreement and appreciation but told her that the king and Parliament would never go for it. Now she was about to expose her ideas to a man who was truly the representation of all that was good about England. His reaction would determine the shape of her fate and her future.

"I wish to propose to the king the creation of a commonwealth of Nations, rather than an empire. Each nation will have its own government and ruler, but all will pay obeisance to His Majesty King of England. Some taxes and dues will be paid, but the expenses for the mother country will be far smaller as she won't need armies to defend her possessions, so England, having a fraternal commonwealth instead of an empire which it must control, can rebuild both its Treasury and its reputation."

Johnson sighed deeply and made a spire of his hands against his mouth. Flora remained silent, waiting for his reaction. Boswell looked to Johnson, but she could see from his eyes that he approved of every word she'd said.

"And each member nation of the British Commonwealth would have its own ruler? And each ruler would be subservient to the king of England?" asked Dr. Johnson.

She nodded. "Ruler or Governor, Parliament or Senate, Congress or Meeting House. I don't know each nation of the empire well enough to advise."

"But why would the king of England, and its prime minister and Parliament, give up their colonies?" he asked.

She explained the reason. "England is a small nation and cannot maintain control of a country like America or any of its other colonies, without having large resident armies. They're costing a fortune and leaving England weak and undefended against its real enemies, the French, the Spanish, and the Portuguese. By having a commonwealth, there'll still be trade between England and its former colonies, and some sort of fee for membership of the Commonwealth in place of exorbitant taxes which won't be necessary because there'll be no army to pay for."

Again, Johnson nodded. "And why should once liberated colonies want to retain their association with England once the umbilicus has been cut?"

She'd thought that issue through and answered, "Because of the strength they'll still retain in the numbers of nations and the populations which will be part of the Commonwealth of England. If they become independent without maintaining their relationship with England, then they'll be prey to conquest by nations such as France and Spain. But if countries view members of the Commonwealth avariciously, then they'll know that should they attack, Britain and other commonwealth nations will come to her aid."

He remained silent. Boswell smiled at her and nodded in appreciation. But could Dr. Johnson see the benefits. At last, he said slowly, "I see great advantages and many problems. But so long as the advantages outweigh the problems, there's no reason why such a brilliant concept can't be proposed. First to Lord North, the prime minister; and then, God willing, to the king. A commonwealth of nations? An interesting idea. Throughout history, all great empires have frayed at their edges; revolts against the central authority begin at the margins of the empire and eventually work their way through to the center of power. This was the case with Assyria, Egypt, Rome, and latterly the Ottomans seem to be stagnating and will soon, I have no doubt, be following the same pathway.

"But that's not what you're proposing, is it? Not an empire ruled by a central government which ultimately must become despotic because such a government can never remain benign, but a commonwealth in which every Nation contributes to the good of the whole." He nodded and smiled. "What an interesting idea. Brilliant, eh Boswell?"

Johnson turned to Jamie and said ostentatiously, "Sir, you have a mother who is a woman beyond price. The name of Flora Macdonald is one which will be mentioned in history, and if courage and fidelity be virtues, mentioned with honor."

His panegyric was interrupted by a servant who knocked deferentially on the door and entered carrying a tray with silver pots of tea, hot water, milk, and lemons. A three-tier cake stand filled with biscuits and pastries of all different shapes and sizes was also on the tray. Jamie looked at it in astonishment. His cookies came out of a pewter cookie jar on a kitchen shelf.

The servant placed the tray on the table, and each took a pastry, Jamie selecting the biggest. Flora poured tea for everybody, and as she sat down, wondering what to say next, Dr. Johnson asked, "Would a child willingly give back his birthday gifts? Would a farmer willingly give away his lands? If not, then what will be uppermost in the mind of the king of England will be the thought of giving away an empire which makes England far greater than the size of its island with all the attendant prestige which it brings? I'm not sure that withdrawing armies and saving a fortune will be uppermost in the minds of the prime minister and his less-than-intelligent king."

She sipped her tea and gave her considered response. "The child will not be giving back his toys, Dr. Johnson. Instead, he will be putting his toys into a big basket filled with the toys of his brothers and sisters. Then all will share in the toys and the child, while he might have lost the exclusive right to the toys, will nonetheless be able to play with all the other children's toys. As to the farmer, he will share the bounty of his lands with all the other farmers, and instead of surviving on just one crop, he will give part of his crop away, but will benefit from all the other crops grown. And as to King George III, he will be father to other kings and rulers and governors, and all kings and rulers and governors will pay tribute to him for being the father. But with respect, I believe that you're underestimating the value and benefit to England if it can withdraw its armies?

"All that money in supporting its empire can be saved. Trade will flourish because it will be on an equal basis, not on the inequitable relationship of a master and his servant. Women in England will still demand beaver furs for their hats and coats, so trappers in American will still gain their livelihood; farmers will still grow tobacco and sugar and potatoes, but it will be a free and fair trade. You will have an assured supply and we in the former colonies will be free to live our lives without the yoke which is breaking our backs. You in England will need to spend less money because you won't have colonies to support. If the French in America continue their assaults against our possessions, we, the American army, will rise up and fight them. And if your army is required because of French or Spanish adventures in Europe, then it can be free of its responsibilities in the colonies. Indeed, the American Army might even come to the aid of its father, the king of England."

She had been speaking longer than she dared hope. When she addressed an audience, she would speak uninterrupted for an hour. Yet this was more a conversation than a speech, and she knew that Dr. Johnson wanted to interrupt.

Instead of speaking, he looked at her for an embarrassingly long moment. Then he turned to Boswell and said, "Call the guards, Boswell, for we have in our presence a dangerous radical, a woman who will upset the very balance of nature itself and will undermine the roots of our civilization. This woman must be taken away to the very furthest island in the world and cut off from all society."

Flora looked at him in astonishment, until he burst out laughing.

"Brilliant, Flora. Utterly brilliant. You argue like an advocate and you think like a philosopher. Yesterday, I met an interesting young man named Jeremy Bentham, whose ideas of social justice called Utilitarianism may inform you better of what kind of society you might wish to see in America. It calls for the greatest good for all. I want you to meet him. Indeed, I want you to meet many men of my acquaintance, for there is much you could teach us and more that you could learn from us. While we base our ideas on thousands of years of Greek and Roman civilization, it must be admitted that we have a tendency to be hidebound in our thinking, ossified in our ideas. You may need us, ma'am, but just as certainly we need you to infuse us with the freshness, verve, and originality which springs from the New World in order to shake the branches of our Old World tree."

She glanced at Jamie, who beamed a grin from ear to ear; then she glanced at Mr. Boswell, who smiled and nodded in appreciation. But it didn't satisfy her.

"Dr. Johnson. I would be delighted to meet with your friends, but I'm here on a mission. I must see the prime minister and the king, in order to prosecute these ideas and turn them into realities. Will you advise me on the best way forward?"

"Of course," he said immediately. "I shall write a note today to Lord North, our esteemed prime minister. You will see him by the end of the week."

She nodded in gratitude. It was what she had hoped for, yet dared not expect. Suddenly, a simple American farmer's wife was destined to see the most important man, after the king, in all of England. She wondered how it had all come to this.

And with her newfound confidence, she decided to ask the next favor. "Sir, what you have offered is more than I could have believed possible when I left America. For that, I am grateful. But there's one other service I wish to ask for, and I will understand why you may prefer to decline. My son, Jamie, and I, have an appointment with destiny. To gain our destiny, we have to seek the assistance of a churchman of England who still harbors Jacobite sympathies. Do you know of such a churchman?"

Surprised, Johnson asked, "Why would you need to see a Jacobite churchman?"

"There are good reasons," she said softly.

"But surely you can't expect me to expose any of my friends to potential danger and imprisonment and accusations of treason against the Crown of England unless you give me more information. That would be most unreasonable."

She looked at Jamie, who nodded.

"Dr. Johnson, Mr. Boswell. May I introduce you to my son, James. He is the only male successor of the Stuart line to the Crown of England and Scotland. He is the last remaining son of the House of Stuart. Jamie is Bonnie Prince Charlie's son. He was conceived in a crofter's hut on the Island of Skye. And I intend to have him crowned in Westminster Abbey on the Stone of Scone as the king of Scotland. I know that Prince Charles is still alive, but no Scottish laird will accept him as king because of his past misadventures. So the Scottish monarchy must miss the present generation and move on to the next, which is my son. Prince Charles has all but renounced his claim to the Scottish throne anyway. He has tried three times and will no longer be considered king by any Scotsman or woman. Jamie, however, is his son and I will make every endeavor to see that he is recognized as the rightful heir.

"I have come to England in order to fulfill Prince Charles' destiny, though God knows not for himself, but for his heirs. It is my intention to have my son crowned as the king of Scotland in the tradition of John de Balliol, Robert de Bruce, Duncan, and Malcolm. Then Scotland will become independent under its king and with the consent of the lairds of Scotland, will join with King George to become a part of the English Commonwealth."

Johnson and Boswell stared at Flora as though she was a lunatic. But in her eyes, they saw an intensity and honesty that made them wonder who was sane and who was mad.

For many long and embarrassing moments, neither of them said a single word, until Dr. Johnson said softly, "And the name of the next king of Scotland? Will it be your son's name? Will he be King James?"

"That is something which will become known to the entire world when he is crowned," she said.

Johnson looked at him, still trying to come to terms with the enormity of what she had told him. "And you believe that King George will welcome your son with open arms?"

She shook her head. "No, I understand that he will perceive him as a threat, just as George I saw Prince Charles' father as a threat and after him, George II saw the prince as a threat. But the difference, Dr. Johnson, is that my son will be presented to the king as the rightful heir to the throne of Scotland. He will be crowned king on the Coronation Chair. He will sit on the Stone of Destiny, and a man of the church will pronounce him rightful king."

"Are you aware, Flora, that the Coronation Chair is in Westminster Abbey; that it is kept in the Chapel of Saint Edward the Confessor and that every day, dozens of priests attend that church. Every monarch of England since the time of Edward III has been crowned in that chair during his coronation. What possible reason would you give for your son to be seated in the chair and a ceremony performed around him, without the guards and priests shouting out and stopping the coronation?"

"I shall enter the Abbey in the dark of night, and the ceremony will be performed when the church is empty. I will have witnesses to attest to its validity, though my son will be the first king crowned in the dark and without his subjects being present."

"But . . ." For the first time in his life, Dr. Johnson was lost for words.

Flora continued, "I know it's very unusual, sir, but these are unusual times. Rather than my son gathering an army and taking what's his by force, he is instead using stealth and guile. But unlike Bonnie Prince Charlie, there will be no bloodshed. Of that, I promise. And anyway, the moment Jamie sits on the Coronation Chair and the Stone of Scone, he will be known as the rightful king. There's a phrase in Latin which I believe is carved into the Stone which means that any lawful pretender who sits on the stone and is crowned becomes king. And my son, the male heir of Charles Stuart, is a lawful pretender to the House of Stuart."

"The phrase, ma'am, is *Ni fallat fatum, Scoti, quocunque locatum; Invenient lapidem, regnare tenentur ibidem*, which in translation means 'if Fates go right, where'er this stone is found, the Scots shall monarchs of that realm be crowned.' But phrases don't make a king, and your son will never be accepted for the role of monarch of Scotland for the simple reason that you and the prince were never married. Despite the fact that you have a husband in America, your son is a bastard of the House of Stuart. I deeply regret, ma'am, that you have had a wasted journey," said Dr. Johnson, still shocked to be in the presence of the illegitimate offspring of Bonnie Prince Charlie.

"But we were married, Dr. Johnson. In the eyes of God, we were married. We gave each other vows of love and formality, and we exchanged gifts. In the ancient Salic tradition, we were wed, even though our marriage wasn't formally recognized. But understand clearly, sir, that it was a marriage, and my son is no bastard."

"Then you're a bigamist," said Boswell, "for you have another husband called Alan in America."

"No, for according to the ancient Salic laws of France, I could divorce my husband within the year simply by declaring him to be gone and returning each other's possessions. I gave birth to Jamie in the Tower of London, and before my Alan and within the year, I declared myself to be divorced. As neither Charlie nor I had exchanged any property, the divorce became final at that moment, and I was free to marry Alan, and I did so when my son was two years of age. So my Jamie is the legitimate heir, and . . ."

"Damn me, ma'am, but Scotland isn't governed by the Salic Laws," said Dr. Johnson.

"No, but France still operates under those ancient laws, and my first husband Charles Edward Stuart resided in France before he invaded England. It was under those laws that I married him," she said.

Again, Boswell and Johnson looked at each other, then at Flora, and then at her son Jamie, who had sat through the entire interchange with a bemused look on his face, understanding virtually nothing of what had been said.

"You're wasted as the wife of a farmer, Flora. You should have been a lawyer," said Boswell.

"And did Bonnie Prince Charlie know about all this when he was undergoing this ceremony of marriage in the Crofter's hut?" asked Johnson.

She smiled and shook her head. "And I knew nothing about it until I discussed the entire matter with Mr. Benjamin Franklin, and he told me of my situation. He's checked it out with Mr. Patrick Henry, who is an American lawyer, and Mr. Henry concurs."

"But the divorce? You said that you divorced the prince within the year. How did you know to do that if you've only met Mr. Franklin recently?"

She laughed and said, "That was both luck and my Alan's genius and particularity. For he needed to know that I entertained no residual feelings for Prince Charlie. Just days after Jamie was born, in the privacy of my apartments in the Tower of London, Alan asked me whether the birth of the babe had in any way re-ignited any feelings that had been dormant since the Charlie went to France. I assured him that there were no such feelings. He joked and told me that as I had supposedly married Charlie in the Crofter's Hut, it was appropriate that I divorce him in the Tower of London. So I told my husband that as far as I was concerned, I no longer wished to be married to Prince Charlie, and I dismissed him. Neither of us had heard of the Salic Laws, yet somehow we applied them as though we were lawyers in the ancient tradition."

Johnson took in a long breath and said, unsurely, "Then I should rise and pay obeisance to His Majesty James, the uncrowned and unknown king of Scotland."

Flora burst out laughing.

Johnson told her, "I hope that this present King George can see the humor in the situation, for if his grandfather George II was still alive, both you and your son would be locked in the Tower and would never see the fruits of your endeavors. But if we prosecute the idea of a commonwealth, and if James here is presented as king of Scotland, who knows what'll happen? Eh, Boswell? Eh, Flora?"

They sipped their tea. A peace descended on the room. Everybody had run out of things to say. Until Dr. Johnson muttered to himself, "Now where in London am I going to find a clergyman who is a covert Jacobite and who would be willing to risk imprisonment for treason by crowning the next king of Scotland? And how on earth do we burglarize Westminster Abbey?"

# Chapter Seventeen

The winter had been penetratingly cold, but despite the previous day's temperature, it was noticeably warmer today than on previous days. Nonetheless, the cold still caused thin ice to form in the banks and shallow margins of the River Thames and killed a dozen vagrants throughout Southern England who stiffened in death as they lay in roadsides and beneath hedgerows. And the cold of the night was still so intense that even thieves and footpads who normally preyed on drunken revelers returning home from Inns as well as prostitutes with bulging purses servicing late night clients were at home or in bed to protect themselves from the ravages of the longest and coldest winter in living memory.

Even the many layers of clothing in which Flora had swathed herself to protect her body failed to shield her from the numbing icy fingers creeping beneath the folds of cloth and assaulting her flesh. Jamie, younger and heartier, was burdened by the weight of two jackets and two capes in an attempt to stave off the bitter chill, but his face and hands felt as though they were being cut by knives. He'd known many severe winters in Skye and North Carolina but none as wicked and unremitting as this.

It was nearing two o'clock in the morning, and London was pitch black. The occasional street lamp that hung high on a wall barely cast more than the most feeble glow in the winter haze that blanketed the immediate area, leaving dark and menacing the large spaces between the lights.

The black River Thames was like a ribbon in the Stygian gloom with only the occasional lantern from a rowing boat carrying a wealthy passenger home, casting tendrils in the water and showing that it was, indeed, a river and not a bottomless void between the two halves of London. Boatmen who normally charged sixpence to ferry passengers up or down river used the excuse of ice and cold to double their charge to the fury of travelers. But when the boatmen told aspiring travelers that if they didn't like the increase, they could walk home, few resisted paying.

The Palace of Westminster, foreboding against the meager river lights, entertained a few still-lit candles and lamps in its windows from officials working late into the night and the nearby Abbey was in almost complete darkness, its vast oaken doors firmly locked for the night against intrusion.

Flora stood in the darkened pools, invisible between the guttering flames of the street lamps, invisible to any eyes that might have been looking. Beside her, also undetectable in the night and shivering like herself, stood Jamie. With him was the Very Reverend Daniel MacPherson, Dean of St. Clair's Church in Cricklegate, who had been meeting with Flora and her son on and off for three days before agreeing to conduct the coronation ceremony. Accompanying him was his wife, Mrs. Angelica MacPherson and Mr. James Boswell and Dr. Samuel Johnson. Two others, both Scottish lords, had promised to meet them, but the cold had obviously prevented them from stepping out into the streets.

So it was these four witnesses who would attest, in the right place and at the right time, that her son was the rightful heir to the kingdom of Scotland and that he had truly been crowned as lawful king. But as Dr. Johnson had been pointing out for many days, merely being crowned didn't make a man into a king. To be a monarch, he had to be accepted and followed by his people, and the Scots were notorious for being diffident at best and combative at worst when it came to a question of who would rule them. Whether or not they would accept a young Scottish-American man called Jamie, even if he styled himself as King James IX of Scotland, was something that nobody but the Scots would decide.

The Rev. Dr. MacPherson took out the huge iron key that the inventive Dr. Johnson had secured from a pickpocket of his acquaintance who had been paid to steal the key from the Abbey's chancellery, and once he'd checked again that there was nobody other than them in the road, he walked surreptitiously across the silent street toward the Abbey's front door. He was followed by his terrified wife, then by Dr. Johnson and Mr. Boswell, with Flora and Jamie at the rear.

The key turned in the lock, made what sounded to the nervous party like an alarm to the authorities, but was only a loud scraping noise in the silence of a central London where all but hopeful prostitutes and returning footpads were asleep in their beds. They entered the Abbey, closed the door quickly, and stood in the freezing and gloomy vestibule, peering down the dark nave toward the choir stands, the Sanctuary, and the Chapel of Saint Edward the Confessor. It was bleak inside the vast building, the only feeble light coming from the moon shining through the high windows that barely illuminated any aspect of the Abbey. And there was a still, deathly cold about the place.

Dr. Johnson took out the lantern secreted beneath his cloak and used a flint to light the wick. Even though it glowed blindingly bright after the darkness, it only managed to illuminate their immediate surroundings and cast monstrous and ethereal moving shadows that danced from the high vaulted ceiling to the columns and pews as they moved forward.

"Come quickly," said Dr. MacPherson. "The Coronation Chair is kept in the very end of this building in the Confessor's Chapel."

He paced quickly forward followed by the party along the Nave, their footsteps echoing through the empty church. Even though they were alone, it took them several minutes to walk to the end of the building, past the Altar, up the stone steps that led to the sanctuary and then into the ornate surroundings of the Confessor's Chapel where the Coronation Chair was plainly visible against the eastern wall.

"It's beautiful," said Flora, gazing at the intricate carving and inlaid gilt. She wanted to reach out and touch it, but the urgency of the moment settled upon them, and they realized that the ceremony had to be performed quickly and they had to leave as soon as possible to avoid capture.

The Coronation Chair, on which kings and queens of England were crowned, had been specially created for King Edward I in 1300. It was painted gold, and inscribed in it were pictures of birds and foliage. The chair rested on four golden lions, and at its base, positioned between the lions, was a huge stone, the famous Stone of Destiny that had been taken from Scone in Scotland by King Edward in his unification of the kingdom. For nearly five hundred years, the Stone of Destiny and the throne which housed it had stood alone and proud, divinely inspired and awesome in Westminster.

The six stood looking at it in wonder, lost in its power. Only the Reverand MacPherson understood the need to proceed immediately. Fully knowing the dangers and understanding the historical and personal importance of the moment to Flora and Jamie, despite his fears of exposure, he said softly, "There, my friends, is the Stone of Scone. They say that this is the stone upon which the patriarch Jacob rested his head when he came to Bethel. The Book of Genesis tells us that 'Jacob rose up early in the morning, and took the stone that he had put for his pillows, and set it up for a pillar, and poured oil upon the top of it.'

"It's said that Jacob's sons carried it to Egypt and then it found its way to Spain, then Ireland where it sat upon the sacred Hill of Tara and the Irish kings were seated upon it for their coronations. The stone was supposed to groan if the monarch was of royal blood, but remained silent if he was a pretender. Fergus Mac Erc carried it to Scotland and gave it to the monks in Scone for safekeeping. Since the conquest of Scotland by King Edward and until now, the monarchs of the joined kingdoms of England and Scotland have been crowned sitting upon it. Pray God that we're not committing a blasphemy by doing what we're about to do," he said.

He turned to Jamie and said gently, "James Stuart, son of Flora Macdonald and Charles Edward Stuart, please sit upon the throne of ancient ways."

Jamie sat down on the ancient throne and settled into the seat. He grasped the arms as though he was insecure and looked to the others for approval. Dr. Johnson smiled and said softly, "It suits you, young man. You are no less entitled to sit there, bearing in mind your parentage, than was King James VI of Scotland, who became our own King James I of England. Pray God that this moment in destiny fulfils its purpose and prevents bloodshed and misery."

Flora looked at her son and shuddered, overwhelmed by the weight and gravitas of the history she was writing. It had all seemed so clear and simple in America and then in London; but now, in the heart of this awesome Abbey, seeing her son imitating the rites of kings and queens throughout time, she was suddenly wracked by doubt. She held her silence, but her mind was screaming. Was all this nothing but a mother's hubris for her son? Was this little more than nonsense, the fantasy of a silly old woman, a naïve episode from a hapless event a lifetime ago? What had been so clear to her yesterday now became muddied and uncertain. She looked at her lovely Jamie and saw not a king but a simple and honest farmer, cutting down trees and plowing the landscape. A sudden and unremitting instinct shouted at her to stop this process immediately, and for her and her son to return to America and forget the nonsense that had driven her for the past months.

For how could a simple man like Jamie, child of a farmer's daughter, possibly be crowned king of the Scots as though he was a Duncan or a Malcolm or an Alexander or a Robert? Her son, just weeks ago, had been nobody and nothing but Jamie Macdonald, a simple young man farming a small block of land in North Carolina, and now he was sitting in the womb of England on a sacred Coronation Chair about to be crowned king of a people who hardly knew him. She had come so far, yet where had she arrived? The doubt was threatening to overwhelm her.

She looked at Dr. Johnson, who smiled at her and nodded encouragement, as though he could fully understand the doubts assaulting her mind. Did he understand that she was in the depths of her winter, yet within her burnt an invincible summer, a prayer that this moment might just be the spark that would generate a new world of peace between England and America and Scotland?

Flora bit the inside of her mouth to feel pain in case she was in the middle of a dream, but she winced, telling her that it was no dream. Her son, the heir of The Pretender to the throne of Scotland, was about to be crowned king in ancient rite. His destiny, the destiny to which he'd been conceived all those years ago in a crofter's hut in the north of Skye, was about to be made manifest. The pain in her mouth reminded her of the reality that she had created. She knew she had to put her doubts aside and deal with them in the privacy of her room. For she couldn't and wouldn't allow her sudden misgivings to affect the ceremony.

The minister turned to the others in the dim light and said, "Friends, I present unto you King James Stuart, the Ninth of that name, your undoubted king of Scotland. Wherefore all you who are come this day to do you homage and service, are you willing to do the same?"

Dr. Johnson, Mr. Boswell, Mrs. MacPherson, and Flora said "God Save the King."

The minister continued, "Sir, is Your Majesty willing to take the oath?"

Jamie said, "I am willing."

"Will you solemnly promise and swear to govern the people of Scotland and of your possessions and other territories, according to their respective laws and customs?

"I solemnly promise so to do."

"Will you to your power cause law and justice, in mercy, to be executed in all your judgments?"

"I will."

"Will you to the utmost of your power maintain the laws of God and the true profession of the gospel? Will you to the utmost of your power maintain in the kingdom of Scotland the true religion established by God through his only begotten son, Jesus Christ the messiah? Will you maintain and preserve inviolably the church and the doctrine, worship, discipline, and government thereof, as by law established in Scotland? And will you preserve unto the bishops and clergy of Scotland, and to the churches there committed to their charge, all such rights and privileges, as by law do or shall appertain to them or any of them?"

Jamie looked at his mother, who smiled back and nodded. "All this I promise to do."

"My gracious king, to keep Your Majesty ever mindful of the law and the gospel of God as the rule for the whole life and government of Christian princes, I present you with this book, the most valuable thing that this world affords. Here is wisdom; this is the royal law; these are the lively oracles of God. By accepting them and all these precepts, I hereby crown you King James IX of Scotland. God save the King."

The minister gave the bible to Jamie, who received it. He then took a newly created brass crown from underneath his cloak and placed it on the new king's head. He took a small vial of holy oil and anointed the king's forehead. He kissed Jamie on the forehead, shook his hand, and whispered, "God save King James IX of Scotland. Now, friends, before we're caught and executed, for the sake of God Almighty, let's leave this place and return to our homes.

## 10 DOWNING STREET, LONDON

JANUARY 22, 1775

The intervention of Christmas and the New Year, the absence of the king in Hanover and Prime Minister Lord North at his home in Wroxton Abbey in Banbury, forced Flora and Jamie to remain in their lodgings in London far longer than they had originally intended. They had spent the time in writing numerous letters to trusted relatives and clan members in Scotland informing them of their visit, as well as telling them the entire truth about Jamie's parentage and his crowning as heir to the House of Stuart, kings of Scotland. Flora had wanted to keep Jamie's parentage and coronation a secret until the time was right, but Dr. Johnson had made the point quite strenuously that for Jamie to be accepted by the Scottish people, his claim on the throne had to be made public. And so the letters had been sent to all and sundry.

Yet in all the time that they had been in London since the coronation in Westminster Abbey, they had only received one letter back. It was from Lady Margaret Macdonald, Flora's elderly aunt for whom she had worked in her youth as friend and companion. Lady Margaret was unusually harsh and told Flora that regardless of the "nonsense" of her son's "so-called" coronation, the fact that the boy was fathered by someone other than Alan was an admission that should have brought shame to the parties of the disgrace, rather than the tone of joyous exultation that she perceived from Flora's letter. She continued by saying that rather than being spoken about freely, such an admission of immorality and sin should be hidden from the public eye and buried in the ignominy that such an event deserved.

No other letters had been received, despite her writing to prominent leaders of the church in Scotland, politicians, city councilmen in Edinburgh, famous members of the faculties of Edinburgh University, and friends of Dr. Johnson and the Reverend Mr. MacPherson. She had also written to the chieftains of the most important clans.

She had expected some opposition, even some ridicule, but at least some support, just as Jamie's father had received when he'd sent letters to the clan leaders all those years ago. What she hadn't expected was an eerie and unnerving silence. Perhaps the problem lay in the fact that it was still January, when people might continue to be involved in, or recovering from, first footing and Hogmanay and the ceilidhs, which seemed to go on forever in January as the Scots welcomed in the New Year. Often they were away from their homes and sometimes took the entire month to slowly return while spending days visiting relations and friends. But to have sent so many letters and to have received only one reply, that being condemnatory, was worrisome.

Her growing depression was lifted somewhat when Dr. Johnson sent round a messenger saying that the prime minister would receive the famous Mistress Macdonald and her son in his residence at 10 Downing Street in Whitehall. At the appointed hour, two sedans carried by chairmen were sent to collect mother and son. They were carried from their lodgings in Great Portland Street to Downing Street where they were met by Dr. Johnson. For the first time in their acquaintance, Mr. Boswell didn't accompany him.

"Good day, ma'am," he said shaking Flora's hand. "Good day, Your Majesty," he said to Jamie. Neither could get used to the appellation and smiled at each other.

"I have no idea what to say to the prime minister," admitted Flora.

"Then simply address him as you addressed me when we first met. But I would desist from mentioning the changed status of your son until you judge his reaction to the concept of the Commonwealth. Lord North is your route to the king, and if North feels that either his position or that of the king will be undermined by a threat to the monarchy, then he'll block you. On the other hand, he's a reasonable man and desperately concerned about the situation in America. The king is another matter and continues to try to interfere in the government of England, to Parliament's growing fury. Poor Lord North is like a juggler at a market fair, trying to keep half a dozen balls in the air and under his control but in grave danger of seeing them slip from his grasp and falling to the ground."

They walked toward the black lacquered door above which a large brass lamp hung; below it was the number of the house and a large brass mouth for letters surrounded by a gleaming mounting saying First Lord of the Treasury. Dr. Johnson, who had been to the house several times in the past, rapped the large iron knocker shaped like a lion. A few moments later, a liveried servant came to the door and invited them inside. The house was much larger than it seemed from the outside. The floor of the entrance hall was covered in black and white checkerboard of marble, and beyond the alcoves and architraves leading into other rooms lay a large ornately sweeping staircase. At the top of the stairs stood Lord North with two of his children.

"Dr. Johnson, come up, come up," he shouted. "And you too, Mistress Macdonald. And your son."

He disappeared and Dr. Johnson led the way upstairs into a series of large private rooms filled with paintings and sculptures and large tables around which were twenty or more chairs. It wasn't so much a home as a very large office. Johnson led Flora and Jamie along a corridor and into a large sitting room with green silk wallpaper and jade ornaments on buffets and sideboards. On the floor were ottomans and footstools. Lord North was standing by the fireplace, warming himself. As they entered the room, he came over and shook their hands warmly, telling them it was a pleasure to make their acquaintance, especially as Mistress Macdonald was so well known in England as the heroine of the '46.

They sat and were served tea by the servant. As they drank, Lord North talked to Dr. Johnson about issues of London life and asked how Mistress Macdonald and her son were enjoying London.

"A change from the life in America, isn't it," he said.

She nodded and said, "America has much to offer in its vitality and richness, but London is and always will be London. The capital has been here for nigh on two thousand years, whereas the town in which I live in North Carolina has been in existence for a fraction of that time. But in two thousand years hence, Lord North, I invite you to come to Halifax and look at our wondrous buildings and monuments."

He burst out laughing, and raised his cup of tea in appreciation of her geniality. "Tell me, Mistress Macdonald, what is the mood of the Americans today? It has been the source of much consternation in Parliament. Indeed, one of my predecessors, George Grenville retained his prime ministership for only two years and was sacked by His Majesty because of the Stamp Tax he introduced and . . ."

"Yes," said Flora, "but he lost his job because he tried to reduce the taxes paid by Englishmen at the expense of raising the damnable Stamp Tax in the colonies. Naturally, we in America were infuriated and rioted. Why should we assist England at the expense of a nation we're trying to build?" she demanded. "And your predecessor as prime minister, the Duke of Grafton, urged King George to remove all taxes from the colonies, because he'd seen the damage that imposing such taxes could do to our relationship without our being represented in Parliament. As I recall, he wanted to remove all taxes except the tax on tea, which is causing much grievance in my adopted country, Prime Minister."

Johnson looked at her in horror. The very last thing he wanted was a heated exchange before the prime minister had become comfortable with her. Why didn't these Americans understand the subtlety of polite discourse, he wondered. But to his surprise, North reacted in quite an unusual way.

"You're right, of course. We should be very careful as to how we raise taxes from our colonies if they are to prosper. Since Mr. Pitt increased the number of our colonies to include India, Canada, the West Indies, and Africa and now we have the islands of New South Wales and New Zealand in the Pacific Ocean, our merchants have been doing very well, but wars with France and Spain have emptied our treasury, and I am treading a fine line, balanced only by the demands of King George on one hand and the demands of my political opponents on the other. And yes, I'm the first to admit that Mr. Grenville was grievously wrong in raising taxes in America to finance our problems here, but you must understand that we were threatened with riots by the dreadful weavers because of their concerns that we were importing silk and putting them out of business. We had to quell their anger, and lowering their taxes was one way. Don't you see?"

Flora shook her head and said, "I see that you caused great alarm and consternation to the colonists of America by your action."

Johnson coughed and tried to pacify the interview by saying, "My dear Lord North, Mistress Macdonald has come here to seek an interview with you because she has developed a remarkable idea which may be an answer to all of our problems. She has done me the great honor of expounding this idea to me, and while I can see the many problems of implementing it, I do believe that it has great merit and that any problems can be overcome by goodwill and negotiations. Ma'am, perhaps you'll explain yourself to the prime minister."

And for the next fifteen minutes, Flora explained her idea of the transition of the British Empire with subservient colonies into the British Commonwealth with England as the *primus inter pares*, the first among equals.

"This would see America, Canada, India, Africa, and these new colonies you mentioned and all the other nations that you must use your armies to control, as independent nations under the protective shield of King George of England. You would spend a fraction of what your army is currently costing you; when you go to war against Spain or France, you can call on commonwealth countries to send troops to support you; while you won't enjoy such a wealthy revenue in taxes, you will have far less expenditure on arms and munitions and soldiers; and best of all, you can trade freely with those member nations in the Commonwealth and import into England all the commodities which your people covet. Understand, Lord North, that Americans don't dislike King George or the idea of being ruled by an English monarch; what they dislike is an English Parliament which rules our land without allowing its American citizens any representation. If you adopt my philosophy, Mr. Prime Minister, you will create a new world which has merit in all ways."

She stopped talking and looked at him. He was thinking deeply and had not said a single word of interruption in the entire time that her discourse took.

"Is there an historical precedent for this?" he asked softly. "I can see precedent for empire and colonies but not for this idea of a commonwealth. The Roman Empire held colonies and client states and ruled the world . . ."

"And lost them all because it was unsustainable," interjected Dr. Johnson. "The more it grew, the more force it needed to sustain it at its extremities, and the more those extremities fought for their independence. Gaul, Germania, and Judea were constant thorns in the flesh of Rome. My friend, Mr. Edward Gibbon, is in the process of writing a monumental tome on the decline and fall of the Roman Empire which proves this point very convincingly."

"The Empire of the Ottomans?" the prime minister continued.

"Is showing signs of stagnation and retreat," continued Dr. Johnson. "Since the adventure against Vienna, it has become an old lady fussed over by sycophantic servants. In fifty years, it will have crumbled and will become nothing more than the sand of Araby."

The Pretender's Lady • 333

Johnson looked at the prime minister who was trying to think of an example of a successful empire but couldn't. So Dr. Johnson continued, "The problem is, Prime Minister, that when an empire grows, it thinks it can control the world, only to see its expansion eaten away at its margins by those who resist the imperial mantle. Look at the crusades and the conquest of Palestine. Look at the glories of the Spanish and Portuguese Empires that initially enriched but have subsequently ruined their nations. Or look back to the ancient world at Egypt and Assyria and the Persians. The common folk in these great imperial powers would have laughed if, during their expansionary period, someone had said that within a hundred or a thousand years, they would be mere notations in the annals of history. Yet who today remembers the Egyptians or the Persians? Where today is the glory of Greece or the grandeur of Rome? No, Prime Minister, you only have to look at history in order to see the future of our British Empire. Mistress Macdonald is right. You would do well to heed her words. Why does England have to follow the certain history of other past empires and look forward to decay and rot? Why can't England forge a pathway to a new way of creating history for mankind and be the first great empire which unshackles its colonies and teaches the world a new way of relating to areas which we have brought to civilization?"

Lord North listened carefully to Dr. Johnson, but instead of responding, he thought longer, poured himself and his guests another cup of tea, and sipped it. The only sound in the room was the large floor clock in the corner of the room, which ticked away the time and became increasingly loud as the silence deepened.

"But the king has already given up all of his income from the royal estates. All the money that he earns is paid to Parliament, and Parliament gives to His Majesty sufficient money for him to live in the civil list. Yet you want to take away everything, even his possessions overseas?"

Flora shook her head and said, "My lord, these are only his possessions because of conquest. These lands belong to those who live there."

He looked at her strangely. "Are you saying, Mistress Macdonald, that the conqueror has no rights over the land which he conquers?"

She shook her head. "No, of course not. But following the conquest, the settlement must take on a partnership rather than a master and servant role. Otherwise, as the servant grows stronger, he'll reject the dictates of the master."

Lord North breathed heavily, wrestling with the huge concepts that were flooding his mind. And then, as though a light had been lit, he said in a strong and determined voice, "You said that your experiment had merit in all ways, Mistress Macdonald," the prime minister said, turning to her as though she was an accused in a court of law.

She didn't know whether to respond. She didn't, and Lord North continued, almost to himself, "Merit certainly, ma'am, but will the king see the merit in it? You expect me to approach the king and suggest to him that he gives away everything he owns in return for filial loyalty— in return for little more than international friendship? And in the state which His Majesty currently finds himself, I feel that such an approach would drive him again into the mad house."

"The mad house?" she said in surprise.

The prime minister nodded. "Four years after His Majesty married Queen Charlotte, he became touched by madness. He was treated by his royal physicians with an emetic tartar. His illness lasted some time, and during that time, he was incapable of governing. He recovered, but all of his ministers fear a repetition of a problem that could see him forced to abdicate.

"God forbid that I should bring such a scheme to him which might drive him again into the arms of the Devil and make his mind wander aimlessly, for then his wastrel son would succeed, and God help us all. No, madam, I shall not approach His Majesty with your experiment, and neither shall you. For fear of you driving His Majesty back into the arms of lunacy, I regret that you will be barred from entry into the palace. My predecessor, George Grenville, tried to make the king into little more than a puppet, and he lost his job as a result. I have no intention of following in Grenville's footsteps. I commend you for thinking about it, and I pay you my most sincere respects, but that is where your idea for a commonwealth shall stay . . . as a hypothesis in social policy."

THE COURT BAILIFF'S HOUSE

BLACKFRIARS PASSAGE, LONDON

JANUARY 25, 1775

Mrs. Angelica Macpherson, wife of the Very Reverend Daniel MacPherson, Dean of St. Clair's Church in Cricklegate, ate another Bath bun to the bemusement of her hostess, Mrs. Josiah Clarke. Mrs. Macpherson was seated on a leather chair in the front parlor of the Clarke's cottage. The front parlor was used only on occasions when important visitors came to the house. Dressed in an intense concoction of fabric and feathers, Mrs. Macpherson was deemed by Mrs. Clarke to be of sufficient import.

Having spent the entire afternoon declaiming on all sorts of matters, Mr. Clarke, a bailiff with the court of Assize in Oyer, and Terminer, was bemused as he sat beside his wife and they listened to Mrs. Macpherson talk at length about the importance of her Reverend husband's living and the compliments that had been paid to him by none other than the Bishop of Aldgate himself.

They didn't particularly like Mrs. Macpherson, who spoke a little too freely for their minds on matters about which she really should have been more circumspect—matters concerning the church and other Ministers and their wives. Were it not unchristian and inappropriate for the wife of a Dean to be so described, Mrs. Macpherson could have been considered a gossip.

Mr. Clarke, on the other hand, was exceptionally circumspect when it came to matters pertaining to the court of which he was bailiff. Whether or not he had his tipstaff in his hand, he was a bailiff every minute of the day, and what was confidential concerning the judges and the barristers-at-law and even the prison guards, remained at all times confidential. Hot irons wouldn't have forced him to divulge one single shred of information to which he was privy if that information had to remain confidential.

Which was why he was surprised, once Mrs. Macpherson had pushed the last bit of the Bath bun into her exploding cheeks and washed it down with a gulp of tea, that she told them what she had done.

She begged them to respect her confidentiality and maintain her secret, but she informed them that a few evenings ago, she had taken part in a coronation. When Mr. Clarke's face showed both disbelief and bewilderment, Mrs. Macpherson assured him that everything she said was the gospel truth and that she had been one of only a handful of witnesses to the coronation of the sole remaining heir of Bonnie Prince Charlie and Mistress Flora Macdonald. Even the renowned Dr. Johnson was there, which showed how important and historical the occasion was, she assured them. But the more Mr. Clarke's face registered disbelief, the more details Mrs. Macpherson was forced to provide until the entire story had come out.

Once satisfied that they now knew in what high matters of state she had involved herself, Mrs. Macpherson went on to another important matter concerning a wealthy gentleman patron of St. Clair's in Cricklegate and a fifteen-year-old female parishioner who had suddenly disappeared and was last heard of on the continent where, no doubt, the child was taking delivery of what Mrs. Macpherson described as "a certain unwanted and unwelcome gift of the Lord."

Mr. Clarke looked at his pocket watch and stood suddenly. "Ma'am, it's been delightful, but duty calls. I'm wanted at the courthouse in ten minutes, so if you'll excuse me . . ."

To the surprise of both his wife and Mrs. Macpherson, Mr. Clarke left the house and walked hastily toward the Old Bailey where he asked to speak to the chief justice in chambers, Mr. Justice Alston.

Annoyed by the unexpected intrusion when he should have been reviewing a case appearing before him in the morning, Justice Alston allowed the bailiff ten minutes of his time. He barely knew the fussy little man but had seen the bailiff from time to time walking with great self-importance about the court and didn't particularly like him. He was a bumptious and officious little man with no breeding or education. But the matter on which he'd requested an interview was said to be very important, and so the door to Justice Alston's chamber opened, and Bailiff Clarke walked in.

"Begging your pardon, my lord, I have received information from an impeccable source regarding a matter of the greatest urgency. A matter of treason against the king and the realm," he said, sounding very pompous and conceited.

Barely able to resist a smile, Justice Alston asked him to reveal the matter. By the time he'd done so, Alston's jaw had sagged with the enormity of the news.

"And is this woman to be believed?" he asked.

"She is very free with her information, but I am convinced beyond doubt her account to be accurate, my lord. Nobody could have made up those details unless they were true. My good lady wife and I had visited the Abbey only last month, and the details she described accorded with my own personal knowledge of the place."

Justice Alston nodded. "Wait here," he said. "Don't return to your home. I'll send a note to your wife saying that you're delayed on urgent court business. This is a matter which must be dealt with immediately and at the very highest levels. I shall try to seek a meeting with the prime minister this evening. You will come with me."

Bailiff Clarke's eyes opened like organ stops. "Yes, my lord. Of course, my lord." He could barely conceal his excitement. Wait until he told the lads at the Crown and Anchor tomorrow night, he thought.

It took less than a day for news of the interview between the judge, the bailiff, and the prime minister to come to Dr. Johnson's attention. He immediately penned a letter to Flora.

> *You are undone, Mistress Macdonald. We have been betrayed. Flee London immediately. The Prime Minister knows about the ceremony concerning young Jamie, and is making the most detailed enquiries. Flee, ma'am. Flee London and these isles for your safety and that of your beloved son.*

Flora looked at the note from Dr. Johnson's servant and read it for the third time. Its urgency was indisputable, but from what was she fleeing?

And to where? She certainly couldn't go to America from a London port because doubtless the authorities would be looking for her even now. Perhaps she could flee from Liverpool, but again, she had no friends or protectors there.

No, she had to travel urgently up to Scotland, and like Prince Charles three decades before, she had to hide in the heather and in crofts and use her name and reputation with loyal Scotsmen and women in order to evade capture for herself and her son.

She would leave London with Jamie within the hour. Perhaps if she could meet with the right people, and if he was recognized as the crowned king of Scotland, enthroned on the Stone of Scone, then everything might come good. But if that was the case, why had almost nobody responded to her letters? What should she do?

Dear God, she thought as she hurried up the stairs to Jamie's room to alert him, am I a fugitive again? Am I doing once more what I did all those years ago, but this time not with Bonnie Prince Charlie, but with his son? How had it come to pass?

# Chapter Eighteen

February 15, 1775

There should have been a feeling of exultation at walking down the roads of Edinburgh again, looking into the shop windows, smelling the sweet cloying aroma of hot honey biscuits roasting over the red coals of a brazier on street corners. The weather was bitterly cold, but the sky was a clear blue and Edinburgh Castle, sitting squat and dominant above the city, looked as though it was encased in an ethereal glow.

So much of her time had been spent in America, with its single story wooden buildings, its makeshift appearance, dirt roads rutted with the tracks of wagon wheels, and men and women whose appearance showed that they would never be more than dirt-poor farmers, that she truly appreciated the permanence of ancient cities like London and Edinburgh. She looked in admiration as ladies in the very finest of satin dresses, bonnets, and fur hand muffs walked alongside gentlemen dressed in black silk top hats, waistcoats, frock coats, and shoes that shone so much they reflected the buildings.

Now, for the first time in the two weeks—it had taken the two of them to travel by carriage and then by horse to Scotland—she felt she could relax. There was a surreal aspect to her journey. When they left the confines of London and traveled the twenty miles north to the city of Luton, she still cast her eyes downwards, not daring to stare anybody in the face in case she was pointed out to the authorities and exposed as a traitor to King George. But people in Luton and Derby and Manchester and further north had either ignored her completely or had smiled at her and her son and bid them good day.

Now that she felt much safer in Scotland, she began to wonder why she had been forced to escape from London. Why had Dr. Johnson been so insistent that she leave immediately? She had seen no signs of panic or alarm or an England militating to catch and imprison her.

And what had she done that was criminal? Why was she being pursued by the authorities? Treason surely was an assault on the monarch or the nation, yet all she'd done was to have Jamie claim his inheritance as Charlie had tried to do all those years before. But unlike the Young Pretender, his very own son Jamie had been crowned King James IX on the Stone of Scone in Westminster Abbey, where he was enthroned as monarch of his land. Why was this treason against the king of England? Scotland should not be part of England. It was an independent nation and now had its own independent king.

Once she was given a chance to explain it to them, and when it was accepted by the lairds of Scotland, it would be clear to everybody that her son was the lawful claimant and owner of the Throne of Scotland! By rights, he should have been welcomed by the king of England himself as a fellow monarch, the successor to the House of Stuart. Yet Flora was fleeing from the English king's authority as she had done thirty years earlier, accused of *lese majesty*, in danger of imprisonment in the Tower of London for the second time in her life. And today there was nobody like the long-dead Prince of Wales who would ensure her safety and comfort. Today's Prince of Wales was only thirteen years old, and the talk in London was that already the boy was little more than a wastrel, and as seemed to be the curse of the Hanoverians, the father was already showing signs of detesting his precocious son.

Yet flee she knew she had to, because Dr. Johnson's letter was so full of tension and drama. He was a considered man, not the sort to spread discontent and panic, so if he gave her a warning that her own and her son's liberty was imperiled, she knew that she had to act upon it immediately. She must establish the extent of the danger to herself and Jamie, which she could do in Edinburgh, and then make passage for America from Liverpool. Going directly to Liverpool would have been the most sensible plan, had she known the exact nature of the danger that faced her. But even though it was tempting, it was impossible, as the last thing she wanted to do was to book passage and then find the authorities waiting for her on the gangplank when the ship was due to sail. The alternative was to find her way to Glasgow on the River Clyde, where trading ships carrying coal, cotton, and iron left regularly for America; but she didn't know whether they carried passengers, whereas she knew that most people leaving England and Scotland to live in America left either from London or from Liverpool.

So first, she had to establish who was seeking her and what would be the consequences were she to be caught. Then she had to plan evasive tactics. Then she had to somehow take a ship to the New World. There were plenty of ships into and out of Liverpool, so she knew that she wouldn't be more than three or four days in the town before she found two berths. Most of the shipping came into Liverpool carrying black African slaves or cotton, tobacco, sugar, or grain. Their masters and owners often sought paying passengers to the New World to ensure some additional income from a ship sailing westwards.

But before she could feel safe in Liverpool, she had to determine the full extent of the reason for Dr. Johnson's fears. And Edinburgh, where she could easily loose herself, was the ideal vantage point. She had known many people in Edinburgh before she left to live in America. Some would still be alive; some would welcome her into their homes. But she was loath to endanger them if she was truly being outlawed by King George and Prime Minister Lord North.

So she and Jamie, having spent the night in a lodging house, breakfasted and took themselves toward a place in the center of Edinburgh where she hadn't been since 1745. She wondered if it would still be there, thirty years on. And more especially, she wondered whether the venerable Mr. David Hume who had been so kind and generous to a naïve young woman asking impertinent questions about the landing of the Young Pretender, would still be sipping bitter coffee at the same table, possibly surrounded by his friends Mr. Adam Smith and Mr. Thomas Reid. She had often told Jamie about her meeting with the three members of the Philosophical School of Common Sense, but she never for one moment thought that she'd accompany him to the place . . . if it still existed.

She could smell the roasted coffee even before she turned the corner of Albemarle Street. It hung in the cold air and insisted itself upon her senses. It was sweeter than the coffee that she drank in America, possibly smelling of cloves or some other herb. And as she approached, she saw the name on the hoarding and beamed a smile, squeezing Jamie's hand and nodding toward it. The shop was bigger than she remembered, and then she realized that Mr. Casaubon had obviously done sufficiently well in business to purchase the adjoining house.

Emblazoned across the double entry, in gold letters upon a black lacquer background was the name:

## *Casaubon's Coffee Emporium and Cigar Caravan*

followed by the legend:

### *Proudly serving coffee to the citizenry of Edinburgh since A.D. 1737*

As she did when she was a naïve girl, full of hope and expectation all those years ago, Flora stood outside the window and peered in to watch the mid-morning coffee drinkers imbibe their nectar. She had become used to coffee while in America and wondered whether English coffee would taste the same. She looked carefully at the faces of the customers, recognizing nobody. And then her eyes alighted on a table in the middle of the room, at which sat a large and solitary gentleman. All the other tables were crowded, yet he was the sole patron at his. Much older, much fatter, and with far less hair, she nonetheless recognized Mr. David Hume, sitting and reading from a book. It was his eyes. For all the dissolution of his sagging body, his now enormous girth, his eyes were still sharp and full of wisdom as he took in all his surroundings, even while reading.

Flora entered and the bell tinkled her presence. People looked up and stared at an elderly woman and her son. But not Mr. Hume, who was engrossed in his book, peering at the words through his thick spectacles, holding it close to his nose as though smelling it. Yet she knew he'd seen her, judged her, and she felt he'd recognized her. She sighed. He hadn't seemed a young man when she'd first met him three decades ago, but now he was obviously elderly, fragile, and suffering from failing faculties. She guessed he'd be in his mid-sixties. She wondered whether or not she'd aged as much and as badly as he, even though she was ten years his junior.

Carefully threading her way around the tables, she stood before Mr. Hume's table and waited for him to acknowledge her presence. Jamie stood beside her, waiting, though with much less patience. But Mr. Hume continued to read his book.

Jamie coughed to capture his attention. Mr. Hume looked up and saw two figures standing there. Was it mischief that caused him to say, "Another cup of coffee, waiter," before resuming his reading.

Flora smiled. "Might we join you, sir," she said.

Again, he looked up, this time with a frown of annoyance. "Forgive me, Madame, but this table is reserved for my sole use. There are a number of other tables if you'd . . ."

He peered carefully at Flora and then to her son. He removed his glasses and stared at them again, this time struggling with the memory of a moment of long-passed history. But even though she knew he didn't remember the details of their first meeting, she knew from his eyes that he recognized her.

Flora smiled. "It was thirty years ago. At this very table. I had longer hair then. It was as black as pitch and not white as it is today. But then, as now, I was very arrogant in my assumption that a man as clever as you would give any time to a silly girl asking silly questions," she said.

David Hume beamed a smile. "No question is silly if the answer enlightens you, Mistress Macdonald." He stood, and shook her hand warmly. Flora introduced him to Jamie, and they all sat. They were immediately served coffee by the waiter—one so young that he wouldn't even have been born when she'd first visited Casaubon's.

"I'm both surprised and gratified that you remember me," she said.

"Your fame in Scotland is remarkable. You're the woman who saved Bonnie Prince Charlie. People still speak of you with admiration," he told her. "I heard many times from many different people about your bravery in setting off in a tiny rowing boat on a terrible sea and braving the elements to save a hapless young man. I often wondered what became of you. Now you will have the opportunity of telling me."

"And tell you I shall, sir, but there are matters which I wish to divulge which can't be said in public. Might I suggest that we enjoy our coffee together, and I'll tell you a brief biography of my life since our first meeting; I would be fascinated to hear how the past thirty years have been for you, and then perhaps we could go for a walk in Holyrood Park where I can divulge certain matters which are delicate and for your ears only."

They drank their coffee and chatted amiably. Flora told Hume about the rescue of the Prince of the House of Stuart, of his escape, of her imprisonment in the Tower and of her years as the wife of a farmer on Skye. She explained how they had decided to transfer their lives to America and that she had returned to visit the old country with her son Jamie.

And for his part, Hume told Flora of his attempts to gain a Professorship at either Glasgow or Edinburgh Universities, and how he was always rebuffed by churchmen who believed him to be an atheist, or worse, a deist like Adam Smith.

Jamie interrupted him by asking what was the difference between an atheist and a deist. Hume gave a bronchial laugh, leaned forward so that none of the other patrons could hear and said, "An atheist believes in no God. A deist believes that a god created this world, but when he saw what man had done to it, he threw up his hands in disgust and left us entirely to our own resources, so that every mistake we make is of our own doing, and we are responsible for clearing up the mess."

"And you?" asked Jamie. "What do you believe?"

"My beliefs, young man, have frustrated all my ambitions for a calm and ordered life. If I've made mistakes, then if there is indeed a good Lord, he, she, or it has played no part in helping to clear them up."

Hume then told Flora of the many years he'd spent in France and Austria working as a civil servant and meeting great philosophical minds and of how he'd returned to Scotland where he intended to live out the rest of his life writing his books, drinking his coffee, and thinking.

"I am a man, Mistress Macdonald, who is of mild dispositions, of command of my temper, of an open, social, and cheerful humor, capable of attachment but regretfully never married, and at my moment of life, it is unlikely that any lady but a dependent widow or a young woman blind from birth would have me for a spouse. I am but little susceptible of enmity and of great moderation in all my passions, yet I attract so many enemies to my ideas. I don't understand why, for that which I have written is little more than sound common sense, and that which is not common sense has not been written by me."

Poor Jamie tried to follow the philosopher's logic, but failed. They finished their coffees, and Mr. Hume suggested that they take a walk along several streets until they reached Holyrood Park near Edinburgh Castle. They slowly made their way to Arthur's Seat, where the small number of people ambulating would ensure their complete privacy.

When they had reached the foothills of the huge cliff face that was in the center of the Edinburgh park, Mr. Hume said, "Well now, Mistress Macdonald, you wish to talk to me in privacy. Few places within a capital city afford as much privacy as does this."

He said, pointing out the vista overlooking Edinburgh. They sat on the grass in the shade of the hill, and Hume waited for her to begin her narration.

"Mr. Hume, my story begins when I first met His Highness Charles Edward of the House of Stuart. We met on South Uist when he was escaping from the Duke of Cumberland . . ."

And Flora told him about the crofter's hut, their time alone together, her conception of Jamie and his birth in the Tower of London and ended her story fifteen minutes later with the urgent note from Dr. Johnson, which is why she had come to Edinburgh.

He remained silent when she had finished the tale, nodding to himself and looking at Jamie.

"And a fine young man he is too," said Mr. Hume. "But whether somebody who has just left a Carolina farm in America, been crowned surreptitiously in an empty Abbey by an obscure cleric and has just managed to escape the ire of the prime minister and King George by hiding in Edinburgh, will be accepted by the Scottish people as their right royal monarch is another matter entirely. Your son might be an admirable man, ma'am, but claiming the Crown of Scotland just because you and Jamie's father had a night of passion is an altogether different thing," he told her.

They were words that Flora had always known might be spoken, but she had hoped that the overwhelming advantage of a commonwealth of English colonies might be the factor that could persuade the Scots to accept Jamie as their king. But since her escape from London, these very self-same words had been growing in her own mind with every mile that separated them from the Palace of St. James.

Flora had come to England with a firm conviction that she could avoid many deaths and revive the passion with which Bonnie Prince Charlie had landed here to claim the Stuart heritage all those many years earlier. Yet Jamie, much as she loved him, was a farmer's son and calling him king didn't make him a king. She loved him dearly, but all his life, he had grown up in the certainty that his lot in life was to follow in the footsteps of his father Alan, which was to live by simple but honest toil. He had none of the skills of conversation or repartee or wit that was required when he mixed with the men whom he would expect to follow him. Lovely, honest, and able as he was, Jamie had always been taciturn with people, and preferred to immerse himself in books and fixing implements and going fishing and swimming, rather than in the art of rhetoric, debate, and politics.

The man who had sired him had grown up in palaces. His mother's milk had been the inalienable fact that one day he would be king of Scotland and England by reclaiming his family's stolen realm. But this wasn't Jamie's dream. Jamie was a man of the soil and the forests and the hills, a lovely but simple person, not imbued with the intrigues of courtly life—one whom she saw settled in a shack in America with a plump and friendly wife who baked pies and hung out the wash on the line to catch the early morning breezes, with children dangling off his legs as he told them stories of his upbringing in Scotland and of their famous grand-mother who had once met a real live prince; a man who spent his life growing crops and not growing a nation, of fathering a family, and not a people.

A realization came to her, too late to save him from her hubris, that Jamie was a son of his upbringing rather than a pretender king in a Scottish castle ruling men of the intellect of David Hume and the proud chieftains of the clans. As she listened to David Hume, she realized that she had unwittingly made her lovely son into a pawn of her own history, the unsuspecting conspirator to her own ambition to rekindle the ember that had been her love for Charlie. It stunned her to think like this, but now that she was back in Edinburgh, she realized that her passion for Charlie had never truly died but had been buried deep in her breast while she lived the life of a dutiful and loving wife to a good man. Dear God, she thought, what have I done?

Hume continued, "I'm afraid that the Treaty of Aix-la-Chapelle and the War of Austrian Succession have rather put paid to any claim that the Stuarts might have had on Scotland. Time and history have marched past your son's pretensions, ma'am. A pity, but a reality. You may try to have him accepted as monarch, but I fear that like his father and his grandfather, the Old Pretender, your son Jamie will never be accepted by us, or by the English as King James IX. He must return to America as a monarch in exile."

Flora sighed. It was what she'd feared. Here was perhaps the most brilliant man in all of Scotland telling her that all of the time and energy and fuss she'd created in order to see her ambitions flourish had been wasted. And worse, she and Jamie were in danger of imprisonment for treason. Silently she cursed herself for involving other people in her long-dormant pretensions.

"Then we must return to America," she said, her voice dry and rasping. "If you believe that my mission is doomed to failure, if you agree with Prime Minister North that King George will never trade the expense of his colonies for the amity of a commonwealth, and if you think that Jamie will never be accepted as heir to the Stuart throne, then what am I doing here?" she asked.

He patted her on the shoulder and said softly, "My philosophy is that of the empiricists. I believe that knowledge comes to a person exclusively through experience. You can only come to an understanding of truth if you have experienced that truth through your senses and on the sole condition that this experience accords with and is consistent and coherent with your previous experience. What this means, Flora my dear, is that you have learned much from your experiment in coming to England and Scotland, and nothing is wasted. You have learned about yourself and your son. You've come to understand why this flame has so long burned in your heart, tiny and insignificant for a quarter of a century, but suddenly rekindled into a flaming passion. Perhaps it's because your beautiful young son was the same age at Bonnie Prince Charlie when he tried to fulfill his destiny. Has that destiny become yours, Flora? Are you trying to relive your life through your son?

"Or perhaps you came to rekindle the passion you once felt for Prince Charles? Perhaps you came because the son that resulted from that passion is now a man and you want your son Jamie to experience the same depth of joy you experienced when you and Bonnie Charlie had knowledge of each other. I don't know, Flora. Only by searching deep within you will you find the answer. But one thing I do know absolutely is that you have grown in knowledge, stature, and wisdom by coming here. What more can you ask from life?"

She mused on his words; *knowledge comes to a person exclusively through their experiences.* She flushed in embarrassment. Was David Hume right? Was it confirmation that she was still in love with Bonnie Prince Charlie? After all these years? She still dreamed of him, but she assumed that it was nothing more than a woman's fantasy. And what of Alan and her children. No, it was impossible. The man she'd met and fallen in love with was an extinct volcano, fulminating in Italy, married and drunk and if the stories were true, he had become as ugly a person as royalty had ever produced. No, it was quite impossible, and she had to concentrate her mind on the love she had for dear Alan and Jamie and her children and her new home of America. But first, she had to leave Scotland in safety.

"Will my son and I be jailed?" she asked.

He beamed a smile. "Not while there's a modicum of hair left on my balding head, nor Scottish blood coursing around my veins. You and His Majesty King James IX will return with me to my lodgings near to Edinburgh University. Mrs. Lindsay will give you a comfortable room, and there you will remain while I sniff out any English troopers who might be sent to find you. Nobody knows of this problem, as far as I am aware, and while Scots people don't know of any accusations made against you, you may feel free to wander the streets." He looked at Jamie. "Provided of course that you don't insist that your subjects in Edinburgh genuflect in your presence."

He burst out laughing. So did Flora. But Jamie couldn't find reason to laugh and remained straight-faced.

"As soon as is practicable, I shall secure passage by carriage for you from Edinburgh to Glasgow, where you can take a packet boat back to America; there you will breathe the sweet air of freedom. America is where you and your son should be, Flora. Unless I'm very much mistaken, America will soon shrug off the mantle of monarchy and flex its young and powerful muscles. I believe that with its youth and vitality and now with thousands of Scots pouring in there to make a new life, America is destined to become a great nation, a very great nation indeed. And you and your son and your other children will contribute to that nation in ways far more beneficial than could Jamie sitting atop a teetering throne, wearing a second-hand crown, and calling himself king."

She sat for many minutes, letting his words settle upon her mind. Jamie looked at his mother and silently thanked the Lord that they would be returning to America imminently—for though he loved his mother dearly, he had never wanted to be a part of this adventure.

She breathed out a sigh of acceptance, smiled at the elderly David Hume, and stood. "I shall return with you to your lodgings, Mr. Hume, and consider our future in light of your wisdom. I thank you for being a friend to me and my son."

While she was resident at Mr. Hume's Edinburgh lodgings, Flora thought very long and very hard about returning to America and to Alan, having accomplished so much, yet achieved so little. While she knew in her heart that Mr. Hume was right and that the Scottish people would find it difficult to accept Jamie as their king, she felt that in fairness to him, to herself, and to her memory of Bonnie Prince Charlie, that she had to make one determined effort. So she decided that before she left Scotland she would find out whether the guttering flame she still carried for Bonnie Prince Charlie would ever endanger her marriage by flaring up again into a searing inferno. She determined that she would test whether or not the Scottish people's love for Bonnie Prince Charlie was truly dead and a thing of the past.

She sent notes again to those members of Edinburgh society whom she knew that she could trust to keep her secret. She wrote to Lady Macdonald, separately to Sir Alexander Macdonald, and to the leaders in Edinburgh of the Church of Scotland and of Edinburgh University. Yes, it was a risk, but it was a risk she was prepared to take. After all, if she was exposed to the authorities, she could always flee and follow Bonnie Prince Charlie's path across the Highlands. She asked those to whom she wrote to meet with her for afternoon tea at four o'clock in the afternoon of Saturday, February 21.

As Flora's notes were being received, another letter, this one more ominous, arrived in Edinburgh from London. It had taken an entire week for the letter to arrive informing the commander of the garrison in Edinburgh Castle that he was to be on the lookout for an elderly matron with white hair called Flora Macdonald and her son James, who had committed an unnamed but egregious act of treason against the person of His Majesty King George III. No reward was offered to the citizenry for their capture, but once they were arrested, they were to be transported to London immediately to be dealt with.

On Saturday, the twenty-first, at half past three in the afternoon, a detachment of guards was sent to be stationed on the London to Edinburgh road and to stop any persons matching the description of the two miscreants and bring them in chains to the Castle.

Flora had no idea that such a body of troops had been dispatched. Instead, as the troopers sorted themselves out on the road in anticipation of their arrival in Edinburgh, Flora sat in her lodgings with her son Jamie and waited. Mrs. Lindsay had laid out a special tea for her and her important guests, with griddlecakes, honey biscuits, a pot of coffee, and a pot of tea ready to be poured. The fire was lit in the downstairs parlor.

The clock ticked ever onward past four o'clock. Her heart raced in anticipation of what might happen. Did she still love Charlie, a brief figment of her life all those years ago? And did Scotland still remember a handsome and daring young man who had tried to reclaim what was rightfully his?

Flora looked at Jamie and smiled. She had advised him of what to say should people call and shake his hand. And she waited. And waited.

Just in case, she opened the front door to the parlor, but the cold hallway was empty except for Mrs. Lindsay, dressed in her Sunday gown, who gave her an encouraging smile. Flora went to the front door and opened it, despite the harsh wind that was blowing. She returned to the parlor, and she and Jamie stared at the open door. And they continued to wait for Jamie's subjects to come and attend on him. And they waited.

# The First Epilogue

All of the newly-liberated American men in the room sat as still as lumps of marble while King George's court artist, Mr. Benjamin West, quickly sketched in charcoal their positions, their clothes, their wigs, the table and its contents. Facing him were Mr. Benjamin Franklin, Mr. John Adams, Mr. John Jay, and Mr. Henry Laurens who, although not a signatory to the Peace Treaty, nervously held the document at the back of the scene. All sat or stood facing the painter enabling him to sketch a good representation of each man before they disappeared for a celebratory lunch and further discussions.

In Benjamin West's opinion, however, the entire scene was unbalanced, because of a tragically absent figure who should have been sitting on the other side of the table. Yet Sir David Hartley, the British Minister Plenipotentiary and Member of Parliament for Kingston-upon-Hull, sent by King George to negotiate Britain's surrender of its colonies to the Americans, had refused to sit at the same table and have his portrait painted. Posterity would never know his part in the historical proceedings nor the shame he felt at Britain's capitulation to such a raggle-taggle mob of flash-harry Republicans masquerading as soldiers. His pointed absence meant that students of this momentous event would never see the face nor disposition of the man who signed away Britain's most precious colonies.

When West finished the sketching, he sought appointments with the gentlemen over the next few days so that he might paint their faces and bodies in oils on the canvas, but in the meantime, he thanked them for their patience and bid them all good morning.

Benjamin Franklin, wearing his customary dark morning suit, waistcoat, and cravat, rose from his chair and stretched. It had been an exhausting few weeks of the final negotiations with the government of Great Britain. Much acrimony, much bombast, and much rending of the flesh; but in the end the British knew that they had to concede, and Franklin, despite his diplomacy and genteel ways—a counterbalance to John Adams' assertiveness—enjoyed turning the knife in the body of Britain one or two more times than was absolutely necessary. He had once been a solid supporter of Great Britain and the maintenance of a cordial relationship, but when he suffered an appalling attack against his character in the privy council, he had begun to refocus his ideals and realized, just as the other compatriots of the Continental Congress had realized much earlier, that Britain's patronizing relationship with its colony simply couldn't last. Taxation without representation was only one issue; the other was the hubris with which England had treated its American colony, as though it was a perpetually filled pantry that the English landlords could pillage whenever they were hungry.

He left the others to continue talking, and walked alone out of the Salon of War into the miraculous Hall of Mirrors where a luncheon banquet had been laid. King Louis XVI had ensured that on this one occasion, none of his courtiers would be present, only his Ministers, the Americans and their advisors, the British negotiators and advisors, and himself.

Franklin walked to the table and saw with delight that the chefs had included his favorite meal of thinly sliced lamb flavored with a sauce of mint and Spanish pimentos. Whenever he came to Europe, be it Britain, France, Italy, or elsewhere, the very first meal he ordered was a well-cooked lamb. For some reason, possibly the grass on which they were fed, possibly the air or the heritage of the beasts, European lamb always tasted infinitely better than American lamb.

Mind you, his disgust with the French monarch and his wife's eating habits had encouraged him to avoid any meal at which Louis was the center of attention. Just a week earlier, he'd been unable to avoid watching the spectacle of Louis and Marie Antoinette being fed a forty-course lunch and their sycophantic courtiers applauding every mouthful. Nauseating was the word that sprang to his mind, and as a description, it didn't just define the gluttony.

He was about to pick up a plate and fill it, as he had rushed his breakfast in order to attend the final negotiations on the wording of the Peace Treaty, when he felt a tap on the shoulder. Franklin turned his bulky form in surprise and saw Charles Gravier, the comte de Vergennes, chief of the council of finance, and one of the most able and important advisors to Louis XVI. He beamed a smile and clasped his hand.

"Well," said Le Comte de Vergennes, "you have every reason to be happy. America today is an independent nation, free of British control. Do you smell the air of liberty, my friend?" he asked.

"I smell liberty out here, but in there," said Franklin, pointing to the Salon of War, "I cut my tongue on the frigid air. I'm afraid that my old friend, David Hartley, feels that King George shouldn't have given up the colony quite so easily."

Comte de Vergennes rattled a laugh and coughed. Even he knew that he had little time left on this earth in which to assist the French king meet the coming deluge and more importantly in which to intrigue so that he would be remembered as a truly French rascal. "The English king is a fool to have imposed the Stamp Tax and the Tea Tax on you. The youth and strength of America demands that it must be treated with respect. We French have failed to treat our own people with respect and soon this will be our cost also."

Franklin nodded. He wondered how long the French monarchy could survive with all the undercurrents of anger among the people. Perhaps America's declaration of independence would presage a revolution throughout the entire world or ordinary citizens against their repressive overlords?

"The present King George III might be a fool, but he comes from a long line of fools," said the Count. "His grandfather, George II was just as much of a fool, as was his Great Grandfather who ruled the men and women of England, but spoke not a word of English," He laughed again, his chest rattling as he convulsed at the absurdity of the Germanic Hanoverians sitting on the British throne.

Franklin sipped a glass of claret and said, "God help England when this George bids his farewells to this troubled world of ours and is replaced by the Prince of Wales. It's said that whenever the young prince dips himself into the well of a woman, he demands a lock of her hair and keeps it in an envelope in a private room. He's only twenty-one, but they say he already has over a two hundred envelopes. When he becomes the next King George, if his current form is a guide to his future, then Britain will have yet another fop and a dandy, a libertine and a numbskull for a monarch. Your neighbor across the channel will be lucky if it retains Scotland and Ireland, let alone its other colonies when an idiot like him places his backside upon the throne."

The old diplomat shrugged and said "France has had its fair share of libertines and idiots." He sniffed and thought for a moment. Then, after further consideration, de Vergennes said, "Yet despite our monarchs, France has survived quite well, though the time of the monarchy seems certain to be coming to an end. The people of France will soon follow America's lead. Our streets are noisy with protests and demonstrations. Our forces put them down quickly, but it's like a plague which is spreading into the dark corners of our cities. Soon, we'll all be washed away in a deluge of righteous anger. Thank God, my time has passed and I won't be here to see it.

"But as to Scotland and perhaps Ireland, I don't see them abandoning their English father. Scotland especially had its chance to leave England's side when the young Prince Charles Edward of the House of Stuart attacked and tried to regain the throne. He failed just as his father before him failed, and now there are no male Stuarts left to claim either Scotland or England," said de Vergennes. "That adventure is well and truly over."

"Don't be so sure," said Benjamin Franklin.

Sublimely attuned to the slightest nuance in a conversation, de Vergennes, France's most experienced diplomat, instantly sensed new and exciting information. "And what does my American friend mean by that?"

Franklin smiled and said, "I mean precisely what I say. You stated that there are no male heirs to the House of Stuart. I warned you not to be so certain."

"Tell me the entire story immediately, Benjamin, or I shall order the guards to skewer you with their bayonets."

Franklin leaned forward conspiratorially, even though there were only the two elderly men in the vast hall and said, "Well, some years ago, shortly after Prince Charles left France on his quest to conquer England and Scotland . . ."

# The Final Epilogue

July 2, 1803

Charles Edward Alan Macdonald, son of Jamie and Bessie, grandson of the late Flora Macdonald and His Royal Highness the late Pretender King Charles Edward Stuart, felt fear grasping his heart as he walked between the soldiers toward the library door in the palace that was home to Napoleon Bonaparte, emperor of France.

Why he felt fear was a mystery to him. He had been born for this moment. Although he'd only known his destiny recently, something about his upbringing, even from his earliest moments, informed him that he was born differently to other men. Perhaps it was the glances and the comments whenever he'd asked about his grandfather and grandmother. Perhaps it was the reason that Grandmother Flora and her children had left America and returned to Skye in the old country when Grandfather Alan had been arrested for fighting on the side of the English; or perhaps it was the fact that whenever he traveled in Scotland and people found out that he was the grandson of Flora Macdonald, they looked at him as though he was the Christ child.

Of course, it might have been none of these reasons; instead, it might have been the way his father Jamie treated him during their play

*357*

together. They were always playing make-believe, and Jamie always played the king and Bonnie Charlie (as his father always called him) played the prince.

Charlie was a bright boy, and he knew that there was an untold story. It was only recently that the mystery that he'd known existed had been revealed to him. When he was a small lad, sitting on his father's knee in their home in Skye, his grandmother Flora had sung him songs of the Highlands and the Islands and told him of the story of a handsome prince and the brave Scottish lass who'd saved the prince's life. He'd grown up knowing the words but had only recently come to understand that they applied to his grandmother.

It was Grandmother Flora who'd joked with him when he was a small child and told him that one day he might be king of England and Scotland. He'd loved her fairy tales and asked her to repeat them time and time again. And when she'd died two days after his tenth birthday, his father Jamie had taken up the role of storyteller, repeating Grandmother Flora's narratives until Charlie knew them so well that they took on a reality.

And then, two years ago, on his twenty-first birthday, his father Jamie had sat him down and told him the extraordinary truth—that many years previously, Jamie had been crowned King James IX of Scotland and that one day, just as America had gained its independence from England so too would Scotland gain its independence; and at that moment, the Stuart family would claim its inheritance.

When Napoleon Bonaparte turned the horrors and the executions and the nightmare of the French Revolution into the conquest of all of Europe, Jamie told his son that it was now time to approach the emperor and reveal to him the truth about who he was and the Stuart's claim to the throne.

"I can't do it," his father had said, "for although I was born in the Tower of London as a prisoner of King George II, I have spent too much of my life in America to be accepted for a king of Scotland, and will never be recognized for my claim. So you, Charlie, who were born in Scotland, must represent me. Are you willing," he'd asked. And Charlie had immediately said that he was willing and eager to go.

That was a year ago. A year in which correspondence had flowed between the Island of Skye and the City of Paris involving ever more important officials within the French government and circles that revolved around the emperor. And as the likely date for Napoleon's invasion of England drew ever closer and more certain, the need to meet with the newly crowned emperor and present his case to be crowned as rightful heir to Scotland grew increasingly important.

Knowing that a meeting must come soon or be too late when French troops stationed themselves in the streets of London, Charlie had been working in the fields when his father came running up the hill, carrying a letter that had just been delivered by messenger. As his father shouted his name louder and louder and told the whole world that Napoleon would grant Charlie an audience, the lad threw down his spade and knew that his moment with destiny had arrived.

Three weeks later, Charles, son of James, grandson of Flora and the Pretender to the Scottish throne, was walking with military precision between tall Imperial guards, wearing a new serge suit that itched mercilessly, new shoes with delicate buckles, and a dark blue silk top hat purchased in Bond Street just before he left London.

As he neared the door, the liveried servants opened it, and to his surprise, he saw the emperor of France, dressed in his blue and white military uniform, kneeling on all fours over a huge map of Southern England and Northern France. The entire floor was covered in maps, as was his vast desk, the walls to his library, and the chairs. Kneeling with him were two men in military uniforms, as well as a man dressed in his shirtsleeves. Under other circumstances, they could have been playing a nursery game, but these were men who were preparing for a war. He had begun his journey full of confidence, but as he'd entered the Petit Palace de Luxembourg, his courage and self-belief quickly began to disappear.

When the door opened, Emperor Napoleon looked up and with great agility sprang to his feet. He was much shorter than Charlie had thought. The guards stood still, enabling the young man to walk forward toward the emperor, hand outstretched in greeting. He realized that his hand was shaking. And sweating. He was pleased that he was wearing gloves.

Napoleon shook his hand and surveyed him. "So, young man, you claim to be the heir to the Stuart family and are rightful king of Scotland and England," he said.

"No, Highness, I am the son of the heir. My father was crowned King James IX of England and Scotland in Westminster Abbey. He is the true heir."

There was a glint of amusement in Napoleon's eye. "But I was under the impression that King George III, despite his recent episodes of insanity, was still the lawful king of England and that his heir was the Prince of Wales."

"With respect, Majesty, I said that my father was the true heir to the throne. As Your Majesty knows, the Crowns of England and Scotland were unfairly taken from King James II of the House of Stuart by . . ."

One of the generals who was kneeling stood up and said caustically, "Young man, His Majesty is well aware of the history of your family."

"Forgive me," said Charlie, his courage having vanished entirely now that he was inside the emperor's private sanctum.

"I have examined your letters and given them to my ministers of State. They have reported back to me that you do indeed have a claim to the throne of England and Scotland if you are who you say you are. Whether or not it's a valid claim is something that needs to be determined. Come, young man. I'll take time off from my duties and have a cup of coffee with you. You may be the heir to the thrones of England and Scotland at the moment, but whether or not you are when I've finished my coffee, depends on what you have to say for yourself."

Napoleon led him over to the far end of the room where the scene was more orderly. There were no maps spread out on the floor, but instead exquisite furniture of a fineness that Charlie had never before seen. Compared to the crude chairs and tables in his own home in Skye, these were superbly delicate.

Napoleon noticed him looking and said, "I took these from the palace at Versailles. I don't think that what remains of the Bourbon dynasty will have any further use for them. Now, sit and tell me why I should assist you in your claim to England and Scotland."

"Majesty," he said, remembering the words instilled into him by his father. "My dear Grandmother, Flora Macdonald, assisted Prince Charles, my grandfather, to escape the clutches of the king of England in 1746 . . ."

"Yes, it was after he'd lost the Battle of Culloden Moor. A disastrous battle fought by an incompetent."

"My Grandmother Flora and Prince Charles had an issue. It is my father, James, who was born in the Tower of London, where my Grandmother Flora was imprisoned for assisting Prince Charles to escape."

"But your father is illegitimate, so what is his claim to the throne?" asked Napoleon.

And Charlie explained the marriage ceremony that under Salic law made the contract legal, and made her son legitimate. And, he stressed, the legitimate heir to the thrones after Prince Charles' death in Rome in 1788.

Napoleon nodded. "And has King George and his Hanoverian family been appraised of your claim?"

Charlie shook his head. "Thirty years ago, my father was crowned in a very private ceremony in Westminster Abbey. But the prime minister and the king found out about it, and my Grandmother and my father only just managed to escape to America with their lives. Some years ago, my grandmother wanted to return to Scotland to end her days, and so my family returned with her. She is buried in Kilmuir on the northern coast of Skye and has a winding sheet in her coffin; she asked to be wrapped in the sheets in which Bonnie Prince Charlie slept when he was with her. She had kept these sheets all her life. Because of the danger of being arrested for treason, we have kept this family secret to ourselves," he said.

Napoleon shook his head. "This doesn't demonstrate for me the bravery of a monarch, young man. This shows me the timorousness of a coward. A true king would have gathered his people and would have put the Hanoverians to flight, as your grandfather attempted and as your grandmother bravely assisted him. But for your father to have buried his ambitions for half of his life doesn't augur well for a man who would be king," he said.

"I know that's how it seems, Majesty, but my father spent almost all of his life in America. He is asking that when you cross the English Channel to attack England that you unseat the Hanoverians, remove them and their successors from the throne, and repair the damage to history which has been done. My father and I are the rightful heirs to England and Scotland."

Napoleon burst out laughing. "Oh, just like that? Simply cross the Channel and attack England? My boats are outnumbered five to one by the English Navy. My army is the bravest in all of the world, but unless I can transport it across to England, it is tethered to France. And if I attempt to cross the Channel, my ships and my army will be sunk. Britannia truly does rule the waves between our nations. I and my generals are working day and night to try to find a way to cross the waters. Until I do, young man, neither you nor I will gaze upon the throne of the king of England, let alone replace its current occupant."

"But if you do, Sire, then my family is the rightful claimant to that very throne," said Charlie.

Impressed by the young man's courage in speaking so forcefully, Napoleon said softly, "but why should I make the House of Stuart into the kings of England and Scotland when I've put my own family and my generals onto the thrones of half of Europe? Why shouldn't I simply conquer England and place one of my cousins on the English throne so that I have complete control?"

Charlie steeled himself for his answer. "Because then you will have not just the English to fight, Majesty, but me and my father and those Scots who will rise up against you. Believe me, sir, that unless a Stuart replaces a Hanoverian, all England and Scotland will oppose you. You may conquer the English armies, but the only way you'll conquer the English people is by capturing their hearts and imposing a foreign king on them will not do it. They have spent years hating the kings from Hanover; they will never accept a king from France. Whereas if you put my family back on their rightful throne, France and England will be as one. Surely you can see the wisdom of supporting the legitimate heirs to the throne, who will then become your closest of allies and who will then end all costly wars between our nations."

He sat back and waited for the sky to fall in. But he had to have taken the gamble. Napoleon looked at him with narrowed eyes, summing him up. Then miraculously he smiled and said loudly for all to hear, "At last. I'm dealing with a man who speaks like a monarch. Come over here, Prince Charles, and I'll show you the maps that will define the coming war with England. Once I've worked out how to beat Admiral Lord Nelson and the British fleet, my soldiers will cross the Channel, and England will be mine. Then, perhaps, I will consider putting your family back on the throne, where you think that you belong."

- END -